The Star Cross: The Dark Invaders

(The Star Cross Series, Book 2)

By

Raymond L. Weil

USA Today Best Selling Author

Books in The Star Cross Series

The Star Cross (Book 1)
The Star Cross: The Dark Invaders (Book 2)

Website: http://raymondlweil.com/

Cover Design by Humblenations.com
ISBN-13: 978-1537008141
ISBN-10: 1537008145

DEDICATION

To my wife Debra for all of her patience while I sat in front of my computer typing. It has always been my dream to become an author. I also want to thank my children for their support.

The Star Cross: The Dark Invaders

Chapter One

Fleet Admiral Kurt Vickers waited tensely for the Star Cross to drop from hyperspace. On the tactical display, he saw the bright green icons of the rest of his fleet accompanying the flagship. From a source on Kubitz, he had learned of a Profiteer attack planned upon a helpless star system just 412 light-years from Newton. If everything went according to plan, Kurt would drive off the Profiteer ships and make that world an ally. It would also be extremely gratifying to deprive the hated Profiteers from pilfering the wealth of the system.

Nearly fourteen months ago he had successfully driven the Profiteers from Earth, freeing the planet. Unfortunately, as they withdrew, the Profiteers had nuked numerous cities across the globe out of spite. Over forty million people died in the reprehensible attack. While it wasn't feasible to attack Marsten, the responsible Profiteer world, due to its alliance with the Gothan Empire, Kurt could hinder their future attacks upon unsuspecting and defenseless planets.

The Profiteers made their money stripping the wealth from weaker worlds and selling their inhabitants at the slave markets on Kubitz, a black market world deep in the Gothan Empire. Kurt was determined to be a major thorn in their side anytime the Profiteers ventured forth from their empire, particularly if it was High Profiteer Creed.

"Hyperspace dropout in six minutes," Captain Andrew Randson calmly informed the admiral. "The Profiteer fleet has just crossed the orbit of the sixth planet in the system and is inbound to planet four." The fleet was already at Condition Two with all hands at their battle stations.

Kurt knew from his sources that planet four held a humanoid race that had already reached out and explored several nearby star systems. Their civilization was just slightly behind Earth in its development. Unfortunately, like Earth before the Profiteer attack, they had as of yet to encounter any other space-going cultures.

"How many ships?"

"Looks like six battlecruisers and twelve escort cruisers," Lieutenant Lena Brooks reported from her sensor station. "Also about a dozen cargo ships with four more escort cruisers are trailing the leading fleet."

"Pirates," muttered Andrew, shaking his head in disgust. "We should drop in on their home world and wipe them out, just like they did some of the cities on Earth."

Kurt knew Andrew was still bitter over the Profiteers taking his wife and daughter prisoner, transporting them to the Gothan Empire and the deplorable planet Kubitz, where anything and everything was for sale, a literal den of thieves. The Profiteers had been training Andrew's wife and daughter to sell as household servants, when Andrew and Kurt had traveled to Kubitz and bought their freedom, as well as the others taken from Earth.

"Are they Marsten ships?" asked Kurt in a low voice.

Andrew had mentioned several times about going to Marsten and dropping a few nukes in revenge. Kurt knew Andrew wasn't the only one to feel that way.

"Unknown," answered Lena, shaking her head as she narrowed her eyes, studying the data on her sensor screen more closely. "We can't identify the individual ships until we drop from hyperspace and close the range."

"Keep an eye out for the Ascendant Destruction," ordered Kurt in a colder voice. "If it's there, I want it destroyed."

The Ascendant Destruction was High Profiteer Creed's ship, which had led the takeover of Earth, and then Creed's men had stripped the planet of much of its wealth. High Profiteer Creed had ordered the nukes dropped on Earth as the Profiteers and the Dacroni mercenaries fled the system. Kurt would never forget the sight, seeing all the mushroom clouds rising above so many of Earth's cities.

"Grantz swore this was a Marsten Profiteer fleet," Andrew said. He didn't like Grantz, but the former-Profiteer-turned-informant had his uses. "The Ascendant Destruction could be here!"

"I hope it is," Kurt replied. It would be a huge morale booster if he could go back home and report the pirate leader was dead.

"Four minutes to hyperspace dropout," Lieutenant Charles Styles reported from the Helm.

"All ships are maintaining formation and should drop out oriented for combat," added Andrew, looking at the long-range sensor screen.

The long-range sensors were capable of detecting ships in hyperspace. Their design had originated in the Gothan Empire but had been modified for use on Earth and Newton warships.

Kurt took a deep breath and activated his comm unit, which could put him in touch with any ship in the fleet, even in hyperspace, as long as they were nearby. "Rear Admiral White, is the Ranger ready for its first combat mission?" The Ranger was the new heavy carrier built at Newton Station. It had all the most modern weapons and incorporated numerous design upgrades to make her the most deadly ship in her class.

"We're ready," answered Rear Admiral Susan White. "Our Lance fighters and Scorpion bombers are ready to launch. Fighters are armed with Thors, and bombers are armed with two Hydra missiles each."

"Keep in mind we have two priority targets, the Ascendant Destruction—if it's here—and capturing those cargo ships."

Kurt intended to make the Profiteers pay dearly for this little venture of theirs. This would be his first opportunity, since driving them from Earth, to hit them where it hurt—in their accumulation of credits. The Profiteers did everything based on how many credits they could earn on their raids. Kurt was determined to make this raid a financial disaster, costing the Profiteers as many credits as possible.

On the sensor screen, twelve planets were now distinct orbs.

"What do we know about this system?" asked Andrew.

Kurt knew Andrew had gotten some of the basics from an earlier briefing, but he probably wondered if Kurt had any additional information. Since a lot of what they knew came from Grantz, Kurt and Andrew felt uneasy fully trusting it. As everyone realized, Grantz was primarily interested in one thing and one thing only: acquiring more gold!

Kurt leaned back in his command chair. They still had a few minutes before dropout. "It has twelve planets with planet number four inhabited by a race very similar to Humans. They've explored several of the nearer star systems but haven't encountered any alien or other humanoid civilizations."

"Well, that's about to change," muttered Andrew with a frown. "What about their space fleet?"

"Supposedly they have a few armed ships but not many."

"Any bases or colonies on the moons or other planets in their system?"

Kurt frowned and shook his head. "We don't know. All Grantz learned was that a group of Marsten Profiteers had discovered a new humanoid world which they intended to exploit. We're here to stop them and extract a little revenge."

"One minute to dropout," spoke Lieutenant Styles.

Kurt nodded and then announced over his ship-to-ship comm, "All ships, set Condition One and prepare for imminent combat."

-

Immediately the alarm klaxons sounded, and red lights flashed. On various ships of Kurt's fleet, crews prepared for combat, hoping that finally they would get revenge on the Profiteers who had so mortally damaged their home planet. Iron cold eyes watched the viewscreens, and white-knuckled hands were poised above the controls. In the fighters and bombers on board the Ranger, pilots sat in their cockpits, their eyes focused straight ahead, waiting for the signal to launch.

Suddenly the minute passed, and the fourteen ships of Fleet Admiral Vickers's task force dropped from hyperspace into the

Julbian System. Four battlecruisers, one heavy carrier, two light carriers, and seven light cruisers were ready to meet the Profiteers in combat.

-

Alarms sounded on the sensor console, and several red lights flashed. "Sensor contacts," reported Lieutenant Brooks, as red threat icons appeared on her screen. "Confirmed six Profiteer battlecruisers and twelve escort cruisers in the lead fleet. The second fleet comprises twelve cargo ships and four escort cruisers."

"The Ascendant Destruction?" asked Kurt, his eyes focused intently on Lieutenant Brooks.

Lena nodded as she turned to look at the admiral. "It's here!"

Kurt let out a deep and satisfying breath. "All ships, the Ascendant Destruction has been detected. Primary targets are the cargo ships and the Ascendant Destruction. One month's leave to the ship that kills that bastard!"

Across the fleet, the gazes of the commanding officers grew determined. Here was the ship and the Profiteer leader who had killed tens of millions of Humans in the nuclear bombardment of Earth. There was no thought of mercy; the Profiteers, due to their callousness, deserved none.

"Rear Admiral White, your job is to capture the cargo ships and annihilate those four escort cruisers. The battlecruiser Trinity will assist you. Captain Watkins, you have command of both light carriers. I want as many of those escort cruisers as possible taken out. You have the light cruisers Alton, Sydney, and Dallas to assist. The rest of us will go after the Profiteer battlecruisers and the Ascendant Destruction. Good luck and good hunting."

-

In space, the Human fleet broke up into three attack formations. From the three carriers, all fighters and bombers launched while the main portion of the fleet raced toward the Profiteer battlecruisers with weapons primed and revenge in their sights.

-

"Sensor contacts!" called out Third Profiteer Bixt from his sensor station on the Profiteer flagship. "They just dropped from hyperspace behind us."

"Another Profiteer fleet moving in on our territory," rumbled Second Profiteer Lantz, showing anger in his eyes. Lantz was bipedal and slightly taller than a Human. His skin was a light-blue color with coarse white hair on his head. His face, while humanoid, had larger-than-normal eyes. "How did our destination leak out?"

"Contact that fleet and see who dares to intrude on us," ordered High Profiteer Creed angrily. "We have a signed contract with the Controllers on Kubitz, claiming this world as ours to exploit. There will be stiff penalties if another Profiteer clan is attempting to infringe on our rights."

The sensor operator's eyes suddenly widened, and his face turned pale. "They are not Profiteer ships. They're Human!"

"Plhtup!" swore Creed, turning toward the sensor operator in disbelief. "Are you certain of that?" This had to be Fleet Admiral Vickers. Creed knew he should have killed the admiral when he had the chance.

"Yes, they've already launched their small attack craft and are moving rapidly into weapons range."

"The Humans seek to destroy us for what we did to their world," said Second Profiteer Lantz fearfully. "We must withdraw. There is no profit to be made here if we engage the Humans."

Still Creed hesitated. Since the Humans had driven his fleet and the Dacroni mercenary ships from Earth, Creed had been searching for a new world to exploit. This humanoid-inhabited planet in the Julbian System, while not as rich as Earth, would have served as a reasonable replacement. Its women would sell well in the slave markets on Kubitz for use in the pleasure houses, and the men would be ideal for hard labor. Now the Humans threatened to ruin everything. Creed regretted not bringing a few mercenary ships with him. He had opted to save a few credits, and now that decision might prove costly.

"They're attacking our cargo ships," cried out Second Profiteer Lantz, as he saw several small explosions on one of the viewscreens on the front wall of the Command Center. The cargo ships didn't have energy shields and were vulnerable to attack. Those ships were expensive, and he could already see his profits plummeting from this venture.

Creed snapped out of his thoughts to save his fleet. He could always find other worlds to conquer and strip them of their wealth. Better to preserve his fleet and return home. "Order all ships to jump into hyperspace and return to Marsten."

-

Strike Commander Captain William Anders felt the power in his Scorpion bomber as he streaked toward his target, a large Profiteer cargo ship. "All bombers, target the engineering compartments. We want to disable the hyperdrives so they can't jump out."

Around him, the nine other small bombers in his squadron were formed up in a diamond formation. "As soon as we get within range, split up and target the cargo ships designated Big Momma and Big Poppa. I don't want to see either of them jumping to safety." Captain Anders knew that other bombers were targeting the other cargo ships.

The bombers flew in, facing no resistance as the escort cruisers were busy with the fighters and the battlecruiser Trinity. Two hundred small attack craft had been launched by the Ranger. One hundred and twenty Lance fighters and eighty Scorpion bombers were inbound toward the Profiteer vessels. The bombers were primarily targeting the cargo ships, and the fighters were headed for the escort cruisers.

A pinging noise on the flight console in front of Captain Anders indicated a target lock on the large cargo ship he was approaching. Pressing a button on his flight control panel, a Hydra missile dropped away from the bomber's wing and headed swiftly toward its target.

"Missile away!" yelled pilot Lieutenant Davis over the squadron comm channel.

"Mine too!" called out pilot Lieutenant Jamie Schmidt.

Other bomber pilots indicated missile launches as well.

Several bright explosions marked the impact of missiles on the largest cargo ship, designated Big Poppa. The cargo ships were not protected by energy shields and were easy prey to the missiles. The warheads on the missiles had been replaced with a weaker one, designed to disable a ship and not destroy it. The cargo ship instantly lost power and began drifting in space. More missiles impacted the other large cargo ship, and soon it too was powerless. The Profiteers had just lost two large and very expensive cargo vessels.

Captain Anders flew low over both ships, inspecting the damage. The hulls were blackened in several sections with a large hole in the hull directly over the engineering spaces. He carefully checked his sensors as he scanned each vessel. While the damage to the engineering sections was substantial, there was no danger of the ships blowing up. If they could be taken back to Newton Station, these cargo ships could be easily repaired and put to good use.

"All bombers, we'll circle our two targets until the battle is over. Keep your sensors focused on the two cargo ships. If there's any indication they're repairing their damages, we'll hit them again." Each Scorpion bomber still possessed a second Hydra missile if needed.

Anders then switched his comm to the frequency used by the cargo ships. "Attention Marsten cargo vessels. Any attempt to repair your damage will result in the destruction of your vessels. Prepare to be boarded. Your crews will be returned to Kubitz unharmed." Anders didn't bother to mention Fleet Admiral Vickers would demand payment from the Marsten Profiteers for the safe return of the cargo ships' crews. Anders allowed himself to smile. Two could play that game of making profits on the black market planet.

-

Captain Cheryl Anniston bit her lip as she anxiously took the eight-hundred-meter-long battlecruiser Trinity in toward the four escort cruisers that were her targets. The Lance fighters had just hit all four of the cruisers with their entire complement of Thor missiles.

"Our shields are at 97 percent," reported Tactical. "Weapons are online and ready to fire. Enemy energy shields have been substantially weakened by the fighter strike."

"Hit target one with a spread of hypermissiles followed up by our particle beam cannon," ordered Anniston, leaning forward in her command chair. The hypermissiles had been purchased at Kubitz and then modified for use on Human ships.

-

On the outer hull of the Trinity, six missile hatches instantly slid open. A sudden flash of light indicated the launch of the missiles, and then they vanished as they entered hyperspace. Moments later they struck the energy shield of one of the Profiteer escort cruisers. Each missile was equipped with a ten-kiloton warhead, and the shield became markedly visible as it strained to withstand the sudden assault of energy. Then a dark blue particle beam slammed into the weakened energy screen, penetrating it and striking the thin armor on the hull.

A jarring explosion shook the small vessel, and glowing debris flew away from the ship. Where the particle beam had struck, a huge hole now resided in the side of the vessel. Secondary explosions shook the ship, and then, with a sudden flash of light, the cruiser exploded as its power systems were compromised.

-

"Escort cruiser is down," reported the lieutenant, sitting in front of the sensor console.

"Switch to secondary target," ordered Captain Anniston, more at ease now that battle had been joined.

The Trinity vibrated, and a console shorted out, sending a shower of bright sparks across the Command Center.

"Hypermissile strike to the energy screen," reported Tactical. "It's holding at 84 percent."

"Captain, enemy target number three is in trouble," the Trinity's sensor operator reported. "The Scorpion bombers are really working it over." A squadron of the small bombers had been diverted to launch a missile strike against the Profiteer escort cruiser.

Cheryl looked up at one of the viewscreens, seeing numerous flashes of light as small Hydra missiles equipped with ten-kiloton warheads impacted the Profiteer escort cruiser's energy screen, which suddenly failed. As additional Hydra warheads detonated, the enemy ship was blown into a million pieces, turning it into a burning pyre of wreckage.

"Escort cruiser is down," reported the sensor operator with a pleased look on his face.

Cheryl nodded. "That's what the Profiteers get for arming their ships so lightly to save money."

That was one of the things Fleet Admiral Vickers had learned from the warships he had purchased from Kubitz. The ships were woefully under armed to save credits. Newton Station totally refurbished the weapons systems on the battleships and battlecruisers Kurt had purchased.

-

High Profiteer Creed seethed with anger. Two of his escort cruisers were down. Both of the large cargo ships had been disabled, and the Humans were attacking the others. This profit venture was rapidly turning into a disaster. "How long before we can jump out of here?" he demanded, turning an icy stare toward Navigation.

"Two minutes," replied Third Profiteer Holbat. "I'm powering up the drive now. We weren't expecting to jump so soon."

"Plhtup," groaned Second Profiteer Lantz as he rolled his eyes. "We'll lose all of our cargo ships in two more minutes. Ships we'll have to pay to replace back at Kubitz."

The Ascendant Destruction suddenly shook violently, and warning alarms sounded. High Profiteer Creed was nearly thrown to the deck. With a snarl, he buckled his safety harness tighter. "All weapons, fire on the Humans." For once Creed was thankful he had spent the extra credits to have his flagship fully upgraded with the most powerful energy shield possible. In hindsight, he should have spent more on his other ships for the same improvements. Now that error would turn costly.

-

In space, the six-hundred-meter-long light carriers Vindication and Dante closed the range on the Profiteer escort cruisers. Already both carriers had launched their bombers and fighters, which were currently on attack runs. Once the bombers and fighters delivered their missile payloads, the three light cruisers accompanying the carriers would move in to finish off the escorts.

"Fighters and bombers are making their attack runs," reported Lieutenant Anthony Dries, the executive officer. "They're meeting very little defensive fire."

Captain Henry Watkins nodded. "That's because the Profiteers aren't used to defending against small attack craft. Most of the races we've encountered from the Gothan Empire don't use them." Henry leaned back in his command chair. He had been friends with Fleet Admiral Vickers for years and knew where his primary focus was in this fight. "What's the status on the Ascendant Destruction?" Everyone in the fleet hungered for the destruction of that Profiteer vessel and the death of its High Profiteer.

"It's under attack from the Star Cross, Carlsbad, and Himalaya. The four light cruisers with the admiral are attacking another one of the Profiteers' battlecruisers," reported Lieutenant Julie Jenkins from her sensor console.

Henry nodded. "Keep me informed. We need to focus on our mission and take out as many of these escort cruisers as we can." However, Henry knew everyone in the fleet waited to hear if the Ascendant Destruction had been destroyed.

-

The fighters and bombers from the two light carriers swept in, facing little resistance, and, from point-blank range, launched their Thor and Hydra missiles. Nuclear fire raged across the shields of three Profiteer cruisers. Then the sixty small attack craft turned and fled back toward the safety of the carriers, knowing what would occur next. From the light cruisers Dallas, Alton, and Sydney, six hypermissiles launched from each one. The missiles jumped into hyperspace to slam into the weakened shields of the Profiteer escort cruisers. Blistering explosions of nuclear energy rolled across the defensive screens. All the hypermissiles had struck a relatively small area.

Almost immediately from the three light cruisers, dark blue particle beams flashed out, penetrating the energy shields and striking deep into the hulls of the Profiteer ships. Explosions shook the vessels, and then the light cruisers fired their bow KEW cannons, hurling dual two-thousand-pound projectiles at 10 percent the speed of light. When the rounds struck the Profiteer vessels, the ships simply disintegrated from the massive release of kinetic energy.

-

"We got three of them!" boasted Lieutenant Dries with a satisfied grin. "That's cutting them down to size."

"Remaining enemy escort cruisers are transiting into hyperspace," warned Lieutenant Jenkins. "We won't get the rest of them."

Captain Watkins turned toward the main viewscreen, showing the remaining escort cruisers disappearing. He also noticed four cargo ships and one of their escort cruisers were escaping as well. He let out a deep sigh; it had been too much to hope to get them all.

Glancing at another screen, he saw the Star Cross and the other Human battlecruisers were heavily engaged with the six Profiteer battlecruisers. The enemy ships were putting up substantial resistance.

"Send our light cruisers to aid Fleet Admiral Vickers," ordered Captain Watkins.

He saw one Profiteer battlecruiser under extremely heavy attack, its energy screen alight with nuclear explosions. There was no doubt in his mind that this was the Ascendant Destruction. With concern, he saw that one of Admiral Vickers's accompanying light cruisers targeted by several Profiteer battlecruisers was in trouble.

-

The light cruiser Badger reeled from the attack of two Profiteer battlecruisers intent on its destruction. Its defensive shield was in danger of failing as more power was required to keep it up.

"Status?" demanded Captain Harris, seeing the frightened looks on his crew.

The ship suddenly shook violently, and the lights dimmed.

"We just lost two of our energy beam turrets, and we have fires in sections seven and eight on the starboard outer hull," the executive officer reported. "Numerous compartments are open to space with heavy casualties."

"Pull us back," grated out Captain Harris, knowing his ship was badly damaged. If they didn't withdraw, the ship would be lost.

"Sublight drive has failed," the helm officer reported grimly. "We're shifting all our available power to the energy shield!"

A rumbling noise suddenly filled the Command Center. Harris looked questionably at his executive officer, who shook her head.

"Secondary explosions. We won't last much longer."

Harris nodded. This was a good crew, and he wished he could have taken them back home one more time. Before he could say anything, a bright light filled the Command Center.

-

"Light cruiser Badger is down," reported Lieutenant Brooks as she saw the cruiser's green icon suddenly expand and then fade away on her sensor screen.

Kurt sucked in a deep breath. There had always been a risk of losing some ships in this battle. "Keep our focus on the Ascendant Destruction and the other battlecruisers. I want to hurt them as much as possible."

"Firing particle beam," said Lieutenant Evelyn Mays as she let loose the deadly weapon on the enemy flagship.

-

"Our surviving escort cruisers and four of our cargo ships have transitioned into hyperspace," reported Second Profiteer Lantz. He had a jagged cut across his forehead from slamming into his control console. "The other cargo ships have been disabled, and their escort cruisers destroyed."

The Ascendant Destruction suddenly rang like a bell, and more alarms sounded.

"Particle beam strike to our hull," cried out Lantz, gazing in horror at the damage control console, lighting up in red warning lights. "Our hull's been compromised."

"Can we jump into hyperspace?" Creed knew, if they couldn't, they were doomed.

"Borderline," reported Holbat. "We may burn out the drive in the process."

The ship shook violently, and several consoles exploded. Third Profiteer Lukon screamed and fell to the floor, leaving the communications console unattended.

"Jump us," yelled Creed, his face stormy. "If you don't, we're all dead!"

Moments later High Profiteer Creed felt the ship jump into hyperspace. The sounds of battle faded away, and the ship settled down. "Report!"

He didn't even want to contemplate how much the Humans had just cost him. It would take tens of millions in credits just to replace the ships and crews he had lost, let alone the assets he sought within the system of Julbian. He fully intended to return to Kubitz and file a complaint against the Humans with the Controllers, though he knew it would do little good since the

Humans were not a part of the Gothan Empire. However, he might get some trade restrictions put on them.

"We've got a problem," reported Second Profiteer Lantz, his face pale. "Our engineer reports the hyperdrive is overheating, and we can't stay in hyperspace for long without burning it out. If we lose the drive, we won't make it back home."

Creed looked worriedly around the Command Center. He didn't dare drop from hyperspace too soon or the Humans might find them. "Tell Engineer Gext to keep the drive online as long as possible. When he thinks we've pushed it as far as we can, then we'll drop from hyperspace and begin repairs."

High Profiteer Creed coughed from the smoke still in the air. He wasn't even sure if his other battlecruisers had made it out. Not until he returned to Marsten would he know the full extent of his losses. He cursed the Humans. Something would have to be done so they couldn't continue to interfere in Profiteer business. When he made it back to Marsten and later to Kubitz, it might be necessary to speak with the mercenaries again.

-

Kurt felt extremely disappointed as the Ascendant Destruction escaped into hyperspace along with four other battlecruisers. The final remaining battlecruiser was under heavy attack from the light cruisers and now the Himalaya. Obviously the ship's hyperdrive was damaged, and it couldn't flee. In an eye-opening explosion the ship blew up, sending fiery debris across space narrowly missing one of the light cruisers.

"Profiteer battlecruiser is down," confirmed Lieutenant Brooks. "The others have escaped into hyperspace."

"We should have used the more powerful hypermissiles," said Captain Randson, showing his frustration at the Ascendant Destruction escaping.

Kurt knew Andrew was right. They only had a few of the powerful fifty-megaton antimatter missiles, and Kurt had been hesitant to use them. Only the battlecruisers were armed with them, and each one only carried a few.

"How many of them did we get?" Even if High Profiteer Creed had escaped, Kurt knew it had been at a heavy cost. "We'll have other opportunities at the Ascendant Destruction."

Captain Randson spent a few minutes examining some data on his command screen as well as speaking to several other ships, including the Vindication and the Ranger. When he was done, he turned around with a huge grin. "We captured eight of their cargo ships, including the two big jobs. We also destroyed six of their escort cruisers and one of their battlecruisers."

"Our own losses?"

Andrew slowly shook his head. "We lost the light cruiser Badger and all hands on board."

Kurt hated losing the crew and their ship, but the Profiteers had lost a lot more. In addition, Kurt now had eight more cargo ships, which could be taken back to Newton as soon as the fleet tugs were called in. Not only that, he intended to contact the world of Julbian. Just maybe, if everything worked out right, Newton had gained their first ally.

Chapter Two

Fleet Admiral Kurt Vickers breathed a long sigh of relief as the Star Cross exited hyperspace in the Newton System. It felt good to be home after their successful mission to Julbian. His only regret was that the Ascendant Destruction and High Profiteer Creed had escaped. Kurt allowed a smirk to cross his face as he thought about the captured cargo ships and the Profiteer ships they had destroyed. Creed's little jaunt to the Julbian System had cost him a fortune, and that pleased Kurt immensely. He would have other opportunities in the future to bring the Profiteer to justice.

On board the Star Cross was a delegation of Humans from Julbian. The Julbians had been shocked to learn of the existence of other humanoid races as well as of the Gothan Empire. Kurt had shown the Julbian leaders some videos of the occupation of Earth and how the Profiteers had tried to strip it of its valuables as well as kidnap men, women, and even children to be sold in the slave markets on Kubitz. Kurt made it very clear what the Profiteers had planned for Julbian. Their leaders had immediately requested to meet with Governor Spalding and see the defenses around Newton. If things went well, the Julbians would be signing a trade agreement as well as laying the groundwork for a future alliance.

"Do you think the Profiteers will attack Julbian again?" asked Andrew as he watched Newton grow larger on the ship's main viewscreen.

Newton was the only other fully Earth-type world discovered in Earth's explorations. Now they knew many others were scattered across the galaxy, and most of them were inhabited.

"No, I doubt it," replied Kurt, folding his arms across his chest as he gazed at the viewscreen and the blue-white world they were approaching. "That's why I left the Ranger and two battlecruisers behind. We'll get the fleet tugs on the way in the next day or two to pick up those disabled cargo ships as well as a passenger liner for the Profiteer crews. The Vindication, along with four light cruisers, will escort the tugs and passenger liner. Two of the light cruisers will stay behind to add to Rear Admiral White's task group. If Governor Spalding's meeting with the Julbians goes as planned, we'll send a cargo ship back with some defensive satellites to place in orbit." Kurt didn't mention they would have to make a trip to Kubitz to replace any satellites they sent to Julbian.

"How long will you leave the Ranger and our other ships there?" Andrew felt uncomfortable having three of their most powerful warships away from Newton. His wife and daughter were on that planet, and, after their harrowing abduction from Earth, and almost being sold into servitude, he didn't want them to worry about it happening on Newton.

"Only a month or two," Kurt answered. He could see Newton Station on the viewscreen now. The massive space station was capable of repairing and building any type of ship Kurt needed for the fleet. "They'll help the Julbians upgrade their own warships with more modern weapons. We'll send some construction people and technicians on the passenger liner to assist with the upgrades. Fortunately they have a small shipyard in orbit that should suffice to do the necessary work. Once that's done, and, with the addition of the defensive satellites, it should discourage any future Profiteer incursions."

Andrew looked pensive. "The Julbians only have six medium-size cruisers to defend their system. Will that be enough?"

"I'll permanently assign one of the battleships we bought from Kubitz to the system," Kurt explained. He had already spent some time thinking about this. "It's been fully upgraded and will have a full load of hypermissiles. That, along with the six cruisers and the defensive grid, should prevent any further attacks from the Profiteers."

"Unless they return with mercenaries," Andrew pointed out.

In the Gothan Empire, several mercenary groups routinely hired themselves out to deal with potential problems the Profiteer clans encountered. The most notorious were the Dacroni mercenaries, who had assisted High Profiteer Creed in his earlier conquest of Earth's solar system.

"We'll deal with that when and if it occurs," answered Kurt, looking at Andrew meaningfully. Kurt didn't want to spread his own forces too thin. The galaxy was a much more dangerous place than many had believed possible.

"We'll dock with Newton Station in twenty minutes," Lieutenant Styles reported as he moved the large eight-hundred-meter-long battlecruiser toward a docking port.

Kurt gazed at the massive shipyard. On one quadrant, he could see new construction. A second flight bay would increase the number of fighters and bombers available to the station for its own defense. Even as he watched, four Lance fighters exited from the other flight bay to go on their patrol route. The space around Newton was heavily protected with a complete and extremely powerful defensive grid encircling the planet. Not even a fully armed Dacroni mercenary fleet could put a dent in the defenses around Newton. Kurt had done everything in his power to ensure the colony was secure and safe from future attacks. It had been expensive and cost a lot of Earth's gold, but it was well worth it.

"Several passenger liners from Earth just dropped from hyperspace," reported Lieutenant Lena Brooks, as two large green icons suddenly appeared on her sensor screen with a smaller one. "They're escorted by the destroyer Malvin."

Kurt nodded. All cargo ships and passenger liners coming from Earth now did so with an armed escort. He had assigned their remaining destroyers to escort duty as they were too small to be effective against Profiteer ships or mercenaries. He also had no plans to build any more of the small ships.

"How many people do we have on Newton now?" asked Andrew, glancing at the tactical screen and the three inbound green icons.

Ever since Earth had been freed from the Profiteers, a steady flow of new colonists were coming to Newton. The living conditions back on Earth were still pretty miserable due to all the nuclear warheads that had been detonated. Chemicals had been brought in from the Gothan Empire to help disperse and reduce the radiation, but it had been expensive and had cost a fortune in gold. However, the use of the chemicals had probably saved million of lives.

"We're nearing twelve million," Kurt answered. "Governor Spalding says he's nearly swamped finding accommodations for all of them. Before we left on this mission, he mentioned sending the Star Cross to Kubitz to see if we can purchase some better construction technology to help with the housing shortage. Tens of thousands of people are living in a few tent cities on the surface, while awaiting permanent housing."

"Kubitz," muttered Andrew, shaking his head disgustedly. "I hate that planet. I still don't understand why all the civilized races in the galaxy tolerate the Gothan Empire. You would think they would join together and take out those Profiteers once and for all."

"Their worlds are too heavily defended," responded Kurt. "You saw what the defenses around Kubitz look like. They dwarf what we've put around Newton."

Andrew nodded, and then shook his head. "How soon are we leaving? I'd like to see my wife and daughter."

"Not for a few days. I still need to talk to Governor Spalding. I also want to take care of this trading agreement and alliance with the Julbians, and the Vindication and the fleet tugs must be sent off. We'll give the crews a couple days' leave before we set out for Kubitz."

"What if we run across the Ascendant Destruction when we get there?" asked Andrew.

Most of the Profiteers routinely visited the planet. "We'll cross that road when we get there," Kurt replied in a steady voice. In the Kubitz System, they dared not engage the Profiteer ship, but outside the system was a different matter entirely.

-

Later that afternoon Kurt walked up to his sister's house. He heard a loud shout from within, and the door flew open. Flying out came eight-year-old Bryan, his eyes wide upon seeing Kurt.

"Uncle Kurt!" yelled Bryan, bouncing with excitement. "You're here!" Bryan ran to Kurt and grabbed him by the hand. "Did you blow up any alien ships? Did you kill that evil Profiteer everyone's talking about?"

"Bryan!" admonished Denise as she stepped out on the porch, frowning at her young son. "You shouldn't ask your uncle those kinds of questions."

"Hi, Denise," Kurt said, pleased to see his sister. "Have you seen Keera the last few days?"

Keera was a Human doctor he had met on Kubitz and had fallen in love with. Most of the time when Kurt was on leave or on planet, the two spent their time together. Keera worked at Newton's main medical center, teaching techniques and medical procedures used across the galaxy to cure various afflictions. She had even talked Kurt into purchasing some very advanced medical equipment from Kubitz to bring back to Newton.

"She was over last night for supper," answered Denise, indicating for Kurt to follow her into the house. "She mentioned something about going to Aston to give a speech on advanced medical practices for the treatment of the elderly."

"Sounds like her," Kurt said as he sat down on the sofa. "She takes her medical profession very seriously." It was one of the things he liked about Keera.

"She's good at what she does," Denise said, as she walked into the kitchen and returned with two glasses of iced tea. She handed one to Kurt and sat down across from him. "Alex is at work and won't be home for a few more hours."

Bryan sat down next to Kurt and glanced at his mother, then his eyes shifted to his uncle. "So, did you blow up any ships?"

Kurt laughed. Bryan was so inquisitive and always full of questions. "A few," he admitted. "We brought some new people from another world back with us."

"Do they have four arms or wings?" asked Bryan, his face lighting up with curiosity. "Are they aliens?"

"Bryan!" exclaimed Denise with a deep frown. "That's not polite."

"Well," Bryan said, defending himself. "Keera told me, on some worlds, people have wings and can actually fly. She promised to show me some pictures when I get older."

"Not these," said Kurt, shaking his head. "They look just like you and me, and I think we'll be good friends."

"Why don't you go play?" suggested Denise to Bryan with a smile. "I'm sure I can talk Uncle Kurt into staying for supper."

"Will you?" begged Bryan, looking expectantly at Kurt.

"Sure," Kurt answered. "I don't have anything else planned." Besides, his sister was a sensational cook.

"Great!" responded Bryan happily. "Maybe we can play some baseball. I'm getting pretty good at hitting the ball with my bat."

Denise sighed and nodded. "He can hit the ball. He broke out the neighbor's window the other night."

"Sure," Kurt said to Bryan. "We'll play some later."

That seemed to satisfy the young boy as he turned and headed toward his room.

Once Bryan left, Denise studied her older brother. "Did you run across High Profiteer Creed?"

Kurt leaned back on the sofa, relaxing. It amazed him how comfortable the sofa was. Nothing like this was in his quarters on the Star Cross. "Yes, it was his Profiteer fleet we found in the Julbian System. Unfortunately he got away, but we captured most of his cargo ships and destroyed some of his other vessels."

Denise nodded. "You'll get him someday. It's only a matter of time."

Kurt hoped Denise was right. A lot of anger remained, particularly on Earth, over what had happened during the

Profiteer occupation. Killing High Profiteer Creed and destroying the Ascendant Destruction would alleviate much of that.

-

The next day Kurt sat in Governor Spalding's office. He had been summoned here to discuss the impending negotiations with the Julbians.

Spalding stood at the large window that overlooked the capital city. In the past year, its inhabitants had grown from six hundred thousand to nearly one million. Most of the growth had been new colonists coming from Earth.

"Things have really changed in the last two years, and they still are," Spalding said as he turned around to face Kurt. "We have more and more people on Earth applying for colonizing visas every day."

"How many more will you allow?" Kurt knew the cargo ships and the passenger liners were hard-pressed to keep up with the demand from people on Earth wishing to migrate to Newton.

"That depends. Things on Earth are still pretty chaotic. It's all President Mayfield can do to keep the North American Union from collapsing. There's a lot of discontent and threats against the government. The same problems have been experienced by the European Union and the Russian Collective, though I understand the Chinese Conglomerate has come through pretty much unaffected. They have a much tighter control on their people."

"What about the gold reserves sent from Earth?" asked Kurt. Most of the major countries on the planet had sent their reserves to Newton for safekeeping.

Governor Spalding's eyes narrowed sharply, and he let out a deep and regretful sigh. "They've been sent back. Every government, including the North American Union, demanded we return what was sent here. They were quite unhappy to find out how much of it we spent at Kubitz and then paid Avery Dolman when he came here. They demanded an accounting of every credit we spent."

"You didn't send it all back, did you?" asked Kurt. They might need that gold at a later date as very little minable gold remained on Newton or on the other worlds and moons of the system. Earth was unique in having gold deposits so close to the surface, making mining it relatively easy.

"No," admitted Spalding with a guilty look. "Earth has no way to know how much we spent of their reserves. I kept 10 percent of what remained, and I have no intention of sending them an itemized list of what we spent."

"That's still quite a bit," answered Kurt, with narrowed eyes. "It should allow us to fund the compound on Kubitz and continue to procure the things we need."

"That's not all," said Spalding, a grin crossing his face. "You recall those Profiteer cargo ships you captured before the battle of Earth and during? We kept all the gold and other precious metals on board those ships as well. We still have nearly all that and should be okay in the immediate future, as long as we don't go overboard procuring any more expensive weapon systems."

Kurt nodded, surprised to hear just how much gold and other precious metals they still had. "We also have a large credit balance with the Controllers on Kubitz. Don't forget we stored a lot of gold in the secret vault underneath our embassy compound too."

Spalding's grin grew wider. He had forgotten about that with everything else going on. "Have you spoken to Marvin Tenner recently?"

"No," Kurt answered. "Not since the last time I went to Kubitz. How's he doing?"

Marvin was a former lieutenant who had been in charge of the First Contact team on the Star Cross. He and a few others had volunteered to stay behind on Kubitz and represent Newton's interests. Over the past year, the embassy staff had been substantially increased, as well as a full company of Marines assigned for security. Kubitz could be a dangerous place for the inexperienced.

Spalding was silent for a moment, and then, opening a drawer on his desk, he pulled out a red folder. Laying it down, he opened it. "Two days ago the light cruiser Concord returned from Kubitz. The ship shouldn't have returned for another two weeks. Tenner is growing concerned about some rumors floating around the planet."

"What kind of rumors?" asked Kurt. Rumors were always afloat on Kubitz. Yet he was also concerned. By sending the light cruiser back early, Tenner had no more warships above Kubitz to aid him if he needed it or had to evacuate.

Spalding's brows wrinkled in a deep frown. "There's something going on in the more civilized regions of the galaxy. Reports tell of attacks on the warships of the Protector Worlds and entire populations going missing from some of the colonies of several Enlightened Worlds."

Kurt leaned forward, his interest piqued. "Surely the Gothan Empire isn't attacking the Enlightened Worlds?" Kurt knew the more advanced worlds tended to ignore the Profiteers. However, an outright attack could cause the Protector Worlds to band together and remove the Gothan Empire as a threat. Kurt couldn't imagine the Profiteers taking such a risk.

"No," replied Spalding, glancing down at the report on his desk. "It's someone else."

"Who?" asked Kurt. Just one super advanced warship from any of the higher civilizations could take on Newton's entire fleet with impunity. The highly advanced Protector Worlds were responsible for the defense of the Enlightened Worlds of the galaxy.

"That's just it," Spalding replied, his eyes narrowing sharply. "No one seems to know. Tenner's tried to find out but keeps running into dead ends."

"Or no one is willing to pay enough for the information," interjected Kurt knowingly. On Kubitz everything was for sale for the right price. If the information was there, it could be bought.

Spalding was silent for a long moment, and then he spoke. "I think it's time you paid Kubitz another visit. Use Grantz—and even Avery Dolman, if necessary—to get to the bottom of these rumors."

"Why are you so interested in this?" asked Kurt. The highly civilized worlds were far away from Earth and Newton. He also hated the idea of dealing with Dolman. The man was conniving and had his hands in nearly everything illegal on Kubitz.

Spalding leaned forward and spoke in a quieter voice. "I received a message from President Mayfield earlier in the week. Fleet Admiral Tomalson detected some mysterious ships on the outskirts of the Solar System. When approached by Earth fleet units, they fled into hyperspace, refusing to communicate."

"You think there may be a connection? It could be Profiteer ships, checking on Earth's defenses."

"I think we need to find out one way or the other," answered Spalding. "While Newton is heavily defended with the defense grid and our fleet, Earth isn't, and Mayfield knows that."

Kurt understood Spalding's concern. Earth was now protected by a minimal defensive grid and a small group of warships purchased from the Kubitz shipyards. Four battleships and six battlecruisers were all the ships currently under Earth's control. The ships had been updated at Newton Station before they were turned over to Earth and Fleet Admiral Tomalson.

"Mayfield tried to talk the other Cabinet members into leaving a major portion of the NAU gold here, but the Cabinet blocked his request," Spalding added. "They won't even approve expanding the defensive grid or buying more ships for Earth."

"Who's blocking everything?"

"It's Marlen Stroud," muttered Spalding unhappily.

Kurt rued the day when Secretary of Labor Marlen Stroud had been returned to Earth. He was supposed to stand trial for subversion and treason. He had bribed the Chinese Conglomerate to get him, his family, his servants, and his faithful cronies to Newton when legal routes had otherwise hindered him. He had also attempted to take control of the Newton government. Unfortunately he still had enough political connections that several Cabinet members decided to side with him and allow

Stroud to be reinstated in his former position. Mayfield had asked for Stroud's resignation, but the secretary of labor had refused.

Due to the events of the Profiteer occupation and the nuclear strikes, Mayfield was in a significantly weakened position, and his popularity was way down. The next election was in sixteen months, and Mayfield expected to lose. It was one of the reasons so many skilled young people were emigrating to Newton. Behind the scenes, both Mayfield and Fleet Admiral Tomalson were encouraging the emigration. They greatly feared events on Earth could take a downward turn, depending upon who the next president was. They wanted Newton able to stand on its own and to have the resources and people necessary to do so.

"What about the new construction equipment you mentioned before I took the fleet to Julbian?"

"Check into it. We have a lot of homes to build as well as new industries. I spoke to your friend Malen Jelk, and she mentioned a number of different automated factories available on Kubitz. The Newton Princess will accompany you, along with a special team of business people who are familiar with what we need."

Kurt nodded. He was surprised that Spalding had talked to Keera, who was known as Malen to Spalding. "We'll leave in two days. I let the crews go on leave, and I still need to take care of a few things."

"What ships will you take?"

Kurt thought for a minute before he replied. "The Star Cross, the light carrier Wasp, as well as two light cruisers. That should be sufficient to protect the Newton Princess and encourage any Profiteers we run across to leave us alone." Kurt knew the Newton Princess would be a tempting target for the Profiteers but not if the passenger liner was well protected. "What about the negotiations with the Julbians?"

"Scheduled for later this afternoon," Spalding answered. "I spoke to their leader earlier, and he seems quite amicable. I don't see any problems with signing a trade agreement, though laying out the groundwork for a future alliance might take a little longer."

"Hopefully this is only the first of many. Do you want me at the meeting?"

Spalding shook his head. "Meetings like this are best left to civilian authorities. If something comes up that needs your expertise, I'll get in contact with you."

Kurt was glad Governor Spalding felt confident enough to handle the negotiations.

"Enjoy your time off. You deserve it."

Kurt was determined to form a large enough alliance so that, someday, they could challenge the Gothan Empire and force them to stop their Profiteering. However, that was a long ways in the future and might be nearly impossible. He recalled how long the Barbary pirates had raided in the Mediterranean, and he was afraid the Gothan Empire would be even more difficult to bring under control.

-

A few hours later Kurt took a short ride to an apartment building and went upstairs to the apartment he shared with Keera whenever he was on Newton. Stepping inside, he was pleasantly surprised to see her sitting on the couch, waiting for him.

"I wondered when you would show up," she said reproachfully as she stood up and kissed him on the lips. Keera had been trained in the medical field on one of the more advanced worlds. She had then gone to Kubitz with her brother and taken a job working in one of the larger medical centers.

Kurt stepped back from Keera. Since meeting her on Kubitz, she had provided something that had long been missing from his life. "I understand you've been giving more lectures."

Keera grinned and nodded her head. "Yes, I've been all over the planet, demonstrating modern medical technology and treatments. I've put together another list of additional equipment I need from Kubitz. It's a rather long one."

Kurt sighed. Keera always desired more of the medical technology available on Kubitz and many other worlds. However, the technology saved lives and was an easy sale when he put in the requests to Governor Spalding.

"I'm leaving for Kubitz in a few days," admitted Kurt, knowing she would expect him to return with her latest equipment requests. "Governor Spalding wants me to bring back to Newton some better technology to help with our housing crisis. We can't build new homes fast enough for all the colonists coming in from Earth. I understand you spoke to Governor Spalding the other day?"

"Yes, he was curious about some of the medical technology as well as the factories used on Kubitz."

Kurt nodded. "I'm escorting a team of businessmen on the Newton Princess to see about these factories and some other items."

Keera was silent for a moment as a strange look passed over her face. "I received a message from my brother when the Concord returned."

Kurt's eyes widened. Keera's older brother worked for one of the Profiteer clans on Kubitz and was heavily involved in the black market. Keera very seldom heard from him, as they weren't on the best of terms.

"What did he say?"

"He's frightened," answered Keera, folding her arms across her chest and tilting her head to one side. "He's heard rumors of terrible space battles around some of the colonies of the Enlightened Worlds. Strange black spacecraft are engaging the warfleets of the Protector Worlds and leaving them powerless in space. He fears it's only a matter of time before these strangers show up in the Gothan Empire and over Kubitz."

Keera was very familiar with these worlds, as she had spent some time on several of them. The Protector Worlds were very advanced worlds, which maintained large space fleets to keep the peace. Their primary responsibility was to protect the Enlightened Worlds that had known peace for thousands and even tens of thousands of years. Each Protector World was responsible for the well-being of up to one hundred Enlightened Worlds.

Kurt didn't know what to say. This sounded like the threat Governor Spalding wanted him to investigate. Maybe it was more than just rumors. "I wouldn't worry about Kubitz. That planet has the heaviest planetary defense I've ever seen. I don't think even one of the warships from a Protector World could penetrate it."

Keera stared at Kurt worriedly. "You don't understand because you've never seen the warships of some of the more highly developed worlds. They are much more powerful than you can imagine. It's why the Profiteer fleets give them a wide berth and never attempt to engage them. When you go to Kubitz, I want to go to. I need to speak to Dalen."

Kurt didn't like the idea of her going back to Kubitz. Anytime he went to Kubitz, it could turn dangerous. He was also curious about these warships Keera had spoken of. How strange that both Tenner and Keera's brother had mentioned them. It could still be just a rumor, but it needed to be checked out. Perhaps when he got to Kubitz, he would bite his tongue and speak to Avery Dolman. If the rumors of the black ships were true, Dolman would know. Of course with Dolman, everything came with a price.

Kurt would also like to get more information on the warships of the advanced worlds. It might give him an idea of what type of danger these mysterious black ships represented if they did exist. His attention shifted back to Keera, still waiting for an answer.

"Please, Kurt, this is important. Even though Dalen and I don't get along, he's the only family I have. I have to speak with him. From his message he sounds really frightened."

"Let me think about it overnight, and I'll let you know in the morning."

Keera nodded. "Kurt, this is important to me." She stepped forward, taking his hand, tilting her head, and gazing deeply into his eyes. "He's my brother."

Kurt let out a deep sigh. When she looked at him like that, it was almost impossible to say no. "I need to think about what you just told me. There's so much I'm trying to understand."

"Your answers lie on Kubitz. Everything can be found there," she calmly reminded him.

-

A few days later, Kurt was on Newton Station, preparing to leave for Kubitz. He was meeting with Colonel Hayworth, who was in charge of ship construction on the shipyard, and Colonel Simms, the commanding officer. They stood in one of the station's two construction bays, watching the construction of a new light carrier.

"That's the Ticonderoga," Hayworth said with a pleased smile. "In two more months she'll be ready to put into space."

Kurt watched as small construction robots scurried around the framework of the vessel. The robots had been purchased from Lomatz, the Kubitz weapons dealer, and were worth their weight in gold. Of course gold was how Newton had paid for them.

"She'll need a commanding officer," commented Colonel Simms, as he shifted his gaze away from the ship. Several of the small robots were welding, and the bright arcs hurt his eyes to watch.

"I have someone in mind," Kurt answered. "Several of the light cruiser captains are in line for a larger command. Captain Bridget Marsh of the Dallas would make an excellent commanding officer for the Ticonderoga."

"I agree," responded Colonel Hayworth. "She's a fine officer."

Kurt paused and then focused his attention on Colonel Simms. "What about the fleet tugs?"

"They left this morning with the Vindication as scheduled," Simms reported. "They'll bring back those two big Profiteer cargo ships first, as well as their captured crews. When will you send them back to Kubitz?"

"Shortly," Kurt replied. "We'll interrogate a few of the officers and then negotiate their return with the Marsten Profiteers."

Simms nodded. That was how things were done on Kubitz.

"What are the plans for the big cargo ships?" asked Kurt. The two ships were each nearly one thousand meters in length, larger than the Star Cross.

"Governor Spalding wants them converted to passenger liners to bring more colonists from Earth," replied Hayworth. "It should take about two months to change them over."

The construction and repair bays on the shipyard had been modernized by Kubitz technology with many of the processes now done by robotics. Ship construction and repair times had been decreased by nearly 70 percent due to these new technologies.

"I think the governor is worried about this next election," commented Kurt with a grim look. "We may find the next president of the North American Union won't be quite as sympathetic toward Newton as Mayfield is."

"How will that work?" asked Simms, cocking his eyebrow. "We're technically a part of the North American Union. We have to do what they ask now that the Profiteers have been driven from the Solar System."

"Independence," answered Kurt softly as he glanced around, making sure no one else overheard. "Mayfield will grant it by executive order in the next few weeks."

"Wow!" exclaimed Hayworth, his eyes opening wide in surprise. "That will cause quite a commotion when it's announced. A lot of people on Earth won't like it."

"How will he do it?" asked Colonel Simms, sounding confused. "I didn't think he had the authority without the approval of the Cabinet."

"The North American Union, as well as most of the world, is still under a state of emergency. That gives Mayfield the authority. Of course there's the danger they may impeach him after he signs the executive order. Governor Spalding will then make an announcement on all video and comm channels to everyone on Newton, informing them of our independence. Once that's done, we'll formally open embassies in the European Union, the Russian Collective, and Chinese Conglomerate. Work is already underway for that to happen within a few days of President Mayfield signing the proclamation. We have some trade deals we'll sign with all three which will ensure they support us in case the North American Union attempts to change its mind about our independence at a later date."

"Mayfield's playing with fire," said Simms, shaking his head. "I just hope he knows what he's doing."

"So do I," answered Kurt.

Thankfully Newton was self-supporting and didn't need supplies from Earth to exist, he thought. Of course trade with the North American Union was a good thing, and he would hate to see it come to an end. Just another reason for signing the other trade deals. At the moment Newton had the only access to the Gothan Empire and the technology that could be purchased there. Earth had been cautioned about going to Kubitz, but some very stubborn and greedy people on the planet might not listen.

Chapter Three

Twelve thousand light-years from the Gothan Empire, the Lakiam battlecruiser Aurelia dropped from hyperspace. Around it 112 more battlecruisers appeared in a tight defensive formation. All the ships were armed with the most advanced weapons known to the Protector Worlds.

"Status?" asked Captain Veer as he gazed calmly at the viewscreens surrounding the Command Center on all sides.

Six other Lakiams sat in front of control consoles. More were in key sections of the ship such as Engineering. Overall only forty-seven Lakiams were on board the 1,700-meter-long vessel. The ship was highly automated and used advanced repair robots to perform maintenance and emergency repairs. The ship also possessed a supply of specialized nanites to repair breaches in the hull in case of major damage to the ship.

"All comm channels are silent," reported Mara from Communications. Mara was a highly specialized communications officer. She was also a very stunning looking woman.

"Sensors?"

"Picking up some debris around the fifth planet," answered Sensor Operator Baryon. "Most likely ship remains. Also several space stations should be in orbit, and the sensors are indicating two massive debris fields in their locations."

Captain Veer frowned upon hearing this. The fifth planet was a colony world of the Visth race. They were an Enlightened nonhumanoid species controlling over two hundred star systems with eighty-six inhabited worlds and moons. They possessed no warships other than light automated intersystem patrol ships to keep pirates at bay. They depended solely on the Lakiams for the defense of their worlds. In return, the Visths furnished the Lakiams with certain types of advanced technology. The Visths themselves were a catlike species who walked erect and had endured over two hundred thousand years of peace. The relationship between the Visths and the Lakiams had been very cordial for generations with the Visth worlds working to uplift the Lakiam worlds to Enlightened status.

"No sign of unknown ships?" demanded Captain Veer. Someone had destroyed the ships and stations around Galian Five, and he wanted to know who was responsible. Attacking an Enlightened World brought serious consequences.

In recent months a number of colony worlds of Enlightened civilizations had been hit by an unknown enemy. At first it was theorized the Profiteers from the Gothan Empire were most likely behind these horrendous attacks, but the technology used against the Enlightened Worlds seemed to cast that theory into serious doubt. Reports of colonies stripped of all life and cities burned to ashes spread across the galaxy. Captain Veer had thought the reports to be exaggerated, and now this unknown enemy had struck one of the worlds the Lakiams were sworn to protect. He was determined to get to the bottom of this mystery.

"Nothing," reported Sensor Operator Baryon. "I'm scanning everything out to fifteen light-years and I can find no unknown contacts. I am detecting a few cargo ships and some passenger liners on the normal interstellar routes, but none heading away from this system or coming toward it."

Captain Veer shifted his eyes toward the ship's primary viewscreen. Veer was quite normal for a Lakiam at nearly seven feet tall and having bright blue eyes, golden hair, and a slim stature. His arms were double-jointed with long nimble fingers on his hands.

"Inform all ships to go to Alert Status One. Something about this just isn't right. This is a very heavily traveled star system, and some cargo ships or passenger liners should have survived the attack. Also several large mining operations are on the moons of planet seven."

"There has been no response from them either," Mara answered. "I have already tried contacting them."

"I'm not detecting any power readings at the sites of the mines," added Sensor Operator Baryon. "I should be able to detect the power for the life support systems at a minimum, but the sensors are showing a lack of any signs of artificial energy."

Veer didn't like the sound of this. "Helm, take us into orbit around Galian Five so we can scan the surface for survivors."

Veer knew Galian Five had a population of nearly 230 million Visth. Surely some had survived and could tell him what happened. He was fully confident his fleet could deal with any adversaries who might still be in the system, though the ship's scanners indicated that whoever attacked Galian Five had long since departed. If they were still in the system, they would show up on the Aurelia's sensitive sensor scans.

"The Andocks supposedly lost a number of their warships to these mysterious attackers," commented Tarnth from Tactical.

The Andocks were another Protector World with highly advanced warships. They too had a number of Enlightened Worlds they provided a protective service to for access to certain advanced technology.

"The Andocks probably lied about their ships being destroyed," Veer said dismissively. "They don't want to admit their ships are not as highly advanced as ours." The Andocks were not quite as far along on the path of enlightenment as the Lakiams.

On the primary viewscreen, the blue-white world of Galian Five rapidly grew larger, only it was not as blue-white as it once had been. Dark clouds of red and brown blotted out the surface over many parts of the planet.

"Where are the major population centers?" demanded Captain Veer, leaning forward in his well-cushioned command chair. He was deeply concerned by what he was seeing on the viewscreen.

"They're beneath the dark areas you see on the screen," reported Sensor Operator Baryon. He increased the magnification on the screen and one of the red and brown clouds was greatly expanded. It was still impenetrable and nothing beneath it was visible.

Veer took a deep breath and shifted his attention to Baryon. "Are we close enough to scan the surface for survivors?" The ship had highly sophisticated scanning equipment, which could detect traces of organic life from several million kilometers.

"Yes," Sensor Operator Baryon replied as he activated the advanced sensors. After a few moments he frowned and, reaching out his right hand, touched several glowing icons on one of his sensor screens. Then he slowly turned toward Captain Veer with a confused look on his face. "I don't understand this. The sensors are not picking up any traces of major organics. They're picking up plant life, insect life, and other simple organisms but nothing else."

"You mean not a single Visth is alive on the planet?" Captain Veer asked incredulously. The attack had only occurred six hours previously! That was when they received the first and only distress call from the planet.

"Not only are the Visth missing but there's no trace of any type of large organic life upon the planet or in the oceans."

Captain Veer looked sharply at the sensor operator. "How is that possible?"

Baryon only shook his head. "Unknown. I know of no weapon or scientific development that could eradicate all major life-forms upon a planet in such a short time."

"Keep scanning," ordered Veer, as he took this data to mind. This unknown threat was turning out to be more dangerous than he had originally thought.

-

The Aurelia and her attending fleet slid into orbit 1,400 kilometers above the stricken planet. Sensor scans from all 113 Lakiam ships had failed to detect how all major life-forms upon the planet could have been so efficiently annihilated. No birds flew in the air or fish swam in the planet's large oceans.

Around the planet was the wreckage of dozens of cargo and passenger ships as well as the large space habitats that had once orbited Galian Five. The only things still intact were hundreds of small satellites, which aided in communication as well as control of the planet's weather.

-

"Captain, the system's primary FTL station has also been confirmed as destroyed," reported Sensor Operator Baryon. The FTL station had been an 1,100-hundred-meter-long station that received and sent all FTL messages. "Only a field of drifting debris remains where the station resided."

Captain Veer looked carefully at each of the large viewscreens in the Command Center. Each showed debris from destroyed ships or stations while the primary viewscreen was focused on the planet. It was unfathomable to him how any civilization could even contemplate doing this to Galian Five. It was barbaric beyond belief.

"Are we detecting signs of explosive damage at the sites of the larger cities?" Somewhere there had to be a clue as to who had committed this atrocity.

"They were definitely hit with something," answered Sensor Operator Baryon. "It wasn't nuclear or antimatter, though the damage is very similar to an antimatter detonation."

This greatly concerned Veer. It seemed to indicate an unknown weapon of vast power. "Not kinetics?" A large kinetic strike could cause as much damage as a nuke or small antimatter explosion.

"No," replied Sensor Operator Baryon, shaking his head. "The damage is widespread, but there's no sign of a blast crater. It's as if the released energy was spread out equally across a large area of the stricken cities. I've never seen anything like it."

"Captain," called out Mara from Communications with alarm in her voice. "The Treliid reports a possible contact coming around the planet."

"Put it on the primary viewscreen," ordered Captain Veer. Perhaps now they would know who had attacked the planet. He was anxious to see who this enemy was.

On the viewscreen, a massive black ship appeared, in the shape of two enormous globes connected to one another by a short cylinder.

"How big is that thing?" demanded Veer. It was by far the largest ship he had ever seen outside of one of the old colony transport ships.

"Each of those globes is two thousand meters, and the cylinder connecting the two is four hundred meters long and three hundred in diameter," reported Baryon, as he studied his sensor data. "That ship doesn't match anything in our records."

"The ancient Destroyers of Worlds," muttered Tarnth from Tactical, his face turning pale.

"What do you mean?" asked Veer, confused, a chill running down his back. He had never heard of this. "Who are these Destroyers of Worlds?"

Tarnth turned to the captain. "An ancient legend on some of the older Enlightened Worlds describe such ships. They come from the depths of intergalactic space every few million years and prey upon the civilizations of our galaxy. They feed upon life, all forms of life, particularly the higher ones. It's as if they find the Enlightened races a delicacy. They wait between attacks to allow such worlds to develop and then come to reap their harvest. They only leave death and destruction behind them."

"I don't believe in legends," stated Veer, shaking his head in skepticism. "It's obvious to me some world has built a giant warship to raid the Enlightened Worlds. It's our sworn duty to protect them. This could all be a ruse by the Gothan Empire and the Profiteers to steal high technology such as what Galian Five possessed."

The trade of such technology was prohibited to any civilization below a certain level of development. Veer knew that none of the worlds within the Gothan Empire could qualify. Perhaps they had resorted to building this new raider, which no one would recognize, in an attempt to circumvent the prohibition.

Tarnth looked with deep concern at the captain. "The ancient legends claim that all attempts to resist the Destroyers of Worlds failed. If we attack, our ships will be destroyed."

Captain Veer remained silent as he contemplated Tarnth's words and then finally spoke. "Do you need to be relieved from your duties?"

"No," answered Tarnth, turning back toward his console. "I will do what is necessary and hope I am wrong."

"Mara, hail that ship, and demand they power down and prepare to be boarded." All Lakiam ships had military combat robots on board. They were equipped with heavy stunners as well as a small energy beam cannons. Lakiams themselves had not engaged in individual armed combat in generations as part of their advancement toward the first stage of becoming an Enlightened World. Only a few members of the Lakiam race were still aggressive enough to operate their large fleet of warships.

After a few moments Mara turned toward the captain with a look of concern in her deep blue eyes. "There is no response. I've tried all communication frequencies."

"Captain, more ships are coming around the planet," reported Tarnth, gesturing toward one of the viewscreens. A dozen black spindle-shaped ships were now visible.

"What do our sensor readings say about their power output?" asked Captain Veer.

"I don't understand," replied Baryon, his eyes showing great confusion. "Those ships do not show up on my sensors."

Captain Veer turned toward Baryon, his eyes narrowing sharply. "What do you mean, they're not showing up on your sensors? We can see them on the viewscreen." The sensors on the Aurelia were some of the most advanced known to science. Nothing should be impervious to their scans.

Sensor Operator Baryon shook his head. "Something is interfering with our sensors. It could be some sensor-dampening field generated by the black ships."

A prickling sensation of impending danger suddenly spread across Veer's neck. "Switch the viewscreens to show views around our fleet! If their ships are impervious to our scans, there could be more of them out there. Order our other ships to do the same."

All the main viewscreens except the primary one changed to show different aspects of the space around the fleet. On nearly every screen, black ships could be seen rapidly closing with the Lakiam fleet formation. They had fallen into a trap!

"Interpolate the data from the viewscreens and put it into the tactical display," ordered Captain Veer, trying to stay calm. "Add the data from our other ships as well."

Instantly on the large holographic tactical display to the right of Captain Veer, a swarm of red threat icons appeared. It took the captain only a moment to realize his fleet was badly outnumbered. There was no way these ships had originated in the Gothan Empire. The Profiteers couldn't build anything like the ships Veer was seeing.

Tarnth turned to face the captain with a chilling look on his face. "Those spindle-shaped ships match the ones in the legend! They are the Destroyers of Worlds, and they have returned to ravage our galaxy. We must send word to Lakiam, informing them of the danger."

Captain Veer could tell Tarnth was visibly fearful of the black ships. Veer had known the tactical officer for most of his career in the fleet and had never seen him act like this.

"Mara, send an FTL message back to Lakiam, informing them of what we've discovered. Send our latest sensor scans as well and our logs of all of our previous scans of the vicinity of Galian Five."

Veer then activated his ship-to-ship comm. "All ships, prepare to initiate combat against the black ships moving in on us. All attempts at communication have failed, and we have to assume these vessels destroyed Galian Five. I am confident our energy shields will protect us and our advanced weapons will make short work of these interlopers. Once the black ships have been destroyed, we will perform a thorough investigation of the wreckage to determine their point of origin."

"Captain," Mara called out anxiously. "Our FTL communications are jammed. I can't send a message!"

Captain Veer reached a quick decision. "All ships, open fire!" These black ships would soon learn Lakiam vessels were heavily armed, and not the defenseless cargo and passenger ships they had destroyed around Galian Five.

-

From the bow of the Aurelia, a powerful force beam shot forth to strike the nearest black ship. Other beams from the other ships in the Lakiam fleet also struck the approaching vessels. The beams impacted energy shields, which seemed to absorb the energy from the beams as if they were nothing more than a mere nuisance. The force beams faded out as their power was absorbed.

Seeing the ineffectiveness of their force beams, the Lakiams quickly switched to their energy projectors. Once more ravaging power struck the shields of the black ships only to be absorbed as well. The unharmed black ships continued to close on the Lakiam fleet.

-

"Their energy screens are siphoning off the power from our weapons," reported Sensor Operator Baryon as he saw the ineffectiveness of their attack. "Our weapons are only making their energy screens stronger!"

Captain Veer realized, if all their energy weapons were useless against the Destroyers of Worlds, he had only one other weapon that might work. It was a move of desperation, but he had no other option. "I'm authorizing the use of a dark-matter hypermissile," he said in a calm voice. The dark-matter missiles had never been used in combat before due to the danger they posed to nearby planets.

"Prepping missile," reported Tarnth as his hands flew over his tactical console. "We're going to be hit by the blast wave due to how close the black ships are."

-

On the outer hull of the Aurelia, a missile hatch slid open. In a sudden flash, the missile inside the tube vanished as it jumped into hyperspace. At nearly the same moment it slammed into the shield of one of the black ships, exploding in a brilliant flash of white light. For a moment the black ship vanished as the ravaging energy spread across its energy screen.

-

"Direct hit!" called out Baryon as his sensor screens blanked out from the sudden release of energy.

Then the blast wave struck the Aurelia, the ship groaning in anguish from the backlash of energy sweeping across the ship's energy shield. Several consoles in the Command Center shorted out, and the ship was severely jarred from the deadly energy. Repair robots rushed to control the fires in the burning consoles.

"Moderate damage to the hull and we have several compartments open to space," reported Daxell from his damage control console. "Repair robots have been directed toward the damaged areas. Repair nanites have been released and are already closing the ruptures in the outer hull."

"Several of our other ships received damage as well," reported Mara as messages flooded her comm station.

On the main viewscreen, the black ship reappeared still intact. The dark-matter hypermissile had failed to destroy it!

"Black ships are firing," reported Baryon. "Enemy ship was unaffected by our missile."

Captain Veer looked up at the primary viewscreen to see what appeared to be a black sphere of nothingness hurtling toward the Aurelia. Around its edges small discharges of energy were evident.

"What is it?" he demanded, leaning forward in his command chair. It was traveling much slower than a normal missile.

"It's some form of antimatter," Baryon reported as he checked his sensor screens. "But it's in a form I've never seen before."

"Move us out of its path."

The Lakiam in front of the helm console quickly moved the battlecruiser to one side to avoid the inbound sphere of antimatter energy.

"It's changing course," reported Baryon, his eyes wide in fear. "It'll strike the energy shield in five seconds."

On the primary viewscreen, Captain Veer watched in fascination as the black sphere of mysterious energy struck his ship's energy screen. The ship seemed to shriek in pain as the screen was hammered and the black energy spread across it. The lights in the Command Center dimmed substantially.

"Shield is down to 48 percent and dropping rapidly," reported Tarnth as he watched one of his data screens in disbelief. "Shield will fail in fourteen seconds! Whatever this weapon is it's absorbing the power from our energy screen."

Captain Veer realized he was powerless to prevent the loss of the ship's all-powerful energy screen. Never before had he ever heard of a Lakiam ship's energy shield being overwhelmed by any known weapon. The shield was powered by antimatter reactors furnished by the Visth centuries in the past. Veer didn't know of a more powerful energy source anywhere in the galaxy.

"Shield is at 8 percent," warned Tarnth in desperation as his right hand moved across one of his screens.

Captain Veer watched as Tarnth stole power from other ship systems in an attempt to keep the shield intact. However, nothing he did slowed the weakening of the energy screen. Veer saw a red warning light appear on one of Tarnth's screens.

"Shield is down," Tarnth said as he gazed at the nearest viewscreen in terror-stricken fascination.

Veer let out a deep breath of frustration. He was about to lose his fleet to an unknown enemy. He didn't know if Tarnth's laments about the Destroyers of Worlds were true or not, but they faced a very dangerous enemy. It disturbed Veer even more knowing he had no way to warn Lakiam of what might be coming their way.

"Many of our other ships have been hit with the same weapon," Mara added as frantic calls came over her comm system. "They're losing power, and some report that nearly all their systems have failed."

"Captain, the primary viewscreen!" called out Baryon.

On the screen, a number of hatches slid open on several of the black vessels, and missiles shot out. The lights in the Command Center continued to dim, and several consoles ceased functioning completely from a loss of power. The black antimatter had reached the hull of the ship.

"Shipwide power is failing," reported Daxell. "Engineering can't provide the necessary power to reinitiate the energy screen or power the ship's systems."

-

In space, the black ship's missiles slammed into the unprotected hulls of the Lakiam battlecruisers. Where each missile struck, a miniature sun appeared, marking the death of a Lakiam ship. Nearly all the Lakiam vessels were powerless and drifting in space, making them easy targets for the deadly missiles of the black ships.

-

"Our fleet's being systematically destroyed," reported Baryon, his eyes showing panic. "It's only a matter of time before we're targeted with a missile."

Captain Veer remained silent, knowing he was powerless to do anything to save his fleet or his ship. On the holographic display, ship after Lakiam ship expanded in a flash of light and then vanished from the display completely. Veer's eyes shifted to Tarnth, sitting quietly at his tactical station with his eyes closed. Perhaps these actually were the Destroyers of Worlds who his tactical officer had warned him about.

With a sudden jolt, the lights in the Command Center died away completely. All consoles ceased functioning, and even the ever-present noise of the movement of air through the vents vanished. For a moment the Command Center was in absolute silence. Veer knew this was the end. If the black ships didn't put a missile in the side of the Aurelia, then the failure of the life support systems would soon accomplish the same thing. Veer took a deep breath, knowing death was inevitable. He had failed in his mission, and the black ships would continue on their rampage of destruction. Veer greatly feared no one could stop them. The Destroyers of Worlds had returned, and they were powerful beyond belief.

Chapter Four

Admiral Kurt Vickers watched the tactical screen intently as the Star Cross prepared to jump into the globular star cluster which contained the Gothan Empire. The cluster was 120 light-years across and contained nearly three thousand stars. The empire was a loose federation of 118 worlds in 87 different star systems that routinely raided many of the civilized races of the galaxy.

Nearly all the planets were heavily fortified with orbital defenses as well as warships. Most of the systems sent out raiding fleets periodically to attack convoys of the richer and more civilized planetary systems. This plunder, including captured crews and passengers, was brought back to Kubitz. In most cases, the crews and passengers were held for ransom. If no ransom was received, the captives were sold in the slave markets to the highest bidder.

"God, I hate this star cluster," muttered Andrew with a grimace as he gazed at the hundreds of unblinking stars on the main viewscreen.

Kurt laughed and shook his head. "You'll get to see Grantz again. I'm sure he'll want to take you to one of the pleasure houses and show you the wanton ways of Kubitz."

Andrew moaned. "You know better than that. I'm happily married. Emily would throw a fit if she heard of such nonsense. I'm not risking my wife's ire." Andrew shook his head. "I hope you brought some gold for your pet Profiteer. I'm sure he'll have some devious plan to get as much of it as he can from you."

"Plotting the next jump," said Lieutenant Charles Styles as his hands moved over his navigation console. "We should enter hyperspace in six to eight minutes."

Kurt looked at Andrew. "I want the fleet at Condition One each time we emerge from now until we reach the Kubitz System."

From here on in, they were in danger of being ambushed by small Profiteer fleets interested in making some quick credits off ships inbound toward Kubitz. It had happened before, and it would happen again. A few small Profiteer fleets always prowled the space inside the cluster, seeking a helpless victim. Ships from all over the galaxy came to trade at Kubitz. Most came with armed escorts.

Kurt glanced at the ship's main viewscreen currently focused on the six-hundred-meter-long light carrier Wasp. In the distance, he could see one of the small fleet's two light cruisers. Their primary responsibility was the protection of the passenger liner Newton Princess.

The Newton Princess wasn't visible on the main viewscreen, though Kurt knew Keera was on board. He had been tempted to have her stay in his quarters on the Star Cross, but then he'd decided she might be too big of a distraction. Keera had grown very proficient at taking his mind off his fleet duties whenever she had the opportunity. They still talked each day, and they would be together most of the time on Kubitz.

"No contacts showing on our short-range sensors," Andrew said as he shifted his eyes to another screen. "Though a number of vessels show up on the long-range sensors on the cluster's edge."

Kurt studied the indicated screen. Nearly twenty small red threat icons were visible. At this distance, they could be cargo ships or Profiteer raiders. One small fleet of about eight ships looked suspicious. "Keep an eye on those long-range sensors." The special sensors could detect a ship for a distance of five light-years, which would give his fleet sufficient time to prepare for an attack.

A few more minutes passed, and then Lieutenant Styles announced they were ready to jump.

"Here we go," said Andrew, staring at the viewscreen, his worry evident on his face. "It seems as if every time we come to the Gothan Empire, something bad happens."

"Let's hope it's different this time," Kurt replied. "Helm, take us into hyperspace."

Moments later Kurt felt a slight twinge in his stomach as the Star Cross transitioned from normal space into hyperspace. In normal space, faster-than-light travel was impossible. However, in hyperspace, different universal laws were at play, which allowed a ship to greatly exceed the speed of light. The 5,500 light-year journey from Newton to the Gothan Empire had only taken eight days. It would have taken longer a few years back, but—thanks to some of the technology they had acquired on Kubitz—all of the hyperspace drives on Earth's and Newton's ships had been upgraded. Kurt knew the hyperdrives on vessels from the Protector Worlds or the Enlightened Worlds were even faster.

-

On board the Newton Princess, Keera was both excited and nervous about her return to Kubitz. She had attended medical training on the Enlightened World of Karash and then traveled to Kubitz with her brother. Practicing medicine on the Profiteer world had been extremely challenging and exciting since hundreds of different humanoid races paid visits to the planet on a regular basis, as well as a few completely alien species. Kubitz was also a very frightening place because one's life nearly always hung in the balance. In many areas of the capital city, it was unsafe to travel without an armed escort. The Enforcers, who were responsible for the law on Kubitz, had a bad habit of looking the other way at times.

She had first met Fleet Admiral Kurt Vickers right after a Profiteer attack on the vehicle carrying the admiral. She had been in the vicinity and rushed to give medical aid to the wounded. In gratitude, Kurt had invited her to supper at the embassy compound, and their relationship had only grown from there. She had traveled to Newton with Private Lucy Dulcet, who had been kidnapped by the Profiteers and put through a horrifying ordeal.

After spending some time on Newton and coming to know Kurt even better, Keera had decided to make it her home. Now she and Kurt were living together, and she couldn't be happier.

Not until she received the message from her brother did she realize she still had unfinished business on Kubitz.

Getting up from the sofa, she removed her clothes and took a quick shower. After drying off, she stood in front of the full-length mirror, gazing at her figure. She had dark shoulder-length hair and a fair complexion with curves in all the right places. She knew Kurt approved. She allowed herself to smile, thinking about how passionate Kurt could be at times.

Running her hands over her flat stomach, she was pleased with the muscle tone of her body. She worked out on a regular basis and was careful to eat as healthy as possible. She still overindulged on occasion. Newton had a form of chocolate she absolutely loved and a number of tea varieties she found nearly addictive. She had mentioned to Kurt that several of the teas she had taken a liking to would sell very well on Kubitz.

Slipping into a robe, she returned to the sofa and picked up the message she had left there, the one from her brother. She read it one more time, sensing the fear in his words. Something ominous stirred in the galaxy, and several of the Profiteer clans were deeply concerned. A number of raids had even been canceled as they deemed parts of the galaxy too dangerous to venture into. Dalen even hinted a number of secret meetings had occurred on the planet Marsten, the capital of the Gothan Empire.

Keera leaned back and closed her eyes. She let out a deep sigh. If the Profiteers were frightened about this mysterious menace, she wondered what it might mean for Newton. She had grown to love her new adopted world. Life there was so much slower than Kubitz. She could walk out in the streets without the need of an escort or a handgun to protect herself. She hoped nothing ever changed that.

Opening her eyes, she looked one last time at her brother's message. She had never known Dalen to be afraid of anything. Just another reason he had gone to work for one of the larger Profiteer Clans on Kubitz. He enjoyed the sense of danger and the thrill that type of life offered. Keera had disapproved of

Dalen's decision, but she had come to Kubitz nevertheless so she could practice her medical skills on a myriad of different humanoid and alien races.

Keera stood up, deciding to go to bed. Sometime tomorrow they would arrive at Kubitz, and she would get her answers. Unfortunately, in order to find out what was happening in the galaxy, it might be necessary to contact Avery Dolman. She despised Dolman as he had his hands in every despicable activity that occurred on Kubitz. However, if something were going on, Dolman would know of it or how to get the information.

-

The Star Cross and her fleet dropped from hyperspace near the large Controller station in the Kubitz System. The Controller station was forty kilometers in length and ten in width. On its surface were a number of small habitable domes one to two kilometers in diameter. The station was profoundly armed with ion cannons, energy projectors, and hundreds of hyperspace missile tubes. In near orbit of the station were twenty squadrons of small police ships, each two hundred meters in length and heavily armed. They were responsible for ensuring the incoming ships caused no problems.

"We're being hailed," reported Lieutenant Brenda Pierce. "They want to know who we are and for us to state our business."

Kurt had been expecting this. The computers on the station would have already identified his ships as from Newton. "Tell them who we are and ask what the current fees are to go into orbit around Kubitz."

All ships had to pay a fee at the Controller station before being allowed to go farther into the system. Failure to do so would result in an immediate attack by the patrolling police ships or by the station itself. Once the fee was paid, Kurt's ships would fall under the protection of the Kubitz government and then would be immune from attack by any ship in the Kubitz System. If an attack did occur, the consequences were so severe that the offending ship would most likely be destroyed, and the world it came from would be severely fined or restricted from future raiding.

"Detecting 287 ships currently in orbit near the station," Lieutenant Lena Brooks reported. "A number of them are not in our files."

Kurt shifted his gaze to the main viewscreen, showing the huge Controller station. He could see a number of ships in close orbits. Many of them he had never seen before—ships from numerous races, and nearly all were of a different size and configuration. "Make sure you add all the unidentified ships to our database."

An alarm sounded on the sensor console.

"We have ten police ships coming to give us the once-over," Andrew reported as he watched the tactical screen and the approaching red threat icons.

"We're being scanned," added Lieutenant Brooks as a red light appeared on her sensor console.

"Ignore them," Kurt ordered. He had the fleet at Condition Three with all targeting sensors off. He had also left the antimatter hypermissiles the Star Cross normally carried back at Newton Station. Ships were not allowed inside the Kubitz System with such weapons.

"The fee is 250,000 credits for all five of our ships," Lieutenant Pierce stated as the information came over her comm.

"They've gone up a bit," Andrew said in disgust, rolling his eyes. "They squeeze every credit they can from you."

Kurt nodded his head in agreement. "Tell them to subtract the fee from our account."

A few more moments passed. "Our account has been debited, and they are transmitting a confirmation of our payment to us as well as the Controller exchange office at the main spaceport on Kubitz. We may proceed to the planet."

"Set a course for Kubitz," Kurt ordered as he settled back in his command chair. It would take them a while to reach Kubitz, even traveling at sublight speeds. Hyperspace travel was not allowed inside the orbit of the Controller station.

"Admiral," said Andrew, showing some concern in his voice. "I did a sensor scan of the ships around the Controller station, and a number of Dacroni mercenary ships are here."

Kurt's eyes widened. No love was lost between the Dacroni mercenaries and Humans from Earth and Newton. "It may just be a coincidence. They come here routinely to sign contracts as well as trade."

For once Kurt was glad the Kubitz government allowed no fighting between ships, no matter how serious the disagreement might be between the vessels. If the Dacroni were to attack any of Kurt's fleet, the Kubitz government would respond by immediately destroying the offending ship and heavily fining the Dacroni clan involved.

"Activating sublight drive," Lieutenant Styles reported from the Helm.

On the main viewscreen, the Controller station fell away as the Star Cross accelerated away from it. Kurt was anxious to get to Kubitz and meet with former Lieutenant Tenner. Kurt was certain Keera was just as anxious to see her brother. Plus he would keep an eye on the Dacroni ships to ensure no further mischief occurred, since the Dacroni had been involved in kidnapping Private Dulcet. Kurt would not forget or forgive that.

-

The next day Kurt, Keera, and Andrew were inside the Controller exchange office at the main spaceport. A squad of heavily armed Marines was outside, waiting for their return. One thing Kurt had learned about Kubitz: he and his crew didn't go anywhere without an armed escort.

It took them only a few minutes to be taken to a small office where a Controller sat behind a desk with two armed Lylan Enforcers. The Enforcers were humanoid with large muscular arms and legs, and a squat chest. They came from a high-gravity world, and Kurt didn't want to get into a fight with one unless he wanted to end up with a broken arm or worse. The Controller was easily seven feet tall and humanoid. His head was slightly larger than normal and completely bald. The Controller's eyes were of normal size, though his lips were a little thinner. His body was slim, and his hands had six long digits. He was also a little pale, as if he very seldom saw any sunlight.

"You are the Humans from Newton?" asked the Controller as he called up information on his computer.

"Yes," Kurt replied. "We've come to Kubitz to conduct some business."

The Controller nodded as he continued to access his data screen. Then he stopped and seemed to be examining something. "A fine has been levied against your planet."

"A fine?" said Kurt, growing suspicious. "For what?"

"The planet Julbian has been claimed by High Profiteer Creed and his clan. Contracts have been filed and fees paid, giving High Profiteer Creed full control of any wealth he finds in that system. From this report, your people have interfered and not allowed Creed to fulfill his contract."

Kurt took a deep breath. He almost wished he had Grantz here to guide him through this. "My planet doesn't recognize High Profiteer Creed's right to exploit the Julbian System. My people are in the process of signing an agreement with the leaders of the system where they will fall under our protection. We will also be doing considerable trading with them."

The Controller seemed taken aback by this statement. He studied more data on his screen. "Your planet is not part of the Gothan Empire and not subject to our laws. However, in order to do trade here, you are expected to recognize the validity of any contracts on file and which have been approved by a Controller. It's stated very clearly here in Section 212, Paragraph 47, of the Contract Laws."

"Julbian is in an area of space claimed by my people," Kurt responded.

"Has there been a contract filed here on Kubitz specifying that?" asked the Controller.

"No," confessed Kurt, wondering how big the fine would be.

The Controller studied more information on his screen before turning back toward Kurt. "Under Section 642, Paragraphs 7–18, any race not associated with the Gothan Empire may claim specific regions of space where their interests lie. While this does not prevent Profiteer clans from conducting business in those regions, it does prevent heavy fines being levied against the aggrieved race if they resist Profiteer raids. Do you wish to file a contract listing the area of space your world claims an interest in? If you do so, I can lower the current fine considerably. It will also prevent this from occurring in the future."

Kurt thought furiously for several long moments on a response. "What is the current fine, and how much will it be reduced?"

"The current fine is one hundred million credits, and, by filing a contract claiming interests in the Julbian region of space, I can reduce it to a mere two million. One other thing you must understand. Even though you file this contract, Profiteer Creed still has the rights to conduct business on Julbian as he sees fit. His contract predates anything you may file."

"How much will it cost to file this contract?"

"That depends on the size of the region of space you claim an interest in. You have until your ships leave Kubitz to file the contract. Failure to do so will result in a debit to your account of the one hundred million credits. I would also recommend that, if you have interests in other regions near your world, you include them in the contract to prevent future misunderstandings."

Kurt let out a deep sigh. "I'll have our people begin working on the contract."

The Controller pressed an icon on his screen, and a small computer disk popped out which he handed to Kurt. "This disk contains the pertinent information on laying claim to a region of space. The two-million-credit fine will be due upon filing your contract as well as whatever the contract fee may be. You may now leave to conduct whatever business you have on Kubitz. If you have gold or other precious metals you wish to convert to credits, it needs to be done here at the exchange."

-

A few minutes later they were back outside the Controller exchange where their Marine guards waited.

"I hate this place," muttered Sergeant Jones, who was in charge of the Marine security detail. "Everything looks so damn gloomy!"

He shifted his heavy assault rifle to his other arm. To allow the Marines to carry such weapons, former Lieutenant Tenner had to pay a hefty fee. Only security people involved with an embassy or trading compound were allowed to carry similar weapons. For the duration of Kurt's mission, Sergeant Jones and his squad had been transferred to the embassy security detail.

-

Kurt looked up and he could barely see the sun. Kubitz was the fourth planet out from its primary, and he was amazed at how much of the sunlight was blotted out by the pollution in the air. Grantz had blamed the factories, operating for decades without any regard to the contaminants being released into the atmosphere. It was one of the reasons most cities had large domes over their more affluent sections. The planet also had a serious weather problem with acid rain. At times it was so acidic it could seriously burn a person. People had died when caught out in the open, away from protection, during an acid rainstorm.

Glancing at the spaceport, Kurt saw dozens of small cargo ships and shuttles parked on the landing pads. Vehicles flew by, and numerous work robots scurried back and forth, unloading and delivering crates to various ships.

"Let's get to the compound," said Keera impatiently, looking up at the hazy sky. "I hate being out in the open on Kubitz. Even here at the spaceport, the air smells of ozone and other contaminates."

Kurt knew this was one of the reasons she disliked Kubitz. While the more affluent citizens could afford to live under the protective domes, the average Kubitz citizen lived in slum neighborhoods with very high crime rates as well as sickness. The air was unsafe to breathe over a long period, and she had told

Kurt stories about all the children she had treated at the medical facility with respiratory problems. Some had even died.

"Yeah, I'm sure Grantz is waiting for us," added Andrew. "I see our rides are here."

Kurt smiled, seeing two old-style Humvees pull up. Each Humvee was capable of holding six passengers in its heavily armored body. A small turret on top held a rapid-fire M240K machine gun, which fired 7.62 mm rounds at a top rate of eight hundred per minute.

The old-style Humvees had been brought from Earth as transports for the embassy compound. Since energy weapons were not allowed on Kubitz unless used by an Enforcer, the old-style M240K machine gun was well qualified to keep any criminal elements from attacking embassy staff. It was also about the heaviest weapon the Kubitz government would grant an embassy or trading compound to possess. Six Humvees were at the compound, and, as with the assault rifles, a heavy fee had been paid to allow them to be armed with the machine guns.

The passenger door on the nearest Humvee swung open, and a Profiteer stepped out.

Andrew groaned, recognizing who it was.

"Fleet Admiral Vickers," bellowed Grantz, rushing forward, grabbing Kurt by the hand, and shaking it vigorously. "It's about time you returned to Kubitz. We have much to discuss."

"Yeah, right," said Andrew with a frown. "What schemes have you come up with now to get more gold?"

"Gold!" cried Grantz in mock consternation. "What makes you think that?" Reaching out, he put his arm around Andrew and grinned. "This time you must accompany me to one of the pleasure houses. If you can't find a woman there to satisfy you, I can guarantee the food, drink, and entertainment are well worth it."

"Captain Randson is married and has a daughter," interjected Keera, looking disapprovingly at Grantz. "You also shouldn't be spending so much of your time in the entertainment area. A lot of people have gone missing visiting those pleasure houses."

Kurt and Keera were well aware that much of the black market activity occurred at those establishments.

"Ah, I'm always armed," said Grantz with a hefty laugh, patting the large handgun strapped to his waist. "Besides, I know my way around the pleasure houses, and I have a reputation to uphold."

"I'm sure you do," said Keera, shaking her head in disgust.

"Let's load up," Kurt ordered. "Grantz, I want you in the Humvee with me. We ran into a situation with a Controller here at the Controller exchange which I need to speak to you about."

"About your run-in with High Profiteer Creed in the Julbian System."

Kurt frowned, wondering how Grantz had heard of that. Knowing Grantz and who he associated himself with, it was probably Dolman.

Kurt reached into his pocket, taking out a gold coin. He flipped it into the air and casually caught it in his right hand. He noticed Grantz's gaze never left the coin, his eyes gleaming with greed. "Yes, let's see if you can help us out of a minor situation we find ourselves in."

Grantz's face took on a serious look as he watched the gleaming gold coin. "A one-hundred-million-credit fine isn't minor."

"Perhaps not," Kurt said, handing Grantz the coin. Kurt had an entire pocketful and more back on the Star Cross. With the current exchange rate, each one-ounce coin was worth about 1,200 credits. That was something else he had learned about doing business on Kubitz. Bribes were expected, and the gold coins would work very well to grease a few hands. "Let's see what we can come up with to get that fine reduced."

Kurt really wanted to hear what the Profiteer knew about setting up the contract for the area of space Newton had a vested interest in. Most likely he would have to speak with Avery Dolman and pay a hefty number of credits to have a contract drawn up that would cover Newton's needs. Dolman would know the necessary experts to ensure the contract was foolproof.

Everyone loaded up into the Humvees with both Andrew and Keera getting in with Kurt and Grantz. The Marine escort divided themselves up among the two transports, and they were soon ready to depart. The Humvees were soon rolling down the busy street, which led from the spaceport to the city proper.

"How come you're still alive?" Andrew asked Grantz evenly. "I would have thought, by now, someone would have shot you for your conniving ways."

"This is Kubitz," Grantz said dismissively with a huge grin. "Everyone is constantly scheming to improve their station in life. Besides, I have the right connections and know who to speak to."

"We may need those connections," Kurt said as he recalled what Governor Spalding wanted him to find out. "Once we get to the compound, there's another matter I wish to speak of."

Grantz grinned. "Whatever you want, I'll find it." Glancing at the gold coin, he placed it in a secure pocket.

Kurt nodded, knowing Grantz was serious. While Kurt might disagree with the Profiteer's methods, Grantz did produce results.

Chapter Five

The trip to the embassy compound took nearly forty minutes. The two Humvees drove slowly through the outlying neighborhoods, which were not under the protective environmental dome. Looking out the thick protective windows, Kurt felt the misery of the people living in some of these areas. Along the streets, brilliant signs advertised various services. Small shops lined the streets, selling everything one could imagine. Food, clothing, household items, and even weapons. The other striking thing was the number of people with handguns holstered to their hips. Even a number of the women were armed. A stark reminder of just how dangerous the streets of the cities on Kubitz were to travel.

"I had forgotten how colorful the people on Kubitz dress," commented Keera, gazing at the people. The sidewalks were crowded at this time of day with the streets full of vehicles.

Kurt nodded. He could see both men and women dressed up in very colorful clothing. While the people might not have much, they certainly enjoyed wearing bright colors. His gaze wandered to the vehicles traveling the crowded streets. There was every type of vehicle one could imagine. Cars and trucks powered by old-time combustion engines, electric vehicles, and even solar. The Humvees used advanced hydrogen fuel cells to power the heavy armored vehicles. They were also air-conditioned, and the air went through filters to take out any contaminants. The filters were even capable of preventing poison gas from coming inside. A gas attack had resulted in the abduction of Private Dulcet.

"You wish to claim the territory around the Julbian System as containing interests your government wants to control," muttered Grantz, shaking his head. He was using a miniature handheld reader to scan the small disk the Controller had given Kurt. "If I read this correctly, to lay claim to an area as large as this may be much more expensive than paying the one-hundred-million-credit fine."

"That's a lot of gold we'll give up," said Andrew meaningfully, staring at Grantz. "It might mean we won't have enough to toss around like we have been. I would hate to see you have to curtail your visits to the pleasure houses."

Grantz's eyes narrowed appreciably at hearing those words. He reached in his pocket to touch the gold coin there. "I will speak to Avery Dolman. We may need to enlist the aid of a Controller he knows. Perhaps we can find a way around this."

It didn't surprise Kurt to hear Dolman had a Controller sympathetic to his organization. He would almost have to in order to conduct all the business he did, much of it illegal. Even on Kubitz some things were frowned upon. That was where all the bribes came in. Some illegal transactions could be tolerated if enough credits changed hands.

"It will be complicated since a contract has already been filed by High Profiteer Creed to remove the wealth from this system," continued Grantz, gazing at the small screen. "I will act as the go-between and see what can be done."

"And how much will that cost?" asked Andrew, gazing sharply at the Profiteer. "I doubt if you're doing this for free."

"It's negotiable," replied Grantz, smiling. "Let's see how many credits I can save you first, and then we'll discuss my fee."

"Just get it done," responded Kurt, trying not to roll his eyes. "But keep me informed of your progress. I don't want this to get out of hand." Grantz's desire for gold sometimes made him take risks and be a little careless. However, he had managed the rescue of Private Lucy Dulcet with Dolman's assistance, which Kurt would always be grateful for. Therefore, he was willing to give the Profiteer some latitude in his actions.

"Nearing the dome," the Marine driver commented as he slowed down and presented an entry pass to the Enforcers guarding the entrance. The numerous entrances to the environmental protection dome were all guarded to keep discontents out.

A soon as they drove in, it was like entering a different world. Tall buildings were everywhere and even a few green park areas. Most of the diplomatic compounds resided inside the dome as well as the Kubitz government offices and it was also home to the more affluent people. However, even here in the dome there were dangerous areas such as the ones that held the pleasure houses that Grantz was so infatuated with. Also located here were the massive slave markets.

It didn't take long to reach the Newton embassy compound as the traffic was lighter. Vehicles with polluting engines were still allowed, but the owners had to pay a substantial fine to operate them. Kurt knew the Kubitz government was encouraging the changeover to hydrogen-powered vehicles across the planet to help curb the atmospheric pollution. More of those vehicle types were evident since they'd entered the dome.

Rolling up to the compound, the two Humvees were stopped by a pair of Marines armed with intimidating-looking assault rifles. After confirming their driver's ID, they were motioned through the gate.

"I get tired of having to show my ID every time I leave or return to the compound," complained Grantz, looking at Kurt. "The guards know who I am. Why do I have to always show my ID?"

"It's a formality," answered Kurt, looking at the Profiteer. "Everyone must go through it."

"You could always move out," suggested Andrew. "You don't have to stay in the compound."

Grantz shook his head. "Tenner needs me. He depends on me for advice on how to deal with the various government agencies, the Profiteer clans, and other humanoid races who have compounds on Kubitz. As much as I would like to move to better quarters outside the compound, I am needed here."

Kurt said nothing. Grantz was paid a sum of credits each month to help Tenner with negotiations on Kubitz. The Profiteer was very familiar with how everything worked on the planet, including the black market. Kurt knew Grantz would never move from the compound, not as long as he could earn more gold.

The embassy compound contained one large building and half a dozen smaller ones. A barracks for the Marine company, which had been assigned to the compound as security, was of recent construction. The entire compound was surrounded by a thick five-meter-high wall with two guarded entrances. Kurt noted razor wire had been added to the top of the wall since his last visit. Also two small guard towers were inside the compound with a pair of M240K machines guns, which could cover the interior. To most, this might seem like overkill, but this was Kubitz, and nearly all compounds were well protected to prevent break-ins. Every Profiteer on Kubitz knew the larger diplomatic compounds kept a considerable number of credits and even some precious metals on hand. It wasn't unusual to hear of robberies.

Pulling up to the front entrance of the large embassy building, Kurt saw Marvin Tenner come out with a Marine captain. Everyone quickly unloaded from the two Humvees with Kurt, Andrew, and Keera walking to Tenner.

"I see Grantz went along to greet you," Tenner said with a frown. "I wondered where he'd vanished to."

"I'm glad he did," answered Kurt. "I had some business I needed to discuss with him."

Tenner nodded and then gestured to the Marine captain beside him. "This is Captain Alan Briar, in charge of our Marine force."

Captain Briar immediately saluted, and Kurt returned the salute.

"Captain," said Kurt, reaching out and shaking the man's hand. "It looks as if you have things well under control here at the embassy."

"We try," Captain Briar replied. "Every day is a new learning experience here on Kubitz."

"Why did you come here?" asked Tenner. "I received a message from Governor Spalding about purchasing some advanced construction equipment and automated factories to help with all the colonists coming to Newton. I seriously doubt if that's the reason you came."

Kurt nodded. "It's one of the reasons, but there's something we need to talk about. Let's go inside. We have a meeting to set up."

-

"I'll give my brother a call," Keera said as they entered the embassy. She was anxious to speak with him so she could better understand why he was so frightened.

"You and the fleet admiral will stay in the main guest quarters," Tenner said. "I'll have someone take your baggage from the Humvee to your room. Since your last visit, we've added quite a few people to the embassy staff. You can make your call from your quarters if you want. Also the cafeteria is open around the clock. Just let the head chef know what you want and he'll prepare it for you."

"Have him come to the embassy if you need to," Kurt said to Keera. "There's no reason for you to go out on the streets here."

Tenner glanced at Keera. "If he does come, let the guards at the gate know he's expected. However, if you do decide to go out, Captain Briar will arrange for a suitable escort."

Keera nodded. She was nervous about seeing her older brother. She also didn't care to be wandering about Kubitz alone. She knew she would be safer with a Marine escort, but, if she did have a military escort, her brother might not show. No, it would be better if she could talk him into coming to the embassy.

-

In high orbit above Kubitz, four 1,100-meter-long Dacroni battleships had just arrived. They positioned themselves a short distant from the Newton fleet.

Dacroni Clan Leader Jarls gazed angrily at the ships on the main viewscreen. The Dacroni home world was a heavy-gravity world. Jarls was humanoid with bulky legs, torso, and arms. His face was similar to a human's but rounder and chunkier. His neck was shorter with his head almost resting on his torso.

"The Humans from Earth are here," growled Salas, Jarls's second in command. They had received a message from the

Controller station, informing them of the arrival of the Human ships. Several informants were on board who were paid to keep the Dacroni clan notified of developments that might be of interest.

"Newton," responded Jarls gruffly. "That one ship is the Star Cross, the flagship of Fleet Admiral Vickers." It had cost some credits, but Jarls had wanted to know the name of the enemy commander who had defeated him at Earth. A few inquiries on Kubitz and the transfer of sufficient credits had yielded him the information.

"They're safe as long as they remain in the Kubitz System," Salas reminded Jarls. "We don't dare do anything aggressive against their warships." Other Dacroni ships were in the system, but they were not of Jarls's clan.

Jarls knew Salas was right. No way would he risk his ships by attacking the Newton vessels. The defense grid around Kubitz would instantly hit his fleet, and he was well aware of what it was capable of.

"Send an FTL message to High Profiteer Creed. I believe he's currently at Marsten with the remains of his fleet. Inquire if he's willing to offer a reward if we destroy the Star Cross."

Even though Jarls wanted the Human dead and his flagship destroyed almost as bad as High Profiteer Creed did, it never hurt to see if some credits could be coaxed from the Profiteer leader. Jarls knew Creed still had a sizable quantity of credits tucked away from his partial looting of Earth.

"You intend to follow them when they leave Kubitz?" asked Salas, realizing what Jarls was planning.

Jarls nodded. "Yes, our long-range sensors can reach out five light-years. When Vickers leaves with his fleet, we'll follow and attack as soon as they drop from hyperspace." Jarls knew the small Newton fleet would have to jump several times as it left the star cluster. Vickers had made a serious tactical error in not bringing along several more of his battlecruisers.

Salas nodded his approval. "I would like to see this Human's death even if credits aren't involved. "Should we send some teams to the surface and attempt to set up an ambush?"

"Yes, send two teams to watch the Newton embassy compound. If Vickers leaves, they're to take him out if the opportunity presents itself. No heavy weapons. I don't want to get the Enforcers or the Controllers involved. This needs to look like a casual hit and nothing out of the ordinary. If we can't get him on Kubitz, then we'll blow his ship from space when he leaves."

-

In orbit above Marsten, High Profiteer Creed listened to the message from Dacroni Clan Leader Jarls. All the planets in the Gothan Empire had advanced FTL communications.

"The Humans from Newton have returned to Kubitz," said Second Profiteer Lantz as he turned to face the High Profiteer. "Dacroni Clan Leader Jarls wants to know what you will pay if he destroys the Star Cross and kills Fleet Admiral Vickers."

Creed stood up and walked to stand next to Third Profiteer Lukon at Communications. "They have an embassy compound in the capital city. It was only a matter of time before they returned."

"This is the first time in over a year the Star Cross has shown up at Kubitz," added Lantz. "We might not get an opportunity like this again."

Creed nodded as he thought over his options. Fleet Admiral Vickers and the Star Cross had cost him potentially billions in credits. Between the loss of Earth and now Julbian, Creed could have been one of the richest Profiteers on Marsten.

If Jarls could destroy the Star Cross along with Vickers, then Creed just might be able to return to Julbian and potentially even Earth. His flagship still needed repairs from the damage suffered in the battle with the Star Cross and Vickers's other battlecruisers. Creed knew the Human was a dangerous adversary and needed to be eliminated.

"They are in the heart of our empire!" Lantz said with feeling.

Creed knew his crew still felt anger about the profits the Humans had cost them. Plus the pleasure houses on Kubitz were expensive, and Lantz especially enjoyed spending quality time there whenever they were on the planet. "They will find it much harder to leave Kubitz than it was to come here. Jarls is prepared to make a move."

"It will be costly," commented Lantz. "Jarls does nothing for free."

Drawing in a deep breath, High Profiteer Creed reached a decision. "Lukon, send a message to Clan Leader Jarls. I will pay him ten million credits if he can destroy the Star Cross and an additional five million if he can kill Vickers."

Second Profiteer Lantz's eyes widened significantly, hearing the amount of credits Creed was willing to offer. Lantz hadn't expected the High Profiteer to offer such large amounts. Lantz realized there might be a simpler and easier solution. After all, he didn't spend so much time at the pleasure houses not to realize how things worked on the black market planet.

"What about offering a two-million-credit reward if Fleet Admiral Vickers were to suffer a life-ending accident while on Kubitz?" suggested Lantz. "A number of mercenaries as well as a few bounty hunters would be interested in such an offer."

High Profiteer Creed slowly nodded his head. "That's an excellent idea. Make a list of our contacts on Kubitz who could handle such an offer."

-

Satisfied Fleet Admiral Vickers would soon be dealt with, Creed made his way through the ship to his quarters. The Ascendant Destruction was inside a repair bay in one of the large orbital stations above Marsten. While he preferred the more elaborate repair bays above Kubitz, Creed had decided to return to Marsten to get some basic repairs done to his ships.

Once that was accomplished, he intended to return to Kubitz and have all his battlecruisers fully updated with the most modern weapons and defenses possible. It would also be necessary to purchase more warships and cargo vessels for his fleet. This would put a sizable dent in his credit reserves, but, if he wanted to continue to operate in the area of space where Earth and Newton were, it was a necessary expenditure.

Already he had heard rumors of two more habitable worlds in that region. If that were true, then that backwater area of the galaxy was much richer than formerly believed.

Creed entered his quarters and stood deep in thought. He had plans to become an important person on Marsten. Successful Profiteers held large estates on the planet and often threw lavish parties to show off their wealth. Creed had been well on his way to buying the land he wanted when Fleet Admiral Vickers had interfered.

Several months back he had sent several escort cruisers to check on Earth and the Newton Systems. He had been discouraged to learn Newton now had a full defensive grid along with dangerous Class Two Orbital Defense Platforms. No doubt Vickers had purchased the defenses from Lomatz, the Kubitz arms dealer. Lomatz had a reputation of being willing to deal with anyone, even if the Kubitz government was against it. Also a sizable fleet was constantly in orbit around Newton. An attack against the planet was now off the table. To attack such a powerfully defended world would be too costly.

However, scans of the Earth System were entirely different. Only a few defensive satellites were in orbit along with two defensive platforms. A small number of battleships and battlecruisers were present and of Kubitz design, but they could be easily handled if he brought Jarls along. He had already recruited a number of Humans to act as spies upon the planet. Promises of riches and power had easily swayed them into providing valuable inside information. He already knew much of the gold taken to Newton had been returned to Earth. He even knew the supposed secret locations of most of it.

If he could take out Vickers and the Star Cross, it would weaken Newton to the point they might be hesitant about aiding Earth if Creed attacked it with an overwhelming force. As much as he hated to spend more credits, it might be worth it to bring in a few more of the Marsten Profiteer clans as well as several Dacroni mercenary groups.

From what his spies on Earth had told him, if Creed attacked the planet and looted the secret gold repositories, after paying off the other Marsten clans and the Dacroni mercenaries, he would still come out with well over one billion in credits. It was a staggering amount and one that would ensure his rise as a prominent member of the ruling class on Marsten, the capital of the Gothan Empire.

Walking to his desk, Creed sat down and activated the computer terminal that sat in the center of his desk. For several weeks he had been planning the reconquest of Earth. He figured—from the time he initiated his attack on the planet, looted the gold depositories, and generally stripped everything of value he could find on Earth—he would need seventy-six hours.

Calling up the ships that would be involved from the different clans, he wanted to finalize just how much this venture would cost. He would also be taking a large number of detainee ships. His plan was to bring back tens of thousands of young nubile women and young men who could be sold at the slave auctions on Kubitz. Between the slaves and the wealth he would take from Earth, he could retire in comfort and live a lavish lifestyle on Marsten.

Of course the first thing to be done before he launched his attack was the destruction of the Star Cross and the death of Fleet Admiral Vickers. If things went as he hoped on Kubitz, all that might be attained in just a few days.

-

Keera waited anxiously for her brother to show up. She had left him a message at his apartment, asking him to meet her at the compound. She was in the guest quarters assigned to her and Kurt. With a deep sigh, she stood up and walked to the window. Their quarters were on the second floor, and she looked out across the compound. There wasn't a lot to see due to the tall security wall. In the distance, she could barely make out some of the city's taller buildings, where much of the business on Kubitz was conducted.

However, the streets and the people were completely hidden. She felt a sudden chill as she thought of the deals and transactions being made in the bars and the pleasure houses only a short distance away. It made her even more grateful to have found Kurt and Newton.

Kubitz was like a second home to her since coming here with her brother. She had learned a lot in the medical center where humanoids from all over the galaxy were treated. Unfortunately a lot of the injuries she saw had been from business deals gone wrong. When Kurt had come to the planet and with the horrifying circumstances concerning Private Dulcet's abduction, Keera had decided to go to Newton to see if it offered any new options. She had never regretted that move. Kurt was everything she had ever wanted in a man and a lover. He always put her feelings first. He was also very committed to his duty as fleet admiral and ensuring Newton stayed safe.

Movement at the main gate drew her attention, and a battered-looking vehicle pulled in. As she watched, she saw her brother get out and walk to the main entrance of the embassy. The guards had instructions to escort him to her quarters. She didn't want anyone around when she talked to Dalen. The last time she had seen him, they had had a terrible argument. They left angry with each other and hadn't spoken since.

Keera walked over and stood by the door. It wasn't long until she heard a tentative knock. Opening it, she saw her brother along with one of the Marines who had escorted him. "Come in, Dalen," she said, gesturing for him to enter the room.

Dalen stepped inside and stood, looking at his sister as she told the guard he could leave, and then she shut the door. He was a little taller than Keera but had the same dark hair and fair complexion. "It's been a while," he said. "I didn't know if you would come or not in response to my letter."

"Sit down. We have a lot to talk about." Keera walked over and sat on a sofa, indicating Dalen should sit next to her. "How is your work with the Profiteers going?"

"Fine," Dalen answered. "Or at least it was until recently. Now everything's changed."

"The black ships?"

Dalen nodded; his eyes clouded over as he looked across the room. He let out a deep breath and then spoke. "Business is way down. A number of Profiteer clans have quit sending raiding fleets into the territories of the Enlightened Worlds. Some are hesitant to even leave the Gothan Empire. It's been weeks since a cargo ship or passenger liner from an advanced world has been seized."

"It's that bad?"

"Yes, and I'm afraid it'll only get worse."

Keera leaned back and looked at her brother. He seemed paler than normal, and his breathing was rapid. Dalen was two years older than she was. Keera had never seen him this worried before, not even when she had gone to work at the medical center. They had argued about that as he wanted her to stay home, and not be out and about on Kubitz. Instead she had gone to work at the center and moved into her own place.

"What else do you know?"

"I'll tell you, but you have to promise me one thing."

"What's that?"

"When you leave and go back to Newton, I want to go with you. I don't think the Gothan Empire will be a safe place to be much longer."

Keera sucked in a deep breath. She hadn't been expecting this. She didn't know what her brother would do on a planet like Newton where there was no black market or Profiteers.

"I'll see what I can do. Now tell me what's got you so scared of staying on Kubitz. The brother I know wasn't even scared of the Profiteers. What's changed?"

Dalen studied his sister and asked, "Have you ever heard of a race called the Destroyers of Worlds?"

Fleet Admiral Kurt Vickers, Captain Andrew Randson, and Envoy Marvin Tenner were in a large conference room. Joining them were Avery Dolman and the weapons dealer Lomatz who had worked with Kurt before.

"I've arranged for Grantz to meet with Controller Nirron over your contract problems with High Profiteer Creed," Dolman said. "I'm sure they'll work up an acceptable contract."

"And how much will that cost?" asked Andrew suspiciously.

"Only a modest fee," Dolman replied with a smug grin. "A lot cheaper than the one-hundred-million-credit fine you're currently facing."

"Does everyone know about that?" muttered Andrew.

Dolman shrugged his shoulders. "This is Kubitz. What do you expect?"

Marvin Tenner turned to Lomatz. "You helped us with the warships we purchased last time, as well as placing the defensive grid around Newton."

"Don't forget finishing your space station," Lomatz reminded him. "A number of people on Kubitz were very unhappy when they learned all I did."

"We appreciate everything you did for us," Tenner replied evenly. "If I remember correctly, you were well compensated."

Lomatz nodded and then turned toward Kurt. "I suspect there's another reason why you asked for a meeting with Dolman and me."

Kurt nodded. "Some mysterious ships were spotted in the far reaches of Earth's solar system. We don't believe they're Profiteer ships. We've been made aware of rumors of a new enemy attacking the Enlightened Worlds. Is there any truth to that?"

"I don't know what you're talking about," said Lomatz, looking uncomfortable. "Rumors always float around Kubitz."

"I understand the Protector Worlds are powerless to stop these mysterious black ships." Kurt stared at Lomatz, waiting for an answer.

Lomatz turned toward Dolman, as if expecting him to respond instead.

"It's complicated," replied Dolman, leaning back in his chair. "I think it's best if Lomatz leaves us. I believe he could face some serious repercussions if he were to speak of the black ships. They're a closely guarded secret."

Lomatz stood, focused on Kurt, and then spoke in a softer voice. "If these black ships have been spotted around your home system, know full well you can do nothing to stop them." With that ominous remark, Lomatz left, shutting the door behind him.

"Crap!" said Andrew, as he watched the door shut. "I don't think I'll like this."

"No, you won't," said Dolman. "What you've heard is true. These black ships are attacking the colonies of the Enlightened Worlds. So far none of the home worlds—either Enlightened or Protector—have been attacked."

"What else do you know?" asked Kurt. If these black ships were a threat to Earth, he wanted to find out everything he could about them.

Dolman leaned forward, and a serious look crossed his face. "This information will be free, but I might need a favor in return someday."

"Agreed," replied Kurt. He was astonished Dolman was willing to share any information without an exchange of credits.

"In the last six months, a number of meetings have been held on Marsten in the Golite System between the leaders of various Profiteer worlds and clans. The shipyards and construction stations in orbit around Kubitz have been working full time, building new battleships, battlecruisers, and defensive stations. The same goes for the shipyards above all the major Profiteer worlds. They're expanding their fleets and increasing the strength of their defensive systems. Even here at Kubitz, the defensive grid has been increased by nearly 20 percent. Hundreds of millions of credits are being spent each week."

Andrew let out a whistle. "I thought the defensive grids around the main Profiteer worlds were powerful enough to stop even a ship from one of the Protector Worlds."

"They are," answered Dolman, his brow wrinkling in a deep frown. "But this threat is not from any of the Protector Worlds."

"Where are these black ships coming from?" asked Kurt. It sounded as if the situation was direr than he had believed possible.

"We know of them only in legends and in vague historical data from eons ago. They are known as the Destroyers of Worlds. Every two or three million years they enter our galaxy and destroy most of the civilized races. They cleanse all major life-forms from the worlds they attack. Only plant life, insects, and a few microbes are left behind."

Kurt felt his breath catch in his throat. He couldn't believe what he was hearing. "These are invaders from another galaxy?"

"No," responded Dolman, shaking his head. "We don't have a lot of information to go on since very few worlds survive their cleansing. Vague references state they live in intergalactic space or are from another universe."

Kurt felt a chill run up and down his back. If these ships were the ones spotted in the outer reaches of the Solar System, what exactly did it mean? Earth wasn't nearly as advanced as the other worlds in the galaxy.

"Why can't Lomatz speak of this?" asked Tenner.

"Panic," replied Dolman. "If word of this got out, it could crash the economy of the Gothan Empire. Trade would stop, and even the black market would be impacted. For now the different planetary leaders are taking a wait-and-see attitude while building new ships and strengthening their defenses. They're hoping the Protector Worlds can stop the black ships."

"And if they can't?" asked Andrew.

Dolman drew in a sharp breath. "Then we're all dead!"

Chapter Six

Keera was deeply concerned about what her brother had told her. She had a strong suspicion the black ships were one of the reasons Kurt had come to Kubitz. Their conversations had been shorter than normal on the trip from Newton to Kubitz, as if something had been weighing heavily on his mind. When he returned to their quarters after his meeting with Dolman and the others, he had been strangely quiet. He hadn't even asked about the conversation with her brother.

That next morning over breakfast, she asked him how things were going. Kurt responded, saying, "Okay. We'll discuss it when I return." Shortly after that Kurt and Andrew had gone off with Grantz to speak to Controller Nirron about the fine and the new contract he and Grantz were working on. With a deep sigh, Keera watched Kurt leave, and then she settled into their quarters to wait. She knew it was best to let Kurt work through this on his own.

The comm unit near the wall blinked, and Keera walked over to answer it. Perhaps Kurt was calling, and he had finished his business quicker than he thought so he could return early. It would be nice if they could eat lunch together.

"Hello?" she said, pressing the answer button on the comm unit.

"Sis, this is Dalen. I think there may be a problem."

Keera let out a deep breath, wondering if her brother had failed to tell her something. Was he in trouble with the Profiteers he worked for? "What is it?"

"It's Kurt. A bounty has been put on his head. Rumor has it that High Profiteer Creed wants him dead."

Keera felt a cold chill wash over her. She forced herself to remain calm. This was Kubitz, and such things were quite common. "How big a bounty?"

"That's just it," Dalen answered. "Most bounties are around ten to twenty thousand credits for a hit. This one is two million credits! Every bounty hunter and unemployed Profiteer on the planet will be looking for Kurt and trying to collect. I've never heard of a bounty this large before. He needs to get off Kubitz now! Hundreds of bounty hunters and Profiteers will be hunting for him. Even some of the smaller clans may become involved."

Keera felt her heart pound, and she suddenly found it hard to talk. Two million credits was a fortune, and she knew some individuals on Kubitz would go to great lengths to collect such a sum. "How soon can you be ready to leave?" As soon as Kurt returned, she would beg him to board the Star Cross. With that large of a bounty, not even the embassy would be safe from attack.

There was silence on the other end of the line, and Keera thought she could hear her brother speaking to someone. "I can be there in an hour."

"Do it," Keera said. "I need to make a call and see if I can warn Kurt."

"I hope you can," answered Dalen. "I'll be on my way shortly." With that the line went dead.

Pressing another button on the comm unit, she was in contact with the embassy communications operator. "I need to speak to Captain Briar immediately!"

"Just a moment," the communications operator responded. "I'll put you through to his office."

Keera just hoped she was in time.

-

Kurt was in one of the Humvees going to his meeting with Nirron, the Controller who was working on the contract to declare the area of space around Julbian of interest to Newton. Grantz had returned earlier and reported much of the work had already been done, and Nirron had a few questions that needed to be clarified before the contract would be ready to be filed. Later in the day, Kurt wanted to make arrangements for some Kubitz factory dealers to go to the Newton Princess to meet with the business people waiting on board. Dolman had mentioned several factory groups who routinely dealt in building and delivering the automated factories Governor Spalding was interested in. These factories were quite common on Kubitz and the rest of the Gothan Empire.

"I saved you a lot of credits," Grantz said haughtily. "I have proven once again how valuable I can be."

"We'll see," said Andrew, shaking his head. "What do you do with all the credits we pay you?"

Grantz grinned and leaned back with a self-satisfied look on his face. "I have a reputation to uphold. The females at the pleasure houses expect a certain flair from me. I tell you, the women, food, and drinks at the pleasure houses are the best on Kubitz, among other things. You should really come with me one time to see for yourself."

Andrew shook his head. "I'm happily married. No way would you catch me near one of those."

"You can skip the women," Grantz said, shrugging his shoulder. "Just come for the food, drink, and the entertainment. I promise it will be an experience you will never forget. I'll even buy the first round of drinks."

"No thanks," said Andrew, frowning at the Profiteer.

"Admiral, we may have a problem," Sergeant Jones said with concern in his voice. He sat in the front passenger seat next to the corporal, who was driving. "I just received an emergency message from Captain Briar. It seems that a bounty has been placed on your head."

"A bounty!" said Andrew, his eyes widening in disbelief.

"Yes," Sergeant Jones replied as he unbuckled his safety harness and stepped through the small armored hatch that separated the driving compartment from the passenger compartment. "A warning was called in to the embassy. They're rolling three more Humvees to rendezvous with us and escort us back."

"How big?" Grantz asked Kurt. Bounties weren't that unusual on Kubitz.

"Two million credits."

"Two million credits!" roared Grantz, his eyes growing wide at the amount, his hand automatically moving to his gun. Taking a deep breath, Grantz brought his hand back to his side.

Andrew watched Grantz. His hand rested on his 9 mm pistol. "Don't get any ideas, Grantz," warned Andrew, tapping his pistol. "Remember who's paying you."

Grantz only grinned and nodded. "I like you, Captain. You have nothing to fear from me, but a lot of bounty hunters and hard-on-their-luck Profiteers will want to collect that bounty. I suggest we turn around and get back to the compound where it's safe before we're attacked."

"Get us back as quickly as possible," Kurt ordered as he listened to Grantz.

While Kurt still didn't fully trust the Profiteer, Grantz was probably right about the danger. Kurt had been through an attack on Kubitz once before and had no desire to go through one again. The report of the bounty deeply concerned Kurt. With a reward of that size, he wasn't sure even the embassy compound would be safe. It might be necessary to return to the Star Cross, making sure enough people witnessed his departure so the embassy would be left alone.

"High Profiteer Creed," Andrew said grimly. "It has to be him. We should have killed the son-of-a-bitch at Julbian when we had the chance."

Kurt's face grew stormy. Andrew was probably right. High Profiteer Creed had to be the one behind the bounty. They should have used the antimatter missiles at Julbian and destroyed the Ascendant Destruction. Kurt wouldn't make that mistake again.

-

The two Humvees were on a busy street, and it took the drivers a few moments to find a place to safely turn around. Tall buildings surrounded them on both sides, and heavy pedestrian traffic was on the wide sidewalks. Glaring signs advertised their wares in the large windows, and it was a busy time of day. With some careful maneuvering, they finally got turned around and started back. They had only gone a few blocks when several large trucks suddenly blocked the road in front of them. Both Humvees braked to a sudden stop.

"We've got trouble," Sergeant Jones said as he chambered a round into his assault rifle. He also drew his pistol and ensured it was fully loaded. "Several trucks are blocking the road ahead."

"We're blocked from behind too," added the driver. "With no side streets intersecting this main road, we can't turn off." The driver reached between the two front seats and picked up his assault rifle, clicking off the safety.

"Corporal Evans, get into the turret and get the 240 ready. We may need it shortly," ordered Sergeant Jones.

Grantz unbuckled the strap that held his handgun in place. "They'll blast us from these vehicles. They wouldn't have blocked the street if they didn't think they could get to us."

Kurt glanced out one of the heavy bulletproof windows. "How soon before the other three Humvees get here?" There was no way to tell what they were up against.

"I've already informed them of our situation," Jones said as he peered through the front windows of the Humvee. "But it'll be a while. They have some busy streets to navigate."

The Humvee suddenly jolted to one side as a loud explosion rang out. A huge dent appeared on one of the armored walls, and two of the small windows cracked.

"I warned you," muttered Grantz as he drew his pistol.

"Where did that explosive round come from!" yelled Jones, looking up at Corporal Evans in the turret.

"Don't know," Evans grated out as he rotated the turret, looking for a target. "Too many people are on the streets to tell."

"Sidewalks are clearing," the driver reported. Out the front and side windows he could see people running hastily toward doorways. Metal shutters were sliding down over the exposed windows and even some of the doors.

Two more explosions rocked the Humvee, nearly tipping it. The 240 machine gun suddenly fired in quick short bursts.

"I've got two targets inside a building doorway," reported Evans. The machine gun fell silent. "Both targets are down."

Kurt looked out the front of the Humvee just in time to see the other Humvee vanish in flames. For a moment he thought it had exploded, but then the fire and smoke cleared, and the Humvee reappeared, seemingly undamaged, though it was heavily scorched. The turret on top of the Humvee swiveled to one side and returned fire at targets behind a large truck parked on the side of the street.

"We're pinned down," reported Sergeant Jones as he spoke to the Marines in the other Humvee over his comm unit. "Large trucks block the street in front of us and behind us. Also our assailants are using several trucks on the side of the street for cover."

The Humvee shook again as another explosive round struck the armored exterior. Each time a round struck, the Humvee rang like a giant bell.

"What are they shooting us with?" Andrew stared at several bulges in the Humvee's heavy armor.

"Some kind of small rockets," Sergeant Jones answered. "From what Corporal Richards in the other Humvee is reporting, the damn things are being launched from behind the trucks in front of us. We can't get a clear shot at the launchers."

"How many more hits can the Humvee take?" asked Andrew, but nobody answered. "I don't suppose you see any Enforcers coming to our rescue?" They never seemed to be any around when needed.

"None in sight," Evans replied as he fired a short burst at an armored figure who appeared around one of the trucks. The figure dropped to the ground and lay there unmoving. Rounds from the M240 were deadly if they struck their target.

"How long can we stay in the Humvees?" asked Kurt. If the attackers penetrated the vehicle's armor, the battle would be over. One explosive round going off inside would kill everyone. Kurt wondered if they would stand a better chance outside.

"Depends," replied Sergeant Jones as he peered through one of the small cracked windows. "If these are just bounty hunters or a small Profiteer group, we may be able to hold out until the other Humvees get here. If we exit the vehicles, we'll be picked off one by one. I can't tell how many are out there. Our best bet is to stay inside the Humvees. At least with the M240s, we have the firepower to keep them back and the armor provides some protection."

Kurt worried they might have encountered a more dangerous opponent; the attack seemed too coordinated. "Four Dacroni battleships are in orbit. These may be mercenaries we're facing."

Sergeant Jones peered out the front windows once more. "I don't think these are mercenaries. Mercenaries would be equipped with more powerful weapons and would have chosen a better location for an ambush. We're in the open with a lot of witnesses."

At that moment an explosive rocket slammed into the windshield of the Humvee, shattering it into a million pieces. The driver screamed and fell over against the door. A jagged piece of glass had penetrated his protective chest armor. Smoke and fire filled the driver's compartment.

Sergeant Jones stepped into the smoke and, leaning forward, checked the driver's pulse. Turning toward Kurt, he shook his head. Ducking back into the passenger compartment, Jones slid the protective armored door shut, sealing them off from the driver's compartment.

"Can't see much now," muttered Andrew, gripping his pistol in his right hand as he stared out one of the small bulletproof windows. Even outside the air was full of drifting smoke from the weapons fire.

"Corporal Evans, keep an eye out!" ordered Sergeant Jones. "They have to force us from the Humvees before our other vehicles get here. Also the Enforcers can't let this go on too long or too many eyebrows will be raised." He could hear the machine gun on the other Humvee firing in longer bursts.

"I'm seeing a lot of movement," Evans reported as he fired at several figures in body armor. "I think they're preparing to rush us."

"They know their time's running short," Andrew said as he pulled his pistol from its holster.

Corporal Evans fired steadily, and then a loud explosion rang out from the top of the Humvee as an explosive rocket slammed into the turret, disabling it. Corporal Evans tumbled out and collapsed to the floor.

One of the other Marine privates checked him and then turned toward Sergeant Jones. "He's only unconscious."

"Crap!" muttered the sergeant, flipping the safety off his assault rifle. We're defenseless now. The other Humvee can't cover our rear."

Kurt could hear noises at the large hatch at the end of the vehicle. Letting out a deep breath, he knew they were in a precarious situation. He wondered if he would make it back to Keera. Looking at Andrew, Kurt wished the captain had stayed on board the Star Cross. It had been a mistake for both of them to come down to the planet.

A sudden explosion shook the back of the Humvee violently as the hatch was blown off, and smoke came billowing in. The Marines fired through the door at the smoke-shrouded targets. One of the Marines cried out and fell, blood spreading across his chest.

"Damn," muttered Andrew, glancing at a red stain on his own uniform. He leaned up against the wall of the vehicle and slowly slid to the floor.

Kurt glanced at the captain, seeing he had been hit in the side. A cold feeling came over Kurt as he realized they might not get out of this.

The firing outside seemed to increase dramatically, then it subsided and finally came to a stop.

"Our other Humvees must have gotten here," Kurt said, stepping to Andrew's limp form. He was still breathing, though a pool of blood grew next to him. "I need a first aid kit. We must stop the flow of blood."

"I'll take care of it," one of the Marine privates said, grabbing a nearby first aid kit. "I've been trained in field medicine."

Kurt stepped back as the private treated Andrew. Kurt didn't know how he could face Andrew's wife and daughter if the captain died from his injuries.

"It's too early for it to be our other Humvees," Sergeant Jones said, confused. He held his rifle pointed at the rear of the vehicle.

A figure suddenly appeared in the shattered hatch. "You should have called on me for an escort," said Avery Dolman, holding a smoking pistol in his right hand. "You're lucky I was in the neighborhood."

"How?" asked Kurt, stunned to see the black marketeer.

Avery pointed toward Grantz, hunkered down in a corner of the Humvee. "Our mutual friend here called me and said you were in a slight bit of trouble."

Grantz stood up and pointed to a small communications device in his left hand. "I knew as soon as I heard about the bounty that we would be hit. I called Avery and requested immediate assistance. I was sure you wouldn't mind paying the extra protection fee."

"The Enforcers are here," Sergeant Jones reported. "Our other vehicle is reporting a large number of them just showed up."

"I'll handle them," Dolman said with a grimace. "I'm pretty sure I can ensure you won't be fined or suffer any repercussions from this little fracas. I have a few connections with the Enforcers."

"Captain Randson is stable," reported the Marine treating him. "We should get him to a medical center as soon as possible."

"I'll take him in one of our other Humvees as soon as it arrives," Sergeant Jones said. "Captain Briar should be here momentarily."

Kurt nodded. This whole incident just reminded him of how dangerous Kubitz was. He found it hard to believe Keera had lived here for a number of years. Someday he would have to ask her how she had survived.

-

Jarls shook his head in frustration. He had just received word a few mercenaries along with a small Profiteer clan had tried to ambush Fleet Admiral Vickers. Unfortunately the attempt failed, and the Kubitz government had just issued a strong warning about attempting to collect the bounty on Vickers. As with most warnings from the planet's government, this one cautioned anyone attempting to collect the bounty with the use of illegal weapons on Kubitz. The use of such weapons would see the offenders heavily fined with other stiff penalties.

"Well, that tears it," muttered Salas, frowning in disgust. "The Enforcers will be on the watch now, and Vickers knows he's being hunted. He'll board the Star Cross, where we can't get to him."

"The Carlton Profiteer Clan will be slapped with a substantial fine for using explosive rockets inside the capital, particularly inside the environmental dome. It will make everyone else much more cautious about attempting to collect the bounty on Vickers's head." Jarls knew the chances of his mercenaries getting to Vickers had been greatly decreased.

Salas studied one of the large viewscreens in the Command Center, which was focused on the Star Cross. "I doubt if Vickers will leave the Newton embassy compound again until he's ready to board his ship."

Jarls nodded his agreement. "He would be a fool to risk his life on the streets of the capital. And Vickers is no fool."

"What about our teams on the planet?"

"Have them watch the Newton embassy compound discreetly. I don't think we have a realistic shot at getting him on the planet now."

Jarls folded his powerful arms across his chest. He would have to take out Vickers and the Star Cross in a space battle. He had summoned several more battleships as he wanted to ensure his targets were eliminated. If all went as planned, he would annihilate Fleet Admiral Vickers and his entire fleet.

-

Keera paced nervously in her quarters. Kurt had arrived at the compound an hour earlier and gone straight into a meeting with Marvin Tenner, Captain Briar, Grantz, and Avery Dolman. She had heard about the ambush and how close she had come to losing Kurt. She felt intense anger at the type of world Kubitz could be at times.

Keera had also called the medical center, where Captain Randson had been taken under heavy guard and had been assured he was receiving the best treatment possible. Fortunately Keera knew several of the doctors and had spoken briefly to one who owed her a few favors. He had promised to look in on Andrew and ensure he made a full and speedy recovery.

There was a knock at her door, and she walked over and opened it. Her brother stood there, and, much to her surprise, a young woman was with him.

"Hi," Dalen said a little hesitantly. "I'm sorry we're late, but we had to do a little packing. This is Meesa, and she'll be coming with us. We've been together for over a year, and I don't want to leave her behind."

Keera frowned, not sure how Kurt would take this. "Come on in. I'm waiting for Kurt to get back from a meeting."

Dalen nodded as he and Meesa entered the room. "I heard about the attack. Was anyone hurt?"

"Three Marines were killed and two others injured," Keera answered. "Also Captain Andrew Randson was shot. He's been taken to the Hatheen Medical Facility for treatment and should make a full recovery."

"The Hatheen Medical Facility," Dalen said, his brow wrinkling in thought. "Didn't you work there for a few years right after we moved to Kubitz?"

"Yes," answered Keera, recalling those early days. Many nights she'd come home only to get into a fight with Dalen over his involvement with the Profiteers. "Sit down and make yourself comfortable. Kurt should be here shortly, and then we can decide when we'll board the Newton Princess."

"That's the passenger liner from Newton?" asked Meesa timidly.

"Yes, and it's very comfortable. So, Meesa, tell me how you met my brother."

-

"You were damn lucky," said Dolman, gazing across the conference table at Kurt. "My sources tell me two Dacroni strike teams are currently in the city searching for you. If you step outside this compound again, you could very well end up dead."

"Dacroni," muttered Grantz unhappily. "They're not someone to be trifled with."

Dolman shook his head. "No, I strongly suspect High Profiteer Creed has offered the Dacroni clan leader a substantial number of credits if he can eliminate you or your ships."

Kurt turned pale at this comment. They would be leaving in a few more days, and Keera would be on board the Newton Princess. "How many Dacroni ships are currently in orbit?" The last he had heard, four were in close proximity to his small fleet.

"It's unchanged," Captain Briar responded. "I've been checking every few hours."

"But that could change at any time," warned Marvin Tenner, with concern in his eyes. "Perhaps it would be best if you summoned more ships from Newton."

"No," answered Kurt, shaking his head. "I don't want to risk any more of our fleet, particularly if these rumors about the black ships are true."

Avery Dolman was silent for a long moment. "There may be a way to get you safely away from Kubitz," he said slowly. "I know of a piece of technology that will mislead the Dacroni as to the dropout point of your first hyperspace jump. The technology is illegal on Kubitz as it's from a Protector World."

"I thought everything was for sale on Kubitz," responded Kurt, wondering why this technology would be prohibited.

Doman shook his head. "No, not everything. There's a level of technology that's forbidden to sell as it might create an imbalance in the power structure of the Gothan Empire. Great care is taken to ensure certain technologies from the Enlightened Worlds and the Protector Worlds are not sold on Kubitz or anywhere else in the empire."

"How do you have access to this forbidden technology?" Kurt suspected who else might be involved, but he wanted to hear it from Dolman.

"Lomatz," Dolman answered in a softer voice. "I can speak to him and make some arrangements. If this technology is installed on your ships, you can never tell anyone where it came from."

Kurt slowly nodded his head. If they could make the first jump without encountering Dacroni warships, then each proceeding jump would make the likelihood of detection less likely.

"Why can't this technology be used on more than one jump?"

"It takes too long to recharge. By the time the system is ready to cloak your second hyperspace jump, the Dacroni will have found you."

Kurt was silent as he weighed his options. This system sounded all well and good, but he knew it would carry a hefty cost. Fortunately they had a large credit account already on Kubitz and a very large quantity of gold in the secret vault beneath the embassy compound.

"If I agree to this, how quickly can Lomatz have it done, and how much will it cost me?"

Dolman grinned and then answered. "Nothing, not one single credit."

"What?" uttered Grantz, his eyes widening in shock. "A system like that should run at least two to four million per ship. It would give the Profiteer who possessed it a tremendous advantage in raiding ships and getting away undetected."

Staring intently at Dolman, Kurt asked the obvious question. "Lomatz must want something. What is it?"

Dolman nodded. "A favor. He will come to the Newton System in a few weeks to deliver some things that recently came into his possession."

"What?" asked Marvin Tenner suspiciously. He had been on Kubitz long enough to know nothing was free or didn't come without strings attached. Some of those strings could be quite expensive.

"I can't say, other than you're the only one he's willing to trust with this."

"Does this have to do with the black ships?"

"I can't say," answered Dolman evenly. "Just trust me. You won't regret it."

Kurt was backed into a corner. "Okay, I agree. If Lomatz is coming to Newton, we need some items. I'll want him to bring them too."

Kurt intended for Lomatz to bring Keera's medical equipment as well as the new building equipment Governor Spalding wanted. Kurt would also ask Lomatz for more fifty-megaton antimatter missiles. If these mysterious black ships were a real threat, Kurt wanted the most powerful weapons at his disposal. He needed to make the arrangements for the automated factories too. The business people on board the Newton Princess were probably growing impatient.

"One more thing," Dolman added. "I did some checking and the ships that were detected on the outskirts of your home system were not the black ships. They are currently not interested in such a backwater area of our galaxy."

"Then who were they?" asked Kurt, growing suspicious.

"They were Profiteer ships." Dolman replied. "The word on the street is that High Profiteer Creed is keeping a close watch on your home system."

Kurt let out a deep breath. He didn't like the sound of that as it indicted the High Profiteer wasn't finished with Earth. It was just one more problem he would have to worry about.

-

Four days later Kurt was back on board the Star Cross, sitting in his command chair, looking calmly about the Command Center. How strange to be here and for Captain Randson to be absent. Kurt had decided Andrew was better off on the Newton Princess under Keera's expert care. The passenger liner had a modern medical facility, much of it designed by Keera. She had informed Kurt there would be no problems in caring for Andrew, and he was well on his way to a full recovery. Even Dr. Willis had agreed that Andrew was better off on the passenger liner.

"All ships report ready to activate their subspace drives," reported Lieutenant Brenda Pierce as she listened to the messages over the comm.

"We can leave at your command," added Lieutenant Styles. He had already programmed a course into the navigation computer.

Kurt shifted his eyes to the main viewscreen, showing six Dacroni battleships in the distance. Two more had arrived the day before. He sure hoped this hyperspace cloaking system worked that Lomatz's engineers had installed. Lomatz had seemed confident it would. Kurt had no desire to face the Dacroni battleships in battle. After what had happened on Kubitz, Kurt was certain the Dacroni battleships were waiting for the Star Cross and the other Newton ships to leave their protected orbit. With a deep sigh, Kurt knew High Profiteer Creed needed to be dealt with.

"Take us out," Kurt ordered, curious to see if the Dacroni ships followed them. They had to cross the orbit of the sixth planet, where the Controller station was located, before they could activate their hyperspace drives. If they activated them any sooner, they could face stiff fines and possible banishment from trading on Kubitz.

They already had permission from Kubitz Orbital Control to leave the planet. Inside the safe in his office was the new contract he had submitted to the Controllers. It specified a few small areas of space Newton claimed an interest in. Several of the areas mystified Kurt as Nirron had included them at Lomatz's insistence. Overall the new contract had cost Newton twenty million credits. They had also worked out an agreement on the automated factories and the building equipment Governor Spalding wanted. Now all they had to do was make it back home to Newton.

-

The Star Cross and the other four ships of her small force rapidly pulled away from the crowded orbital space above Kubitz. A few minutes after their departure, all six Dacroni battleships set out in pursuit. Everyone else watching in other ships and upon the planet knew, if the Dacroni were successful in catching the Newton vessels at their first hyperspace dropout, there would be a battle, and no one defeated six massive Dacroni battleships.

For several hours the two fleets kept their distance. The Newton fleet was satisfied to stay a few minutes ahead of the pursuing Dacroni warships, and the Dacroni were confident they would net their reward when Fleet Admiral Vickers dropped from hyperspace. It would be sweet revenge for the fleet losses the Human admiral had inflicted on Clan Leader Jarls in previous engagements, as well as evening the score for the hundreds of millions of credits he had lost when they were driven from Earth.

-

"We're crossing the orbit of the sixth planet," Salas reported as he watched the ship's sensors closely. "Human ships are activating their hyperdrives."

"Track them on the hyperspace sensors," ordered Jarls, growing impatient to kill the Human admiral and his paltry grouping of ships.

"Ships are jumping," Salas said as the ships vanished from the regular sensors only to appear moments later on the hyperspace one. "We have them on the long-range sensors."

"Prepare to enter hyperspace," ordered Jarls, feeling victory within his grasp. Even as he watched the long-range sensor screen, the five red threat icons slowly faded away and vanished.

"What happened?" demanded Jarls, standing up and striding to the long-range sensor screen in disbelief. "What's wrong with the sensors?"

"I don't know," stammered Salas as he ordered the sensor operator to run a diagnostic. "They've never done that before."

A few minutes passed, and the sensor operator shook his head. "There's nothing wrong with the sensors. We just can't seem to detect the Newton ships."

Jarls returned to his command chair, slamming his fist on the armrest, shattering it. "Lomatz!" he roared. "The weapons dealer has to be behind this. No one else would have access to such technology."

"We can file a complaint at Kubitz," suggested Salas. "If he's sold forbidden technology to Vickers, Lomatz will suffer the consequences for his actions. The Controllers will ban him from ever selling anything on Kubitz again."

Jarls gazed angrily at the now empty long-range sensor screen. "No, we can't do anything as we have no proof. Set a course for Dacron Four. We've been away from home far too long. Fleet Admiral Vickers and the Star Cross will have to wait for now. I'll contact High Profiteer Creed once we get back home. Perhaps between the two of us, we can set a trap for Vickers. Our day will come, and Vickers will learn of the wrath of the Dacroni."

The Dacroni clan leader slowly brought his anger into check. Once again Fleet Admiral Vickers had demonstrated his resourcefulness. However, Jarls knew, at some point in time, not even that would save the crafty Human admiral.

Chapter Seven

The black ship dropped from hyperspace into the unsuspecting system of Golithia. The ship was dumbbell-shaped, with two enormous globes at each end connected to one another by a short cylinder. The ship was painted a matte black, and no starlight reflected from its hull. A powerful energy screen protected it, and a sensor-dampening field ensured it could not be detected.

This was a Vorn mothership with only one priority: food procurement for the Vorn race, particularly the Royal Caste. Around it other black warships exited hyperspace in a defensive formation around the behemoth-size vessel. The spindle-shaped ships were five hundred meters in length and extremely deadly. They were armed with the most powerful weapons known to the ancient race.

The Vorn race was divided up into three castes: The Royal Caste, which consisted of the Queens, their consorts, the Queens' extended families, scientists, and top military leaders. The Military Caste was made up of warriors who were specially bred to fight for the Royal Caste. They were intelligent, loyal, and quite deadly. Last of all was the Working Caste. This caste consisted of nearly mindless drones bred for specific functions.

Over the eons, the Vorn race had become known as the Destroyers of Worlds. They lived in huge artificial constructs in intergalactic space. However, the Vorn had not originated in this universe. They were from a bubble universe where they had fled a great enemy. In a desperate battle, the Vorn Queens had fled with their surviving ships into the heart of a black hole. They had traveled through the singularity and arrived in a new universe, one where their weapons were supreme and where the inhabitants of the multitude of galaxies were a prime food source for the Vorn.

The Vorn stood upright, having a basic humanoid form with two legs and two arms. That was where the Human resemblance ended. The average Vorn looked like a cross between a humanoid and a wasp. The head was covered in very short hair and triangular-shaped with two antennae. Its eyes were multifaceted and could see in a number of different light wavelengths. They had small wasplike wings normally folded on their backs. Their hands consisted of seven thin digits with which to manipulate equipment. However, the most shocking aspect of the Vorn race was that they were telepathic. They could sense each other's thoughts over short distances.

The military commander of the mothership waited patiently for the other ships to arrive. Once the fleet was assembled, it would move toward the single inhabited world in this system. Time for another world to die and to procure more food for the always-hungry Vorn race.

-

Commander Halk Lakor stared with deep concern at one of the viewscreens of his flagship. Commander Lakor was of the Andock race, and his fleet was responsible for protecting the Enlightened World of Blisth. Computer simulations run on Andock had predicted Blisth was the next most likely target for the Destroyers of Worlds.

"We got lucky," Second Commander Torrel commented as he gazed at the viewscreen. "The enemy dropped from hyperspace near a research satellite and was captured on its video input. We're getting a live feed of what's happening in the outer system."

"Send a drone to Andock with the data," Lakor ordered as he watched more of the black ships exit hyperspace. He wanted to ensure the home system knew exactly what they faced. "Send a message to Blisth to evacuate. I want every cargo and passenger ship crammed full of civilians and exiting this system within the next hour."

"You don't think we can hold the system?"

"No one's stopped the black ships yet," Lakor said evenly. "We'll do our best, but I fear all we can do is give the evacuating ships time to get away. I also want an FTL drone launched every ten minutes with the latest tactical data. Perhaps the information we send back to Andock will give our military leaders and scientists a clue as to how to stop the black ships in the future."

Second Commander Torrel nodded and passed on the orders.

Lakor thoughtfully studied the viewscreen. It was doubtful the black ships knew they had been detected. Perhaps this time it would give the Andock fleet an advantage. In the last six weeks, three Enlightened World colonies under Andock protection had been destroyed by the deadly enemy. Not a single inhabitant survived on any of the three worlds. Nearly one billion Enlightened World inhabitants had been killed.

"Set our viewscreens to display any aberrations that might appear. Have our ship computer correlate the aberrations and project them into the tactical display. We'll then use the information from the display to determine targets."

Taking a deep breath, Commander Lakor addressed the ships of his fleet. "All ships, set Alert One. Enemy ships have been spotted in the outer system. As discussed in earlier strategy sessions, we will use the images from our viewscreens, which our ship computers can interpolate and plot in the tactical displays, to determine targets. Hold your fire until I give the order. Perhaps we can draw the enemy in close enough for our weapons to be effective."

Commander Lakor had 120 ships under his command. Of that total 110 were 1,200-meter-long battlecruisers and the remaining 10 were 1,500-meter-long battleships. As he watched the viewscreen, more of the deadly black ships dropped from hyperspace. Already he was outnumbered two to one.

"The Lakiams lost a fleet a few weeks ago," Second Commander Torrel said as he gazed at the viewscreen. "Not a single ship survived."

Commander Lakor nodded. "It's been the same everywhere the black ships have struck. From the latest reports fourteen Enlightened World colonies have been hit."

Torrel turned toward Commander Lakor. "What happens when the black ships strike one of the actual Enlightened Worlds and not just a colony?"

"The Enlightened Worlds and various Protector Worlds have communicated a lot over the last few weeks. We know more about the black ships than we did. One of the older Enlightened Worlds escaped the black ships the last time they came to our galaxy. They were a Protector World back then. Even so, they didn't have a lot of information. However, when the black ships previously attacked the worlds of our galaxy, they started out small and random, just like these raids."

"Like they were searching for the best targets?"

"Possibly," Commander Lakor replied. "Then, after a while, the black ships appeared everywhere. World after world succumbed and were stripped of their higher life-forms. The only living things that remained, once the black ships left a planet, were the plant life, insects, and microorganisms. Every other life-form was gone. Only a few civilized worlds escaped the death and destruction spread by the black ships. Even those worlds suffered a collapse of their civilizations as the rest of the worlds around them were gone."

Torrel slowly shook his head. "They take so much. I wonder if they leave the lower life-forms so new civilized species will someday evolve to become new victims."

"That's the theory." On the viewscreen, Commander Lakor saw no more black ships dropping from hyperspace. "Move the fleet closer to the planet. Perhaps we can give the evacuation fleet sufficient cover fire to allow them to escape."

-

In space, the Andock fleet moved to within one hundred thousand kilometers of Blisth. Already cargo ships and a few passenger vessels had lifted off the planet and fled into hyperspace. Other ships were still being loaded and would be launching as soon as they were full of evacuees.

The fleet put the planet to their back, and then the ships turned to face outward, waiting for the appearance of the black ships, ready to fulfill their sworn duty to defend the Enlightened Worlds under their protection. A defense that in every recent case so far had failed.

Minutes passed as the fleet waited with all sensors scanning the space around them and the planet. However, the Andocks knew from previous reports their sensors would be useless against the enemy ships. Instead they would depend on their ships' computers and viewscreens to spot and plot the location of the black ships when they arrived.

On the surface of the planet, dozens of small and large cargo ships were hurriedly loaded with panicked citizens. Blisth had been colonized for over six hundred years and, in all that time, had never faced any threats. As a peaceful world, Blisth was dedicated to the advancement of knowledge, living in harmony with nature, the environment, and all other species. Now that peace was about to be shattered by a deadly enemy who knew no mercy.

Large passenger liners dropped to the surface to take on evacuees. Normally the large ships didn't land but were loaded at one of the three orbital stations above the planet. However, in this instance, there wasn't time to load passengers in shuttles, take them to a station, and then board one of the liners. Therefore, the large ships came to the planet's spaceports. It was the first time many of the ships had ever entered a planet's atmosphere, but they had been designed to do this in case of an emergency. Even so only about 2 percent of the population could be evacuated; the rest were doomed to wait and hope the defending fleet was successful in stopping the incoming black ships.

-

"Contacts!" called out the sensor operator as the ship's computer began putting red threat icons into the tactical display. "Enemy ships detected on a number of viewscreens throughout the fleet. They'll be in weapons range in fourteen minutes."

"What's the status of the evacuation?" demanded Commander Lakor. The black ships had arrived much sooner than he had expected.

"Not enough time for some of the ships," Second Commander Torrel responded as he checked with the planet's Space Control. "They need another forty minutes to get every available ship fully loaded, off the planet, and into hyperspace."

Commander Lakor took in a deep breath and then slowly let it out. "We need to find a way to buy them the extra time."

He studied the tactical display for a long moment. The enemy's mothership was in the center of the approaching formation of 311 small and deadly cruisers.

"We need to stop the enemy's advance," Lakor said. "I want all ten of our battleships to do a short hyperspace jump to just behind the black fleet. Once we emerge from hyperspace, I want every weapon we have focused on that large ship in the middle of their formation. Our battlecruisers will advance and attack the front of the enemy formation at the same time. They'll fire an initial barrage and then transit into hyperspace, coming back out in an englobement formation around the black fleet."

"Englobement?" stuttered Second Commander Torrel, his eyes growing wide. "We don't have enough ships."

Commander Lakor shook his head. "It doesn't matter. We're just buying some time." He didn't go on to say he expected to lose his entire fleet. All he could do was delay the black ships, before they destroyed his task force. In the end, he knew they were all most likely going to die.

-

The black ships continued their steady approach. On board the mothership, the Vorn watched as cargo ships and passenger liners lifted from the surface of the planet and vanished into hyperspace. Somehow the defending fleet had detected them. The Vorn's telepathic abilities allowed them to communicate across their fleet without the need for primitive comm systems. It gave them a decisive edge in all battles as the fleet could move in unison with just a single command from the fleet military commander. The fleet moved closer to the defenders and prepared to attack.

The Andocks waited until the last possible moment, and then ten battleships vanished into hyperspace only to reappear directly behind the Vorn fleet. As soon as the Andock ships' weapons and shields came online, force beams flashed into being, slamming into the massive mothership at the center of the Vorn formation. Its powerful shield flashed to life as it glowed brightly. However, the deadly energy transmitted in the force beams was only absorbed. The mothership had been designed to resist such an attack in force. Since coming to this universe, not a single Vorn mothership had been lost in battle.

-

"No effect!" yelled Second Commander Torrel in disbelief. "Ten battleships and that thing is untouched. How's that possible?"

"The enemy ship is absorbing the power of the force beams," announced the Andock officer at the sensor console. "Our weapons are only making the screen grow stronger."

On the tactical display, the other Andock ships now fired their own force beams and energy projectors at the leading enemy ships. Their beams also were absorbed by the black ship's energy screens, and no damage was caused. What a disheartening development as Commander Lakor had expected to at least damage a few of the enemy vessels.

"Fire missiles!" he ordered, finding it difficult to believe his attack was having no effect. The only chance they had was to overload the energy screens. Surely there had to be a limit to how much energy they could absorb! If he couldn't destroy at least a few of the black ships, how would he stop them from advancing on the planet?

On all the Andock ships, missile hatches slid open, and powerful antimatter hypermissiles jumped into hyperspace to instantly slam into the shields of the black ships. Each missile contained a two-hundred-megaton warhead. Space lit up in a fury of brightness as antimatter energy washed across the screens of the enemy ships. But even these powerful weapons were ineffective. After a few moments, the antimatter energy faded away as its power was absorbed by the enemy ships.

"Hypermissiles ineffective," reported Second Commander Torrel, gazing at the viewscreens in disbelief. "None of our weapons are penetrating their shields."

Looking at the tactical display, Lakor saw the green icons representing his battlecruisers vanish only to reappear around the black fleet. As soon as their weapons and shields stabilized, the battlecruisers fired upon the black ships trying to inflict some damage.

"Jump us back over Blisth," Commander Lakor ordered as he thought over the dilemma he was now in. "I want all ten battleships between the planet and the inbound enemy fleet." Every minute of time he bought for Blisth meant thousands of innocent lives could be saved.

"Our battlecruisers?"

Commander Lakor turned toward Second Commander Torrel. "Our weapons are ineffective. We're not slowing down the enemy much. All battlecruisers are to continue their attack for thirty more seconds and then jump from the system. There's no point in sacrificing them needlessly." If his ships had been able to cause any significant damage then they would have remained. As it was, to continue the battle was pointless.

Lakor felt a slight dizziness as the flagship suddenly made the short hyperspace jump back to Blisth.

"Commander, the black ships are firing black energy spheres toward our battlecruisers."

"All battlecruisers, jump now!" ordered Lakor over the comm system, linking him to all of the ships in his fleet. He greatly feared for the safety of his warships. He had heard rumors about an unstoppable black energy sphere that was fatal to any ship it struck. "I want detailed sensor scans of those energy spheres. I want to know what they're made of, and the strength of the explosion if and when they strike any of our battlecruisers."

On the main viewscreen, he could see the spheres of black energy hurtling toward his battlecruisers. Small discharges of energy were visible around the periphery of the weapons. Just as the battlecruisers began to vanish into hyperspace, the weapons smashed into the screens of those in the process of jumping, paralyzing the ships. The black energy seemed to spread across the screen as if it were alive. There were no explosions!

"Those spheres are some type of black antimatter," reported the sensor operator, shaking his head in disbelief. "I've never seen it in this form before."

"The black antimatter is preventing our remaining battlecruisers from entering hyperspace," Second Commander Torrel reported as he listened to frantic reports coming in from the stricken ships. "It's siphoning the power from the energy shields and causing some type of interference that won't allow our battlecruisers to activate their hyperdrives."

Commander Lakor knew, by jumping his battleships when he did, he had spared them this fate. "How many of our battlecruisers managed to jump into hyperspace?"

"Only eighteen," replied Second Commander Torrel, his face turning ashen. "Many of the remaining ships are reporting their shields are down, and power is fading."

"So this is how they've destroyed the fleets which came up against them." Commander Lakor knew he had no real choice about what to do now. "Contact Space Control on Blisth, and tell them all cargo ships and passenger liners must leave now, whether they're fully loaded or not."

"Black ships are firing missiles," warned the sensor operator.

On the tactical display, the green icons representing the powerless Andock battlecruisers began rapidly to expand and vanish, On the viewscreens, bright flashes of light indicated the detonations of the black ships' small antimatter missiles and dying Andock warships.

Commander Lakor sat in silence as he watched his fleet die. Many of the commanding officers on those vessels he had known for years.

"The black ships are coming straight toward us," the sensor operator said nervously. "I estimate they'll be in weapons range in less than four minutes."

Commander Lakor let out a deep and regretful sigh. He had reached a decision counter to his orders. "All battleships, jump to Haycort Seven. We'll rendezvous there and decide upon our next course of action."

"What about Blisth?" asked Second Commander Torrel. "It's our sworn duty to protect it."

"We can't protect it," uttered Commander Lakor, his shoulders drooping. "We can do nothing to slow the advance of the black ships. It's best for us to flee and report back to Andock Prime with what we have learned here. Perhaps our scientists can come up with a way to protect our ships from the black antimatter. If they can't, then I fear our galaxy and all of its races are doomed."

-

Moments later the ten Andock battleships vanished into hyperspace just as the black fleet entered weapons range. On board the Vorn mothership, the Vorn military commander watched as his prey disappeared from the large holographic tactical display. *The enemy has fled*, he thought, turning toward a Vorn prince, a member of the Royal Caste, who only traveled on the huge motherships as they were heavily armed and protected with an impenetrable shield of energy.

They detected us somehow, the prince thought back. By focusing, the Vorn could make other Vorn hear their thoughts, a form of telepathic projection. It could be directionally aimed at one individual or a general projection that all Vorn in the fleet could understand.

It is unfortunate, the military commander said. *Now they will know the weapons our ships are equipped with.*

Not all of them, the prince replied. *We have not used some of our more powerful ones upon their ships.*

The military commander nodded his agreement. Time to move upon the planet and secure its abundant food source.

-

As the black ships neared the planet, powerful energy beams flashed out, blowing escaping passenger liners and cargo ships into glowing wreckage that fell back toward the planet. The three orbital stations were all annihilated in bright flashes of light as antimatter hypermissiles blasted them into drifting wreckage.

On the surface, the populace fled the spaceports, seeking shelter in the tall, slender buildings, which rose up nearly a kilometer into the bright blue sky. From communication centers across the planet, frantic pleas for help were broadcast on all known FTL frequencies. However, the black ships had blocked all channels, ensuring their cries were not heard.

The black mothership moved closer to the planet, and fourteen large hatches slid open. From each a black ray flashed forth to strike the surface of the planet below. Wherever it struck any usable organic material, it was transformed and transported to the ship. As a black beam swept across an inhabited city, all its inhabitants were transformed into a black ashy substance, which the beam sucked up.

For several hours, the mothership orbited the planet with the deadly beams covering every square kilometer of the land's surface and its deep oceans. Even in the seas, fish and other sea creatures were transformed, and their substance beamed up to the mothership. At last, when the final usable organism had been transformed, the beams shut off. Not a single bird flew in the sky; not a single animal roamed the land, and all the cities were lifeless.

From the orbiting black cruisers, spheres of white energy fell toward the now empty cities on the surface of the planet. Wherever a white energy sphere struck, it burst like a bubble, spreading out across the land. Buildings collapsed, and other structures burned as the slowly spreading energy ravaged the surface. When it finally died out, all that remained of the targeted city was smoking rubble and ruins. Not a single structure was undamaged. The same destruction occurred numerous times across the entire planet, annihilating all visages of a civilized culture.

-

On board the mothership, the prince had watched expectantly as the tractor beams inside the black rays brought the converted organic substance into the mothership and fed it into the convertors. The convertors classified the different organic components and then changed them into the appropriate food for each of the castes.

The prince walked over and pressed a button on a small control panel. Instantly a receptacle slid open, and a gray pellet in the form of a small cube was ejected onto a tray. The prince took the pellet and popped it into his mouth, crunching the pellet with his mandibles and feeling the invigorating strength that instantly flowed through him. This pellet was made from the organic material of one of the civilized inhabitants of the planet they had just culled. Gray pellets were for the Royal Caste and the other privileged few; black cubes were for the Military Caste, and finally the brown cubes were for the Working Caste. Each cube would provide sustenance for a full day—or two days if necessary—without the Vorn experiencing any hunger pains.

Time for us to rendezvous with a Collector Ship, the prince thought toward the ship's military commander. *When we return, we will bring more of our brethren. This galaxy is once more ripe for a full culling.*

-

In space, the black ships jumped into hyperspace, their mission complete. This galaxy was once more full of civilizations that were a prime food source for the Vorn. Behind them, they left a shattered and nearly dead world. The Vorn would show no mercy, nor expect any. Since coming to this universe from their own, they had decided long ago that no civilized race would be spared which could ever threaten the Vorn. The Destroyers of Worlds had returned to the galaxy, and they were hungry.

Chapter Eight

Fleet Admiral Kurt Vickers was in his quarters, studying the contract Controller Nirron had filed on behalf of Newton. Kurt was still mystified why two small sectors of space consisting of only a few stars had been included. One was 460 light-years from Newton, and the other was nearly 600 light-years away. One thing they both had in common, they were farther out in the Orion Arm than Newton was. It also suggested these two small sectors might not have been visited by any of the Profiteer clans. Kurt was well aware the Profiteers considered this section of the Orion Arm to be a backwater area as the star density was far less than those farther inward.

Since Controller Nirron worked for Lomatz, Kurt suspected the weapons dealer had something to do with including these two sectors. Kurt strongly suspected there was a lot more to the arms dealer than Lomatz let on. Once the fleet returned to Newton, it might be a good idea to send some ships out to explore both of these regions just to see what Lomatz was hiding or wanted Kurt to find. Every time he went to Kubitz, it seemed as if he came back with more questions than answers.

It would be four more days before they reached home. Kurt was still coming to grips with Keera's brother and his girlfriend returning with them. Keera had told Kurt everything her brother had told her about the black ships and the secret meetings going on in the Gothan Empire. It pretty well matched what Dolman had said. There was no doubt in his mind that the empire was preparing for war.

Reaching forward, Kurt activated the computer screen on his desk. After touching a few icons, Kurt pulled up the defensive grid that surrounded Newton. Numerous violet symbols surrounded the planet. Newton Station was the largest, followed by the Class Two Command and Control Center for the sixteen Orbital Defense Platforms. There were also sixty-four defensive satellites armed with dual-firing energy turrets. On the surface of

Newton were eight large Planetary Defense Centers. Twelve of the defensive satellites were most likely going to Julbian to bolster that planet's defenses.

He had tried to purchase more while at Kubitz, but the order had been turned down due to an unusually high demand for them and production schedules at the orbital construction stations. Dolman hadn't been surprised when Kurt had mentioned the failure to purchase more of the powerful defense satellites. The black marketeer had promised to look into it and see if some of his contacts could wrangle the satellites for Newton. Dolman had casually mentioned the cost for obtaining the satellites this way would run about 40 percent more. With reluctance, Kurt had agreed. Newton needed the satellites, as did Earth and Julbian.

"Is that enough?" he said aloud, thinking of this new and mysterious enemy, attacking the Enlightened Worlds. Kurt was also very concerned about the mysterious ships Fleet Admiral Tomalson had detected in the outer regions of the Solar System. If these were Profiteer ships, as Dolman had claimed, then High Profiteer Creed could be considering another attack. As weak as Earth was now, they would be helpless against a determined attack by the Profiteers. He wanted to put at least a dozen more of the defensive satellites around Earth to augment its defenses. Just maybe that would be enough to keep the Profiteers away.

Once he returned to Newton, he planned to send two battlecruisers, a light carrier, three light cruisers, and four cargo ships back to Kubitz to pick up the defensive satellites he hoped Dolman would procure. Kurt doubted if he could purchase any more of the large Orbital Defense Platforms due to the Profiteers' own fear of the black ships, but Kurt did want as many of the smaller defensive satellites as he could get. They also needed to somehow speed up the transfer of colonists from Earth. Newton's population wasn't big enough to fight a major war against an established enemy, particularly one not worried about their profit margin.

-

"What did you do on Kubitz?" Keera asked Meesa, while they sat with her brother in the main lounge of the Newton Princess. Keera was curious as to this woman's background since her brother seemed so infatuated with her and who looked to be six or seven years younger than Dalen.

The girl looked questioningly at Dalen, a deep flush spreading across her face. She seemed embarrassed, as if she didn't know how to answer the question.

"It's all right," said Dalen, taking her hand and squeezing it. "I trust Keera. She worked at several of the medical centers there and knows what goes on. She won't be shocked by anything you say."

Meesa took a deep breath and nodded. "I worked for a while at a trading shop, where we sold off-world products, but the pay was so bad I couldn't afford my apartment or even proper clothes. I tried to find a roommate to help with the bills, but that didn't work out. My best friend worked at the Newland Pleasure House and suggested I apply for work there."

Keera's eyes widened. She had heard this story before while working at the medical centers. Many young girls out on their own turned to the pleasure houses to supplement their income. It was a sad story but part of the accepted culture on Kubitz. Working at a pleasure house, in most instances, paid very well.

"How long did you work there?" asked Keera.

"Six months," Meesa answered timidly. "I made enough to make my rent, buy some really nice clothes, and even a vehicle. Then I met Dalen." Her eyes shifted to him, and he smiled encouragingly.

"Let me guess," said Keera, shifting her gaze to her brother, who looked at the floor. "He came to the pleasure house as one of your clients."

Meesa nodded, tears in her eyes. "Dalen talked me into quitting my job. At the Newland Pleasure House many of the girls worked month long contracts, which they could either renew or cancel. I canceled mine and moved in with Dalen. He got me a job working as an inventory clerk for the Profiteer clan he was associated with. It paid decently—a lot more than what I made at the trading store."

Keera looked from one to the other. "You both need to understand that the planet we're going to is nothing like Kubitz. Newton has no Profiteer clans and no pleasure houses. The people even walk about on the streets unarmed."

"Unarmed?" gasped Dalen, his eyes widening in disbelief. "What's to stop them from being robbed?"

"Crime is almost unknown on Newton," Keera explained. "A police force is responsible for maintaining the laws set forth by the planet's government. They're nothing like the Enforcers on Kubitz."

"Everything sounds so different. What will we do on Newton?" asked Meesa. "Will we be forced to live in poverty?"

Keera recognized the fear in Meesa's eyes. She had seen it often enough on Kubitz. "Don't worry. I'm sure I can arrange jobs for both of you. Newton has a booming economy, and there's virtually no unemployment. Our biggest problem right now is building enough housing for all the colonists coming to live on Newton. It's a beautiful world, and I think both of you will find it far different from anything you've encountered before."

"No black market?" asked Dalen unbelievably. "There's always a black market of some type."

Keera looked suspiciously at her brother. "No, there's no black market, and, while you're living on Newton, you will not be involved in anything unlawful. Am I clear enough on that?"

"Yes," answered Dalen, nodding his head. "I'm just trying to understand how the planet works."

Leaning back in her chair, Keera considered her next words carefully. "There's a library on this ship. I would suggest you both check out some audiobooks that will teach you about Newton. Your translators will easily convert the words into something you can understand."

Keera had provided both Dalen and Meesa with the small egg-shaped translators, which hung from their necks so they could understand what other people said on the ship. In time, they would be expected to learn the language spoken on Newton, which was Earth-normal English.

-

Back on Earth, President Mayfield had just finished a tumultuous meeting with his Cabinet. In a highly contested vote, Secretary of Labor Marlen Stroud's request to have Fleet Admiral Vickers arrested and court-martialed had failed by the narrowest of margins. Mayfield had been deeply concerned when the votes had been tallied, the measure failed by an eight-to-six margin.

A previous measure by Stroud to have Governor Spalding removed from office had also failed. Both votes had resulted in a lot of arguing and finger-pointing by different Cabinet members. Of course if either measure had passed, Mayfield would have vetoed it immediately. It was the third time Stroud had introduced the two measures, and this was by far the closest vote. It greatly concerned Mayfield that Stroud had gained more support from the other Cabinet members.

Currently President Mayfield, Fleet Admiral Tomalson, and General Braid sat in Mayfield's office, discussing the meeting.

"That damn Stroud and his supporters will be a problem," muttered General Braid, standing up and walking to a small bar, where he poured himself a stiff shot of whiskey. He downed it and turned around to face the other two. "We should have taken him out and had him shot when he returned from Newton."

Tomalson shook his head. "That would make us no better than him."

"We still have a slight majority on the Cabinet who support us," Mayfield reminded the other two. "I can always veto any measure Stroud or his cronies pass if I have to."

"For now," commented the general. "But what happens after the next election? We may all find ourselves out of a job."

Mayfield knew General Braid was right. His popularity was at an all-time low, with calls to move up the election due to the current state of the North American Union and the rest of the world. Over eighty million people had died as a result of the

Profiteers' nuclear warheads, which had exploded on numerous cities across the planet during the Profiteer invasion. The first warheads had fallen when the Profiteers arrived and then a final barrage had been launched as they left.

"We may have to move on the Newton independence issue sooner than I'd thought," Mayfield said with a deep sigh. "Right now we have the votes to pass it. If we wait much longer, that could change."

"It'll be very unpopular with the voters," Admiral Tomalson said. "Newton is considered to be the North American Union's shining colony. It's the only habitable world we've ever discovered. To give it up will result in repercussions, both politically and militarily."

"I've spoken to the leaders of the European Union and the Russian Collective," Mayfield said. "And they're both aware of what I plan to do. As soon as I make the announcement, they'll sign trade agreements with Newton as well as recognizing the planet as an independent entity."

"What about the Chinese Conglomerate?"

Mayfield shook his head. "They've agreed to remain silent. They greatly fear that, if we grant Newton its independence, the Chinese colonies on the moons of Saturn may demand the same."

"They're not self-sustaining," pointed out Admiral Tomalson. "They still rely heavily on supplies from Earth for many of their basic necessities."

"I think," Mayfield said, "the Chinese fear just the thought of possible independence may cause problems on their colonies. They've asked me to hold off announcing Newton's independence for as long as possible."

"How much longer can we wait?" asked Braid. "Stroud is working on several other Cabinet members, trying to sway their opinion. He has some very powerful connections, and he's not hesitating to use them."

Mayfield stood up and walked to the large window, overlooking the ruins of Washington, DC. The radiation was gone, thanks to the chemicals and a dust they had purchased from Kubitz. Tall cranes were visible everywhere as the capital was being rapidly rebuilt.

"Two weeks," Mayfield answered as he turned around. "In two weeks I'll submit a measure requesting we grant Newton its independence. If it fails, I'll do it by an Executive Order."

Fleet Admiral Tomalson nodded, knowing when that announcement was made, all hell would break loose. He also knew the future of the people on Earth resided not in the Solar System but on Newton and with Fleet Admiral Kurt Vickers.

-

A few hours later Fleet Admiral Tomalson climbed rapidly through the Earth's turbulent atmosphere in a shuttle on his way to his flagship, the Retribution, a battleship purchased from Kubitz and then updated at Newton Station. The Retribution was 1,100 meters in length and 220 meters in width, it was the most powerful ship Tomalson had ever commanded.

"We'll rendezvous with the Retribution in twenty minutes," the pilot informed the admiral.

Tomalson nodded as he looked out the small viewport next to him. In the distance, he could see the ruins of Earth's former shipyard. He had pushed for its rebuilding but had been blocked by Secretary of Labor Stroud as a waste of resources. Why spend all the money to rebuild the station when they could purchase completed warships from Kubitz? The only problem with that was all requests to purchase additional warships had been blocked by Stroud and his group.

Rumors were that the Chinese Conglomerate was considering building a shipyard to construct their own warships. Some speculation was circulating that the Chinese Conglomerate, the Russian Collective, along with the European Union, were preparing to send a mission to Kubitz to see about purchasing a small fleet to protect their interests. Tomalson didn't like the idea of others traveling to the Profiteer world, but, if it would add more ships to protect the Solar System, then he could accept it.

Looking out the viewport, he could see Earth. In some areas black burn marks indicated where nuclear weapons had detonated. A large portion of the population now believed the entire situation with the Profiteers had been grossly mishandled. Of course a lot of that was due to the propaganda Marlen Stroud and his cronies were spreading. Every media station spouted more and more of Stroud's carefully orchestrated lies every day. President Mayfield had made several attempts to correct the misinformation, but the public had rejected his explanations. They wanted a scapegoat to blame for what had happened to them, and the president and Fleet Admiral Vickers were it.

Tomalson was greatly concerned about what would happen after the next election. The Profiteers were still a threat, and Tomalson strongly suspected the unidentified contacts his ships had detected on the Solar System's periphery belonged to the Profiteers. It had been a mistake to move all the gold and other valuable metals from Newton back to Earth.

Tomalson had secretly used some connections he had in the various Earth governments, so he knew where much of the returned gold was hidden. He had already decided, if the Profiteers returned before the election, Tomalson would arrange for much of the gold to be seized and returned to Newton. After the election, he suspected he would be powerless to do anything. One other thing he had decided: if President Mayfield lost the election, he was moving to Newton.

-

Back on Earth, President Mayfield was examining some photos General Braid had furnished him of the damage done in the nuclear attacks, along with reports on how long it would take to rebuild the affected cities. None of the news was good. His Cabinet, led by Marlen Stroud, obstructed nearly every measure Mayfield put forward to aid in the reconstruction. The explanation used by Stroud was that the country had lost so much of its wealth to the Profiteers and by the wild spending of Fleet Admiral Vickers that there wasn't enough money to spend on everything that needed to be done. Stroud had suggested they only do a few projects at a time and only those that showed a potential good rate of return. Strangely enough, it seemed any project applied for by a company or associate of Stroud's was quickly approved.

With a deep sigh, President Mayfield stood up and walked to the large window. The sun would soon be setting, and the construction lights throughout the city would be turned on. Work to restore the capital was going on around the clock. In the distance, he could see a dusty haze in the air. Much of this was caused by the total lack of vegetation across the countryside for miles around the capital. Plans were being made to restore the ground cover and even plant new trees in the spring. Regardless there was so much to do that Mayfield doubted it would ever look as it once did.

Looking upward, he didn't see any stars; it was still too early, but he knew in which direction Newton was. The colony was like a bright beacon on the horizon—the future and the only hope for Earth's eventual salvation.

-

Fleet Admiral Kurt Vickers breathed a sigh of relief as the fleet dropped from hyperspace into the Newton System.

"Receiving standard challenge," reported Lieutenant Brenda Pierce as her communications console lit up with the incoming message.

"Acknowledge it and inform Newton Station we'll be there in about two hours," Kurt ordered.

Twenty hyperspace detection buoys orbited the Newton System. Each could detect a vessel approaching in hyperspace out to a range of five light-years. Newton Station kept a close watch on the long-range sensors, and a small, fast response fleet was always ready to move out and challenge any unknown contact.

As soon as they arrived at the station, Kurt had a few things he needed to take care of, and then he planned to take a shuttle to brief Governor Spalding on what he had learned at Kubitz. The situation they now found themselves in was disheartening. Kurt had thought Newton safe against any attack with the defenses they had installed. However, with the potential threat of the black ships, that might no longer be true.

-

Two hours later the Star Cross docked at Newton Station, along with the Newton Princess. Entering the station, Kurt was pleased to see Keera, Dalen, Meesa, and especially Andrew, who was walking a little tenderly, but he looked much better than the last time Kurt had seen him.

"What are the plans?" asked Andrew.

Kurt knew Andrew was anxious to take a shuttle to the planet to see his wife and daughter. Emily would be quite upset when she learned he'd been shot—a near-death event. A few inches to the right and he would have died in the Humvee.

"I'll meet with Governor Spalding and report on our mission, and then I'm taking a few days off." Kurt wanted to get away from fleet business to allow his head to ponder what he had learned on Kubitz. "All the ships' crews who went with us will get a two-week leave."

"So I get you for two weeks?" asked Keera, obviously not believing what she heard. She grinned and reached out, taking Kurt's hand and squeezing it.

"For most of it," replied Kurt, smiling. "We need to get Dalen and Meesa settled in, and I have a few other things to take care of, but, for the most part, I'll just hang around our apartment and take it easy."

Keera nodded. "As soon as we get to Newton, I'll call your sister and tell her what you said. I'm sure Bryan will make some plans for the two of you." Keera knew Denise would ensure Kurt actually took the time off and didn't end up working.

"Bryan?" asked Dalen, looking confused. "Who's Bryan?"

Keera grinned. "He's Kurt's eight-year-old nephew, and he's quite a handful."

"Children!" Meesa said, her eyes brightening. "I've always had a way with children." She focused on Dalen meaningfully.

Dalen glanced away, refusing to meet her eyes.

"Maybe you'll both meet him later," Keera said. "Right now let's arrange for a shuttle to Newton. We need to get the two of you registered with the colonization department. I suspect Kurt will meet with the station's commander before coming to the planet."

Kurt looked at Keera; she knew him so well. "Yes, I want to speak with both Colonel Hayworth and Colonel Simms about a few things. It shouldn't take more than an hour or two."

"Call me when you reach the spaceport," said Keera, releasing Kurt's hand. "If we have time, I would like for us all to go out to eat together tonight. It would be a good way to introduce Dalen and Meesa to Newton."

"I will," promised Kurt, leaning forward and kissing Keera on the lips. "I'll see all of you later." With that Kurt turned and hurried off. He had sent a message earlier to Colonel Hayworth and Colonel Simms, informing them that he wanted to meet with them immediately.

"Is he always so busy?" asked Meesa, watching Kurt enter a turbolift and quickly disappear from view. "How do you ever find time to be alone with each other?"

Keera smiled. "Most of the time he's busy, but he does work in time for the two of us. Now let's get down to Newton. A lot of surprises await you."

-

Colonel Hayworth and Colonel Simms just stared at Kurt as if they couldn't believe what they had just heard.

"Ships from another universe?" blurted out Colonel Hayworth, his eyes wide in shock. "How's that possible?"

"A damn black hole?" muttered Colonel Simms, shaking his head. "I've heard a few theories that, if you enter a singularity at the center of a black hole, you can traverse the wormhole safely if its exit point is a white hole. Theoretically it can transport you vast distances across space and even into other bubble universes. It's also conceivable that, by traveling through such a wormhole, time could be affected."

Hayworth shook his head, his face turning pale. "This sounds like someone's worst nightmare. How certain are we these black ships really exist and it's not a Profiteer trick to get more credits from us?"

Colonel Simms stood up and activated one of the viewscreens in the conference room, checking one of the sixteen Class Two Orbital Defense Platforms. The platform was one hundred meters across and twenty meters thick. On top sat a massive ion cannon, four large energy projectors, and eight smaller defensive energy turrets. Each of four missile pods contained six hypermissiles with an automatic reloading system. Everything was computer-controlled, and a crew of six could operate the entire platform. However, the living quarters were set up to hold a crew of twenty to allow for routine maintenance and crew rotation in the small Command and Control Center. The platform was protected by a very powerful energy screen.

"So you're telling us that not even one of these can stop one of the black ships?

"We don't know," answered Kurt, gazing at the powerful defensive station on the viewscreen. This was one of the reasons he'd felt Newton was safe.

Colonel Hayworth stood up and walked to the viewscreen with his hands clasped behind his back. He spent a moment staring at the defensive station and then turned toward Kurt. "What would happen if the black ships attacked Newton?"

Kurt's face took on a somber look. "They've reportedly attacked a number of Enlightened World colonies. In several instance ships from the Protector Worlds have engaged the black ships. In every instance, the Protector World fleets have been wiped out. We don't know what type of weapons the black ships possess or even what they look like, other than a few vague descriptions."

"But a race that attacks every two to three million years," said Simms, folding his arms across his chest, "what culture would do that? How have they existed for such a long period of time?"

"They may be so alien we can't understand them, particularly if they came from another universe," replied Kurt. "There's not much anyone knows about them."

"What do you want us to do?" asked Hayworth, focusing his attention on the admiral.

Kurt took a deep breath. "Get your engineers together and see what can be done to strengthen the defenses around Newton. Find out if anything can increase the firepower of our warships. For the moment, it seems as if the black ships are more interested in the Enlightened Worlds than anyone else, so we may have time."

All three of them fell silent as they thought about the evil that might be in their future. Just the fact they might be dealing with an alien civilization called the Destroyers of Worlds was frightening enough. However, knowing the most powerful ships in the galaxy had failed to stop them was even more appalling. If the Protector Worlds couldn't stop the black ships, then what chance did Newton have?

Chapter Nine

High Profiteer Creed had taken his fleet to Kubitz. Repairs had been made at Marsten, but now Creed wanted all his warships updated to the highest levels possible. He was a little aggravated when he had been told it would be over a week before one of the numerous orbiting shipyards could work his ships into its busy schedule.

"A full week before even the first of our ships can enter one of the shipyards?" muttered Second Profiteer Lantz in disbelief. "What's going on with the shipyards? We've never had to wait before!"

Creed stood, gazing at the primary viewscreen, which was focused on one of the huge orbiting shipyards. "I don't know, but I intend to find out. I've never heard of all the shipyards being this busy with new construction and ship updates before."

"Could it have something do with those secret meetings going on?"

"Possibly," Creed said, crossing his arms as he thought.

Over the past few months leaders from most of the Profiteer planets as well as the largest clans had been meeting secretly on Marsten. Creed had found out about this from several sources he had on the planet. However, he hadn't found out what was going on and why the need for such secrecy. Now all the shipyards above Kubitz were busy. Thinking about it, even the ones above Marsten had seemed busier than usual.

This might pose a problem as Creed wanted to increase the size of his Profiteer fleet. Normally he operated six battlecruisers and sixteen escort cruisers along with the cargo and detainee ships he maintained. In the last battle with Fleet Admiral Vickers over Julbian, Creed had lost one battlecruiser, six escort cruisers, six medium-size cargo ships, and two large ones. All of those losses needed to be made up, and it would be quite costly.

"Do we have the latest prices for new warships?" asked High Profiteer Creed, looking at Third Profiteer Lukon, who had spoken with one of the primary weapons dealers on Kubitz.

Lukon turned his attention to Creed. "Yes, but it's not good. Prices have been marked up by nearly 20 percent. For all the upgrades you want, it'll drive up the price almost 40 percent."

"Forty percent," groaned Second Profiteer Lantz. "How can we afford that? We didn't make any credits off the Julbian debacle."

Creed turned to glare at Lantz. All he cared about was having plenty of credits to spend at the pleasure houses on Kubitz. Lantz had a reputation as a wild spender, wasting thousands of credits on exquisite food, entertainment, and, of course, women.

"We'll get the credits back when we retake Earth," Creed said pointedly. "There'll be plenty of credits for the pleasure houses."

Walking back to his command chair, the High Profiteer sat down, considering the number of new ships he wanted to purchase. He was disgusted with the price increases, but he didn't see where he had any other choice. After he had been ambushed by Vickers in the Julbian System, Creed realized he needed a larger and more powerfully armed fleet. He had a feeling the Newton Humans would be a thorn in his side for quite some time.

Lantz took a deep breath and shifted his gaze from the viewscreen to the High Profiteer. "So, how many ships are we ordering?"

"I want our new fleet to consist of ten battlecruisers and twenty escort cruisers, all updated to the latest specs. I also want to add some defensive weaponry to handle the small attack craft the Humans are so prone to use."

Lantz took only a moment before he replied, "That's five new battlecruisers and nine more escort cruisers, plus new cargo ships as well." Lantz's eyes widened as he realized the cost. "That's nearly two hundred million credits!"

"I also want a top-of-the-line battleship to serve as our new flagship. Vickers heavily damaged the Ascendant Destruction, and it would be wise if we moved to a larger and better armed vessel."

"Good idea to move to an updated battleship." Then Lantz frowned. "A first-line battleship, fully updated, will run about twenty-five million credits."

High Profiteer Creed nodded his acceptance of the costs. "That's over half of our credit reserves for our new fleet. Once our attack on Earth is finished, we'll replace the credits spent for upgrading the fleet plus a lot more."

Lantz nodded his acceptance. "I hope you're right. We'll have to find new crews for the warships as well as the cargo ships."

"We can find them on Kubitz or even Marsten," Creed responded dismissively. Turning toward Lukon, he added, "Inform Toblan that I will get back with him shortly on the ship order as well as the updates."

Toblan was the weapons dealer Creed was most familiar with and had done business with before. He was pretty certain, with the size of the order he was placing, he could work out a better price than what the weapons dealer had currently quoted. In all business deals on Kubitz, the initial price was always much higher than what the final settlement price would be. Creed knew that transferring a substantial sum of credits to Toblan's personal account would help in the negotiations too.

Once the agreement was settled, it would take several months for his ship order to be completed. In the meantime, he had various other Profiteer clans to meet with as well as Dacroni Clan Leader Jarls. In order for his plan to work, Creed knew he had to overwhelm Earth's defenses quickly and then move in to plunder the planet.

With a conniving smile, Creed thought about the conspirators he had on Earth who would help him. With their aid, Creed would know exactly where all the gold and other valuable metals were hidden on the planet. If all went as planned, his fleet would be in and out in seventy-six hours or less. By the time Fleet Admiral Vickers heard Earth had been retaken, it would be too late for him to do anything about it.

-

Several days later Grantz was in the Haslen Pleasure House, enjoying an expensive meal consisting of several of his favorite delicacies. As he ate, he saw the target he sought. He had heard rumors of High Profiteer Creed's second in command coming to this particular pleasure house due to the opulent food and drinks it served. If everything went as planned, he would garner some valuable information, which just might result in more gold coins coming his way.

Grantz finished his meal, stood up, and sauntered over to Second Profiteer Lantz's table. Lantz was eating with a gorgeous scantily clad woman, both laughing loudly.

"I understand they serve a drink here called the firebreath," said Grantz, sitting down across from Lantz. He motioned for a server and ordered two of the drinks as Lantz looked with confusion at Grantz.

"And just who are you?" asked Lantz suspiciously, sliding the woman off his lap.

"Third Profiteer Blaxton," answered Grantz, giving a false name. "I understand you're looking for some new crews?" Grantz knew this was a risky question.

The server returned with the drinks, placing one in front of Lantz and then Grantz.

"Hey, how about me?" the girl asked plaintively. "I love those drinks."

"Not now," said Lantz, glancing at the girl. "Why don't you disappear for a while? We have an appointment for later."

The girl looked miffed and then nodded. "Don't be late."

Lantz watched the girl saunter off, moving her hips. He shook his head, then turned to this strange Profiteer. "How did you hear we might be looking for some new crews?"

Grantz sucked in a deep breath. "Rumors. I heard several other Profiteers speaking about it earlier. You're with High Profiteer Creed. Isn't that correct?"

"What's it to you?" asked Lantz, his eyes narrowing.

"I want to join," Grantz said with a grin. "I heard he's made some big credits in the past year or so, and I want in."

Lantz eyed Grantz carefully and then asked, "What's your specialty?"

Grantz knew what Lantz was thinking. After all, they were a lot alike. Lantz was thinking, if he could find some well-qualified crewmembers for Creed, it would improve his standing with the High Profiteer. There was also the possibility of working out some side deals where new crewmembers recommended by Lantz would have to pay him a percentage of their take for a significant period of time.

"Sensor operator," Grantz said easily. "None any better."

Lantz was silent for a moment, deep in thought.

In the background loud music was playing, and on the small stage several women were dancing very provocatively.

All that Lantz ignored. "Do you have any friends who might be interested in long-term work on a Profiteer ship?"

Grantz leaned forward, knowing he had Lantz within his grasp. "My former crew is out of work at the moment. I can get hold of about sixty if the offer is decent. I believe a deal could be worked out, giving you a small percentage of our take if you can get us all hired. I may also know a few others who just might be interested. How many crews do you need?"

Lantz licked his lips, greed coloring his expression, which Grantz knew all about.

For the next hour Lantz told Grantz about the new ships High Profiteer Creed had ordered and the upgrades being made. When he finished, he looked at Grantz expectantly.

"Fully updated Profiteer warships," Grantz said, feigning excitement. "Your High Profiteer must be planning a really big score."

"The biggest," Lantz said with a nod. "I'm talking about gold, other precious metals, gems, and women. The women from this world are beautiful and will bring the maximum prices at the slave markets."

Grantz gestured and had the server bring another drink for Lantz. This would be his fifth one, and, by now, Lantz should be feeling the effect. Grantz watched as Lantz gulped down the drink. He was already swaying slightly just sitting in his chair. Leaning forward, Grantz asked his next question. "Just where is this world that contains all this treasure? I've never heard of such a place."

Lantz laughed, nearly falling from his chair. "High Profiteer Creed has been there before, and so have I."

"Where is that?" Grantz asked softly.

Lantz's eyes seemed to clear slightly. "Earth," he said drunkenly. "We'll take a big fleet to Earth and plunder the entire planet."

Before Grantz could ask another question, Lantz leaned forward and laid his head on the table. Almost instantly he began snoring loudly. Satisfied with what he had learned, Grantz stood up and gestured to their server. He handed her two hundred credits, per their earlier arrangement to spike Lantz's drinks. "Thanks for your help."

"What about your friend?"

It wasn't uncommon for servers to be highly tipped when negotiations were going on. Grantz grinned and handed the girl another one-hundred-credit note. "Let him sleep it off. When he awakens, tell him Third Profiteer Blaxton will contact him later."

Of course Grantz had no intention of keeping that appointment. He had all the information he needed, and now it was time for a meeting with Marvin Tenner. Fleet Admiral Vickers had left some of the gold coins he had been flashing around with Tenner, and Grantz wanted his just reward for the valuable information he had just pumped out of Second Profiteer Lantz.

-

A few hours later Marvin Tenner and Captain Briar were in Tenner's office, listening to the tale Grantz spun. Neither knew whether to believe what the greedy Profiteer said or not.

"How do we know what you're telling us is the truth?" demanded Briar with a deep frown. "After what Fleet Admiral Vickers did to High Profiteer Creed's fleet at Earth—and more recently in the Julbian System—Creed would be crazy to attack Earth again. Fleet Admiral Tomalson has ten powerful warships, and he could probably hold High Profiteer Creed at bay long enough for reinforcements to arrive from Newton."

Grantz stubbornly shook his head. "It won't only be High Profiteer Creed. I got the impression from Second Profiteer Lantz that this attack would involve a much larger fleet than what Creed currently possesses. If I were to guess, he's bringing in other clans as well as more of the Marsten mercenaries. This will be a snatch and grab. The fleet will destroy Fleet Admiral Tomalson's ships, then spread out and loot everything they can from Earth before Vickers can respond. Even with the updates done to Fleet Admiral Vickers's ships, it will be a good day before they can travel to Earth once news of the attack reaches Newton. By then, High Profiteer Creed will have pillaged the planet and could either be gone or in the process of leaving."

Tenner shook his head. He couldn't risk ignoring what Grantz had told them. There was only one way to find out for sure. Pressing the comm unit on his desk, he asked to be put in contact with Avery Dolman. If anyone could confirm if Grantz's information was authentic, it would be Dolman. Tenner let out a deep sigh. No doubt this information wouldn't be free. It would be costly, but, if it were true that High Profiteer Creed was preparing to attack Earth again, it would be worth it.

-

A little later Grantz was back in his quarters in the visitor's wing of the main compound building. He preferred staying here as it was quieter, and he could come and go as he pleased. In his hand, he held five of the one-ounce gold coins Fleet Admiral Vickers had left with Marvin Tenner. It hadn't taken long for

Avery Dolman to confirm High Profiteer Creed's fleet was in orbit, and Creed had inquired about purchasing new warships. Dolman also confirmed Creed had met with several other Profiteer clans to assist him in a big raid he had planned that would bring huge riches to all involved. While Dolman couldn't confirm Earth was the target, all the rumors circulating on Kubitz pointed to that.

Walking to a wall, Grantz removed a picture, which was hiding a safe he had installed. Pressing his palm to the identification pad, the light above it glowed green, and a clicking noise could be heard as the steel pins inside the safe unlocked. Opening the small safe, Grantz carefully placed the five gold coins alongside the others. Several small gold bars were also inside as well as piles of currency. Grantz took out some of the currency and then locked the safe.

If things continued, very soon he would have enough credits to ensure his retirement. He would live out the rest of his years in comfort and semi-luxury, something every Profiteer strived for. He just needed the Humans of Earth and Newton to survive for another few years and to continue to pay him in gold when he came up with important information, like what he had shared today.

-

On the outskirts of the Gothan Empire, three medium-size cargo ships dropped from hyperspace. They had been rebuilt and armed. Even so their weapons were only slightly more powerful than an Earth destroyer. The three ships were from the European Union, the Russian Collective, and the Chinese Conglomerate. Their mission was very simple: open up trade negotiations with the leaders of Kubitz, buy a small fleet of warships to help protect their colonies in the Solar System, and see what other technological innovations might be available on the planet. The captains of the three ships didn't believe the planet could be as corrupt and dangerous as Fleet Admiral Vickers had let on. They were convinced this was a gambit by Vickers to keep other Earth powers from Kubitz and to retain all the new Kubitz technology for Newton.

-

"What do you think we'll find?" Second Officer Mathew Quinn asked his captain.

On board the largest of the cargo ships, the European Union's Athenia, Captain Amos Fulbright waited as the navigator plotted the next jump.

Quinn was impatient to reach Kubitz and see for himself this famous black market planet.

"A civilized world with rules and laws," replied Fulbright. "I don't believe all the stories from the North American Union about the Enforcers, the dangerous Profiteers, and these mysterious Controllers who maintain power through a series of contracts that dictates their way of life. It all sounds too fantastic."

"But what if there is an element of truth in the rumors?" Quinn was deeply concerned they were in over their heads. Much of the crew felt the same way. He still didn't understand how Captain Fulbright had been given command of this mission. Other officers were better suited.

"No civilization could exist under the conditions Fleet Admiral Vickers described," replied Captain Fulbright dismissively. "It's all a sham to give Newton and the North American Union an advantage over the rest of us."

Quinn only shook his head. For as long as he could remember, the North American Union and the European Union had gotten along well together. Why this sudden animosity?

An alarm suddenly sounded on the sensor console.

"Contacts!" called out the sensor operator. "I have seven ships exiting hyperspace. Estimated distance is two million kilometers."

Fulbright grinned. "Now we can open communications and see who these people are. As close as we are to the Gothan Empire, it's bound to be one of their fleets. I'm sure they'll welcome us and be excited about the opportunity to open up trade with the other nations of Earth."

He smiled and cleared his throat. "Communications, open contact with those ships. Inform them we're a peaceful trading mission from Earth and would like permission to continue on to Kubitz."

"Message sent," replied the communications officer.

"Ships have changed their course and are accelerating toward us," reported the sensor operator uneasily. "Ships have been identified as one battlecruiser and six escort cruisers."

"A protective force patrolling the approaches to the star cluster," Captain Fulbright said confidently.

"No response to our message," added the comm officer. "I'm retransmitting it."

"Captain, we should go to Condition One and raise our energy shield," suggested Second Officer Quinn. The Athenia had a weak energy shield, but it was better than nothing. "It might also be a good idea to be prepared to make an emergency hyperjump."

"Ridiculous," scoffed Captain Fulbright. "We don't want to appear threatening or afraid."

"We're being hit by targeting scans," reported the sensor operator nervously.

"I'm sure it's just a precaution on their part," Fulbright said as he watched the seven red threat icons on the sensor screen. "We're strange vessels, and they're only taking precautionary measures."

"We should take our own," suggested Quinn a little heatedly. "At least bring our energy screen and weapons online.'

"We'll do no such thing!" growled Fulbright, turning toward Quinn. "I have orders not to provoke these people. Communications, inform the Yangtze and the Kirov not to take any provocative actions."

Quinn only shook his head and turned his attention toward the incoming ships. For several long minutes he watched as they rapidly closed the range with the three cargo ships. Quinn felt a cold chill run down his spine. The way the ships approached, they were definitely on an attack vector. He studied the small tactical station, wanting to rush over and raise the ship's energy shield and power up the weapons. It was all he could do to restrain himself.

On the ship's main viewscreen, one of the approaching ships became visible, and it was obviously heavily armed. Even as Quinn watched, several hatches slid open on the hull.

"Crap!" yelled Quinn. "Those are missile tubes! They're going to fire!"

"What?" stammered Captain Fulbright, his face turning pale. "That's impossible. Why would they do that?"

On the screen, a small missile appeared and then vanished as it transitioned into hyperspace.

A sudden bright light filled one of the other viewscreens, which was focused on the cargo ship Kirov. In a fierce explosion the Kirov blew apart; in its place a raging fireball swirled and then died away.

"Kirov has been destroyed," reported the sensor operator in dismay. "Detecting more targeting scans."

"We're getting a message," the comm operator reported. The comm operator had one of the egg-shaped translation devices, which they had gotten from the Profiteers who had attacked Earth. "The commander of that fleet is a Tellurite, and he's demanding our immediate surrender. If we fail to do so, he will destroy us."

"But we came in peace," cried out Captain Fulbright. "How can this be happening?"

"Because Fleet Admiral Vickers spoke the truth!" Quinn said angrily. "You have led us to our doom."

"Captain, what should I tell the Tellurite commander?" asked the comm officer.

Fulbright gazed at the viewscreen, still showing the glowing wreckage of the Kirov, too paralyzed to speak.

With a deep and resigned sigh, Second Officer Quinn turned away from the captain to face the comm officer. "Inform the Tellurite commander we surrender. Our ships are his." Quinn knew this was the only option he had to save the crews of the Athenia and the Yangtze. He was greatly afraid none of them would ever see Earth again.

-

On Kubitz, Marvin Tenner was very relieved to see a fleet, especially the Vindication from Newton, go into orbit above the planet. The light carrier Vindication, along with the battlecruisers Vesta and Trinity, three light cruisers, and four medium-size cargo ships were now overhead. Captain Henry Watkins was one of Fleet Admiral Vickers's oldest and most trusted friends. Watkins would know what to do with Grantz's information, which had been confirmed by Dolman.

Contacting the compound's communications center, Tenner had a message sent to Captain Watkins to meet with him as soon as possible. As an afterthought he contacted Captain Briar and informed him of Captain Watkins's expected arrival and that he would like three Humvees sent to pick up the captain. After the incident with Fleet Admiral Vickers, Tenner wasn't risking anything happening to Watkins.

-

On board the Vindication, Captain Watkins gazed at the ship's tactical screen in amazement. Over eleven hundred ships were in orbit above the planet. At the Controller station, there had been close to six hundred. Henry had never seen so many ships in a single place at one time. It made him realize how minuscule Earth and Newton were in the grand scheme of galactic politics and power. This was his first trip to the Gothan Empire, and he was well aware of the dangers.

"Damn, that's a lot of ships," muttered Lieutenant Anthony Dries, the executive officer. All viewscreens in the Command Center were on, and each one was focused on a different type of spacecraft. Some were obviously warships, but, for the most part, the others were cargo ships and passenger liners.

"Any Dacroni mercenary ships in orbit?" Henry asked.

"No, none detected," reported Lieutenant Julie Jenkins from her sensor console.

"Captain, I'm receiving a message from our embassy compound," reported Ensign Paul Lasher from Communications. "Marvin Tenner requests you come to the compound immediately due to some emergency."

"Is the compound under attack?" asked Lieutenant Dries, turning toward Ensign Lasher.

"No, nothing like that. Ambassador Tenner has some important information he needs to brief you on. He says it's highly sensitive, and he doesn't want to broadcast it over the comm channel."

Henry sighed. He had hoped to avoid going down to the chaotic planet. "Inform them I'll be down shortly. Lieutenant Dries, arrange for an armed escort and prep one of the shuttles."

Henry wondered what Tenner was so excited about. While Henry was at the compound, he might as well ask Tenner about setting up a meeting with Avery Dolman. Henry's main reason for coming to Kubitz was to acquire more defense satellites for Newton. He hoped that, by now, Dolman had come through on his promise to Kurt.

-

Two hours later Captain Watkins was ushered into Marvin Tenner's office. With a groan, he saw Kurt's pet Profiteer Grantz was also in the room.

"Captain," said Tenner, indicating Henry take a seat in front of his desk next to Grantz.

"Where's the fire?" asked Henry, ignoring Grantz. "Your communications officer indicated there was an emergency."

Marvin nodded. "Grantz, tell the captain what the Profiteers are preparing to do."

Grantz nodded and spent a few minutes detailing his conversation with Second Profiteer Lantz.

When Grantz was finished, Henry shook his head and spoke to Tenner. "How sure are we this information is correct and that Grantz isn't just trying to get more gold?"

Grantz replied angrily to Captain Watkins. "I have an agreement with Fleet Admiral Vickers as well as a written contract. I will abide by those, and this information has nothing to do with gold."

"You did get some gold coins for this information," Tenner reminded the Profiteer. Shifting his attention back to Henry, Tenner continued. "We confirmed the information through Avery Dolman. It seems High Profiteer Creed is buying new ships to replace the ones Fleet Admiral Vickers destroyed. Creed is also updating all his ships to the highest standards allowed for a Profiteer vessel. Also enough rumors are floating around that appear to indicate Creed's bringing in some of the other Profiteer clans as well as the Dacroni mercenaries."

"He'll smash the fleet protecting Earth's solar system and then ransack the planet before Fleet Admiral Vickers can respond," Grantz said, his eyes focusing on Captain Watkins. "In most cases Profiteer fleets don't work well with one another. This has seldom been done before. However, Creed has promised huge riches for those willing to follow him to Earth."

Henry leaned back in his chair as he thought over what Tenner and Grantz had just told him. "How soon before High Profiteer Creed can be ready to attack Earth?"

Tenner looked questioningly at Grantz.

"He has to update his ships," Grantz said, hesitating. "Not only that, he's ordered some new warships. It will take several months for those to be ready. At the earliest, I would say you have three months to prepare for his attack.

"Three months," mused Henry as he thought over what that might mean.

In three months they could substantially increase the defensive grid over Earth and even station a quick reaction force close to the Solar System. If everything worked out right, they might just put a surprise in place for the Profiteers.

"I'll take this information back to Fleet Admiral Vickers," promised Henry. "However, while I'm here, I need to meet with Avery Dolman and possibly Lomatz. Kurt wants to purchase more defensive satellites to put over Newton, Earth, and Julbian. After what you just told me, we may want to increase the size of our order." Henry knew about the large cache of gold bars stored beneath the embassy. It would only take a fraction of that to pay for the defensive satellites.

-

Second Officer Mathew Quinn looked despairingly around him. The entire crew of the Athenia had been tossed into a large cargo hold on board the Tellurite battlecruiser. The furnishings broadcast its sole purpose was to hold prisoners.

"What'll happen to us?" asked Ensign Barbara Jones. "Did you see how these people stared at us?"

Quinn let out a deep breath. They were in a jam, and he didn't see a way out. Before he could say anything, the door to the hold opened, and a number of armed Tellurites entered. They were very similar to Humans, only slightly shorter and with more skin hair. Their eyes also seemed to be a little larger.

"Who speaks for this crew?" one of the armed Tellurites asked in very stilted English.

Quinn turned toward Captain Fulbright, but the captain just sat there with a glazed look in his eyes. "I do," Quinn said.

The Tellurite nodded and, walking over, handed Quinn one of the egg-shaped communication devices, telling him to put it on.

Quinn put it around his neck and then looked expectantly at the Tellurite commander.

"Your ships have been confiscated and now belong to my clan. They will be taken back to our home world and refurbished for Tellurite purposes. All of their contents will be sold."

"What about us?" asked Quinn. He already suspected the answer if the stories Fleet Admiral Vickers had told were true.

"You will be sold at the Kubitz slave markets," the Tellurite commander replied. He looked at Ensign Jones and continued. "Some of your women may be trained to work at the pleasure houses."

"If we object?"

The Tellurite commander shrugged his shoulders. "You will be killed. At least at the slave markets most of your crew might be bought by a trader interested in acquiring some skilled spacehands." The Tellurite then turned and left, leaving Quinn with the communications device still around his neck.

"What did he say?" asked Barbara, her eyes filled with fear and uncertainty.

"They're taking us to Kubitz," Quinn answered. "We won't know until we get there what'll happen to us."

"We're never going home, are we?" Barbara asked plaintively.

"Don't give up hope," Quinn said, trying to sound positive. But, in his heart, he knew there was very little hope. In all likelihood his crew, as well as the one from the Yangtze, would be sold into slavery. However, women, like Barbara, would suffer a far more humiliating fate. Quinn closed his eyes, wishing he had never volunteered for this mission.

-

Two days later Second Officer Quinn was crammed inside a large truck with other members of his crew. It was nearly suffocating inside.

"Where are they taking us?" asked Barbara. Then in a lower voice, she asked, "Will we be sold as slaves? The rumors are the Profiteers do that."

Quinn hated lying to Barbara, particularly if they were taken to one of the slave markets. "Possibly," he said evenly. "I guess we'll know when we get to where we're going."

Barbara reached out and took Quinn's hand. "Don't let them sell me."

Quinn held her hand but didn't reply. Their future was out of his control.

After what seemed like several hours, the truck slowed down, and Quinn thought he could hear the driver speaking to someone. Then the truck moved forward again and, after a few moments, came to a stop. He heard more voices, and then the doors to the back of the truck were opened. Fresh air flooded in, and he blinked his eyes. He stared out in disbelief. A full platoon of Marines stood outside, their weapons held at the ready. A man in civilian clothes stepped closer to the back of the truck, looking inside.

"I'm Marvin Tenner, the Newton Envoy to Kubitz," he announced. "Your ships were captured by the Tellurites, and they brought all of you here to be sold at the slave markets."

At this revelation everyone in the truck gazed at one another in alarm and started talking. "Quiet!" Quinn ordered. "Let's hear what Mr. Tenner has to say."

"Thank you," Tenner said. "Fortunately for all of you, we were informed of your capture by an acquaintance, and we've bought your freedom. We have facilities here where you can clean up and stay until we can arrange for your safe return to Earth."

"We won't be returning to Earth," a gruff voice said, as Captain Fulbright pushed his way through the crowded truck. His eyes seemed clear and his self-assurance was back. "We have business to conduct here on Kubitz."

Tenner gazed at Captain Fulbright for a long moment and then gestured to several of the Marines. "Your business on Kubitz is over. Corporal, take this man into custody for questioning."

"You can't do this!" protested Captain Fulbright in a loud and boisterous voice. "I'm a representative of the European Union, and you have no authority over me or my crews."

Tenner slowly shook his head. "No, Captain, in that you're wrong. This is Kubitz, and here you have no authority over anything."

-

Later Marvin Tenner spoke to Second Officer Quinn in his office. Quinn had come forward and offered to explain to Tenner what their mission was about and what had happened.

"You were very fortunate," Tenner said, after he had listened to Quinn's report of the attack upon the three cargo ships and what the Tellurite commander had told him about being sold as slaves. "A number of Profiteer clans would have air-locked your crews and just taken the ships. The Tellurites are one of the clans who believe in selling their captives on Kubitz at the slave markets. We have an associate who keeps track of such things and informs us when any Humans from Earth are up for sale. We had to pay a fairly hefty fee to free both of your crews."

"What happens to us now?" Quinn couldn't believe how lucky they had been.

"We'll summon a passenger liner from Newton," Tenner explained. "It will take several weeks for it to get here with the next ship exchange. We keep at least one warship in orbit at all times. When the next replacement comes, I'll arrange for the passenger liner to accompany it."

"How long will we be here?"

Tenner thought about that. Captain Watkins could take the request back to Fleet Admiral Vickers. Kurt would be angry over the Tellurites destroying one of the cargo ships. He also wouldn't be happy about Earth making the attempt to go to Kubitz after he had warned them not to. Finally, he would have to arrange for a fleet to protect the passenger liner on its trip to and from Kubitz.

"A month," Tenner said evenly.

Quinn nodded. At least they would be going home. However, he still felt uncomfortable with Captain Fulbright's actions. Something didn't feel right, and he had mentioned that to Tenner.

-

After Second Officer Quinn left his office, Tenner called in Captain Briar. "This whole thing smells. Captain Fulbright is hiding something from us as well as his crews."

"I expected as much after talking to a few of them," Briar responded. "What do you want me to do?"

Tenner grinned. "Let's have Grantz talk to him. Maybe he can make the Captain reveal why they came to Kubitz."

Briar nodded and grinned in anticipation. "We'll let Grantz scare him a little."

Tenner nodded. This would probably cost him another gold coin or two. However, Grantz had a way of getting people to talk, and Tenner really wanted to know what was going on. The only way to find out was from Captain Fulbright.

"I'll call Grantz," Tenner said. Looking at Captain Briar, he shook his head. "He'll probably enjoy this."

-

Later Tenner sent a message to Captain Watkins aboard the Vindication. Captain Fulbright, under Grantz's interrogation, had confessed to being hired by someone in the NAU to travel to Kubitz. This individual had paid for the updates for all three cargo ships. Tenner strongly suspected this lead would go back to Marlen Stroud. Fleet Admiral Vickers and Governor Spalding would be highly aggravated when they heard this.

Tenner hadn't told Quinn a small fleet of Newton ships was currently in orbit. Tenner could have easily enough arranged the two crews transportation back to Earth on Watkins's ships, but Tenner wanted to teach them a lesson, and the best way to do that was to strand them on Kubitz for a month and let them think over how close they'd come to never returning to Earth again. Such an action might discourage the Earth governments from trying this in the future. With a deep sigh, Tenner leaned back in his chair. There was never a dull day on Kubitz.

Chapter Ten

The Vorn Mothership Reaper dropped from hyperspace in a small lonely star system just outside galaxy X241. Around the mothership, other spindle-shaped cruisers appeared until the entire force of 412 ships was assembled.

Fleet is present, thought Military Commander Mardok toward Vorn Prince Brollen, standing in the center of the large Command Center. The area remained quiet as the Vorn did not voice their words but thought them. They did have a spoken language, but it was very seldom used among the upper castes unless they were in the home system. There, verbal communication was encouraged to prevent an overload of telepathic messages where over one trillion Vorn were present. Spoken language was sometimes necessary to give directions to the nearly mindless drones. They seemed to respond better to a voice command rather than a telepathic one.

Prince Brollen turned his triangular-shaped head toward the military leader. *The Collector Ship*? The ship was supposed to be in this system, waiting on the return of the prince from his sampling survey.

Already evident on the long-range sensors. We can be at its location in four hours.

Make it so, Prince Brollen commanded. *We must send word back to our Hive Queens that this galaxy is once more ripe with food.* It would be a message that would bring joy and relief to the Vorn Queens.

Our fleets will come and begin the harvesting, the military commander acknowledged. Our food reserves are running low, and this galaxy will serve to replenish our stocks.

It is the will of the Hive Queens, answered Prince Brollen in reverence. *It is our destiny to continue as the dominant race of this universe.*

-

The mothership and her fleet proceeded deeper into the system until the ships arrived in orbit around the star's only planet. The planet was a dead husk without an atmosphere or even a single moon. Above the planet were two other massive ships and a swarm of the spindle-shaped cruisers. One of the large vessels was the Collector Ship that dwarfed the mothership. The second large ship was the vessel used for intergalactic travel. All ships in the fleet had to be docked to it in order to be transported intergalactic distances. It was powered by Zero-Point Energy and capable of traveling much faster than a ship in hyperspace. A hyperspace journey of one week could be done in hours with the Zero-Point Energy drive.

-

Dock us to the Collector Ship, ordered Prince Brollen as he gazed at the massive vessel on the viewscreen with his multifaceted eyes. *We must unload the results of our harvesting to be analyzed by our scientists. If found acceptable, then the harvest of this galaxy can begin.*

If approved, the food would advance the standing of the prince with all the Hive Queens. Perhaps high enough that someday he might be allowed to mate with one, and his progeny would become an important component of the Vorn.

The military commander bowed slightly and then passed on the orders to the command crew to begin docking procedures. It would take two days to unload and process all the organic cubes the ship had on board. As the cubes were unloaded, they would be classified as to their purity. Only the purest would be set aside for the Hive Queens to sample.

-

Prince Brollen had gone to the Collector Ship to check on the processing. He was part of the Royal Court of the primary Hive Queen and, as such, was ushered immediately into the main processing facility, where several scientists and technicians of the Vorn race were busy analyzing the food cubes that had been unloaded.

How goes the processing? asked the prince, broadcasting his thoughts directly toward the lead scientist.

More than satisfactory, replied the scientist, bowing toward the prince. He clicked his mandibles. *I have tried several samples of the processed food cubes, and all are acceptable. Nearly 12 percent of the cubes thus far processed are suitable for the Royal Caste and 2 percent for our Hive Queens.*

Prince Brollen gazed around the huge processing facility. Members of all three castes were present. Scientists and technicians operated the equipment. The military stood guard; and the nearly mindless drones ambled about, keeping everything clean and sanitary. One of the drones suddenly staggered and fell down. It lay on the floor, twitching, until one of the military walked over and shot it with an energy pistol. Two other drones scurried over and quickly carried the lifeless body to a disposal chute, depositing it to be fed to one of the ship's antimatter reactors.

We have a problem with the latest batch of drones, the lead scientist projected, noticing the prince's focus. *Our food supplies are getting low, and I fear they are greatly malnourished.*

Feed them some of the cubes we have processed and classified as suitable drone food, ordered Prince Brollen. No need for anyone to go hungry now, not even the drones. While the drones could be reproduced in abundance, the prince saw no point in wasting resources needlessly.

-

Two days later the prince was on board the mothership, watching the ship's main viewscreen. The Collector Ship was docked to the Intergalactic Transport Vessel. It would take the food gathered to the artificial habitats the Vorn race occupied to be sampled by the Hive Queens. If they approved, then a general harvesting of this galaxy's organics would begin.

As the prince watched, the transport vessel accelerated away from the planet as it could not activate the intergalactic drive near a body of mass. For nearly an hour, the ten-thousand-meter-long vessel headed outward, away from the star, and then suddenly the space around the transport seemed to shimmer. In the blink of an eye, it was gone, along with the Collector Ship docked to it.

Soon there will be plenty to eat once more, projected Military Commander Mardok.

In recent months even the prince had heard of the growing dissatisfaction about the shortage of quality food. Some of the military had been forced to eat food cubes normally reserved for drones. While distasteful, they were nourishing enough to allow for survival.

Other nearby galaxies lack quality food for our race, thought back the prince. He had been involved in a general discussion among several of the Hive Queens as well as other princes. *There is more in abundance in this galaxy than ever before, if our brief sampling is an indicator of what resides around its stars.*

The military commander was in agreement.

The princes and the Queens had discussed recently how major deletions of the drone population might be necessary if the needed quantities of proper quality food were not found. Several of the upper-level scientists had claimed the nearby galaxies had been harvested far too often, and enough time had not been allowed for their worlds to recover and to develop proper life-sustaining food. It had even been suggested that the Vorn race consider moving to another location in this universe.

The Hive Queens had been hesitant as this would mean abandoning the massive artificial habitats the Vorn race occupied. Habitats that had taken thousands of years to build and had been their homes for millions more. A compromise had been reached, and, after the harvesting of Galaxy X241, the time between harvests would be substantially increased. Several more distant galaxies would be harvested to allow the nearer ones to recover sufficiently.

The transport ship will be gone for ten days, Prince Brollen projected to the military commander. *When it returns, we shall begin the harvest in earnest. Prepare our cruisers for long-term deployment to Galaxy X241. I expect this mothership to exceed any other in our entire fleet in the amount of high-quality food procured.* As one of the leading princes in the Hive Queen hierarchy, he expected superior effort from all who served him.

-

Military Commander Mardok bowed slightly and then left the Command Center. While he had a good relationship with the prince, it was always prudent to be aware of how callous the Royal Caste could be at times. To the Royal Caste, all other castes were tools to be used and then discarded. Too often, valuable members of the military, scientists, and technicians had their lives ended on a whim of a Royal Caste member.

With the worker class, it was even worse. The average worker drone, once it reached maturity, lived for only six years. To the Royal Caste, worker drones were easily replaceable. It was not uncommon to see one eliminated for just being in the wrong place at the wrong time. The military commander, while perfectly willing to sacrifice his life for his Hive Queen, did not want to die a needless death.

-

Four days passed, and, deep in the space between galaxies, there was a shimmer, and then the transport ship appeared from what seemed to be a rift in space. The intergalactic drive allowed the vessel to travel in the space between the bubble universes, where physical laws were virtually nonexistent. While it wasn't possible to leave this universe completely, it could skim along the border that separated this universe from others.

On board the transport ship, Prince Ortumad watched the main viewscreen attentively. Hundreds of stars seemed to appear, but he was well aware these were not individual stars but entire galaxies. A few had distinct spiral shapes, and others were globular, but many were so far distant they appeared only as a single point of light. A few red dwarfs were in the immediate vicinity, and the transport ship had exited near one of them.

Transition to normal space successful, thought the Vorn, standing at the helm controls.

Take us to the Conclave Habitat, Ortumad ordered.

The Conclave Habitat was where all the Queens would gather to taste samples of the food he had brought. He had already tasted several himself, and he was confident the Queens would agree to the harvesting of Galaxy X241.

On the main viewscreen, a number of huge black constructs appeared. One of the viewscreens showed a close-up of the nearest massive spherical object. Each was over ten thousand kilometers in diameter, and the same dark metal that covered the hulls of the Vorn warships covered this metal behemoth as well. Ortumad knew 116 of these massive habitats were in orbit around the red dwarf star. A number of these small long-lived stars had been located in this region of intergalactic space when the Vorn had first arrived. Many of them once had planets or asteroid fields in orbit. Those planets and asteroids had been pulverized and used to build the habitats where the Vorn race lived.

On the tactical display, thousands of icons became visible. Most were spacecraft traveling back and forth between the habitats, and a few were large cargo ships. Less than twenty thousand light-years distant was a small globular cluster rich in planets, moons, and asteroids. The Vorn had established a number of massive mining operations there millions of years in the past after annihilating the one spacefaring race who resided in the cluster. Now the cluster was void of life and only served as a source of valuable minerals, used to expand the habitats and build more Vorn warships.

"Queen Alithe has requested your presence," the Vorn at Communications said in a voice filled with clicking sounds from his mandibles.

Near the habitats, most Vorn used their spoken language as it could become quite stressful with over one trillion Vorn broadcasting their thoughts. The use of telepathy inside the system was strictly controlled. Only members of the Royal Caste were allowed unrestricted use of that ability or caste members who were within eyesight of one another where the telepathic broadcast could be easily directed.

Prince Ortumad nodded. *Inform Queen Alithe that I will be at the Conclave Habitat shortly and will bring a large number of food samples for her and the other Queens.*

There was no doubt in Ortumad's mind that, once the Queens had sampled the food, they would order the immediate harvesting of Galaxy X241. When he returned, he would bring a fleet of motherships with him. Once enough motherships and cruisers were gathered, then the harvesting could begin in earnest.

-

Back on Earth, President Mayfield looked around the large conference table where all fourteen Cabinet members sat in stunned silence. Some feigned shock, while others were truly upset by his announcement. A select few had been called in earlier to the president's office and briefed on the proposal.

"What the hell do you mean by proposing we grant Newton its independence?" demanded Secretary of Labor Marlen Stroud, rising to his feet and pointing an accusing finger at the president. "There's no way we should even consider this proposal."

"Newton owes us too much money to even consider granting them independence," added Secretary of the Treasury Dwight Michaels. "When you figure up what Fleet Admiral Vickers and Governor Spalding have spent on ships, their defenses, and that embassy they set up on Kubitz, it will be decades before we get all of our money back. No, there can be no independence until they have repaid their debt."

President Mayfield leaned back in his chair and took a deep fortifying breath. "Over twelve million people reside on Newton, and it is a self-sustaining colony. It no longer needs supplies or other materials from Earth. It's time to let them go their own way. They have earned their independence after what they have done for us."

"I second the resolution," spoke up Fleet Admiral Tomalson, his eyes focusing sharply on Marlen Stroud.

"As do I," added General Braid in a powerful and uncompromising voice. "We owe Newton our freedom, and their independence will be a just reward."

"No!" stammered Stroud, shaking his head defiantly. "Fleet Admiral Vickers and Governor Spalding must continue to answer to this Cabinet. They have committed grievous crimes against this planet which must be adjudicated."

-

Stroud was still extremely angry over how he had been treated on Newton—arrested by Marines in front of others and forced to work in a fishing village. He couldn't let the two people responsible for that slip through his hands unpunished. He was so close to having enough votes to remove both of them from power. Just a few more weeks and Vickers would be back on Earth, going through a court-martial. Stroud would see to it that the book was thrown at Vickers, and Stroud would gleefully have Vickers sent to prison for the rest of his natural life.

"We vote," said Raul Gutierrez, the Secretary of Homeland Security. "The motion has been seconded, and the second upheld by General Braid."

Stroud knew he had been outmaneuvered. Looking around the table, there was no doubt the resolution would pass. "This is a mistake," he grumbled as he sat back down. "Newton is ours and must remain under our control. The people will not stand for this!"

-

President Mayfield stood and looked gravely at the Cabinet members. "All in favor of granting Newton independence raise your hands."

Six hands went up immediately, and Mayfield felt his heart stutter. He needed eight votes for the resolution to pass. Then hesitantly one more hand was raised and then another.

"No!" yelled Stroud, shaking his head in anger. "This vote was rigged in advance. I won't let you get away with it. When the people hear what you've done today, heads will roll."

"Be that as it may," President Mayfield replied as he passed the resolution around the table to be signed, "this matter is settled, and, as of today, the Newton colony is now an independent world. I will go on all media stations later this evening to make the announcement." What a relief that no Executive Order from him would be needed to grant Newton its independence. It would make challenging Newton's independence much more difficult or nearly impossible.

"This will be the end of you," threatened Stroud, his face flushed with his growing rage. "If you sign this resolution, you'll be impeached and removed from office within the month, and I'll lead the effort to do it!"

"Perhaps," Mayfield replied as the document made its way back to him. With a flourish, he signed his name and handed it to his secretary to notarize. She had been standing by and listening to the entire exchange. "File that and distribute the necessary copies."

As the secretary left the room, President Mayfield had one more piece of business to attend to. "Yesterday I received a message from Governor Spalding. It seems that three modified cargo ships from the European Union, the Chinese Conglomerate, and the Russian Collective attempted to go to Kubitz and meet with its government."

"They have every right to do so," grated out Stroud, still fuming from the stunt Mayfield had pulled to give Newton its independence. "Vickers and Spalding don't own the rights to Kubitz. Anyone can go there. It's about time some Earth ships were sent to represent us. It's only a shame those ships couldn't have come from the North American Union."

Fleet Admiral Tomalson slowly shook his head, gazing at Stroud. "Kubitz is in the heart of the Gothan Empire, and, to reach it, you must go through Profiteer space. Hell, even Kubitz is dangerous. Fleet Admiral Vickers says it's a den of thieves and pirates, and should be stayed away from if one wants to live a long life."

"All lies," Stroud said dismissively. "The Profiteer attack on our planet was from one Profiteer world. I'm sure the rest are peaceful, and it won't be a problem to set up diplomatic relations with many of them. Those horror stories from Vickers are just to limit access to any advanced technology we might procure by going around Newton. I'm glad to see someone finally took the initiative to travel to Kubitz, where I'm sure they'll be enthusiastically received, and we will soon have confirmation of the lies Vickers has told."

Fleet Admiral Tomalson slowly rose to his feet and pointed to a piece of paper in his hands. "The three cargo ships were intercepted by the Tellurites, a Profiteer world that preys on cargo ships coming into the Gotham Empire. They are one of the smaller Profiteer worlds and operate a number of raiding fleets, searching for laden cargo vessels inbound to Kubitz."

Stroud's face turned pale. "What are you saying?"

"The Tellurites destroyed the cargo ship Kirov, and all members of its crew were killed in the attack. The Athenia and the Yangtze were seized, and the two crews sent to Kubitz to be sold in the slave markets."

"Sold as slaves! The Kirov destroyed!" cried out Secretary of Education Connie Saxon, her eyes showing shock. "We must rescue them!"

"Yes!" called out Stroud, seeing an opportunity. "We can send our fleet to Kubitz and demand the release of the two crews."

Fleet Admiral Tomalson shook his head. "We don't have the ships to spare. I have asked this Cabinet a number of times to expand our fleet, and each time I have been turned down. We barely have enough ships to protect Earth."

"We don't have the money to waste on warships we'll never need," said Secretary of Treasury Dwight Michaels. "The rebuilding of our cities and infrastructure will take everything we currently have in our treasury and more."

"Well, it seems as if we need them now," replied Tomalson, glaring at Michaels. "Don't forget the mysterious ships we detected a few months ago on the outer edges of the system. What if we're attacked again?"

"We're getting away from the subject of this conversation," Connie Saxon said, not wanting to get into an argument. "Is there any way Newton can help, since they already have an embassy on Kubitz?"

President Mayfield cleared his throat and spoke. "Fortunately the people in charge of the Newton embassy learned of the seizure of the cargo ships and their crews. They arranged to pay the necessary fees to free both crews. The men and women who were on board the Athenia and the Yangtze are now safe at the Newton embassy compound on Kubitz. A passenger liner from Newton will go to Kubitz shortly to pick them up and return them safely to Earth. I have already notified the European Union, the Chinese Conglomerate, and the Russian Collective of what happened. For now, they have agreed to leave Kubitz and the Gothan Empire to Newton and Fleet Admiral Vickers."

-

Marlen Stroud leaned back in his chair, shaking his head in disbelief. It seemed that Fleet Admiral Vickers and Newton had come out ahead once more. It would be quite some time before any Earth country risked sending another ship to the Gothan Empire. He had helped to secretly finance the mission to Kubitz. He had never expected it to end this way.

-

Later President Mayfield, Fleet Admiral Tomalson, General Braid, and Secretary of Homeland Security Raul Gutierrez were in the president's office, discussing the results of the Cabinet meeting.

"Did you see the look on Stroud's face when you informed the Cabinet of the failure of the three cargo ships to reach Kubitz?" asked Raul. "I got the distinct impression he already knew about them."

"Do you think it's possible he had something to do with sending them?" asked General Braid.

"It's possible," Mayfield replied with a nod. "We know he has deep connections with the Chinese Conglomerate. That's how he got to Newton to begin with."

"Still say we should have shot him when he first returned from Newton," mumbled General Braid. "What the man did was treason."

Fleet Admiral Tomalson stepped to gaze out the large window at all the construction going on. It would be years before Washington was restored to its former glory. "We upset Stroud considerably today. I suspect he's already working on impeachment. He'll call in every political favor he can to reverse the resolution giving Newton its independence."

"Won't matter," responded Mayfield. "I'll make a speech in a couple of hours notifying the world of Newton's independence. Within the next few days, both the European Union and the Russian Collective will sign trade agreements with Newton, as well as recognizing their independence status. Once that's done, Stroud nor anyone else will be able to do anything to reverse it."

"Except get you thrown out of office," Raul suggested. "The next president could make things very difficult for Newton. He or she could also put a stop to all immigration."

"We have the two large Profiteer cargo ships that Fleet Admiral Vickers captured that will be ready to make passenger runs in another few days. Each one of those ships can carry ten thousand colonists. With the other ships we have available, we can move nearly one hundred thousand colonists a week to Newton."

Raul only shook his head. "We're stripping the country of some of its brightest and most talented people. Some will say we're destroying any hope of a restored future."

"Our goal is to send eight million more people to Newton," said Mayfield, folding his arms across his chest. "That will give them a population base of slightly over twenty million people. That's what we feel is needed to allow them to grow on their own at a reasonable rate as well as to defend the planet."

"What about the other countries of the world? How many colonists from them will Newton accept?" asked General Braid.

"Some have already been approved," Fleet Admiral Tomalson answered as he turned away from the window to look back at the others. "Several ships a week leave the United Kingdom, Australia, Germany, and even South America. All the applicants are thoroughly screened before being granted colonists' status."

"What about those ships your fleet detected a few months back?" asked Raul. "What do we make of them?"

Fleet Admiral Tomalson turned toward the president, who nodded his head. "We may have a bigger problem than Marlen Stroud. We received a message from Fleet Admiral Vickers yesterday, and it's quite disturbing. Evidently High Profiteer Creed is organizing a major attack on Earth. He's bringing in other Profiteer clans as well as more of the Dacroni mercenaries."

Raul and General Braid stared at each other, both their faces turning pale. They knew the struggling economy of Earth would collapse completely if the Profiteers returned.

"How soon?" asked Braid.

"Two more months at the outside," President Mayfield answered. "Fleet Admiral Vickers wants to put more defensive satellites in orbit around Earth as well as station a quick-response fleet close to the Solar System."

Raul blinked his eyes and then asked, "Will that be enough?"

"It depends on how determined the Profiteers are," Tomalson replied. "If they bring a truly large fleet, there may be nothing we or Admiral Vickers can do."

"What if they nuke us again?" Raul asked.

Tomalson looked gravely at Raul. "If the Profiteers succeed in taking over the planet that may be a very real possibility."

Everyone in the room grew quiet.

The planet had already lost over eighty million inhabitants to Profiteer nukes with more dying daily from radiation exposure. The effects of the nuke attacks would be felt for generations. Just the thought of another, and possibly worse nuclear attack was appalling. If the Profiteers nuked Earth again, the planet might not ever recover.

-

Marlen Stroud sat in his office, his face full of anger. He had just talked to one of his allies in the Chinese Conglomerate. They had confirmed the failure of the Kubitz mission. They had received a message from Governor Spalding, informing them of the Tellurite interception of the three modified cargo ships and the loss of the Kirov. Spalding had informed them their cargo ship crew would be returned in about four more weeks.

"What now?" asked Dwight Michaels. "It looks as if we cannot count on Kubitz technology to dig us out of this mess Mayfield's put us in."

Stroud glared at Michaels, his strongest ally on the Cabinet. "We move immediately for impeachment," growled Stroud. "Mayfield will make his speech later today, and we can do nothing to block that. However, once the speech is over, we'll launch a multimedia campaign on how giving Newton its independence is bad. We'll run ads on every media outlet, detailing all the money Newton has spent to protect itself while leaving us nearly defenseless."

"That's not true," objected Michaels, his eyes narrowing. "We've blocked all the defense appropriations that Tomalson and the president have requested."

"We know that, but the people don't," replied Stroud with a conniving grin. "When we're through, President Mayfield will be lucky if the people don't lynch him."

Michaels was silent for a long moment and then spoke. "Who will be the next president?"

Stroud didn't answer. If all his plans came to fruition, then, in a few more months, he would sit in the Oval Office, fully in charge of the North American Union and then later the entire world. He had operatives in both the Russian Collective and the Chinese Conglomerate. While the European Union and some of the other independent countries might be a problem, he was confident they would all come around eventually.

Then, once he had control of Earth, it would be time to move on Newton. Governor Spalding and Fleet Admiral Vickers hadn't heard the last of Marlen Stroud. Sometime in the not-so-distant future, they would rue the day they had refused to turn Newton over to him. Leaning back in his plush office chair, he could already see the reactions on their faces when he removed them from power. The only thing Stroud needed to decide was whether to have them hung or put before a firing squad.

Chapter Eleven

Prince Brollen aboard the mothership Reaper gazed in satisfaction with his multifaceted eyes as four intergalactic transport ships reappeared in the system. Even more pleasing was seeing the three other motherships and the two Collector Ships docked to the massive vessel. All the other docking ports held the helix-shaped cruisers. This was an invasion fleet.

The approval for the harvesting of Galaxy X241 must have been approved, Mardok, the Reaper's military commander projected. *This is a good beginning.*

We will know soon, Prince Brollen replied, his two antennae waving slightly, anticipating the orders to begin the harvest. *Prince Ortumad aboard the transport ship will be in range shortly, and then we will know for certain.*

Telepathy was limited in range. The longer the distance, the more exhausting it was to project one's thoughts. For most purposes, a maximum limit of fifty thousand kilometers was feasible. Any further than that and a Vorn risked brain damage or collapsing from exhaustion. The only exceptions were the Hive Queens; they could reach out much farther.

Prince Brollen watched as the four massive transport ships steadily came closer and then went into orbit around the planet. Already he could taste the new food they would be harvesting from the worlds of Galaxy X241.

Hive Queen Alithe has agreed to the harvest, Prince Ortumad sent to Brollen. *All the Hive Queens were at the Conclave Habitat and thoroughly enjoyed the food samples you gathered. Queen Alithe is quite pleased with you.*

Prince Brollen turned in the direction he sensed Ortumad's thoughts came from. *There is an overabundance of food in Galaxy X241. It will take us a long time to complete this harvest. We will feast for many years to come.*

We will deploy a total of ten mothership fleets initially, Ortumad responded. *More transport ships will arrive in the next few days. Within two years we will have over one hundred mothership fleets assisting in the harvest.*

What are the wishes of Queen Alithe?

You are to take your fleet and harvest one of the primary food worlds of this galaxy. A second mothership will be placed under your command as well. The Hive Queens are anxious to receive more high-quality food from different food species.

Prince Brollen remained silent for a moment. *The food species in Galaxy X241 are quite advanced. Much more so than those we have encountered previously. There may be some danger.*

Not to our vessels, answered Ortumad dismissively. *In all the secondary worlds you have harvested, not one of your warships was ever damaged. We know the type of weapons we face, and, while they are powerful, they cannot penetrate our energy screens. You also did not use several of our more powerful offensive weapons. While there will doubtlessly be some great battles fought by the food species, in the end, they all will be subjugated and serve as nutrients for the Vorn.*

I will ready my vessels, replied Prince Brollen, anxious to begin the harvest. *As soon as the second mothership is ready, we will depart for Galaxy X241. I already have a target picked out. I am sure the Hive Queens will find the food gathered from this particular system to be highly pleasing.*

The second mothership will be ready for departure in two hours, Prince Ortumad responded. *Tomorrow I will send the others.*

My fleet is ready, proclaimed Prince Brollen. *The Vorn will feast well on the food from this galaxy*!

Prince Brollen turned toward Military Commander Mardok. *The word has been given from the Hive Queens. Galaxy X241 is to be harvested. Prepare the fleet to journey to the homeworld of species 822.*

Military Commander Mardok bowed slightly and then issued orders to the command crew of the mothership as well as to the cruisers. While in Galaxy X241, they had cataloged hundreds of different intelligent food species. Mardok knew their survey was far from complete as Galaxy X241 was overrun with species suitable for food, such as species 822, also known as the Visth.

-

In the Newton System, Fleet Admiral Kurt Vickers was once more in Governor Spalding's office. The two were discussing the recent change in the status of Newton.

"I still can't believe the president pulled it off," Spalding said as the two stood at the large window in his office, looking out across the capital city.

"He's not our president now. You're fully in charge," Kurt reminded Spalding. "I'm just worried about the ramifications of what he did and what'll happen on Earth."

Spalding nodded and then answered in a grim voice. "There will be repercussions, probably some serious ones. Marlen Stroud will see to that."

"I can't believe Stroud weaseled himself back into power. Sometimes I despair of the politics that occur on Earth. Why can't they place the people first?"

"It's a sad situation," admitted Governor Spalding. "But some good people are in government, such as President Mayfield."

"How did the people take the announcement of our independence?"

"Most seemed happy about it," answered Spalding as a buzzer sounded on the comm system on his cluttered desk. "It took nearly all the people by surprise, and it will be a few days before everyone fully understands what our independence means."

Spalding walked over and answered the comm, holding the receiver to his ear. With a satisfied nod, he hung up and turned toward Kurt. "That was Colonel Simms. The Vindication and her ships just dropped from hyperspace and will dock in about two more hours."

Kurt nodded. "I expected them back shortly. They're a little ahead of schedule."

A light cruiser had returned a few days earlier bringing the warning from Marvin Tenner about the coming Profiteer attack. They had informed President Mayfield of the impending danger so he could begin making preparations for Earth's defense.

"That's not all," Spalding said, his face creasing in a concerned frown. "A number of very large ships are with the Vindication. The same ships Lomatz came to Newton with last year, only this time a lot more of them. Were you expecting Lomatz to show up?"

Kurt felt a sudden chill. "While I was on Kubitz, Lomatz indicated he might come to Newton with something I would find interesting. I never did find out what. I wasn't expecting him to arrive unannounced."

"Whatever it is, you better get to Newton Station and the Star Cross. I'll feel a lot better with you there to handle this situation. I never did trust Lomatz the first time he was here."

Walking across the room, Kurt paused and then turned toward Governor Spalding. "I don't know what Lomatz brought me, but I have a feeling we won't like it." Kurt knew Lomatz had a reputation as a weapons dealer willing to do business with anybody. Lomatz and Avery Dolman were thick as thieves, and both were probably involved in this unexpected visit. Kurt wouldn't be surprised to find Dolman on board one of Lomatz's ships as well.

"Keep me informed," Spalding said as he sat down behind his desk and picked up a thick folder. "I have some trade agreements with the European Union and the Russian Collective to go over. If everything goes well, I should have them approved in the next few days."

Promising to keep Spalding informed of developments, Kurt left the Capitol building for the spaceport, taking a shuttle to Newton Station. The Star Cross was still docked to the station, and he was anxious to get on board and find out what Lomatz was up to. It was a little reassuring that the Vindication was here too. Kurt was confident, if there were any danger, Henry would never have brought Lomatz and his ships to Newton.

-

As Kurt stepped into the Command Center of Newton Station, he saw a frantic amount of activity. Both Colonel Simms and Colonel Hayworth were present and speaking animatedly to one another.

"I'm not sure we should let those ships come so close to Newton," Hayworth argued. "We have no idea what they want here."

"Captain Watkins has vouched for them," Colonel Simms pointed out.

"Let them approach," Kurt ordered as he stepped closer to the two men, who hadn't noticed he had entered the crowded Command Center. "Lomatz told me, while I was on Kubitz, that he would be coming to Newton. I just didn't expect him this soon."

Colonel Simms grimaced. "But look at what he brought with him. If we're reading these scans correctly, he's brought two of his big construction ships as well as ten of those massive cargo vessels. Also we can't identify the other six ships."

"Put them up on a viewscreen. Let's look at them." Kurt was curious about the six unidentifiable ships.

On the screen, the massive construction and cargo ships appeared. Each was two thousand meters in length and four hundred meters in diameter. However, what stunned Kurt were the other six ships. He hadn't been expecting this. They were obviously warships—and very large ones at that. He had never seen ships of this design before. Two of them were easily 1,700 meters in length, and the other four were 1,200. Kurt felt uneasy, wondering what Lomatz was up to. The only way to find out was to talk to the weapons dealer.

"See if you can contact Lomatz," Kurt ordered. "Maybe he can explain what's going on." Kurt folded his arms across his chest as he studied the ships on the viewscreen. Lomatz had never given any indication of owning warships, though his construction and cargo ships were moderately armed.

Ensign Paul Simmons worked his communications console, and, in just a matter of a few seconds, he had Lomatz on the comm. "Mr. Lomatz is requesting a meeting on board his ship. He says he has brought you some gifts."

Kurt let out a deep sigh. He wondered how costly these gifts would be. However, since Lomatz had furnished the hyperspace stealth technology that had allowed Kurt and his ships to escape the Dacroni mercenaries, he at least owed Lomatz this meeting.

"Tell him that I'll board his ship as soon as it goes into orbit around Newton."

"Message sent," replied Ensign Simmons. "Lomatz says he's looking forward to your visit and suggests bringing an engineer or two who's familiar with ship construction."

Kurt turned toward Colonel Hayworth. "I guess that means you're coming with me."

"I'll go round up a few ship engineers," replied Hayworth, taking a deep breath. "I'm sure they'll be interested in going aboard one of Lomatz's vessels."

"Ensign Simmons," said Colonel Simms with a disgruntled frown, "have Lomatz's ships go into close orbit to the station. I want to keep an eye on them. I also want a few ion cannons focused on his command ship."

"Why the hostility?" asked Kurt. "After all, Lomatz and his construction people helped build a major portion of this station."

"Yeah," Simms replied. "I'm just concerned about what he wants this time."

Kurt nodded. "Contact the Vindication and tell Captain Watkins that I need him here at the station. Perhaps he can help clarify what's going on."

-

Three hours later Kurt was on board Lomatz's ship, the Golan Four. Kurt was afraid to ask what had happened to the first three ships with the Golan name. With him were Colonel Hayworth, several ship construction engineers Hayworth had suggested bringing along, as well as a full squad of heavily armed Marines. Kurt had spoken briefly with Captain Watkins, but he was unsure himself what Lomatz was up to. All Watkins knew for certain was that Marvin Tenner had said it was important Lomatz travel to Newton and that Kurt would understand after he spoke to the weapons dealer.

No comment was made by the ship's crew as Kurt and his party were led to the meeting room, where Lomatz waited. Most of the crew were of the same humanoid race as Lomatz. They looked Human, except their eyes had a strange yellow tint to them. One thing Kurt did notice was that nearly every crewmember wore a sidearm—a definite indication they were from the Gothan Empire. While the weapons dealer might not be classified as a Profiteer, he was pretty damn close.

After about twenty minutes they reached a large ornate wooden door. Kurt was surprised to see this type of door inside a spacecraft. Their escort opened the door, and Kurt and his people stepped inside.

"Fleet Admiral Vickers!" called out a familiar voice.

Kurt winced, recognizing Grantz's loud booming voice. It seemed as if every time something unexpected occurred, the greedy Profiteer was present. Unconsciously Kurt touched his pocket, making sure he had no gold coins Grantz could weasel from him. "Grantz, why are you here? Shouldn't you be back at the embassy with Marvin Tenner? How will he survive with you leaving him on his own?" Kurt thought maybe, by trying a little flattery, he could encourage the Profiteer to remain on Kubitz the next time an opportunity arose for him to sneak off to Newton. It seemed every time Kurt turned around, the Profiteer showed up with some scheme to get more gold.

"No, Tenner suggested I tag along. He still has his hands full with the two Earth ship cargo crews he's holding." Grantz grinned as he looked at Kurt and the others. "Besides, I've brought you something that's nearly priceless this time."

Kurt sighed. Tenner had probably wanted some peace and quiet or else Grantz had connived some way to get all the gold coins Kurt had left behind with Tenner. Grantz was very good at sniffing out gold if it was around.

Lomatz stood, taking note of the armed escort the admiral had brought. "Your Marines will be comfortable outside this meeting room," Lomatz said. "You're quite safe on board my ship."

Kurt knew Lomatz didn't have a problem with him bringing an armed escort; Lomatz would have done the same. Nodding to the Marine sergeant in charge of the security detail, Kurt told him to wait outside in the corridor. If there were any hidden danger, Grantz wouldn't be around.

"If all of you will have a seat, we'll get this meeting started," Lomatz announced as he sat down at the head of the large wooden table.

Kurt took his seat, noticing how comfortable it was. The chair seemed to adjust itself to his physical form. "I'm a little confused," he began. "Why are you here? And where did those six warships you brought come from? I wasn't aware you possessed such ships. They don't match anything in our ship database."

"It's a long story," said Lomatz, leaning back in his chair and moving his gaze across the Humans who had come with the admiral. "First off, I must confess I know a lot more about the black ships than I've let on."

"Is that what this is about?" Kurt wasn't surprised the weapons dealer had additional information. It was one of the ways Lomatz and Avery Dolman made their living.

Lomatz nodded. "If one knows where to look, there's evidence of attacks by the black ships going back over twenty million years."

"Twenty million years!" gasped Colonel Hayworth in disbelief. "People didn't even inhabit Earth twenty million years ago."

Kurt studied Lomatz with renewed interest. Any information Kurt could get on this new and dangerous enemy he wanted to hear. "What do you know about the black ships?"

Lomatz let out a deep breath and placed his hands palm down on the conference table. "The black ships come from a race called the Vorn. The species is insect-based and very similar to what your people would call wasps. The Vorn stand upright, having a basic humanoid form with two legs and two arms. The average Vorn looks like a cross between a humanoid and a wasp.

The head is covered with very short hair and triangular-shaped with two antennae. Its eyes are multifaceted and can see in several different light wavelengths. They have small wasplike wings that normally stay folded on their backs. Their hands consist of seven thin digits with which to manipulate equipment. However, the most shocking aspect of the Vorn race is that they're telepathic. They can sense each other's thoughts over a short distance. What their exact telepathic range is, I don't know, but I believe it's well over fifty thousand kilometers."

"A telepathic race," said Kurt, finding it hard to believe. "Where did they come from?"

"Another universe," Lomatz answered gravely "They were involved in a great battle with that universe's controlling intelligences and on the verge of defeat. In desperation, a group of their motherships, with Hive Queens on board, attempted to transit the singularity at the heart of a black hole. When they emerged, they were in our universe."

Colonel Hayworth's eyes were wide and puzzled. "Why are they attacking the Enlightened Worlds?"

Lomatz placed his hands together and looked directly at Fleet Admiral Vickers as a strange and almost frightening look crossed his face. "For food. Their motherships convert all organic substances found on a planet into food for their race."

Silence filled the room as Kurt and the others with him sat stunned at this revelation.

"For food?" asked Colonel Hayworth in disbelief.

"Yes, they have a weapon that dematerializes life-forms and breaks them down into a basic organic compound. This compound is transmitted to their ships and converted into small food cubes to feed their race."

"How do you know all this?" asked Kurt, finding it hard to believe what Lomatz was saying. It all sounded so fantastic. A race that fed on all other civilized species? This sounded like some old twentieth-century science fiction movie. "Can the Vorn read our thoughts? Why don't they raise their own food?"

Lomatz's eyes took on a haunted look. "Many years ago I was on a trading mission to one of the Protector Worlds. This particular Protector World was near the heart of the galaxy. Before arriving there, my ship detected another vessel in distress. We dropped from hyperspace to render assistance. The ship we found was unlike any I had every encountered before."

"I'm sure you haven't seen every ship type," said Kurt, confused. "Tens of thousands of inhabited worlds are scattered across the galaxy." He had learned this startling fact on Kubitz. He had never imagined how much intelligent life there was.

Lomatz shook his head. "Actually there are many more than that. However, this ship was more like what you would call a space-going yacht. We brought the ship into our main cargo hold and found only one person on board. The science on that ship was far beyond anything my crew or I had ever run across. Not just a few years ahead of us but thousands of years more advanced. With the help of the being piloting the vessel, we repaired it.

"For our assistance he paid with pure gold, gold purer than any I had ever seen before. He also took me aside and warned me about a great menace soon to return to our galaxy. He told me of the Vorn and the black ships. He told me, while the Vorn could speak to each other telepathically, they could not read the thoughts of other races. Only their own."

"How did this being know so much about the Vorn?" Kurt found Lomatz's story highly intriguing—if it were the truth and if the weapons dealer wasn't making up the whole thing.

"His race was very old. They had been an Enlightened World before the Vorn first put in an appearance."

"Twenty million years ago?" asked Hayworth, his eyes widening. "If this race is so old and their science so great, why haven't they done something to stop the Vorn?"

"His race was spared the harvesting by the Vorn the first time they came to our galaxy. They were so terrified of what the Vorn had done to all the other races that they immediately took it upon themselves to hide once the Vorn left. They learned who the Vorn were and why they had come to our galaxy from a disabled Vorn cruiser. In sheer fear, their entire civilization relocated to a place where the Vorn would never find them. To ensure no one revealed their hiding place, they very seldom venture forth. The small ship I aided was a research vessel that had gone out into the galaxy to see if the Vorn had returned."

"These people just ran, not telling anyone about the Vorn, leaving everyone else in the galaxy to die?" uttered Hayworth disgustedly. "What kind of people are they? With their advanced science and knowledge of the Vorn, surely they could have helped."

"I asked the same question," Lomatz replied. "He said it wouldn't make a difference. There was nothing they or anyone could do to stop the Vorn and their black ships. He claimed the Vorn were like a force of nature, and the only sure defense against them was to stay hidden."

Kurt leaned back and gazed speculatively at Lomatz. There had to be another reason why the weapons dealer had come to Newton. While his story was fascinating and told a lot about the Vorn, there had to be something else. He couldn't imagine Lomatz coming all this way just to talk about the black ships.

"Why are you here, Lomatz?" Kurt asked bluntly.

"The harvesting by the black ships has already begun," replied Lomatz, his eyes focusing sharply on Kurt. "I have confirmation of at least fifteen Enlightened World colonies that are now nothing more than empty worlds, their populations converted into food for the Vorn."

"Why should that concern us?" asked Colonel Hayworth. "We're not an Enlightened World, not even close. Perhaps the Vorn won't come here."

"All worlds are in danger," Lomatz responded, his yellow-tinted eyes shifting to Colonel Hayworth. "In time, the Vorn will spread their harvesting to include all space-going species, including the Gothan Empire, Newton, and Earth."

"If the Protector Worlds can't stop the black ships, what can we do?" asked Kurt.

Since returning from Kubitz, this fear had been haunting Kurt the entire time. Against a regular enemy, such as High Profiteer Creed or even the Marsten mercenaries such as Clan Leader Jarls, Kurt could come up with a plan. But the black ships were something else. How could he stop a race that has spent tens of millions of years conquering and destroying countless civilizations?

"You noticed the six strange ships that accompanied my vessels when we dropped from hyperspace. What you don't know is that all six of those are Protector World warships. My cargo vessels have been watching the areas of space where battles between the black ships and the Protector Worlds have occurred. We salvaged six vessels that were relatively unharmed. The power had been drained from their ships, killing the crews. I brought with me two Lakiam and four Andock battlecruisers. My crews and I are willing to teach you how to operate these vessels and explain the advanced science behind their systems."

"What's in it for you?" asked Kurt, finding it hard to believe what Lomatz offered. Kurt wanted the ships, but what was the price? This was too big of a deal for the weapons dealer to be offering for free. Kurt wondered how many hundreds of millions of credits Lomatz would demand for the six warships.

Lomatz's eyes narrowed. "It will take time for the Vorn to reach this area of space. I will turn over those six warships to you as well as what I've brought on my cargo ships. All I ask in return is that you pay for the cargo, and the six warships are yours free of charge. I still have a business to run on Kubitz, at least for a little while longer."

"And?" asked Kurt, knowing there was bound to be more.

"A group of us want to come to Newton to live out our lives. That includes family members as well. In total, nearly twenty thousand of us. If we come here, there is a good chance we can live out the remainder of our lives before the Vorn find us."

Kurt closed his eyes, unsure of what to say. Did he dare agree to allow twenty thousand of Lomatz's people to come to

Newton? Many of them were probably associated with the Profiteers or might even be Profiteers!

"I'll need to speak to Governor Spalding first," Kurt finally said. This was too big of a decision for him to make on his own.

"I understand," answered Lomatz. "We would even be willing to settle on an uninhabited part of Newton away from your people. However, before you speak to Governor Spalding, let me show you one of the Lakiam warships. I think you will quickly see the wisdom in accepting what I'm proposing."

Colonel Hayworth shrugged. "It wouldn't hurt to look."

With a deep sigh, Kurt nodded. "We'll see, but I'm not promising anything." Kurt glanced at Grantz, who had a big grin on his face. Kurt wondered just how much the greedy profiteer was involved in all of this. Standing up, Kurt motioned to Lomatz. "Let's go. I have to admit I'm curious to see a Protector World warship."

-

Kurt, Colonel Hayworth, a bevy of ship construction engineers, several of Newton's top scientists, and a few technicians walked through the Lakiam battlecruiser in awe. Lomatz was with them, along with a few specialists familiar with the ship's systems. One of the first things Kurt noticed was how wide and bright the ship's corridors were. Hell, even some carpeting was on the deck.

Lomatz stopped and opened a door by sliding his hand over a sensor. It opened silently, revealing living quarters. "This is for the crew," he stated. "You will find the quarters are quite comfortable and even luxurious compared to what you're normally accustomed to."

Kurt stepped inside, glancing around at several comfortable-looking chairs, some super modern viewscreens, and a kitchen setup he wasn't familiar with. "How large a crew does a ship like this take?"

"This is the flagship Aurelia of one of the Lakiam fleets that engaged the Vorn," Lomatz explained. "It normally takes a crew of forty-seven."

"Forty-seven?" one of the construction engineers said, his eyes opening wide in disbelief. "How do they conduct repairs on the ship if it's damaged?"

One of the specialists accompanying Lomatz turned toward the engineer. "The ship is highly automated and uses advanced repair robots to perform maintenance and emergency repairs. The robots are currently in their storage cabinets since we temporarily deactivated them. The ship also possesses a supply of specialized nanites used to repair breaches in the hull in case of major damage to the ship."

"Submicroscopic robots," commented Colonel Hayworth as he thought of the applications. "Those might be useful."

"Can the ship handle a larger crew?" asked Kurt. He didn't know if he would feel comfortable with such a powerful warship having only forty-seven people on board. What if it were boarded by the enemy? There should at least be a company of Marines on a vessel this size.

Lomatz smiled. "Yes, the living quarters can accommodate up to one hundred and twenty. The Lakiams very seldom have full crews on their ships as they deem it unnecessary and inefficient."

Colonel Hayworth shook his head. "It's hard to imagine a ship this size could be operated by only forty-seven people. How many warships like this do the Lakiams possess?"

"I don't know," admitted Lomatz, frowning. "They're responsible for protecting eighty-seven Enlightened World civilizations. So their fleet must be very large, probably numbering in the thousands."

Kurt only shook his head at hearing this. He was just beginning to realize how powerful the Protector Worlds were. What was frightening about all this was that the Protector Worlds seemed to be powerless to stop the black ships.

Continuing on through the ship, they finally reached the Command Center. Stepping inside, Kurt paused as he looked around. It was unlike any Command Center he had ever been in. The entire room was circular with six control consoles sitting in a small semicircle in front of what appeared to be a slightly upraised command dais. On the walls, numerous screens showed views of space. At the moment several were focused on Newton Station, Newton, some of the ships in orbit, and even one of the Orbital Defense Platforms.

Kurt stepped up on the dais and sat down in the command chair. The chair adjusted itself until it fit Kurt's form perfectly. "What type of weapons does this ship have?"

"Some of the most powerful weapons known to the Protector Worlds," Lomatz answered. "Its primary weapon is a force beam that's capable of disrupting the atoms holding a ship's hull together. It's also equipped with direct energy projectors, similar to a Dacroni battleship but ten times more powerful."

"What about missiles?" asked Colonel Hayworth. "Or are the Lakiams so advanced they no longer use them?"

"No, they still use missiles," Lomatz replied. "Their primary offensive missile is a dark matter hypermissile with a five-hundred-megaton warhead."

"Dark matter," one of the scientists said, shaking his head in amazement. "How did they ever harness that?"

"Their science is very advanced," one of Lomatz's technicians explained. "They're one of only a few races who have developed this technology."

"What is the ship's power source?" asked another of the scientists.

"The ship has two antimatter chambers which supply power to the ship's systems as well as the weapons."

Hayworth considered Lomatz. "If this ship were to attack High Profiteer Creed's fleet, what would the result be?"

Lomatz looked long and hard at Colonel Hayworth before replying. "This ship, by itself, could destroy all High Profiteer Creed's ships without suffering any damage to itself. Nothing currently in the Gothan Empire could be a legitimate threat to this vessel. The only system that might have a chance of turning this vessel away would be Kubitz with its massive orbital defenses and perhaps Marsten."

Kurt closed his eyes. This ship and the others that Lomatz was offering him were the solution to keeping High Profiteer Creed from attacking Earth again. The question now was, how did he convince Governor Spalding into allowing possibly twenty thousand humanoids from Kubitz into settling on Newton and bringing with them their corrupt way of life? Kurt knew what Kubitz was like, and there was no way would he allow that to happen to Newton.

Studying Lomatz, Kurt knew a lot of negotiating would happen over the next few days or even longer. With a deep sigh, he felt a headache coming on. He strongly suspected that, somehow or another, Grantz would play a huge role in what was to come. Kurt knew he might as well delve into his supply of gold coins as the greedy Profiteer would be expecting payment.

Chapter Twelve

Captain Dreen of the Lakiam battlecruiser Basera gazed with great worry at the multiple viewscreens scattered about the circular Command Center. He had a fleet of 208 warships sitting in the home system of the Visth. The Visth themselves had nearly four hundred small automated patrol craft scattered about the system, watching for any signs of the Destroyers of Worlds. Across all the Enlightened Worlds of the galaxy, fear had spread like wildfire. The Destroyers of Worlds had returned, and the civilized galaxy was reeling from their first attacks. Seventeen worlds had reportedly been attacked, two more in just the past week, and all upper life-forms taken. In their wake, the black ships had left planetwide destruction and no survivors.

"Anything on the long-range sensors?" Dreen's fleet had been in the Visth home system for nearly two weeks, waiting for an attack they all hoped would never come.

"Nothing," replied Sensor Operator Laylem as he checked his screens one more time. "If reports from previous actions are accurate, we won't pick them up on any of our sensors, not even the hyperspace one."

Dreen nodded as he thought over the meager information they had on the enemy. The Andocks had shared what had happened at Blisth, particularly since a number of their ships survived, including Commander Lakor and his flagship. Crystal-clear videos had shown the combat and how ineffective the weapons on the Andock ships had been. Dreen knew, from the reported losses to the Lakiam fleet units at several Enlightened World colonies, that their ships had fared no better. Captain Veer's fleet at Galian Five had been completely wiped out. Dreen didn't intend for his fleet to suffer the same fate.

"What's the current situation on Visth Prime?"

"They're scared," replied Sheera Keenol from Communications, using her right hand to move several long locks of golden hair that were out of place. Sheera was nearly seven feet tall and very beautiful, as most Lakiam women were. "Many of their media stations are discussing the recent attacks from the black ships and what may be in store for the galaxy. The general consensus seems to be that the black ships can't be stopped. More reports of the Destroyers of Worlds are appearing all the time. Many of them are from other worlds and can't be substantiated."

"Old legends and fears," muttered Captain Dreen with a deep frown, wondering how to tell what was truth and what was simply unfounded rumors.

It was much the same across many of the Enlightened Worlds and their colonies. When his fleet had left the system of Lakiam, he had been astonished at all the effort being put into shoring up the defenses in the system. All Protector Worlds sat behind a defensive grid of some sort, mainly to ensure the Profiteers didn't raid. Now those defenses were expanding, and warship production had been greatly accelerated. Dreen had been told by a close acquaintance that many of the Protector Worlds had planned a strategy meeting in the near future to discuss how to deal with the growing threat of the black ships. Dreen couldn't ever remember the Protector Worlds coming together for such a meeting before.

Captain Dreen saw Sheera's eyes suddenly widen. She spoke rapidly into her comm and then turned toward Dreen. "We have an unconfirmed report of unknown ships spotted in the Alurr System. The ships didn't appear on sensors but were spotted by an observation satellite, studying a large comet."

"Where's the Alurr System from here?" asked Dreen, shifting his gaze to the navigation officer.

"Eight light-years," replied Jalad as he put a star chart up on one of the viewscreens. A blinking red icon designated the Alurr System. "The system has no inhabited worlds or outposts."

"Where's the nearest Enlightened World colony?"

The navigation officer spent a few moments checking his computer console. "Procom Four has a Visth colony with nearly one billion inhabitants, but it's fourteen light-years away. If the report of the unknown ships is correct, they've already passed it."

Captain Dreen felt as if ice water had just been poured over his head. If this was a black fleet, and, if it had passed up the large Visth colony world, the only other major target in this region of space was Visth Prime itself!

"Contact Visth Traffic Control and inform them we may have a black fleet dropping from hyperspace shortly." Dreen knew this would greatly increase the fear on the planet and would cause panic.

Captain Dreen slowly examined each of the numerous viewscreens in the Command Center, searching for any sign of the enemy. It was highly aggravating knowing his fleet's powerful sensors were all but useless.

"Captain, Visth patrol ship V-214 has just dropped off the sensors," reported Laylem, his eyes widening. "It was there a moment ago, and now it's gone."

The Basera was tracking all ship movements in the system. Cargo ships, passenger vessels, the patrol ships, and hundreds of other vessels which moved about. As the homeworld of the Visth, numerous ships were both inbound and outbound.

"Direct the two patrol ships nearest that quadrant of the system to investigate."

The Visth had turned control of their unmanned patrol ships over to Captain Dreen and the Lakiam fleet. He had dispersed the patrol ships across the system, hoping they could spot the black ships if they put in an appearance.

"May not be necessary," Sensor Operator Laylem spoke, his eyes showing great concern. "Two more ships in the same area have also ceased reporting."

"All crews, set Alert Status One throughout the fleet," Captain Dreen announced over his ship-to-ship comm, sitting up straight in his command chair. "Prepare to fire weapons. From all indications, a black fleet has entered the system. Already three Visth patrol vessels have been destroyed."

"Visth Traffic Control is bringing the planet's defense grid online," reported Sheera from Communications. "Command of the grid has now been transferred to Lakiam control. All cargo and passenger ships currently in the system are being ordered to jump to Procom Four. All visiting ships are being told to leave the system as soon as possible."

Dreen nodded. Visth Prime had one of the most powerful defensive grids in the entire galaxy. Thirty-two Class One Orbital Defense Platforms orbited the planet along with two hundred defensive satellites. The entire defensive grid was commanded from a Class One Command and Control Station, which in itself was more heavily armed than ten Lakiam battlecruisers. For this emergency, full Lakiam crews had gone on board the defensive platforms as well as the Command and Control Station to ensure maximum utilization of the powerful weapons systems.

After hundreds of thousands of years of peace, the Visth were incapable of ordering the death of other intelligent beings, even if it meant their own demise. In normal times only the Command and Control Station had a small crew of Lakiams on board. The rest of the defense grid could be operated by remote control, and not once in the Visths' long history of peace had it been necessary to actually activate the defense grid—until today.

"Order the patrol ships to return to Visth Prime," commanded Dreen. While the small ships were only lightly armed, he would take every warship he could get his hands on. "Send out a general distress call on all hyperspace channels requesting more ships."

"Hyperspace channels are jammed," Sheera replied a few moments later as her nimble fingers moved across her console. "All we have is short-range communications inside the system."

Captain Dreen leaned back in his command chair, knowing help wouldn't be coming. His gaze shifted to one of the larger viewscreens showing the world of Visth Prime, a beautiful world with large oceans, islands, and two major landmasses—home to nearly four billion Visth. Large artificial habitats orbited around the planet as well as several of the other planets in the system.

The Visth System had eight planets and twenty-one moons. On most of the planets and larger moons were domed cities. The total population in the system was well above six billion. Captain Dreen didn't want to think about what would happen if he couldn't stop the black ships. Six billion Visth were depending on him to keep them alive.

"Any further contacts with the inbound black fleet?" It was maddening that the ultramodern sensors on his flagship were so impotent against the black ships.

"Nothing," said Sensor Operator Laylem, shaking his head. "I've tried every type of scan we have, and they've all come back negative. If the black ships are out there, I can't detect them."

Captain Dreen nodded. So the rumors of some sensor-dampening field were true. It was also possible the hull material the black ships were constructed of interfered somehow with the scans. All of his ships' targeting computers had been reprogrammed to take either of these possibilities into account. The Andocks had found limited success using their viewscreens to locate and plot the black fleet. Dreen's ships would do the same when the black ships drew near enough.

-

Minutes passed and then turned into an hour. Captain Dreen watched with calm nerves as the crew in the Command Center attempted to locate the black fleet. On the two tactical hologram displays, hundreds of ships had jumped from the system, and more were doing so every minute. A number of large passenger liners had been launched from the orbital stations around Visth Prime with evacuees. Across the system, every ship the Visth had was being loaded with evacuees and sent to Procom Four.

"Contact!" called out Alborg from Tactical as he pointed to a viewscreen, where a black spindle-shaped ship appeared.

"Confirmed," reported Sensor Operator Laylem as a red threat icon suddenly appeared in the holographic tactical display. Seconds later more red icons flashed to life as other ships spotted inbound enemy vessels.

"How accurate is that?" asked Captain Dreen, peering sharply at the display, which was rapidly filling with red threat icons. It was true then; the Destroyers of Worlds had come to Visth Prime. He felt a chill run through his body as he realized what was at stake. Visth Prime was one of the oldest Enlightened Worlds and was well respected throughout the galaxy.

"It's accurate," Sensor Operator Laylem replied. "Our ship's computer has been programmed to use the viewscreens to correlate the exact locations of the black ships. It should be accurate to within a few meters."

"Black ships will be in weapons range in nine minutes," reported Alborg as he checked his weapon systems. "All weapons are charged and ready to fire."

"Now we wait," said Captain Dreen as several more black ships appeared on the viewscreens. On the planet and across the system, frightened Visth would be rushing to board any available starship to escape the coming of the Destroyers of Worlds. He could well imagine the panic that was now sweeping the system.

-

In the large Class One Command and Control Station, Captain Drale Latium watched as red threat icons appeared in the two large holographic displays in front of him.

"All systems powered up and working at optimum levels," reported Mal Drume from Tactical. "Energy shield is at 98 percent, and energy reserves are at 64 percent and rising."

Energy reserves were the stored power that could be called upon if the antimatter reactors were compromised or failed.

Captain Latium walked to stand just behind Drume, who was busy with his console. "I'm concerned about these black antimatter spheres we've heard rumors about."

"They're more than rumors I'm afraid," Drume responded. "I've seen the video and sensor readings from the Andock fleet that was decimated in the Blisth System."

"Can we defend against them?"

Drume slowly shook his head. "It's a form of antimatter we've never encountered before. The science behind it is totally alien to our way of thinking. I've spoken to a few weapon specialists and even a couple research scientists. They believe this black antimatter doesn't even originate in our universe."

"How long can our energy shield stand up to it once we've been struck?"

"We have a lot more power available to us than one of our battlecruisers," Drume answered. "We also have our energy reserves."

"Any recommendations?"

Drume drew in a deep breath. "From the data we received from the Andocks on the Blisth attack, we know energy weapons are ineffective against the black ships. The only weapons that might be effective are our dark matter hypermissiles. Even an energy screen such as the black ships have must have a limit to the amount of energy it can absorb."

"So are you suggesting multiple dark matter missile strikes on just a few of the black ships in an attempt to overload their shields?"

"I think it's our only hope of success. I've taken the initiative to have dark matter missiles distributed to every orbiting defensive platform. All of our missile reserves have been committed."

Captain Latium shifted his gaze from Drume to the two tactical displays, now showing hundreds of red threat icons. Latium greatly feared that, even if the dark matter missiles worked, they didn't have enough to make a difference. Dark matter missiles were very expensive and not easy to build.

-

Captain Dreen stared in awe at the two ships now on one of the primary viewscreens. They were massive, larger than any vessel he had ever seen before. "Mark those two motherships as our primary targets."

"Captain, I just spoke to Mal Drume on the Command and Control Station," reported Sheera, turning toward the captain. "He believes by hitting the black ships with multiple dark matter missiles we can overload their energy screens."

"Weapons range in two minutes," reported Sensor Operator Laylem.

"Locking on targets," reported Alborg from Tactical. "Do we use the dark matter missiles as Tactical Officer Drume has suggested?"

Captain Dreen stared at all the red threat icons on the tactical display. He felt a sinking sensation in the pit of his stomach, seeing how badly outnumbered his fleet was. "I want 40 percent of our fleet's missiles targeted on the two motherships and the rest on twenty of the spindle-shaped cruisers. Perhaps if we can damage or destroy a number of their vessels in the initial exchange, they'll withdraw." Dreen knew that was unlikely, but it was their only hope.

"Allocating targets with the rest of the fleet," answered Alborg as he sent targeting information to the other ships.

"How many are we facing?"

"The two motherships and five hundred and seventeen spindle-shaped cruisers," answered Sensor Operator Laylem.

On the main viewscreens, the images shifted to show more of the black ships. They looked deadly and were advancing with a confidence that was disconcerting. Captain Dreen knew the decisive moment was rapidly approaching. He had his fleet assembled into five lines, forty ships wide, with a reserve of eighteen directly behind the center of his formation.

"Dark matter hypermissiles are ready to fire," reported Alborg, looking back at the captain. "This will be a coordinated strike from all ships."

"What about the Visth-automated patrol ships?" asked Sensor Operator Laylem. "A number of them are nearby, with more arriving every minute."

Captain Dreen paused as he considered what could be done with the lightly armed ships. All they had in the way of armaments were a pair of direct energy cannons.

"Weapons range!" called out Laylem.

"Fire hypermissiles!" ordered Dreen. He'd figure out what to do with the Visth patrol ships later.

-

On the Lakiam battlecruisers, small hatches slid open. In a blur of movement, the dark matter hypermissiles seemed to vanish from their missile tubes as they transitioned into hyperspace. From the 208 battlecruisers, nearly two thousand missiles flashed from their tubes to slam into the powerful energy shields of the Vorn ships. Huge five-hundred-megaton explosions of energy washed across the energy screens of twenty Vorn cruisers and the two motherships. The Vorn screens had been designed to withstand nuclear explosions, antimatter explosions, and every type of energy weapon imaginable. However, the massive release of energy from dark matter was unexpected.

Vorn energy shields glowed brightly as they absorbed the tremendous quantities of energy. The shields grew brighter and brighter, and then flickered. They had reached their saturation point, and, in titanic blinding explosions, they collapsed, releasing the energy they had absorbed. Glowing nova like explosions suddenly appeared in the Vorn formation as all twenty spindle-shaped cruisers were obliterated. The entire Vorn formation was lit up from the brilliance of the explosions.

In the center of the Vorn formation, dark matter explosions covered the energy shields of the two motherships, obscuring them from view, but their shields had been designed to withstand any conceivable onslaught. Even so, the shield on one of the large ships struggled to stay intact. The shield glowed as bright as a sun with the amount of energy it was absorbing. Some of that energy leaked through, striking the black hull of the massive starship. Huge rifts were torn in the battle armor, and large sections were left open to space. Several secondary explosions rattled the Vorn mothership, causing the vessel to falter in its advance toward the Visth homeworld.

-

On board the Vorn Mothership Reaper, Prince Brollen recoiled in shock when twenty of his indestructible cruisers exploded as their energy screens collapsed, releasing incalculable amounts of energy and annihilating them instantly.

The Scythe has suffered considerable damage to its outer hull, Military Commander Mardok reported uneasily. He wasn't sure how Prince Brollen would receive this. Military commanders had been deleted for reporting less upsetting information than this in the past to Vorn princes. *Some secondary explosions have damaged the vessel's sublight drive. Repairs are underway.*

Prince Brollen looked at the viewscreen, which showed the other mothership. He felt growing anger and disbelief at the damage done to the vessel. It was inconceivable that a food species could inflict damage on one of the Vorns' most valuable and powerful ships!

What type of missiles are those? he demanded in a shrill thought directed at the military commander. On the main viewscreens, the shattered and fiery remains of twenty of his cruisers were visible.

The same as they used on us once before, Military Commander Mardok reported. *Only this time they changed their tactics and concentrated their firepower on just a few of our ships.*

Sensor scans indicate dark matter in the warheads of the missiles, one of the scientists reported. Yield is in the five-hundred-megaton range.

Dark matter, thought Prince Brollen, his twin antennae standing straighter. *We've never encountered such a weapon in previous harvests of this galaxy. This is a worrisome development.*

All ships, commence black antimatter bombardment of the defending fleet, broadcast Mardok. His order, transmitted telepathically, was received instantly. He would destroy the enemy fleet before more Vorn vessels were lost.

-

Captain Latium watched with interest as he saw the successful attack launched by Captain Dreen. "You were correct," he said to Mal Drume at Tactical. "By concentrating our dark matter hypermissiles on just a few targets, our battlecruisers overloaded the enemy's energy screens."

"Captain, enemy ships are launching their dark antimatter spheres at our cruisers," warned Besel Molk from his sensor console.

Latium shifted his attention to the large viewscreens on the front wall of the Command and Control Center, seeing what looked like black spheres of nothingness hurtling toward the battlecruisers. Around the edges, small discharges of energy were evident. "Order the cruisers to fall back to the defense grid. Our defense platforms can give them covering fire with their dark matter missiles." Latium had overall command of the Lakiam forces in the Visth System, though he was allowing Captain Dreen considerable latitude with the fleet.

"Sending the order," replied the communications officer.

Captain Latium watched tensely as the battlecruisers reacted to his order. Hundreds of black antimatter energy spheres hurtled toward the Lakiam vessels. "Target ten of the enemy ships, and fire enough missiles to bring down their shields and destroy them." Perhaps he could take some of the pressure off Captain Dreen's ships until they reached the defense grid.

"Twelve dark matter missiles on each target should be sufficient," Mal Drume responded. "I'm directing ten of the defense platforms to fire their missiles."

"Some of our battlecruisers have been struck by the enemy fire," pointed out Besel Molk.

On several of the main viewscreens, black antimatter spheres slammed into the powerful energy screens of Lakiam battlecruisers. The spheres seemed to flatten out and spread across the screens, turning them dark. Other Lakiam battlecruisers turned and fled back toward the defense grid and the hoped-for safety provided by the powerful defense platforms.

"Thirty-two battlecruisers have been hit by the dark antimatter spheres," reported Besel Molk.

"Ships report massive power losses," the communications officer added.

"Send out all of our tugs to tractor those battlecruisers beneath the defense grid," ordered Captain Latium. "Perhaps that will give them time to reinitiate their power systems."

"Too late," Molk said dejectedly. "The black ships are launching antimatter hypermissiles."

Captain Latium turned toward the viewscreens, knowing he could do nothing to save the valuable warships.

-

In space, dozens of hypermissiles left the missile tubes of the black ships to strike the unprotected hulls of the Lakiam battlecruisers. Brilliant fireballs of antimatter destruction spread across the hapless ships as they were annihilated ruthlessly from existence. In moments all thirty-two powerless battlecruisers had been reduced to molten wreckage and wisps of glowing gas.

Even as the warships died, the ten designated Class One Orbital Defense Platforms launched their black matter hypermissiles. Microseconds after leaving the missile tubes, they slammed into the ten black ships the Command and Control Center had designated as targets. Massive five-hundred-megaton explosions ravaged the enemy ships' energy screens, bloating them with energy. Then, in brilliant flashes of light, the screens seemed to implode. In each location where a black ship's energy screen collapsed, a miniature nova appeared.

-

We've lost ten more vessels, and the enemy ships are retreating to the planet and its orbital defenses, Military Commander Mardok projected. *It was a mistake to wait so long to harvest this galaxy once more. The added time has allowed some of their races to develop weapons that are dangerous to our ships.*

Prince Brollen was in agreement with Military Commander Mardok's assessment. The Hive Queens had hoped, by putting off the harvesting of Galaxy X241, the food species would be more plentiful. Part of that plan had succeeded. The food species were much more abundant, but they were also much more powerful and dangerous.

After we harvest this world, we will send word back to the Conclave Habitat of the danger of some of the food species in this galaxy. It may be necessary to deploy more of our ships.

Military Commander Mardok nodded his agreement. *I have ordered our ships to close the range with the planet's orbital defenses. We will deploy our black antimatter energy beams. They should make short work of the planet's defenses.*

I leave the battle up to you, Prince Brollen replied. After all, that was what the military leaders had been created for.

-

Captain Dreen gripped the edges of his command chair as his flagship moved behind one of the large defensive platforms. All his remaining ships were taking up positions around and behind the platforms to aid in their defense and to increase the amount of firepower available.

"We have a lot of frantic messages being broadcasted from the surface of Visth Prime," Sheera announced as her comm console was nearly overloaded with anxious calls. "The Visth want to know if we can hold back the black ships from the planet."

Dreen took in a deep breath. They had destroyed thirty of the black ships, but he knew they didn't have enough of the black matter hypermissiles to destroy the rest. They might get fifteen or twenty more, but that would still leave over 460 of the enemy, plus their two motherships.

"Do the defense platforms and the Command and Control Station have the necessary firepower when combined with our remaining fleet to stop the enemy?" asked Dreen, looking at Alborg, who was in front of the large tactical console.

Alborg slowly shook his head. "We might get a few more of them, but force beams and direct energy cannons won't overload their enemy screens. Once we've used up all of our dark matter hypermissiles, we'll have to fall back to our antimatter ones. I estimate it will take sixty of those missiles to overload the shields of the black ships. If you add all our energy weapons, we could reduce that to maybe forty concentrated hits, but it will have to be well-coordinated."

Captain Dreen ran some quick calculations in his head. Even at the most optimistic result, too many of the black ships would be left when the battle was over. He and Captain Latium could do nothing to save the Visth homeworld. "Do what you can," he ordered.

-

Prince Brollen stood with his multifaceted eyes staring expectantly at two large viewscreens directly in front of him. The fleet was rapidly nearing the orbital defenses protecting the planet. This food species was probably feeling confident in repelling them since destroying some of the Vorn ships. They were about to learn not all the Vorns' most deadly and destructive weapons had been revealed.

We're in weapons range, Military Commander Mardok sent. *All ships, fire black antimatter energy beams. Destroy the orbital defenses first and then the defending battlecruisers. The planet they defend is a food world, and our Queens and our warriors need the nourishment it will provide.*

Prince Brollen nodded his approval. Mardok was a fine military commander. That was one of the reasons Brollen had chosen him for that role on board the Reaper.

-

From the black ships, energy beams flashed out to strike the protective screens of the Orbital Defense Platforms and the Command and Control Station. The beams were black and ominous and reeked of deadly power. As the beams struck the platforms, their energy screens suddenly flared as their power was drained, and then the beams penetrated. In massive explosions, the large Orbital Defense Platforms began to blow up.

-

Captain Latium felt the Command and Control Station rock violently as several of the black beams penetrated the station's energy shield. Alarms sounded, and red lights flashed. On the damage control console, red lights glowed. On several viewscreens, he saw defense platforms exploding in massive releases of energy, sending debris careening across space.

"Order all platforms to fire their remaining black matter missiles!" he ordered. "Follow up with antimatter missiles in auto mode."

Latium wanted every remaining missile fired as rapidly as possible while they still had the firepower to damage the black fleet. He was devastated to see how powerful this new beam weapon of the enemy was. He hadn't expected to lose so many of his defense platforms so quickly. Without the defense platforms, the Visth homeworld was doomed.

"Those beams are composed of the same type of energy as the black antimatter spheres," Drume reported as his hands flew nimbly across his tactical console. "Only it's more focused and much more intense. Our energy shield won't hold up long, even with our energy reserves." As he spoke, the lights in the Command and Control Center dimmed, and the station shook violently once more. In the distance came the sound of tearing metal.

"We have numerous compartments open to space," reported Lela Graft, the damage control officer. "We're losing life support in parts of the station."

"Firing missiles in auto mode," reported Drume. "Force beams and all energy projectors operating at full power. We have enough energy for three minutes of operation."

Captain Latium considered his command crew. All of them knew they were not getting out of this alive. Their duty was to defend the Visth from harm. They would fail miserably in this, but they would all give their lives in the effort. However, Latium saw no point in Captain Dreen sacrificing his ships needlessly, as they would be needed to defend other Enlightened Worlds and possibly even Lakiam. The vital information gleaned from this battle must be shared with all the Protector Worlds. The black ships could be destroyed but at a terrible cost.

In a calm and decisive voice, he turned toward the communications officer, seeing the fear in her eyes. "Tell Captain Dreen that he's to take his fleet and jump into hyperspace when the last orbital defense platform has been destroyed. He's to proceed directly to Lakiam and inform them of what transpired here. Perhaps what we learned today will allow other Enlightened Worlds to survive."

The Command and Control Center grew quiet as the Lakiam officers realized there would be no escape for them.

-

In space, the intensity of the battle increased tenfold as the besieged Orbital Defense Platforms fired their missiles in sprint mode. Each station in range targeted just a single black ship. Even as the platforms died in titanic explosions of pure energy, a few black ships met their deaths as well. Dark matter hyperspace missiles slammed into energy shields, followed by weaker antimatter ones. Energy shields on the black ships became engorged with energy, only to detonate violently when they finally reached their saturation point. Every time that happened, the black ship died instantly.

Force beams and energy beams lashed out at the black ships in a vain effort to destroy more of the enemy. On ships where energy screens were already engorged from absorbing energy from black matter and antimatter missiles, the screens failed, releasing their stored-up power. More black ships died in fiery explosions.

The black ships ignored their losses and pressed on doggedly, playing their deadly black antimatter beams across the Orbital Defense Platforms. Platform after platform died as their screens were overwhelmed, and then their very structures were blown apart. In a matter of only a few minutes, all that remained were the beleaguered Command and Control Station and the Lakiam fleet.

-

Captain Dreen felt the blood drain from his face upon seeing the destruction wrought by the black ships. He had never dreamed the large Class One Defense Platforms could be destroyed so easily. These same platforms were deployed above all the Protector Worlds. Nothing was stronger.

“All vessels, standby to jump,” he ordered over the ship-to-ship comm. “As soon as all hypermissiles, both dark matter and antimatter have been fired, you’re to jump into hyperspace and proceed immediately to Lakiam.”

On one of the viewscreens, he saw two more black ships explode. It was a muted relief to know they had at least one weapon which was effective against the enemy ships. It was essential word of this reach Lakiam and the other Protector Worlds.

"Some of the enemy ships are targeting our battlecruisers," warned Sensor Operator Laylem.

On the large tactical display, Dreen saw four green icons representing his battlecruisers vanish. "All ships, jump now," he ordered. If he waited another few minutes, he could lose the rest of his fleet.

"Jumping," reported Jalad from the Helm as he pressed several icons on one of his computer screens. Instantly the flagship accelerated and transitioned into hyperspace.

The last scene Captain Dreen saw would be etched into his mind forever. The black ships brutally attacking the Command and Control Station, which was still valiantly fighting back. Much of its armor had been stripped away, but its remaining force beams and direct energy projectors were still firing defiantly. Then everything faded out as the flagship jumped to safety.

-

Captain Latium watched as Captain Dreen's flagship vanished from the viewscreen into the safety of hyperspace, leaving the Command and Control Station alone to face the black fleet. He was relieved the majority of Captain Dreen's ships had escaped. Shifting his gaze to the damage control console, he noted nearly every light was red. All their missiles had been launched, and most of the station's force beam and energy projectors were gone. Nothing could be done now to protect Visth Prime. Even the communications console had fallen silent as the world below realized its protectors had been defeated.

With a deep sigh of resignation, Captain Latium leaned back in his command chair, awaiting death. He wished he could have seen Lakiam one last time. His last thoughts were of his wife and daughter, and then a black beam swept through the Command and Control Center, wiping everything out of existence.

-

All enemy forces have been eliminated, reported Military Commander Mardok. *We lost sixty-two of our cruisers, and the other mothership suffered moderate damage as reported earlier. They further report they can still carry out the mission against the planet.* Mardok was concerned for his own well-being as Prince Brollen could order Mardok's deletion. No military commander had ever lost as many ships as he had in a single battle since coming to this universe.

Prince Brollen nodded. This battle had been much more costly than he had believed possible. The report of the strength of some of these food species would have to be sent to the Conclave Habitat to ensure all motherships on harvesting missions were adequately protected. Thousands of cruisers still remained at the Vorn habitats. For a moment he toyed with the thought of ordering Military Commander Mardok's deletion. However, he had fought the battle well and could not have known the danger of the food species' deadly missiles.

Take us in, broadcast Prince Brollen telepathically. *It's time to begin the harvesting.*

-

The two motherships and the remaining black cruisers went into orbit above Visth Prime. The energy beam satellites and the small patrol ships opened fire and were instantly annihilated. Their meager weapons were useless against the black ships. It only took the black fleet a few minutes to destroy all of them. In space above Visth Prime, small bright antimatter explosions marked their passing.

Huge hatches on the two motherships slid open, and the black harvester beams lashed out to strike the planet below. In moments nutrients for the Vorn race reached the ships via the tractor beams inside each of the harvester beams. It would take hours, but the planet would be fully harvested and its bountiful food collected. Then the ships would move out and continue the harvest of the orbiting habitats, the other planets, and the moons of the system. When the Vorns left, there would be no surviving higher life-forms. They would have all been converted to food for the hungry Vorn race and their Hive Queens.

Chapter Thirteen

"I can't believe that both Grantz and Lomatz are here at Newton," said Keera, shaking her head in disapproval. "What do they want? Is this one of Grantz's schemes to get more gold from you? You're way too generous with him as it is." She stood in their apartment with her hands on her hips, waiting for an answer.

Kurt let out a deep sigh. He had just finished a long and difficult meeting with Governor Spalding. For over a week they had been negotiating with Lomatz over the six Protector Worlds' warships he had in his possession. Kurt had taken both Governor Spalding and General Mclusky to tour the Aurelia to see exactly what Lomatz was offering. The technology on the Lakiam warships was breathtaking and necessary for Newton and Earth's defense, and both men had been impressed, particularly when told about the firepower the six ships possessed. Having them in the Newton fleet would mean future threats from the Profiteers would come to an end.

Governor Spalding was still not fully convinced and had scheduled another meeting with Lomatz for later in the day at his office. The governor had a few more questions he wanted clarified before he agreed to anything with the Kubitz weapons dealer. Kurt had taken a few hours off to rest and spend some time with Keera.

"I'm not sure what Grantz is up to," admitted Kurt, reaching out his arms to take Keera by the waist. He pulled her closer to him and kissed her gently on the lips. "Andrew is keeping an eye on him."

Keera looked into Kurt's eyes. "How is Andrew feeling?"

"Better," answered Kurt, running his right hand gently up Keera's back. "Since he checked out of the medical center, he's been spending most of his time at home with his wife and daughter. He's been aching for something to do, so I assigned him to keep on eye on our Profiteer."

"Knowing how he feels about Grantz, you couldn't have a better person watching your greedy friend." Keera leaned up against Kurt and closed her eyes. "How much time do you have before this next meeting?"

"A couple of hours," Kurt answered in a softer and more suggestive voice.

Keera leaned back and smiled. "That should be just long enough. You know what kind of mood running your hand across my back puts me in."

Kurt nodded. That had been the general idea.

-

Keera took Kurt's hand and led him into their comfortable bedroom. Some passionate lovemaking would take her mind off her brother and his girlfriend. She had found the two of them a nearby apartment and Dalen a job working in construction. He was very good at programming and operating the small work robots now currently used to help build homes and other infrastructure on the planet. She still worried about her brother since Meesa had mentioned that, on several nights, he had come home very late.

Her attention was brought back to Kurt as he unbuttoned her blouse. Already her breathing was heavier, and her heart was beating faster. She would worry about her brother later; for now she wanted to concentrate on Kurt and what they were about to do.

-

Governor Spalding was in his office with General Mclusky. "Well, what do you think?"

Mclusky sat down in one of the comfortable chairs in front of the governor's desk. "Those ships are damn impressive. The Aurelia by itself could keep the Profiteers away from Newton and Earth. If we could apply that technology to the rest of our fleet, we'd have a hell of a lot of firepower."

"Lomatz is offering us all six of those advanced warships if we agree to allow some of his people to settle on Newton." Spalding knew Fleet Admiral Vickers wanted those ships, particularly if the mysterious black ships put in an appearance. "I'm just not certain allowing Lomatz's people access to Newton is worth the change in our society. Most of these people will be from Kubitz, and you know what that planet is like."

Mclusky stood up and walked over to a large map of Newton on one of the walls. He put his finger on a big island off the coast of one of the planet's main continents. "This island is uninhabited and large enough to hold the people Lomatz wants to bring to Newton. There's enough room to allow for considerable expansion of their population without having to worry about them spilling over onto the mainland. We could put a couple military spy satellites in geosynchronous orbit above the island to keep an eye on them."

Spalding walked to the map and gazed thoughtfully at the island Mclusky had pointed out. "This will be a very advanced culture we're inviting to Newton. There's a lot we could probably learn from them."

"As you said earlier, many of the people Lomatz wants to bring will be from Kubitz," cautioned the general. "They'll have to agree to abide by our laws."

"I think that can be arranged," Spalding answered. "If Lomatz wants to come here desperately enough, he'll have to agree to some restrictions on his peoples' activities."

Mclusky nodded. "Just keep in mind Lomatz is used to tough negotiations, and I'm sure he expects to come out ahead in anything we agree to."

After Kurt had first brought up the subject of the advanced warships in Lomatz's possession, Spalding had known all along that he would be forced to accommodate the weapons dealer's request to bring twenty thousand of his people to Newton. Spalding just wanted to ensure Lomatz didn't have some ulterior motive. It also concerned him that all of this was due to the black ships. If Lomatz felt the Gothan Empire wasn't safe from them, what about Earth and Newton?

"I'll have some information on that island put together for the meeting later today," Spalding said, realizing the island might be the ideal solution. It had a nice climate and was large enough to accommodate whatever Lomatz and his people might need. However, one thing he had learned from speaking to Kurt about Kubitz, in any deal was to get as much from it as possible. Governor Spalding wanted to know what Lomatz had in those ten large cargo ships he had brought to the Newton System.

-

It was mid afternoon when Kurt arrived at the governor's office. He had grabbed a quick bite to eat after leaving Keera in bed sound asleep. Kurt wished he could have stayed in bed with her instead of coming to this meeting. However, he hoped Governor Spalding was finally ready to make a deal with Lomatz. If they wanted to make Earth and Newton safer, Kurt needed those ships and the technology they represented.

Entering the governor's office, he saw Spalding, General Mclusky, Grantz, Colonel Hayworth, and Lomatz were waiting. "Sorry I'm late," Kurt said. "I had some business I had to take care of."

"You're not late. You're right on time," said Spalding, indicating for Kurt to sit. Taking a deep breath, the governor turned toward Lomatz. "We may have found a place to settle your people. However, before we discuss that, I want to know what's on board those cargo ships of yours and why you brought two of your construction ships to Newton."

Lomatz looked long and hard at the governor before replying. "Profiteer Grantz suggested I sweeten the pot with additional incentives. If my people come to Newton, I want to ensure they're well-protected. With your permission, my two construction ships will build an additional construction bay onto Newton Station. This bay will be capable of constructing ships with the same technology and weapons as the Aurelia. It will also be able to convert your current ships to the new technology."

"How long to build this new construction bay and one battlecruiser based on Lakiam specifications?" asked Colonel Hayworth, his eyes glowing with interest.

"Two months to build the bay and it will be capable of building two battlecruisers every six weeks since the entire process will be almost completely automated. It also won't be necessary to build the new battlecruisers as large as the Lakiams did for the Aurelia. The new battlecruisers will be a combination of Lakiam, Andock, and several other Protector Worlds' technology. My ship construction people have already worked up a main design for your approval, based on your current battlecruiser configuration."

"Would it be possible to convert our other two construction bays?" asked Hayworth, thinking of the possibilities.

"It would," confirmed Lomatz with a slow nod of his head.

"I thought this technology was banned in the Gothan Empire," interjected Kurt, trying not to sound too excited about building new advanced warships at such a high speed.

"We're not in the Gothan Empire," Grantz pointed out. "The Protector Worlds didn't want their technology used against them in raids. For generations they have made it plain that, if certain types of technology were to appear in the empire, the Protector Worlds would come and remove it. But Newton isn't in the Gothan Empire, and that's why Lomatz can give you the technology."

"I also won't be telling anyone what I'm doing," Lomatz added.

Kurt slowly nodded his head. "How did you become familiar with the technology from the Protector Worlds? I thought they guarded their advanced sciences to ensure none of the Gothan Empire worlds could get their hands on it." Some things Lomatz and Grantz had mentioned were confusing to Kurt.

Lomatz looked directly at Kurt and then replied. "Every since my encounter with that mysterious advanced race, I've been looking into Protector World and Enlightened World technology. Some of it, when modified so it's not quite as advanced, can be sold at a handsome profit. I have a complete staff of research scientists and technicians who work on this full time. Whenever a

Profiteer fleet captures a cargo ship or passenger ship from an advanced world and brings it back to Kubitz, I send several of my people on board to see if any technology might be of interest. So my people have a decent understanding of the technology used on the Protector Worlds and even to a point that is used on the Enlightened Worlds as well."

"You still haven't told us what's on board your cargo ships," Governor Spalding reminded the weapons dealer.

Lomatz took a small metal disk from one of his pockets. "If I bring my people here to be part of your civilization, I want to ensure they're protected from retaliation. I want this planet to be as strongly defended as possible."

"What do you mean, retaliation?" demanded Governor Spalding suspiciously. "I thought you said the Gothan Empire would do nothing since we're not a part of it."

Lomatz looked uneasily at Spalding before replying. "The technology I'm willing to give you is banned by both the Protector Worlds and the Enlightened Worlds to civilizations below a certain level of advancement. However, due to the threat of the Destroyers of Worlds, I don't believe it will be an issue. Also the defenses I'm willing to provide you with will most likely prevent any repercussions from the technology I'm willing to share."

"Who would retaliate?"

"Possibly several of the Protector Worlds if they learn what I've done," Lomatz admitted. "But, like I said, as far out as Newton is, the odds of that occurring are very low. The Protector Worlds are too busy worrying about the black ships and their attacks on the Enlightened Worlds. The odds of any of them finding out what we're doing out here is infinitesimal. Also, if you ever want to stand a chance at protecting your worlds from the black ships, you need this technology."

Kurt leaned back in his chair and gazed fixedly at Lomatz. "And just what type of defenses are we talking about?"

Lomatz placed the small disk on Governor Spalding's desk and activated it. Instantly a massive defensive platform appeared.

"This is a Class One Defensive Platform. It's ten times more powerful than the Type Twos you currently have. I can provide you with sixty-four of these. Pressing a small button on the side of the disk, another massive structure appeared. "This is a Type One Command and Control Station. It has the firepower of ten Lakiam battlecruisers. I can also provide you with an additional two hundred dual-firing energy beam satellites."

"How much will this cost us?" asked Kurt, knowing these types of defenses must cost a fortune. However, the satellites alone would solve some of their problems. It would allow them to place sufficient satellites above both Earth and Julbian to deter any future Profiteer attack.

Lomatz focused his eyes on Kurt. "It's expensive, but I'm willing to reduce the cost to 70 percent of what it took to build them. The Protector Worlds, as well as a number of Enlightened Worlds, recently placed massive orders for Class One defensive systems. Numerous construction yards across the Gothan Empire are currently in the process of building hundreds of these systems. It wasn't hard for me to get these, using my connections with those who owe me some favors. With the right inducements, I can ensure no one will know where this particular system went."

"Bribes," commented Grantz approvingly. "They will have to be quite large to ensure everyone keeps their mouths shut."

General Mclusky looked hungrily at the massive structure displayed above Governor Spalding's desk. "What would this type of defensive system mean if the Profiteers were to attack Newton?"

"They wouldn't," answered Lomatz with a confident look. "A system like this would wipe them out before they could even open fire. It would also discourage most Protector World ships from entering the system as well."

Governor Spalding let out a deep breath. He couldn't turn Lomatz's offer down, not now. Purchasing this system would also come very close to depleting their gold reserves. "There's a large island off the coast of one of our primary continents that would be ideal for your people. It's big enough to allow space for future development as well as population expansion."

Lomatz's eyes lit up. "Can you show me this island? I would like to visually inspect it before I agree."

"It can be arranged," replied Governor Spalding. He just worried about what the effect would be of having twenty thousand of Lomatz's people on Newton. Many of them, if not all, having had past dealings with the Profiteers and were no doubt used to the pirate like culture which prevailed on Kubitz.

"One other question," said Kurt, focusing his eyes on Lomatz. "In the contract I signed on Kubitz you added two small sectors of space to it. Why?"

Lomatz looked long and hard at Kurt. "Have you sent ships to inspect those two sectors?"

"Yes," Kurt answered. "They should be back any time. But I would still like to hear from you what we're supposed to find."

Lomatz hesitated and then spoke. "I'm not 100 percent certain, but Avery Dolman heard some rumors on Kubitz. If they're true, I believe you'll be very pleased with what your ships find. I would rather not say anything else until your ships return. I promise you there is nothing of danger in either of those two small sectors of space."

"Very well, I'll wait," replied Kurt. "But as soon as the ships return you and I will be sitting down to discuss what they found."

Lomatz nodded. He had been expecting this.

-

Kurt was back on board the Aurelia with an inspection team from the shipyard. This time they were going to take a detailed tour, inspecting every area of the massive warship. Even Andrew had come along since Grantz was on board.

"Damn, this ship is big," muttered Andrew as they walked down a wide and brightly lit corridor. "Is this carpeting on the floor?" Andrew stopped and bent down, running his hand across it.

"Not like you're used to," replied one of Lomatz's technicians, who was accompanying the inspection team. "It's a metallic fiber that resembles carpeting and is very resistant to wear, yet feels like an actual floor carpet. This type of material is quite common on most Protector World ships."

Grantz grinned at Andrew. "The Protector Worlds are rich from all their colonies they possess as well as from the services they provide the Enlightened Worlds. They spare no expense to make their ships as comfortable as possible."

Kurt had already noticed. Walking through the ship, one would never know this was a warship. In many ways, it resembled a luxury passenger liner. He had already been shown a large comfortable lounge area with massive windows where one could look out into space. One of the technicians had pointed out the clear material of the windows was nearly as strong as ship armor. Plus the windows had blast shields, which slid down during combat for additional protection.

Kurt was surprised at how much effort the Lakiams had taken to make the ship as comfortable and as luxurious as possible. The personal quarters were all unbelievably comfortable with every modern convenience imaginable. Every workstation had chairs that conformed to its occupant. Repair robots could do the standard preventative maintenance on the ship as well as conduct most emergency repairs.

"This ship is a marvel of construction," commented Colonel Hayworth as they turned a corner and came to a large sealed hatch.

"What's behind this hatch?" asked Kurt, turning to face one of Lomatz's engineers. This was the first hatch they had come to that was locked and protected by a security code that had to be entered on a touchpad on the wall.

The engineer hesitated and then answered, "The Lakiams don't indulge in hand-to-hand combat. It's part of their commitment to becoming Enlightened. Instead they use combat robots. The robots are equipped with heavy-duty stunners so they don't have to take a life."

"What happens if the stunners don't work?" asked one of Hayworth's ship construction supervisors, who had been asked to come along on the inspection.

"Each combat robot has a small energy beam cannon in the center of its chest," the engineer replied. "It's quite capable of penetrating any metal unless protected by an energy shield. The beam can be adjusted to specific intensities, depending on the type of combat situation the robot finds itself in."

"How are they controlled?" asked Kurt, wondering if it was some automatic function controlled by the ship's computer?

"The ship's commander is the only one with authority to activate the combat robots," replied the engineer. "As I said before, they are very seldom used."

"How many of them are on the Aurelia?" asked Hayworth, peering at the closed hatch and wondering what the robots looked like.

"Two hundred and forty," the engineer replied. "I've never seen them in action, and I couldn't tell you when the last time was a Lakiam captain deployed any."

Grantz gazed at the closed hatch and shook his head. "As far as I'm concerned they can stay in there."

"What's wrong?" asked Andrew. "Afraid they might take your gold?"

Grantz only glared at Andrew and then turned away.

"What's back the other way?" asked Kurt. He was anxious to get to Engineering and see how the setup compared to the Star Cross.

The engineer hesitated with an unsure look on his face. "We're not supposed to go there."

"Why?" asked Kurt, growing instantly suspicious. Was there something in one of the compartments Lomatz didn't want them to see?

With a droop of his shoulders, the engineer replied, "It's the detention area for prisoners."

"Detention area," Kurt echoed, surprised. "Why shouldn't we go there? The detention area is empty."

"That's just it," replied the engineer, grimacing. "It's not."

Kurt thought the engineer was probably wishing Lomatz were here right now to explain this. "What to you mean?"

"Two detainees remain," the engineer continued, "until Lomatz determines what to do with them."

"I want to see them," Kurt demanded. He had a strong feeling he knew why the two were being held and he wanted to see if his suspicions were correct. If he was right, it would explain why Lomatz hadn't mentioned this before.

The engineer seemed to fidget. "Why don't I summon Lomatz, and he can clarify?"

"Why don't you?" Kurt said. "I think your boss has some serious explaining to do."

-

A short time later Lomatz arrived, and, from the look on his face, Kurt could tell the weapons dealer wasn't pleased about being here.

"Why did you bring them down here?" Lomatz demanded, glaring at the engineer. "You know this area is off-limits."

"They wanted to see the entire ship, and I was showing them where the combat robots are stored. I didn't know they would ask about the detention area."

"What are you hiding?" asked Kurt, expecting an answer from Lomatz.

With an exasperated sigh, Lomatz turned his attention to Kurt. "When my cargo ship found the Aurelia, we found two survivors from its crew. Normally any survivors would be taken back to Kubitz and held for ransom or sold in the slave markets. I kept these two in detention because, in this situation, neither of those two alternatives would work."

"Why not?" demanded Kurt, not caring where this conversation was going. He was reminded once more that, in many ways, Lomatz was a Profiteer.

"Because this is a Lakiam warship and not a cargo or passenger vessel," Lomatz replied. "This has never been done before, and I seriously doubt if the Lakiams would agree to us keeping their warships. If I were to release these two, and they return to Lakiam, there's a good chance—in just a few weeks—a Lakiam fleet would appear in the Newton System, demanding we return their vessels."

Kurt wondered just what Lomatz had gotten them into. From the meeting earlier, everything had seemed to be worked out, and there were no problems. Now, with the discovery of Lomatz's two captives, all of that had changed.

"I want to speak to them," Kurt said in a determined voice.

Lomatz looked as if he would object and then appeared to change his mind. "Follow me."

They went down a long corridor and came to another sealed hatch. Lomatz stepped forward and entered a pass code into the wall-mounted security pad. The large hatch instantly swung inward without making a sound.

Following Lomatz inside, Kurt marveled at how spotless everything was. A large desk was in the center with a single comfortable chair. Some type of security console was beside the desk, but, other than that, it looked like a normal room. The walls were a sterile white with bright lights in the ceiling. At the far end of the room were four metal doors with large windows in them.

"Those are the retention cells," said Lomatz, crossing his arms over his chest. "Go speak to the two Lakiams if you want. All I get from them is silence."

Kurt, Andrew, and Colonel Hayworth walked over to the nearer cell and looked in through the window. A tall Lakiam with bright blue eyes and golden hair sat in a comfortable chair, watching a viewscreen. The screen had some documentary playing which Kurt didn't even try to figure out.

"How do I speak to him?"

"Depress the green button next to the cell. It will allow for two-way communication," said Lomatz, stepping a little closer. "He won't say anything."

Kurt pressed the indicated button and then took a deep breath. "I'm Fleet Admiral Kurt Vickers, and I wish to speak to you about your current situation."

The Lakiam glanced in Kurt's direction and then turned back to the viewscreen, ignoring him.

"That's all he does," commented Lomatz, stepping up next to Kurt and peering in at his prisoner.

Kurt stepped over to the other cell, and his eyes widened. This cell contained a Lakiam female, and she was one of the most beautiful women he had ever seen. She was tall, well-proportioned, and her skin was unblemished with a golden tan. For a moment Kurt was too stunned to even speak.

"The Lakiams have advanced to the point where they use gene modification to ensure their children are born nearly perfect. All the Lakiam women are very similar. A few have been sold to serve in the pleasure houses on Kubitz, and they bring in a fortune in gold. Their services are in high demand, and it may take a year's advance notice to make an appointment with one."

Kurt shook his head. He disapproved of so much on Kubitz. The slave markets and pleasure houses were only two of them.

"I'd pay the price," commented Grantz who was staring at the women through the glass. "I've heard of these women before and they're proud and haughty."

Kurt frowned at Grantz, indicating for him to step back.

Grantz shrugged his shoulders and went to stand next to Andrew.

"Hello," Kurt said, after pressing the green button to allow for two-way communication. "I wish to speak to you about your current situation and possibly getting you back home."

The woman sat, reading a tablet. Her head turned toward Kurt, and her deep blue eyes seemed to study him for a moment.

"I don't mean you any harm, and I'm not the one who imprisoned you in this cell. You've been brought to my planet, and I wish to speak to you about the black ships."

"The black ships!" spat the women in anger, rising to her feet and throwing the small reading tablet across the room, where it shattered against the wall. "I don't know who you are, but when the black ships come here, you and your kind will die."

"I don't believe in an enemy that can't be defeated," answered Kurt, seeing the woman's anger. "If you're willing to talk to the leaders of my world, I can get you out of this cell."

"Then what? Will you sell me at the slave markets on Kubitz? I will not work in one of the planet's pleasure houses. I will die before I suffer such humiliation."

"No, you won't be sold," promised Kurt. "If you agree to speak to my people, you will be treated with the full decorum you deserve."

The woman stepped closer to the door where she could see Kurt better through the window. "I see the Profiteer standing by your side. Will he agree to what you just said?"

Kurt turned toward Lomatz, who had a disgusted look on his face. Lomatz reached forward and pressed the communications button so the Lakiam woman couldn't hear him speak. "Be wary of what she says," Lomatz cautioned. "The Lakiams have a very arrogant reputation toward races less developed than their own. She will try to manipulate you into doing what she desires."

Kurt nodded. "I'll take the risk. Now open the door."

"It's your world you're putting at risk." Lomatz quickly entered a security code into the small screen next to the door, and, with a clicking sound, it swung open.

"I'm Fleet Admiral Kurt Vickers and welcome to the Newton System."

The Lakiam woman stepped from the cell and looked around before her eyes focused on Kurt.

"I'm Mara Liam, the communications officer of the Lakiam battlecruiser Aurelia, which you have seized illegally. My people will not tolerate you taking one of our warships."

"That's debatable," Lomatz said. "Your ship was adrift, powerless, and in a field of wreckage. Under galactic salvage laws, such a ship can be taken and sold."

"Back to the planet it came from," responded Mara pointedly. "Where are we exactly? I've never heard of the Newton System."

"Out where your people will never find us," Lomatz said smugly.

Mara focused her attention back on Kurt. "If I tell you about the black ships, will you release me and let me return home?"

Kurt had the feeling this woman had another motive behind her question. "We'll talk about it. What can you tell me about the black ships or the Destroyers of Worlds?"

"Tarnth knows more about them than I do," Mara replied. "He recognized the ships as soon as we encountered them. He needs to be released as well."

"What does Tarnth do on this ship?"

"He's our tactical officer."

Kurt considered Mara's request. "If I agree to let him out, will the two of you promise not to try to escape or to contact your people until such time as I deem appropriate?"

"We're Lakiams," spoke Mara in a voice of superiority. "Acts of violence are distasteful to us. We will not attempt to escape or send a message to our fleet. However, I must warn you that we expect to be allowed to return home, or there will be severe consequences for your world."

"Very well," Kurt said. "Lomatz, let Tarnth out of his cell. I want to know what happened to them in their battle with the black ships and if they have any ideas on how to fight them."

Kurt just hoped this wasn't a mistake. The two Lakiams were probably much smarter than the people he normally dealt with. He would have to be extremely careful how he negotiated with the pair. It would also be wise for him to keep in mind the two Lakiams would have their own agenda and probably one not in the best interest of Newton.

Chapter Fourteen

High Profiteer Creed was growing impatient. Once more, his order for new ships had been denied. Creed wasn't certain what was going on, but the shipyards were operating around the clock as well as all the orbital construction facilities for defensive platforms. Something was in the air, and Creed suspected it was bad news. He wondered if some Profiteer had offended one of the Protector Worlds or, even worse, one of the lofty Enlightened Worlds. Great care had always been taken in raids not to risk the ire of either. While those worlds would endure the hijacking of an occasional cargo ship or even a passenger liner, they wouldn't tolerate anything beyond that.

"A lot of rumors are going around Kubitz," Second Profiteer Lantz said. "I've never seen it like this before."

Creed turned his attention to Lantz, who was well-known for his lavish spending at the capital's pleasure houses. Probably where he heard all these rumors.

"At least we've gotten all our ships repaired and updated," Creed said. It had cost 20 percent more than normal, but they were all done. "What are these rumors you've been hearing?" Creed knew Profiteers and other humanoids from across the galaxy could be found indulging in the wanton entertainment the numerous pleasure houses offered. With all the intoxicating drinks available, people might say things they normally would keep secret.

Lantz leaned closer to Creed, as if he didn't want the rest of the crew to hear. "Something's spooked the Protector Worlds. Of all the defensive platforms being built, many of them are being shipped out. Suddenly all the Protector Worlds and Enlightened Worlds are concerned about the defenses around their home planets. I was at the Haslen Pleasure House the other night, and I overheard two Profiteers from the Ormot clan, talking about some mysterious black ships which are attacking Enlightened World colonies."

"Plhtup!" swore High Profiteer Creed, shaking his head. "I don't believe any of those rumors about a mysterious ancient race wiping out entire Enlightened World colonies. If you ask me, some Protector World is just spreading those rumors to force the Enlightened Worlds to pay up more for their defense. It's good business strategy."

"I don't know," Lantz replied doubtfully, his eyes narrowing. "You've heard about all the meetings going on between the different worlds of the empire. Something's going on, and it's not good."

Creed went silent, lost in thought. Lantz was correct about that. A lot of secret meetings had been conducted on Marsten between various planetary leaders of the empire as well as some of the largest Profiteer clans. Something was definitely going on, and it was making people nervous. Creed shifted his eyes to the main viewscreen. It showed many more ships than normal. Even the tactical screen was full of ship icons. It seemed as if everyone had suddenly turned up at Kubitz, shopping for weapons.

"Ready my shuttle," ordered Creed, reaching a decision. "I'm going to Kubitz and meeting with Toblan. There has to be a way to get the ships I want."

Lantz looked long and hard at the High Profiteer. "Just be careful around Toblan. He may jack up the prices for the warships based on increased demand."

Creed didn't reply. Second Profiteer Lantz was concerned about too much of their credit reserves being spent on the new fleet. All Lantz wanted was enough credits for the pleasure houses and the women he had in his little menagerie. Creed was more interested in getting to Earth and stripping it of its remaining wealth. If he were successful, he would be set for life. Others could worry about this supposed threat from the mysterious black ships.

-

Later that afternoon High Profiteer Creed was in a noisy bar, waiting for Toblan to show up. The weapons dealer had insisted on meeting at this establishment near his place of business. Creed took a long drink of the strong alcoholic beverage he had ordered. It burned slightly going down, but it created a pleasant buzz in his head. The music in the bar was loud and the place was full of customers. Most were drinking, and some were watching the stage where several scantily clad women performed. One thing nearly everyone had in common were the sidearms strapped to their waists. Even the women in the bar were armed.

Watching the door, Creed saw Toblan enter, flanked by two guards. The weapons dealer didn't go anywhere without an armed escort.

Spotting High Profiteer Creed, Toblan made his way to his table. "I see you made it," said Toblan, taking a seat across from the Profiteer.

"Yeah," responded Creed, taking another long drink. Setting down his nearly empty glass, he looked at Toblan. "What's going on with my ship deal? Why am I getting the runaround?"

Toblan let out a deep sigh and shrugged his shoulders. "Ships are in high demand. Every world in the empire has placed orders for more warships. The demand is more than our shipyards can handle."

Creed leaned forward and slid an envelope across the table. Toblan picked it up and glanced inside at the thick wad of credit notes.

"I'll double that if you can get me the ships I want." Creed knew the fifty-thousand-credit bribe he had just given Toblan might be enough to push the weapons dealer into arranging for the ships. Bribes, sometimes very large bribes, were quite common on Kubitz, particularly with large business deals involving a lot of credits.

Toblan handed the envelope to one of his security people, who placed it in a secure pouch attached to his belt. "I might be able to do something," Toblan said slowly. "It will be expensive, and it won't be the ships you originally ordered."

"What type of ships can you get me and how much?" Creed knew, from the way Toblan was acting, this would be expensive.

Toblan reached into his pocket and removed a contract. "I took the liberty of drawing this up. The Profiteer world of Lumoz ordered some fully updated ships to add to its fleet. Unfortunately, due to a recent fine from the Controllers, they no longer have the credits to pay for the ships. They're currently in my possession, and I would be glad to turn them over to you if you're willing to pay a premium price."

Creed gritted his teeth, knowing he was about to be taken to the cleaners by the weapons dealer, but he was over a barrel with little he could do if he wanted the extra ships. "What type of ships and how much is this premium price?"

"I can get you six battlecruisers and ten escort cruisers for three hundred million credits."

Creeds eyes glowed red with anger. "That's nearly double the normal price!"

"Sorry," said Toblan, shrugging his shoulders. "That's the going rate. You can take it or leave it. Others are interested in the ships as well, but, due to our past relationship working out arms deals, I'm offering you first choice."

"What about a battleship as a new command ship?" Creed really wanted to move to a more powerful ship for his own protection. The last battle with Fleet Admiral Vickers had demonstrated very plainly he needed one.

Toblan shook his head. "I can't get one. Battleships are at a premium, and it will be months before one becomes available."

"I'll need some new cargo ships and detainee ships as well." Hopefully the modifications made to his ships would be sufficient. It was disappointing to hear a battleship wasn't available.

"Those I can get at the standard rate," Toblan answered as he called up some information on a hand computer pad. "They're not in very high demand at the moment."

After a few more minutes haggling over prices, Creed finally signed Toblan's contract. This would put a big dent in his credit reserves, but all would easily be replaced from the raid on Earth. When Second Profiteer Lantz heard how much the new ships cost, he would scream in disbelief. Creed could already hear Lantz lamenting how he couldn't go to the pleasure houses and how his reputation would suffer.

A commotion near the stage drew their attention. A large man stood up and slugged the man near him in the jaw, sending him flying backward, crashing to the floor. "I saw her first!" he yelled, pointing to one of the nearly naked women on the stage. "Stay away from her!"

The other man staggered back to his feet, drew his sidearm and promptly shot his attacker in the chest. The man fell to the floor, unmoving. "You can have her!" Holstering the gun, the shooter turned around and exited the bar.

Creed turned toward Toblan. Shooting incidents of this kind were quite common. The Enforcers would look into it, and fines would be assessed. The bar had security cameras, which would have recorded the incident. "How soon can you deliver the ships?"

"As soon as payment has been confirmed, they're yours," answered Toblan as several Enforcers entered the bar and walked over to the dead man.

"You'll have your credits tomorrow," promised Creed. He was still angry at the cost of the warships, but he could launch his attack on Earth much sooner. When he got back to the Ascendant Destruction, he would send some messages to several of the smaller Marsten Profiteer clans, which had shown an interest in the raid on Earth. He would also contact Dacroni Clan Leader Jarls. He had also expressed an interest and was willing to commit more of his ships to the attack. The mercenary was demanding payment up front for going on the raid as well as a percentage of the take. It would be expensive, but Creed needed Jarls's battleships.

-

Back on Earth, things were going very badly for President Mayfield. Thanks to Marlen Stroud and his cronies, the North American Union was reaching a crisis point over Newton's independence. Riots had happened in several cities, and online petitions for Mayfield's resignation had reached twenty million signatures. The Internet and other media platforms were full of rumors and false innuendoes.

"Both the European Union and the Russian Collective have recognized Newton's independence and signed trade deals," said Mayfield, speaking to the three men on the other side of his desk. "A number of other countries have followed suit. I don't think there's anything Marlen Stroud can do to reverse Newton's independence."

"No, there's not, and I think he accepts that," replied Raul Gutierrez. "He's just using the Newton issue to stoke the fire for your removal."

"What's the latest word on the Cabinet?" asked Mayfield, looking at Raul.

"Not good," Raul replied, his face showing concern. "Stroud's been picking up support as the public outrage over Newton's independence grows. He's pushing for a Cabinet vote to remove you from power for treason."

"Treason!" roared General Braid, his face turning red in anger. "How can granting Newton independence be considered treason? The man's mad."

"Several constitutional scholars have weighed in, supporting Stroud's accusations," Raul said. "I've used some of my connections, and Stroud may have bought their testimony."

"How many more votes does he need in the Cabinet before he can remove me from power?" Mayfield had hoped to buy a few more weeks or even several months' time before a vote was called. A lot of colonists wanted to go to Newton, and, once Stroud succeeded in taking the presidency away, all immigration would come to a screeching halt.

"One," Raul answered gravely. "There's a chance he may already have that vote. He met in private last night with Connie Saxon and had a long talk with her over dinner. I'm afraid she will be joining his side."

President Mayfield stood up and walked to the large window. He hadn't expected things to move so quickly. Newton didn't have enough colonists yet to fight a prolonged war against the mysterious black ships if it came to that. He watched for a moment as several cranes lifted steel beams into place on a building a few blocks away. He wished it were possible to speed up the construction. He would have liked to see Washington DC, returned to its former glory before he was removed from office.

"How long can we delay the vote?"

"Only a few days," Raul replied. "Once Stroud is confident he has the necessary votes, he'll call an emergency meeting of the Cabinet. It can be done without your presence. A vote of 'no confidence' will result in your immediate removal as president. The Cabinet will then vote to elect someone to finish out your term until new general elections can be held."

"One guess who that will be," muttered General Braid disgustedly. "This is Stroud's attempt at a legal coup."

President Mayfield left the window and sat back down behind his desk. "Admiral Tomalson, what will happen to the fleet if Marlen Stroud takes over as president of the North American Union?"

"He'll remove me immediately and put someone he can control in charge of the fleet. I'm afraid whoever he replaces me with won't understand the danger the Profiteers represent—and particularly those mysterious black ships. We'll be in a substantially weakened position to defend ourselves."

President Mayfield took a deep breath as he realized what needed to be done. "General Braid and Raul, I need you to leave the room so I can speak to Fleet Admiral Tomalson in private."

The two men stood up and left as instructed, leaving the president alone with the fleet admiral.

"I think we need to put our plan for Fort Knox into operation."

"If Stroud finds out what we've done, he'll hang both of us out to dry," answered Tomalson, his eyes watching the president. "We're talking about real treason here. If we're caught, he'll imprison both of us and throw away the key."

Mayfield shook his head. "Only me. Once Stroud succeeds in removing me from office, you're to take the Retribution and go to Newton along with the cargo ships." Mayfield pulled open a drawer in his desk and took out an envelope. "Inside are your official orders from me as president. It will protect you from any charges of treason Stroud may attempt to bring up. It states specifically that you were operating under my direct orders."

Tomalson took the envelope and put it in one of the pockets of his fleet uniform. "We'll need to move fast."

"General Braid has made sure the right people are at Fort Knox. They'll look the other way when your people arrive."

"Who knows what we're planning?"

"Just General Braid, you, me, and Major Aldrich."

"Who's Major Aldrich?"

"A Marine. He made many of the gold transfers to the Profiteers when they were on Earth. Once you send the signal, he'll ensure the right guards are at the facility. They'll let you and your people in, no questions asked."

Tomalson let out a deep breath. "I can't believe we're doing this. We're talking about stealing all the gold at Fort Knox."

"I would rather see that gold at Newton where Governor Spalding and Fleet Admiral Vickers can put it to good use. With Stroud in charge, it's only a matter of time before the Profiteers hit us again. He still doesn't see them as an actual threat."

"Kurt will try to stop them," Tomalson said knowingly. "Even with Stroud in charge, he'll come to Earth's defense."

"I know," answered Mayfield with a sigh. "But by then the gold may be gone. This way we keep it safe."

Tomalson stood up and saluted the president. "We'll set the operation up for tomorrow night. I'll get the gold safely to Newton." Tomalson turned and left the office, planning to immediately take a shuttle up to the Retribution.

As the door shut behind the fleet admiral, President Mayfield let out a deep and frustrated breath. In the last few weeks he felt as if he had aged one hundred years. It was a damn shame politics would send Earth back to the Stone Age. If the

Profiteers did return, as Fleet Admiral Vickers said they would, they might very well nuke the planet once again.

If they did, Mayfield didn't think the planet would recover. Unfortunately all Marlen Stroud was interested in was power. The lives of the people on the planet meant little to him. Mayfield firmly believed Stroud's lack of concern for the people of the North American Union would eventually be his undoing. Regrettably, by then, it might be too late for Earth.

-

Major Nathan Aldrich stood outside Fort Knox at the small military airfield that served the gold depository. It was just after midnight, and, looking up into the night sky, he saw the shapes of half a dozen large shuttles descending. Their engines were baffled to limit light, and they were running in stealth mode so their descent was nearly silent. The shuttles came down, making vertical landings.

A hatch on the nearest one opened, and a ramp slid down to touch the tarmac. From the hatch and along the ramp came a number of large trucks. The first truck pulled to a stop next to Aldrich.

"I'm Captain Latimer of the Retribution," said the Marine driving the vehicle. The Marine had his hand on his pistol as he waited for a response.

"Major Aldrich," Nathan replied. "Everything's been arranged. I have my Marines at the gate and posted at key positions inside. I've passed the word we're running a top secret security drill for tonight."

"Let's hope everything goes smoothly," the captain said. "Hop in and let's get this show on the road."

Stepping inside the truck, Nathan took his seat. "The main gate is shut, but it will be opened when we approach."

From within the six shuttles, a total of twenty-four large trucks headed up the road toward the gold depository. As they approached the main gate, the soldiers on guard duty opened it and saluted as the trucks drove by. As soon as the trucks were inside, the gates were shut, and the guards continued on as if nothing unusual had occurred.

Reaching the main loading entrance, the trucks came to a stop. Marines jumped out from the back of the vehicles and lowered ramps. Instantly small work robots emerged, pulling fully loaded antigravity sleds.

"Robots!" said Major Aldrich in surprise. He hadn't seen robots like these before.

"Yes, how else did you think we could move so much gold in six hours?"

Nathan nodded. "Follow me inside, and I'll clear the way to the vaults."

Entering Fort Knox, they went down a wide and long corridor. The gold depository had been remodeled a few years back for added security and to allow more gold to be stored in its vaults. They reached the first of four twenty-one-inch-thick heat-and-blast-resistant metal doors. Nathan stepped up to a glowing security panel and placed his hand in its center. After a moment the panel turned green, and then Nathan entered a security code. With a number of loud clicks, the massive door slid open.

"Three more," said Nathan, returning to Captain Latimer and indicating they could proceed forward.

As the Marines, robots, and antigravity sleds continued down the corridor, they passed several guard stations. The guards watched as everyone and everything passed but didn't say a word. These Marines had been handpicked by Major Aldrich. They were completely loyal to the major.

"I wonder what's going on?" asked Private Malone as he watched several small robots pass by, pulling an antigravity sled. The sleds reminded him of how the Profiteers transported the gold to their shuttles when they had been on Earth. Malone had been involved in several of those transactions.

"None of our business," replied Marine Corporal Lasher as the last robot and antigravity sled passed. "I trust the major, and I know when to keep my mouth shut."

"How do we enter this in the logs?"

"We don't," replied Corporal Lasher as he slid a miniaturized computer flash drive into his security console. The small flash drive would change the images on all the security cameras to show nothing unusual had occurred. It would also shut off all the alarms and motions sensors inside the vaults.

-

Major Aldrich watched with interest as the small work robots unloaded and loaded the antigravity sleds. A total of 380,000 four-hundred-ounce bars of gold were to be removed, nearly 150 million troy ounces. From the incoming loaded sleds, they took identical-looking bars to replace the ones they removed. The gold bars looked exactly the same and even had a small layer of gold on the outside. However, once past the outer layer, the rest of the bar wasn't gold but a specially created alloy, which weighed the same and had many similar characteristics.

If anyone looked at the bars or even picked one up, they wouldn't notice any difference. To find out the bars had been substituted, they would have to drill inside one. Care had even been taken to ensure the bars had the correct identification markings.

"How will you get all these gold bars to the Retribution?" asked Aldrich. He couldn't see how all this would be loaded on board the six shuttles, not unless they wanted to leave the trucks behind.

"We're not," replied Captain Latimer. "We have several small cargo ships on standby, and the first will land shortly. They also contain more of our fake gold. If everything goes as planned, we should be gone before the day-shift guards arrive."

Nathan nodded as he watched several of the small work robots pick up a pallet of gold and place it on one of the antigravity sleds. In its place, another pallet of fake gold was set down. "It's a good thing the nearby army post is mostly empty, with its soldiers sent to help in the rebuilding effort."

"Wouldn't matter," responded Captain Latimer. "Our stealth systems on the shuttles and the cargo ships make our vessels undetectable to Earth-bound detection systems."

-

For six hours the work proceeded at a frantic pace. The two cargo ships came down and landed next to the shuttles. Heavily loaded trucks made numerous trips to the airport and back to Fort Knox at a steady pace. Finally, just before the sun rose, the last truck delivered its load of gold to one of the cargo ships and then proceeded to a waiting shuttle.

"That's it," Major Aldrich said as he watched all the Marines board their respective vessels.

"Thanks for your help, Major," Captain Latimer said. "You have no idea how important this mission is."

"I suspect I do," answered Nathan. "If the rumors going around are true, and President Mayfield is removed from office, then this gold is better off somewhere else."

Nathan watched as Captain Latimer and the rest of his Marines boarded their respective vessels. Moments later the two cargo ships and the six shuttles rose straight up to vanish into the slowly lightening sky. Nathan would return to Fort Knox and double-check to ensure everything was as it needed to be. No one could suspect what had transpired here overnight. Nathan felt a little odd knowing he had just participated in the greatest theft in modern history.

-

A few hours later the day-shift guards reported. "How was the night shift?" one of them asked Marine Corporal Lasher.

"Just routine," Lasher replied with a yawn. "Had a security drill we ran last night, but, other than that, nothing exciting ever goes on around here. This has to be the most boring post of my career."

The corporal replacing him nodded. "That's why I like it. What could ever go wrong here?"

Lasher nodded, and then he and Private Malone left. A good meal and then some rest were in order.

Malone grinned at Lasher. "Like the corporal said, nothing of interest ever goes on around here."

Lasher nodded. "I wonder what they'll do with all that gold?"

"Take it someplace safe, I hope," Malone answered. "If the Profiteers come back, they're sure to hit this place first. I'm ready to leave this post."

"Me too," Lasher responded as they climbed into a jeep to make the short drive to the barracks. "I have a strong suspicion the major feels the same way."

As they drove off in the military jeep, behind them lay 150 million troy ounces of fake gold. President Mayfield and Fleet Admiral Tomalson had ensured the gold from the North American Union would never fall into the hands of the hated Profiteers. Instead it would go to where it could be put to the best use for both the people of Earth and Newton.

-

Fleet Admiral Tomalson had taken the Retribution and two battlecruisers far out into the Solar System. The three ships were just beyond the orbit of Neptune. He had left Earth orbit on a planned patrol of the outer system due to several unknown ship contacts picked up on the Retribution's long-range scanners. What no one knew but the command crew of the ship was that the sensor contacts were fake.

"Report!"

"All sensors are clear of unknown contacts," Lieutenant Bridgette Gaffney reported promptly. "The battlecruisers Swiftfire and Sturgeon have taken up flanking positions."

Admiral Tomalson nodded. All three ships had handpicked crews on board whose loyalty was beyond question. He had already made arrangements for the families of the three crews to be transferred quietly to Newton.

"The cargo fleet?"

"Just crossing Neptune's orbit. They should be here in another two hours."

Five cargo ships were under the protection of the battlecruiser Lexington. Tomalson had arranged for the families of those six vessels to be transferred to Newton as well.

"How soon before we depart the system?" asked Captain Lindsey Hastings, the Retribution's commanding officer.

Tomalson studied Lindsey. She was a young woman in her late twenties who had a knack for military strategy, particularly where starships were concerned. She also had a knockout figure, which helped to explain why she was such a strict disciplinarian.

"We'll wait until we hear the results of the Cabinet vote early tomorrow. As soon as it's been confirmed President Mayfield's been removed from office, we'll make the transition into hyperspace and proceed to Newton."

Lindsey let out a deep breath. "I can't believe so many people believe all the lies being spread. What happens when the truth finally comes out?"

Tomalson leaned back in his command chair, folding his arms across his chest. "By then it'll be too late. From Fleet Admiral Vickers's latest messages, the Profiteers are planning a massive attack against Earth. It could come within the next month."

Lindsey's face paled. "Will they nuke the planet again?"

"It's a distinct possibility." Tomalson looked toward the front of the Command Center at one of the large viewscreens. The battlecruiser Sturgeon could be seen against a background of unblinking stars.

"So what do we do now?"

Tomalson shifted his eyes back to Lindsey. "We wait. We'll know tomorrow what the decision is on President Mayfield." Tomalson didn't say it was already a foregone conclusion that Mayfield would be removed from office. At the last count Marlen Stroud had the votes to ensure the president's removal.

-

Early in the morning President Mayfield was in the large conference room where the Cabinet was meeting.

"We're here to vote on whether President Mayfield will continue on as the leader of our great country," announced Marlen Stroud, looking defiantly at Mayfield. "His lack of leadership during the Profiteer occupation which resulted in this planet being attacked with nuclear weapons, his reliance on Newton to save us, and the failure to require Newton to pay back all the gold and other treasure they spent without the express permission of this Cabinet are sufficient grounds for his removal."

"They had permission to spend that gold as they saw fit in order to free Earth," Mayfield said in a calm voice. "If not for Fleet Admiral Vickers and what he did, we would still be under the heels of the Profiteers."

"That's your opinion," Stroud said dismissively. "I think we could have negotiated with the Profiteers and perhaps given them enough gold and other valuables so they would have left us alone. The planet never would have been nuked! Tens of millions of people died due to your lack of leadership. That lack of leadership has further been demonstrated by your granting Newton its independence."

"Let's vote," demanded Dwight Michaels, the Secretary of the Treasury.

"I second the motion," said Andrew Sallow, the Secretary of Energy.

"All in favor of removing President Mayfield from office raise your hands," Stroud said, raising his own.

Eight hands were raised in favor of removal.

"Opposed."

Only Secretary of State Anne Roselin, Secretary of Defense General Braid, and Secretary of Homeland Security Raul Gutierrez raised their hands in opposition. Fleet Admiral Tomalson was on board the Retribution and wasn't present to vote.

"The motion is carried by a majority vote of the Cabinet," said Stroud, gazing at the president with a smirk. "Do you have anything to say?"

"No," replied Mayfield, disgusted with the proceedings. "You'll bring this country to ruin, and I want no part of it." With that Mayfield stood and walked from the conference room, not looking back.

General Braid stood up and laid a sheet of paper on the conference table in front of him. "This is my resignation, effective immediately. I'll have no part in what this Cabinet's doing. This country is a democracy, and you're violating our founding principles with this cowardly action."

"Same with me," Raul added as he laid down his own resignation on the table. "I want no part of any of this."

The two men turned and left the conference room without saying another word.

"Good riddance," Stroud said, pleased the two had resigned their posts. It made what he planned to do next much easier. "Now we need to pick a replacement for president, and we have two Cabinet positions that also need filling."

-

Later that afternoon Stroud sat in the president's office. He leaned back in his new chair, enjoying the feeling of power that was now his. He had won the nomination easily by a majority vote of the Cabinet. Since he was now in power, he fully intended to stay. It wouldn't be that hard to manipulate the general population to ensure he won the next election. He had also sent a message to the vice president demanding his immediate resignation. He would choose his own vice president, someone who would do whatever he demanded.

However, he had one other order of business he needed to take care of. Tomalson needed to be removed as fleet admiral, and someone more sympathetic to Stroud's own ideas put in charge. Once the former fleet admiral was safely on Earth, Stroud would have him arrested and eventually court-martialed for treason. It wouldn't be hard to trump up a few charges.

-

Fleet Admiral Tomalson read the latest messages from Earth. He still had a few friends in high places in the military, and they were recommending he leave immediately.

"Are all ships ready to make the jump into hyperspace?"

"Yes, Admiral," replied Captain Hastings. "Admiral, once we leave, there will be no coming back."

"I know," Tomalson said with a deep and regretful sigh. He had never imagined abandoning Earth. "We all know that, but it's not safe here for any of us. Give the order. We jump in ten minutes."

Tomalson leaned back in his command chair as he thought about the events of the last few years. So much had changed on Earth, and the knowledge of other humanoid races and even aliens had been a shock to most of the people on the planet.

Around him the command crew worked at their stations, preparing to jump the fleet into hyperspace. On the main viewscreen, a view of Earth appeared as seen from an orbiting satellite. Tomalson spent the next few minutes gazing at Earth and reflecting on what had occurred.

"Jump in ten seconds," Captain Hastings reported as she sat down in her command chair.

Tomalson felt the Retribution accelerate and make the jump into hyperspace. On the viewscreen, the image of Earth faded away, to be replaced by static. With an ache in his heart, Tomalson wondered if he would ever see the home planet again.

Chapter Fifteen

Prince Brollen waited patiently as the final repairs to the Scythe were completed. His report of the food species' possession of dark matter weapons had been received with annoyance by Prince Ortumad, who promptly sent one of the large intergalactic transport vessels to the Conclave Habitat to inform the Hive Queens of this disturbing and possibly dangerous information.

What will the Queens decide? asked Military Commander Mardok. *The harvesting of the food species in Galaxy X241 will be much more costly than we had originally estimated.*

Prince Brollen turned toward Mardok, his multifaceted eyes gazing at the military commander. *More ships will be sent, and the size of our harvesting fleets will be increased. The dark matter warheads are dangerous to our ships, but our weapons are still superior.*

Brollen knew food stocks were running dangerously low in the Vorn habitats, and, to avoid wholesale deletions of some caste members, this harvest had to occur. There wasn't time to turn to one of the other galaxies, which had been harvested in the past. Galaxy X241 had the abundant food species needed to sustain the Vorn race for the next several thousand years, until the next galaxy was ready to harvest.

Shifting his gaze to the forward viewscreens, Prince Brollen could see myriads of spindle-shaped cruisers in orbit around the dead planet. Six of the large intergalactic transport ships circled the planet as well.

We have sixteen motherships and four Collector Ships here, Mardok sent telepathically. *I am sure the other military commanders and princes are ready to harvest in earnest. Galaxy X241 is rich in food species and will provide valuable nutrients for our Queens and the rest of our species for many years to come.*

The food is good, agreed Prince Brollen. *We allowed this galaxy extra time to develop, and it has paid off. Our harvest ships will be full, and the Collector Ships will have much sorting to do. All the castes will eat well.*

He had kept a supply of samples from the different food species the Reaper had harvested. He had found several that were quite enjoyable. He had listed which species these had come from, and, when the opportunity arose, he planned on adding considerably to his private stock.

Alarms sounded, and Prince Brollen's twin antennae twitched at the noise. On the main sensor display, Vorn ships exited hyperspace.

Switching his gaze to one of the large viewscreens, he saw numerous intergalactic transport ships appearing and setting course for the planet.

Fourteen additional transport ships have exited hyperspace, Mardok reported excitedly as he studied the data on a computer screen. *They are loaded with more motherships, cruisers, and two more Collector Ships.*

It has been decided then, sent Prince Brollen confidently. *This is the beginning of our take-all harvesting force.*

Prince Lantoll, how soon will the Scythe be ready to leave the system on a harvesting mission? The Scythe was only four thousand kilometers away and within easy telepathic range.

Two more days and all the repairs will be finished, Lantoll replied instantly. *We are ready for the harvest.*

I expect we will leave this system shortly, so hurry your repairs. I intend for our fleet to lead in harvesting when compared to the others.

It will be done, Lantoll replied.

Prince Brollen was satisfied with Prince Lantoll's response. Brollen was a senior prince and the favorite of several Hive Queens as well as being in the court of Queen Alithe, the ruling Hive Queen. Brollen was high enough up the hierarchy that his orders would be obeyed. However, Prince Ortumad was even higher, and, with the newly arrived ships, there might be other high princes.

-

Captain Dreen of the Lakiam battlecruiser Basera was aboard his flagship after meeting with the fleet officers in charge of Lakiam's military. The officers had watched in horror as the videos from the battle over Visth Prime were played back in detail. The sheer power of the black ships' weapons was a shock. There had been a much-heated discussion on how best to defend the Enlightened Worlds, the Enlightened Worlds' colonies, as well as Lakiam's own systems. It had been a shock to realize there were not enough ships in the fleet to defend all the systems the Lakiams were responsible for. The Lakiams controlled thirty-two star systems and had large populations on sixteen habitable words, fourteen terraformed moons, with mining operations in all thirty-two systems. They were responsible for defending eighty-seven Enlightened civilizations. Those eighty-seven civilizations had over 1,400 colonies to protect as well.

"What is the decision?" asked Alborg, turning away from his tactical station where he had been running battle simulations. He was determined to find a better way to defeat the black ships.

Captain Dreen sat his seven-foot-tall frame in his command chair and let out a deep breath. "It's not good. The general consensus is we don't have enough warships to protect all the worlds we're responsible for."

"The Destroyers of Worlds are real," said Sheera Keenol, listening to several media stations on her comm station. "Scholars are searching the ancient archives for any information on past appearances. It seems they have made a number of visits to our galaxy over millions of years."

Dreen looked around the circular Command Center. He had everyone's attention. "It seems a couple worlds escaped the last appearance of the black ships. They have come forward with information about what we're up against."

"A Couple?" said Laylem from his sensor console. "Are you saying that only two worlds in the entire galaxy survived the black ships the last time they put in an appearance?"

"Two civilized worlds," Dreen clarified. "They were Protector Worlds at the time. After the black ships left, the two planets' civilizations collapsed. Their galactic wide economy was gone as well as all their colonies. It took them thousands of years to recover and venture back into space. They are now

Enlightened Worlds, and the black ship information was held in secret for fear of hampering this galaxy."

"I don't understand," said Sheera, looking confused. "Why keep the existence of the black ships a secret? If we had known, we could have prepared for their return."

"They were afraid of what that one fact would do to the new civilizations rising up across the galaxy. If the new spacefaring races knew of the black ships, there would be no striving for enlightenment. Instead all available resources would have been put into building warships and massive militaries in preparation for the next return of the Destroyers of Worlds."

Sheera shook her head in disbelief. "So they left us defenseless instead?"

"They thought they had made the right decision, and it was possible the black ships wouldn't return."

Alborg looked disgusted. "What do the black ships want?"

Captain Dreen looked gravely at his crew. "Food. They consider all higher life-forms a source of food."

Sheera's face turned a ghastly white in shock. "They want to eat us?"

"Not exactly," Dreen answered. "From what we've learned, they convert the organic compounds in our bodies into a food substance they can consume. By harvesting our galaxy, they can obtain enough food to last for thousands of years."

"That's what happened to Visth Prime and all the Enlightened World colonies that were stripped of life," said Laylem, looking ill. "They were turned into food. How will we stop them?"

"We don't know if we can," confessed Dreen, his eyes narrowing. "All the defensive grids around our main planets are being reinforced. The construction of dark matter missiles has been given a high priority. There's some talk about seeing if it's possible to increase the yield to one thousand megatons."

"A warhead like that could destroy a planet or, at the very least, knock it from its orbit," warned Alborg with a shake of his head. "The warheads are also difficult to produce and extremely expensive."

"Unfortunately it's the only weapon we have that seems to work against the black ships. We have to overload their shields with energy in order to cause any damage."

"What are our orders?" asked Sheera.

"Our fleet is being substantially reinforced, and we'll carry twice the black matter hypermissiles than we normally do. The plan is to find a black fleet and destroy it, which might buy us the time to finish fortifying our worlds and find a better weapon to use against the enemy."

Sheera looked at a viewscreen showing Lakiam. The planet was blue-white with several large oceans and three major landmasses, the home of the Lakiam race. "We can't save everything, can we?"

Captain Dreen slowly shook his head. "No, we'll suffer some losses, probably major ones."

What Dreen didn't tell his crew was that a victory over the black ships was considered essential. The survival of his fleet was a low priority if he could substantially damage or defeat the Destroyers of Worlds in battle.

-

Above Kubitz, High Profiteer Creed nodded in satisfaction. Four small Marsten Profiteer clans had agreed to provide ships for his raid against Earth. Dacroni Clan Leader Jarls had driven a hard bargain but, after negotiations were finished, had agreed to bring a substantial fleet of battleships on the venture. Creed was forced to put up twenty million credits as an advance payment to the Dacroni mercenary.

"The raid on Earth had better be profitable," muttered Second Profiteer Lantz. "You've spent nearly all of our credit reserves on this. If it fails, we'll be subject to the will of the Controllers for lack of funds to continue to operate our fleet."

High Profiteer Creed turned toward Lantz. The entire crew of his flagship was concerned over the credits Creed had spent. "We have our new ships, and our fleet is more powerful than ever before. The four clans, which have agreed to accompany us to Earth, have put up forty vessels. Along with Jarls's battleships, this raid is assured of success. Intelligence from our spies on Earth indicates a fracture in one of their leading governments. The escort cruiser Balisk just returned and reports only ten warships defend the planet—four battleships and six battlecruisers."

"Don't forget about Fleet Admiral Vickers."

"His ships won't matter," Creed responded, looking at Lantz. "Earth is far enough away from Newton that our battle and raid will be over before Vickers can respond." Even if Vickers did respond, Creed was certain he had the ships and firepower to defeat the aggravating fleet admiral once and for all.

-

Lantz nodded but didn't reply. He saw no point in angering the High Profiteer by reminding him they had lost nearly every battle that involved Fleet Admiral Vickers. If Vickers somehow reached Earth before the raid was over, it could change everything. If they returned from this raid with little or no gold, his days as a big player at the Kubitz pleasure houses would come to an abrupt end. Lantz had already decided he would go on one final spending spree before the fleet left on its raid.

-

Prince Brollen watched the main viewscreens of the Reaper as the ship dropped from hyperspace in its target system. For now the decision had been made to leave the primary worlds of the food species alone. They would harvest the colony worlds instead, which would still furnish a plentiful bounty for the Vorn race. By harvesting the colony worlds first, it would substantially weaken the primary worlds, making them more susceptible to Vorn attack and eventual harvesting.

All ships have exited hyperspace, reported Military Commander Mardok.

Prince Brollen nodded. His new fleet consisted of his own flagship, the Reaper, two other motherships, the Scythe and Hetel, and six hundred cruisers. The orders from the Hive

Queens had been very simple: harvest as many of the secondary worlds as possible, and then the entire Vorn fleet would move on the primary worlds of Galaxy X241.

-

The Vorn fleet entered the System of Ralla, a colony world of the Bollons, a race with a distinct avian heritage. They were warm-blooded with very short feathers covering their bodies. Their heads were humanoid, yet their mouths formed a beak but rounder than most avian species. The Bollons still possessed their wings and were capable of flight over short distances. They were an Enlightened Race and had been for over two hundred thousand years. The Bollons controlled twenty star systems with fourteen inhabited worlds, with a total population in excess of forty billion. Their cities consisted of extremely tall and slim towers that reached up into the clouds on their worlds.

The System of Ralla contained one habitable world with automated mining operations on several of the moons of the system. Four planets orbited the K-Class star with only a small asteroid field between the orbits of the third and fourth planets.

What's showing on our sensors? demanded Prince Brollen as he watched his fleet gather protectively around the three motherships. He was anxious to begin the harvest as he had not tasted this food species before.

Military Commander Mardok checked with several other Vorn in the Command Center before turning toward the prince. *We're not detecting any warships and only a small defensive grid surrounding the planet. A number of what appear to be cargo and passenger ships are in the system. Some are already jumping into hyperspace and fleeing. Our fleet must have been spotted.*

-

Undetected by the Vorn ships were the forty Dacroni battleships on the outskirts of the system, operating in full stealth mode.

"They're here," softly reported Raster, Clan Leader Masak's second in command.

Masak nodded as he stared at the numerous red threat icons in the tactical display. His face was similar to a Human's but rounder and chunkier. His neck was shorter with his head almost resting on his torso. Masak was dressed in dark gray battle armor, impervious to most weapons fire. His flagship, the Iron Victory, was the most modern battleship in the Gothan Empire. He had spared no expense to arm it with the most powerful weapons possible and an energy shield stronger than those possessed by other clans.

"This is a dangerous mission we're undertaking," said Raster as he adjusted a viewscreen and one of the spindle-shaped black ships appeared. They had seeded the system with small, inexpensive satellites, capable of transmitting a video feed over long distances. Several of them were in range of the recently arrived black fleet.

"We must know how big a danger these new aliens are," responded Masak. "The Profiteers, the Controllers, and all the great clans grow more worried about what these invaders may mean to our profits. Already many clans refuse to leave the empire on raids for fear of leading this new enemy back to our worlds."

Raster gestured toward the viewscreen, showing the spindle-shaped black ship. "At least we know they're real."

"Yes," said Masak, standing up and striding over to the viewscreen to look more closely at it. "But where did they come from? Look at that fleet! Over six hundred vessels, and three of them are larger than anything we've ever seen before."

"Rumors are flying around Kubitz how these are the ancient Destroyers of Worlds," Raster informed Masak. "A lot of loose tongues at the pleasure houses tell the tale and even a few reports about raiding parties encountering fleets of these vessels. Entire fleets of raiders in several instances have failed to return home after traveling to Enlightened World colonies to pick off a cargo ship or take over a passenger liner."

"That's why we're here," Masak said as he turned and went back to his command chair. "We've been paid a handsome sum to test the strength of our battleships against these black ships. Nearly all their vessels are of cruiser size and should be no match for our warships."

"But the Protector Worlds have engaged the black ships and reportedly been defeated in every instance," protested Raster with deep concern. "What can we hope to do against these vessels?"

"Plhtup!" roared Masak, his face showing anger. "What do the Protector Worlds know of war? Most of their captains have never been tested in battle. I believe that lack of experience led to their defeats. All our ships are battle-tested, and we have experienced crews. We will show these black ships the Dacroni mercenaries are not to be trifled with."

Masak felt confident in his words. He and his fleet had been sent here to assess the danger posed by the black ships, and to gather information on their weapons and battle tactics. The only way to do that was in combat mode. Masak intended to jump in, engage the enemy, gather the necessary information, and then, if the battle went poorly, he would jump his fleet back into the safety of hyperspace and return to the Gothan Empire.

"Enemy fleet is inbound toward Ralla," reported the sensor operator. "They're not in any hurry. It will take them nearly two hours to reach the planet."

"The planet has a small defense grid," reported Raster as he studied the information they had on the system. "It has a few Class Two Defense Platforms and less than twenty orbital dual-energy cannon satellites. Everything is controlled from the ground."

"I'm picking up messages from Ralla being broadcast to the black fleet," reported the communications officer. "The planet is offering to surrender if the black fleet will promise not to bombard the surface."

"Is there any response from the enemy fleet?"

The communications officer listened for a few moments and then shook his head. "No, there's no response at all. I can't pick up any type of communication signals between the black ships. It's as if they're not communicating at all."

"That's preposterous," said Raster in disbelief. "Some communication must go on between their warships. How else can they adjust their strategy in battle?"

The communications officer shook his head. "It's possible they're using some form of communication we're not familiar with."

The lack of communication between the black ships bothered Clan Leader Masak. It was inexplicable. "We'll wait until the enemy engages the defensive grid around Ralla and then jump in behind them. All ships will open fire with every weapon as soon as they exit hyperspace."

"We have two hours then," muttered Raster as he settled down to wait.

-

The Vorn fleet continued to close with the planet Ralla. All across the star system, various cargo ships, mining ships, and passenger liners fled in panic as they heard reports of the black ships' presence. The ships had been detected visually on several satellites as well as the orbital astronomical stations above Ralla. From Ralla the message was plain and simple: flee now; spread the word of the presence of the black ships, and ask all available Protector World ships to come to our aid before it's too late.

On the planet's surface, alarm and panic spread. From the tall city towers, citizens stepped off balconies, spreading their wings and fleeing into the countryside. Many headed toward the distant mountains, hoping to take refuge in the huge aviaries that had sheltered their race in the distant past.

The government continued to broadcast their willingness to surrender, but it fell on deaf ears as the black ships refused to respond. In the government communications center, which maintained FTL communications with thousands of worlds, there were no incoming messages. All communications had been cut off. The Rallians responsible for governing their world knew doom was in front of them. There would be no escape from the black ships, and very soon the world of Ralla would join the growing list of dead and destroyed Enlightened World colonies.

-

Prince Brollen watched the viewscreens with anticipation as the Reaper and her attending fleet steadily drew closer to their target world. An avian species was not often found that was civilized enough to be harvested.

Only light defenses surround their world, Military Commander Mardok reported as he readied the fleet to attack.

On one of the viewscreens, a large defensive platform appeared. Even as Prince Brollen watched, several energy projectors fired upon his ships. He was not concerned as he knew the energy would only be absorbed by his fleet's defensive shields.

Destroy their orbital defenses as well as all structures around the planet, sent Prince Brollen. In orbit above the planet were a large number of structures. Prince Brollen knew some of these would be shipyards, others research stations, and even a few were artificial habitats. It was standard procedure for the Vorn to wipe out all visages of a civilization.

Suddenly alarms sounded, and the crew tensed up. On the main tactical display, large red threat icons appeared behind the fleet.

What are those? demanded Prince Brollen. These ships had not been detected by the mothership's sensors.

Unknown vessels, Military Commander Mardok responded as he checked the ship's sensors. *They're firing on us.*

-

The forty Dacroni battleships opened fire with their energy projectors, direct energy cannons, and their powerful sublight antimatter missiles. Fifty-megaton antimatter missiles struck the shields of the black ships, releasing torrents of deadly energy. Across the black fleet, massive explosions washed across their energy screens as thousands of megatons of antimatter energy was released. While the amount of energy released was huge, the shields of the black ships drank it up as if it were nothing.

-

"We're not causing any damage!" gasped Raster, his eyes opening wide in disbelief. "It's as if the energy from our weapons is being absorbed by their defensive screens."

Clan Leader Masak leaned forward in his command chair. He hadn't expected their weapons to be so ineffective. "Have all ships switch to targeting just one ship. We must know if we can knock down their shields." If they couldn't at least inflict some damage, this would be devastating news to the Gothan Empire and all the Profiteer clans.

"New target located, and coordinates sent to all ships," replied the tactical officer. "I'm ordering a full spread of antimatter missiles fired, followed up by a complete barrage from the fleet's direct energy cannons."

Masak gazed at the ship's primary viewscreen, which was focused on the target. He held his breath, waiting for the first antimatter missiles to strike. Suddenly the screen flared up with brilliance as the spindle-shaped cruiser seemed to vanish under the tremendous amounts of energy released by two hundred antimatter warheads. As the energy faded away, Masak was astounded to see the ship was still there, though its energy screen glowed brightly. A direct energy beam struck the dark ship's screen, and then dozens more, until all forty Dacroni battleships were pouring every erg of power available into the beams. The shield flared brighter, and then suddenly it seemed to shatter. A massive explosion lit up space as the energy held in the screen was released, obliterating the black ship and leaving behind nothing but a drifting cloud of glowing gas.

"We got it!" roared Raster, his eyes glowing with satisfaction.

"Enemy is firing!" reported the Dacroni at the sensor console. "It's some type of black energy sphere."

"All ships jump into hyperspace immediately!" ordered Clan Leader Masak. He had heard rumors about this weapon. If it struck any of his ships, they were dead.

The Dacroni ships rapidly reversed course, but, for many of the battleships, it was too late. The spheres of black antimatter accelerated too fast for the ships to escape into hyperspace. Fourteen Dacroni battleships were struck by the deadly spheres. The spheres spread out across the ships' screens, absorbing the energy and then attaching to the armored hulls of the ships themselves. In just moments fourteen deadly warships were drifting powerless in space. From the black ships, hatches slid open, and small antimatter missiles flew out to strike the helpless vessels. In brilliant explosions the ships died, leaving behind shattered wreckage and wisps of glowing plasma.

-

The enemy fleet has withdrawn, Military Commander Mardok reported. He was aggravated that another Vorn warship had been destroyed. *We destroyed fourteen of their vessels before they fled into hyperspace.*

The food species of this galaxy are learning fast, sent Prince Brollen as he gazed at the glowing wreckage on the viewscreens. *Finish the destruction of the planet's orbital infrastructure. I grow impatient to taste this new food species.*

-

In hyperspace, Clan Leader Masak stared in shock at the long-range sensors showing his ships. Fourteen of his valuable battleships were missing.

"Destroyed in less than a minute!" said Raster, his eyes wide open in shock and disbelief. "How can that be?"

"We face an old and ancient race," replied Masak, settling back in his command chair. "Their weapons are far superior to our own."

"At least we know they can be destroyed."

"Yes, but at what cost? It would take nearly every ship possessed by all the Profiteer clans as well as our own to stop a fleet the size we saw back in the Ralla System. What if they attack with two or three fleets of that size?"

Raster remained quiet as he thought over the significance of those words.

Masak knew this information would not be well received by the Gothan Empire. Only the main worlds of the empire and the strongest clans knew of this new danger. He didn't know if it would even be possible to get the entire empire to work together for its common defense. The Controllers and the desire for credits held the Gothan Empire together. This was something else entirely. He had a nagging worry that the way of life in the empire was about to change and not for the better.

Chapter Sixteen

Kurt was at his sister's along with Keera. It had been an exhausting two weeks with both Mara and Tarnth refusing to cooperate with the Newton government. Both had demanded they be allowed to return home immediately. Until that demand was guaranteed, there would be no discussions on the Destroyers of Worlds or of the Aurelia. This was different from what Mara had agreed to earlier, and Kurt strongly suspected it was due to her speaking with Tarnth. After an argument with Lomatz, Kurt had confined the two to their personal quarters on the Lakiam ship. Lomatz had wanted to put them back in detention.

"So you have an alien battleship," stated Bryan from across the dinner table where they all sat. "Are you learning to fly it so you can kill a lot of the bad aliens?"

Kurt laughed. Bryan had such a simple way of putting things. "We're still learning. It's a big ship and much different than what we're used to."

"Can you take me to see it?" asked Bryan, his face lighting up with excitement. "I bet I could learn to fly it. There's bound to be some buttons to push to make it go."

Keera gave Bryan a gentle smile. "We all wish it was that simple. But there's a lot more involved with flying a spaceship than just pressing buttons."

"But you have the alien woman to teach you," said Bryan, looking confused. "Why won't she help?"

"She's not like us," explained Alex, reaching for the gravy to pour over his mashed potatoes.

Denise looked at her husband and Bryan, who was sitting next to him. "Your father's right. Not all people are like us. I'm sure, after a while, she'll come around and help Uncle Kurt with the ship."

"Do you really need her?" asked Alex, shifting his attention back to Kurt. "I thought Lomatz's people knew how to operate the Lakiam vessel."

Kurt let out a deep sigh. "It would make everything a lot easier. The engineers and technicians Lomatz brought know a lot. However, none of them have ever operated a warship like the Aurelia. I have a crew on board that's working on learning everything they can teach them, but it's not the same as having an experienced crewmember explaining and demonstrating how all the controls work. We have no idea what some controls on the panels do."

Denise spoke to Keera. "You're more familiar with these types of people. Didn't you do your medical training on an Enlightened World?"

"Yes, Karash," answered Keera. "The Lakiams are a very proud people and well on their way to Enlightenment. As a result, they have become arrogant and look down on people less civilized than they are. I can talk to her, but I don't know if it will do any good."

"What about this Tarnth fellow?" asked Alex. "Would he be any easier to speak with?"

"I doubt it," Keera answered, frowning. "Our best shot would be with Mara. She's more likely to listen to reason than Tarnth will."

Kurt focused on his plate, stirring his mashed potatoes with his fork. Fleet Admiral Tomalson had arrived from Earth with a fortune in gold. After what they had agreed to pay Lomatz for the new defensive system, the additional gold had replenished their gold reserves plus much more. Tomalson had been stunned when Kurt took him on board the Aurelia for a tour.

Kurt had another meeting with Tomalson scheduled on the Star Cross to discuss the upcoming Profiteer attack on Earth. When the passenger liner returned—carrying the crews from the two cargo ships captured by the Tellurites—Marvin Tenner had also sent word that the Profiteer attack could happen any day. The Human crews had already been sent back to Earth. Kurt was certain their harrowing story of what had happened to them would ensure there would be no more ships heading toward the Gothan Empire for quite some time.

"What does this alien lady look like?" asked Bryan. "Does she have wings?"

Kurt laughed. Bryan always asked about winged aliens. Keera had told him there were some on a few distant worlds. "No, not Mara. She looks very Human."

"She's extremely beautiful," said Keera, glancing at Kurt meaningfully. "The Lakiams use genetic manipulation to ensure their bodies are perfect. Mara is nearly seven feet tall and has deep blue eyes. She also has golden hair."

"What's genetic manipulation?" asked Bryan, carefully pronouncing the words.

"You'll learn about that when you get older," Denise said.

"It's an adult thing then," said Bryan, nodding his head in understanding.

They were interrupted by Keera's cell phone ringing. Frowning, she answered it, and then a very upset look swept across her face.

"What is it?" asked Denise, sensing something was wrong.

"It's my brother," Keera said in an exasperated voice. "He's been arrested."

"Arrested!" Alex said. "For what?"

"What else?" responded Keera, anger spreading across her face. "He was setting up a black market to sell stolen information."

"How the hell did he get involved in something like that?" asked Kurt, frowning. "He's working with construction robots."

Keera stood up, looking at Kurt. "We'll find out when we talk to him. Meesa is down at the main police station, waiting for us."

Kurt let out a deep breath. Police stations on Newton very seldom had to deal with crime. They spent most of their time making sure nothing illegal came in from Earth on all the cargo and passenger ships going back and forth. They also helped explain to new colonists the laws on Newton and occasionally issued fines for minor violations.

"Is Uncle Dalen in jail?" asked Bryan, his eyes growing very large at the thought.

"No," Denise said, shaking her head. Bryan started calling Dalen his uncle as soon as he learned Kurt and Keera were living together. "He's just in a little bit of trouble. Uncle Kurt and Aunt Keera will take care of it."

"Good," said Bryan. "I like Uncle Dalen. He's a lot of fun and a good ballplayer. Maybe they can just put him in a time-out."

-

It only took a few minutes to drive to the main police station, a tall building that dealt in law enforcement as well as indoctrinating new colonists into life on Newton. Inside, they were ushered into a waiting room where a nervous Meesa sat, her hands clasped tightly together.

"Keera!" she cried out, standing up and rushing to hug her. "I'm so glad you could come. I don't know what to do. The police here aren't like the Enforcers back on Kubitz. On Kubitz you would just pay a fine, and that would be all."

Keera nodded her understanding. "I told you and Dalen everything's different here. What's he done now?"

"I'm not sure," Meesa replied. "He's been coming home late, and all he would ever say was he was working overtime."

An officer walked in and paused, waiting for Kurt to acknowledge him. After all, Kurt was the fleet admiral.

"What are the charges against Dalen Jelk?" Kurt was anxious to find out how much trouble Dalen was in. Meesa was highly upset, and he knew Keera was as well.

"He's been taking apart the small work robots he's in charge of. He's been building some high-tech devices that allow you to spy on people kilometers away. We found out about it when some local businessmen complained about some of their trade secrets being stolen and offered for sale."

"Snoopers," commented Keera in disgust. "He's built snoopers to spy on people."

"What are snoopers?" asked Kurt. This was something he had never heard of.

"They're small flying robots a little larger than your thumb. They're highly complicated, but they can record sound and video. They're widely used on Kubitz to spy on everyone and everything."

Kurt wished Keera had mentioned this before. He would have to warn Marvin Tenner about this and have him take some additional security precautions at the compound on Kubitz. "What do we need to do to get him released?"

"I can release him into your custody," the officer replied. "If you will just sign a few forms, he can go home with you now."

"How serious are the charges?" asked Keera. The legal system on Newton was just as confusing to her as the one on Kubitz.

"I think I can arrange for all the charges to be dropped," the officer replied. "But if this happens again, he could lose his colonist status."

"What would that mean?" asked Meesa worriedly.

"He would have to go back to Kubitz," answered Kurt. He didn't want that to happen. Keera had been happy with Dalen safely on Newton and supposedly working a decent job. Kurt knew the only way to fix this was to have a heart-to-heart talk with Dalen. He would also assign a security guard to watch Dalen for a few days to help stress how serious he was. Perhaps if he put a scare into the man, it would force him to straighten up.

After signing some papers, the officer brought a quiet Dalen to them.

"Dalen!" said Keera, her eyes looking stormy. "What did I warn you about? How could you do something like this?"

"I'm sorry," answered Dalen, looking nervously at Kurt. "I didn't think this was that big of a deal. It's standard business practice back on Kubitz."

"This isn't Kubitz!" Keera said angrily, her hands on her hips and her eyes focused so intently on her brother that he had to turn away. "If you do anything like this again, you'll be returned to Kubitz!"

Dalen turned pale at hearing this. "It won't happen again," he promised, looking pleadingly at Meesa, who had tears in her eyes. "I'll do whatever it takes to stay here on Newton and keep Meesa safe."

Kurt nodded. "Walk with me, Dalen. We'll have a little man-to-man talk."

Meesa watched as the two men went through the exit. "What'll happen? What's Kurt going to do?"

Keera allowed herself to smile. She could just imagine what Kurt was saying to Dalen. If anyone could force Dalen to change his path in life, it was Kurt. "Don't worry. I suspect everything will be fine. We'll give the men a few minutes and then go join them."

"Thank you, Keera," Meesa said. "You've been so helpful since we came to Kubitz. I don't know what I can do to ever repay you."

"Just keep my brother happy," Keera replied. "And, if you ever suspect he's up to something illegal, call me immediately, and I'll come over and kick his butt."

"I will," promised Meesa, her eyes wide. "I won't let anything like this happen again."

Keera nodded. She hoped not. Her life on Newton was exciting enough without her brother causing problems.

-

The next day Kurt was aboard the Star Cross, meeting with Fleet Admiral Tomalson, Rear Admiral Jacob Wilson, Rear Admiral Susan White, Colonel Simms, and Colonel Hayworth. Admiral White had just returned with the Ranger from the Julbian System after being relieved by the light carriers Wasp and Ticonderoga.

"I just toured the Aurelia," commented Susan with a look of amazement in her eyes. "I can't believe such a ship exists."

"It's real," Kurt replied. "As well as the other five Protector World ships Lomatz has made available to us."

Colonel Hayworth only shook his head. "They're wonderful warships if we can figure out how to run them. We've spent days training people on the Aurelia, and I would still be afraid to even move her out of orbit without Lomatz's technicians assisting."

"It's that complicated?" asked Rear Admiral Wilson, looking at Kurt. Wilson's flagship was the heavy carrier, Kepler.

"It's not that it's so complicated. The entire ship is almost completely automated. We're still figuring out what some of the controls on the main consoles do. You can push a button or touch a computer icon on one of the screens, and nothing happens."

"Is there any chance the two Lakiams will cooperate and show us how to operate their ships?" asked Fleet Admiral Tomalson. Since coming to Newton, he had been amazed by everything he had seen.

"We're still working on that," Kurt answered. "Colonel Simms, how's installation of the new defensive platforms and command station going?" Kurt was anxious to get them operational as it would make Newton impervious to any attack except from the black ships.

Colonel Simms stood up and walked to a viewscreen. Activating it, a huge defensive platform appeared. The platform was two hundred meters across and forty meters thick. On top sat a pair of massive ion cannons, four direct energy cannons, and eight large energy projectors. Six pods contained eight hypermissiles with an automatic reloading system. Everything was computer-controlled, and a crew of twelve could operate the entire platform.

"With the help of Lomatz's ships we've installed sixteen platforms. We estimate it will take another three weeks to have the rest up and operational. The Command and Control Station is already being worked on and should be fully functional when the last defense platform goes online."

"That's good news," said Kurt, pleased with the progress. "In the contract we signed on Kubitz a while back, Lomatz included two regions of space. Do we know what's there?" Two light cruisers had been sent out to investigate both regions and were due back any day. After speaking with Lomatz, Kurt was highly curious as to what was in the two regions of space.

"We do," Rear Admiral Wilson said, laying his right hand palm down on the table. "The light cruisers Crescent and Olympia returned today from surveying both regions. The regions only contain about twenty stars each, but what they found is exciting. Two inhabited worlds of humanoids who are at approximately the same technological level as the Julbians. They've only just begun to explore the stars around their systems."

Kurt leaned back, staring incredibly at Rear Admiral Wilson. "Are you telling me that we could form an alliance with two more systems which the Profiteers don't know anything about?" No wonder Lomatz had hinted that Kurt would be highly pleased with what was in the two mysterious sectors.

"It seems that way," Wilson replied. "I would recommend we get a diplomatic mission on the way to both immediately."

Kurt nodded his agreement. "Gather all the information from the mission and condense it into something I can show Governor Spalding. I want to move quickly on this."

"What about the Profiteer attack on Earth?" asked Fleet Admiral Tomalson. "With Marlen Stroud in charge, anything could happen. I would also like to know what happened to President Mayfield and General Braid."

"As do I," Kurt responded.

He was worried Stroud might have had them arrested or something worse. Since Stroud had taken over the North American Union, all trade and immigration had been cut off. Still some trade and even colonists continued to come from other countries, but the flow had been drastically reduced compared to what it had been. Stroud had even threatened to use his remaining warships to destroy any Newton ship that entered the Solar System.

Kurt looked back at Colonel Simms. "How's progress on the new construction bay Lomatz promised us?"

"On schedule," answered Simms. "Just watching how Lomatz's people work is astonishing. They have robots that can do about anything. I was amazed at how quickly they finished up the station last year, but this is something else entirely. Lomatz has offered to keep the two construction ships here permanently to help us add anything to the station we want."

"Any ideas?" Kurt was curious to hear what Simms would like to see done to the shipyard.

Simms took a deep breath and then spoke. "If this menace from the black ships is real—and, as frightened as Lomatz seems to be, I'd say that it is—I want to add two more repair bays. The bays will be built to handle civilian craft arriving from the Solar System as well as elsewhere. In the future, we may have a lot of ships that need repair work done, and we must do it as rapidly as possible. I've already talked part of this over with Colonel Hayworth, and he agrees with what I've outlined. There may be other recommendations later."

Kurt looked slowly around the group. There was another reason for this meeting, and it was the most important one. "We have to assume the Profiteers will hit Earth within the next month. From what we've been able to learn, High Profiteer Creed has enlisted at least four other small Profiteer clans to assist him in the raid. Also rumors on Kubitz claim that Dacroni Clan Leader Jarls will be involved as well."

"That's bad," Rear Admiral Wilson said, his eyes narrowing sharply. "Jarls will bring battleships, and, after what happened to him in the last battle in Earth's solar system, he'll bring enough to ensure we don't get another chance to damage his fleet."

"What will we do?" asked Fleet Admiral Tomalson, shifting his gaze over to Kurt. "Even though Marlen Stroud is the new president of the North American Union, I don't want to see Earth hurt more than it already is."

Kurt looked at Tomalson and then replied. "You will take a fleet to Proxima Centauri. That's close enough that our long-range hyperspace sensors will detect any ships entering or leaving the Solar System. Your battleship, the Retribution, will act as flagship and all three of your battlecruisers will go as well. In addition, Rear Admiral Wilson will be under your command. He will have his flagship, the heavy carrier Kepler, the battlecruisers Carlsbad and Far Star, the light carrier Princeton, as well as four light cruisers as escorts."

Fleet Admiral Tomalson nodded as he thought about the firepower on the ships being placed under his command. "What are our orders?"

"If the Profiteers show up with a fleet too large for you to handle, send back one of the light cruisers. Hopefully by then we'll have the Aurelia up and running."

"You think High Profiteer Creed will hit Earth with a massive fleet," Tomalson said in understanding. "That's why you're not sending more ships."

Kurt nodded. "I'm afraid so. With the potential threat from the black ships, we can't afford large ship losses at the moment. Lomatz has indicated it won't be possible to purchase additional warships from Kubitz. Everything they're building is for their own defense against the black ships. They're not selling anything to anyone."

"When do we leave?" asked Fleet Admiral Tomalson.

"Two days," Kurt replied. "Your main duty is to preserve your fleet. I know how badly we all hate the Profiteers for what they did to Earth, but, if we fight them, I want to be able to win, and, for that, we need the Aurelia." Kurt was determined to speak to Mara one more time. Keera was also going to meet with her, and Kurt hoped she would have some success in encouraging Mara to help them. If she didn't, Kurt had one more card to play, and that one might just work but it was one he didn't like. If Mara continued to refuse to cooperate, she and Tarnth would be put back in the detention cells on board the Aurelia until the menace posed by the Profiteers and the black ships was over. Kurt had no intention of actually doing that, but perhaps just the threat would be enough to persuade Mara to cooperate.

-

Keera was on board the Lakiam ship. The luxury and comfort of the ship didn't surprise her as she had been on Enlightened World vessels in the past while attending medical training on the Enlightened World of Karash. She knew how Enlightened civilizations acted, but Mara was from a Protector World, a planet thousands of years away from achieving enlightenment.

Identifying herself to the two Marines at the door to Mara's quarters, Keera was allowed in, after introducing herself to the Lakiam woman over the comm.

Stepping inside, Keera allowed her senses to take in all the comfort and extras in the room. A short hallway with several other open doors was to her right. Mara's quarters were very spacious, which Keera had expected.

Mara's eyes examined Keera for a moment, and then she spoke. "Why have you come? I've already told your people that I will not help them until they can guarantee I will be allowed to go home."

Keera sat down across from Mara, almost jumping as the chair adjusted itself to her form. She had forgotten what real comfort was. "I'm not from here nor am I a member of this species of humanoids. I was trained in medicine at the medical training center on the Enlightened World of Karash."

"But you are not Enlightened," Mara stated critically. "Many humanoids and members of other species travel to the Enlightened Worlds for training."

"Yes, that's true," confessed Keera. "But the people of Newton are so different from others I've met in my medical career. I worked at the Hatheen Medical Facility on Kubitz for a number of years."

"Kubitz!" spat Mara, her blue eyes narrowing. "Why would you go there?"

"It offered me the opportunity to treat members of many different humanoid races as well as alien ones."

"A noble gesture," admitted Mara, showing a little respect. "Why did you come here?"

"I met a man who was everything I had always dreamed of. I fell in love and came here to Newton. I never expected to find such a world, where civilians don't need a weapon to protect themselves. The streets are safe to walk without an escort, and children play in the yards and numerous parks in their cities. If not for the Profiteers, the people of Newton would be a peaceful civilization."

"The Profiteers," repeated Mara, frowning. "What does this have to do with the Profiteers?"

-

For the next hour Keera explained to Mara what the Profiteers had done to Earth and how Fleet Admiral Vickers did everything in his power to drive them from the Solar System. When Keera was done, Mara had a thoughtful look on her face.

"I'm willing to admit Fleet Admiral Vickers sounds like an honest and trustworthy individual from what you've just said. However, the facts are that I'm being held against my will, and the arms dealer Lomatz is here. I don't like that connection to Kubitz."

Keera took a deep breath. "Lomatz is here because of the black ships."

"The black ships," said Mara, leaning forward, wanting to hear more. "Tell me how the black ships are involved."

-

Several hours later Kurt was in Mara's quarters, ready to plead his case once more. He had already decided, if she refused to help them, he would arrange for her safe return to her home world.

"The Profiteers are preparing to attack Earth," he said without preamble. "They've gathered a massive fleet to take all the planet's wealth and kidnap a large number of its inhabitants to be sold at the Kubitz slave markets."

Mara stood up, towering over Kurt. "You don't have the ships to stop this attack?"

"I have the ships, but I will lose many of them in the battle." Kurt took a deep breath. Keera had told him that she thought her conversation with Mara had been positive. Now he just needed to build on that, perhaps it wouldn't be necessary to threaten Mara with detention. "If you agree to help me save my home planet from the Profiteers, I will see to it that you're returned to Lakiam."

"What about the Aurelia and the Treliid? Will you release them to me as well?"

"I don't know," Kurt answered honestly. "Everyone says the black ships are coming. The technology on your two warships is the only chance we have of keeping our people safe from the Destroyers of Worlds."

"You seem to know a lot about the black ships," Mara commented.

"I have my sources," admitted Kurt. "Will you help us against the Profiteers?"

Mara looked long and hard at Kurt. "If I agree, how do I know you'll keep your promise to free Tarnth and me afterward?"

"I'm the fleet admiral, and I don't go back on my word."

"You're also the man Keera talked about earlier," Mara said with a slow nod of her head. "I can see why she feels as she does." Mara leaned back in her chair, her eyes focused on Kurt. "Have your people ready in the morning. I'll speak to Tarnth, and we'll show you how to operate the Aurelia."

"What about the Treliid?"

"No," replied Mara, shaking her head. "It will take both Tarnth and myself just to make the Aurelia ready for combat."

Kurt nodded. "If we're successful in defeating the Profiteers, I'll send you back home as soon as we return to Newton."

"We'll be successful," replied Mara confidently. "There's a reason why the Gothan Empire doesn't risk offending any of the Protector Worlds. You will find that out when we engage High Profiteer Creed."

Kurt stood up, preparing to leave. "I'm truly sorry about what happened to you. I'll do everything in my power to get you home. You have my word on that."

As Kurt left Mara's quarters, he felt excited. In a few days the Aurelia would become part of his fleet. When Profiteer Creed attacked, Kurt would use the Lakiam battlecruiser to ensure the hated Profiteer never left the Solar System but would instead die there.

Chapter Seventeen

High Profiteer Creed watched the ship's viewscreen as more Profiteer vessels arrived. The latest was High Profiteer Mott, who had brought twelve ships. Creed looked jealously at one of the screens showing Mott's flagship, the Jablan—a fully updated battleship.

"That's everyone except Dacroni Clan Leader Jarls," reported Second Profiteer Lantz.

Creed knew Lantz was impatient to get underway. The sooner they replaced the fleet's gold reserves, the sooner Lantz could return to the pleasure houses. He had already mentioned the girls he would miss while he was on this Earth raid.

Creed turned away from the viewscreens. "Jarls should be here shortly. How many cargo ship and detainee ships do we have?" All four of the other clans had brought vessels to haul plunder from Earth.

"Thirty-four cargo ships and eighteen detainee ships," replied Lantz as he checked a data screen.

Creed was satisfied with that number. "We'll form all the noncombat ships up into one fleet with a few escort cruisers to keep them safe."

Alarms sounded, and lights flashed. Creed's eyes instantly went to the sensor console.

"Contacts!" called out Third Profiteer Bixt as his sensors detected the arrival of more ships. Then in a calmer voice, he said, "It's Clan Leader Jarls."

High Profiteer Creed shifted his gaze to the tactical display as large green icons representing the Dacroni mercenaries' ships appeared.

"Twenty-eight battleships and four cargo ships," Lantz said with satisfaction. "That should be enough to ensure Fleet Admiral Vickers stays far away."

The Dacroni had the most powerful battleships in the empire. Just having Clan Leader Jarls on the raid greatly enhanced the success of the venture.

As Creed gazed at the numerous green icons on the tactical screen, he felt pleased with the fleet he had assembled. Overall he had twenty-nine battleships, twenty-four battlecruisers, and forty-five escort cruisers. That was far more vessels than Fleet Admiral Vickers had in his entire fleet, and, with a solid core of twenty-nine battleships, Creed could handle anything Vickers might throw at him. Already Creed could feel the riches piling up that he was about to loot from Earth. He would become one of the richest Profiteers on Marsten, and his exploits would be talked about for generations.

"Clan Leader Jarls says he's ready to depart," Third Profiteer Lukon reported from Communications.

Looking back at the tactical display, Creed noted all the green icons. This was by far the largest fleet he had ever commanded. If his spies on Earth had furnished him with the correct information, the planet had far more gold still on it than he had imagined possible. Hell, when he got back from the raid, he might just buy Kubitz itself!

Activating his ship-to-ship comm, he spoke. "All ships, this is High Profiteer Creed. In ten minutes we will depart for Earth. This raid will go down in Profiteer history as the richest one ever recorded. Prepare to fill your cargo ships with gold, your detainee ships with nubile women and sturdy workers." Creed felt elated. Soon he would be back at Earth, and, if Fleet Admiral Vickers got there in time, Creed would ensure the upstart Human admiral died there.

-

Ten minutes passed, and then the combined fleet jumped into hyperspace. The raid had begun to strip Earth of its wealth and to capture countless numbers of its citizens to be sold at the Kubitz slave auctions.

-

Ten thousand light-years away, Prince Brollen felt elated at the success of his mission so far. Six food worlds had been harvested with no losses to his fleet. In all six harvests they had only encountered light resistance from the defensive grids, which protected the planets. The fleets of warships that had once attempted to block the harvest had disappeared.

Hyperspace dropout in two minutes, Military Commander Mardok reported, standing in front of the ship's long-range sensor display. He was looking for any threats ahead in the system they were fast approaching. The sensors are not picking up any enemy warships.

Excellent, sent Prince Brollen.

If they could harvest four more food worlds, the storage facilities on all three motherships would be full, and then they could journey back to the system where the Collector Ships waited. He doubted if the other harvesting fleets had been as successful. His earlier food-collecting survey had indicated where the richest harvest areas were located in Galaxy X241, and these areas he had targeted.

-

Fleet Commodore Dreen—formerly Captain Dreen—of the Lakiam battlecruiser Basera watched his tactical screen nervously. He had been promoted to this new rank due to the number of warships now under his command.

"Estimated time for black fleet emergence from hyperspace is two minutes, twenty seconds," reported Sensor Operator Laylem.

They'd found a way to track the black ships while they were in hyperspace. Lakiam hyperspace scientists had discovered a particularly unique energy signature given off by a ship's hyperdrive was impossible to mask. The sensors on all Lakiam ships had been recalibrated to note that particular energy.

"Can we detect the use of their subspace drives?" Dreen hoped so as it would allow them to track the black ships' movements throughout the system.

"Unknown," replied Laylem, shifting his eyes from his console to the commodore. "Our scientists have programmed our sensors to look for several different types of radiation which the drives may give off. We won't know until they arrive."

Fleet Commodore Dreen leaned back in his command chair. They were risking a lot on this mission. Around the Basera were 1,400 Lakiam battlecruisers. This was by far the largest fleet Lakiam had ever assembled for a single mission. The ships had been pulled away from their defensive responsibilities in several Enlightened World systems to ensure Dreen had enough warships. Currently all the ships were stealthed and hidden behind a large gas giant, which should make it impossible for the black ships to detect them until it was too late.

"Has the warning been transmitted to Kanop?"

Kanop was the single Enlightened World colony in the system. The Kanop System had seven planets with planet number two being inhabited. Planets five, six, and seven were all gas giants, and Fleet Commodore Dreen had his fleet hidden behind number six.

"Yes, sir," replied Sheera. "I transmitted a warning as soon as we confirmed we were expecting the black fleet."

Dreen looked back at the nearest tactical display. On the surface of the planet, every ship that could hold passengers was rapidly being filled. As soon as the black fleet dropped from hyperspace, a mass exodus would occur across the system as every hyperspace-capable vessel fled.

"What's the status of our weapons?"

"All ships have full loads of dark matter missiles," confirmed Alborg from Tactical. "We have 40 percent of all the dark matter missiles Lakiam has produced in recent years. The rest are on ships protecting our primary worlds."

Commodore Dreen studied one of the main viewscreens on the curved front wall of the Command Center. A massive world of swirling clouds and vicious storms covered the screen. Dreen knew from earlier scans that the wind speeds in some of those storms exceeded six hundred kilometers per hour, strong enough that, if a man were standing on the surface and was struck by winds of that speed, he would die instantly. Even as Dreen watched, jagged bolts of lightning flashed between the swirling cloud layers.

"Contacts!" called out Laylem as glaring red threat icons appeared in one of the tactical displays. The black ships had been picked up visually by recon drones, which had been deployed earlier by several of the Lakiam battlecruisers.

"Numbers and types?" Dreen already knew the approximate number from the long-range sensors, but the types of ships were unknown.

"Three motherships and six hundred and four cruisers," reported Laylem.

"Three motherships," muttered Alborg, his eyes widening. "Think of how many Enlightened Worlds inhabitants will die to serve as food in order to fill those three ships."

Dreen shook his head. "More than I want to think about. We know this fleet has already attacked four Enlightened World colonies and possibly others." These attacks had led to Fleet Commodore Dreen coming to the Kanop System. His ship's computer had predicted Kanop was the next most likely target.

"The black fleet has activated their subspace drives and are inbound toward Kanop," reported Laylem as a warning alarm sounded. "Our sensors have detected and I have confirmed subspace contacts on one of the radiation bands."

"Excellent." This was good news, as it would now be possible to detect the black ships both in hyperspace and normal space. One of their big advantages had just been taken away. "How soon before they reach Kanop?"

"Three hours," Laylem answered as he checked one of his data screens.

Dreen studied the tactical display for several moments. "When will they reach their closest approach to us?"

"Sixty-two minutes."

"Jalad, plot a short hyperspace jump that will put us just behind the black fleet as it passes. We'll jump in and hit them with our dark matter missiles before they even know we're here."

"Plotting jump," responded Jalad as he got busy on his navigation computer.

-

Prince Brollen focused his multifaceted eyes on the tactical displays. Numerous ships rose from the second planet, making the jump into hyperspace. *In the future we should exit a portion of our fleet nearer the planet to prevent so many of the food species from escaping.*

It is only a small fraction, pointed out Military Commander Mardok with a clear thought. *Estimates indicate that, in any system, there are not enough ships for more than 1 percent of the species to escape.*

Perhaps it is best, Prince Brollen sent. *They can colonize other food worlds, and someday, when we return, they will be ready to be harvested.*

Both Scythe and Hetel report ready to harvest, one of the other Vorn in the Command Center reported.

Sensors indicate a moderate-size defensive grid around the planet, added Mardok. *It is not strong enough to cause us any problems.*

Assign enough cruisers to ensure its destruction as well as any other orbital structures, ordered Prince Brollen. *I am anxious to complete the harvest of this system and then move on to the next. I want the food from our ships to be what the Hive Queens taste next.*

It will be done, promised Mardok.

-

"Five minutes to closest approach," Laylem reported as the black fleet steadily drew nearer to the gas giant. The fleet would pass the planet by many millions of kilometers, which allowed the Lakiam fleet to stay hidden until the last possible moment.

"All ships, set Alert Condition One," ordered Fleet Commodore Dreen. The fleet was already at Condition Two; the setting of Condition One was only a formality.

"All ships report ready for combat," said Sheera as ships across the fleet complied.

"Black matter warheads are loaded in all missile tubes," added Alborg. "Ten of our warships will target just one black ship with all their missiles. If our data from the battle at Visth Prime is accurate, ten ships launching all their dark matter missiles simultaneously should overload the energy retention ability of the enemies' screens, collapsing them."

"Two minutes to closest approach," reported Laylem as he watched his sensors intently.

"I want to hit them with two full barrages of missiles before they can react," ordered Dreen. "We can't let them launch their dark antimatter spheres, or the battle will be lost. Once the second wave of missiles has been fired, I want to jump out of combat range of the black ships. We will then reassess our strategy before engaging them again." Dreen could sense the heightened tension in the Command Center. He could even feel his heart start to beat faster.

"One minute to closest approach," reported Laylem calmly.

"All ships are ready to make the jump into hyperspace," added Jalad. The final seconds sped by, and Jalad reached out on his control console, depressing a flashing yellow button.

Fleet Commodore Dreen felt a slight dizziness as the Basera made the short hyperspace jump. It seemed as if only a second passed before the viewscreen stabilized and the tactical display updated.

"Target lock!" cried out Alborg as he launched all twelve of the black matter missiles in the Basera's missile tubes.

Fleet Commodore Dreen clenched his fists as he gazed expectantly at the viewscreens. This was it. The dark matter missiles just had to work, or the galaxy was doomed. Leaning forward in his command chair, he stared anxiously at the viewscreen, showing one of the targeted black ships.

-

Alarms wailed loudly in the Command Center of the Reaper as one of the tactical displays filled with deadly red threat icons, all behind the fleet!

Who are they and how many? demanded Prince Brollen with a piercing thought, his antennas waving widely.

Food species 236, Military Commander Mardok sent back as he frantically transmitted new orders telepathically to the fleet ships. *They have the dark matter weapons*!

On the main viewscreens, blasts of dark matter energy pummeled a large number of the fleet's warships.

First priority is to protect all the motherships, ordered Prince Brollen, watching two Vorn cruisers explode in brilliant fireballs as their engorged energy screens collapsed.

Mardok suddenly grew deeply concerned. More Vorn ships under his command were being destroyed. He glanced at Prince Brollen, worried this time that he might not escape deletion.

-

Across the Vorn formation, the cruisers targeted by multiple Lakiam battlecruisers died in fiery funeral pyres. One hundred and forty Vorn ships were struck by numerous five-hundred-megaton explosive warheads. Seventy-eight of those ships were annihilated as their screens were overloaded and collapsed. In the Vorn battle line, small novas glowed briefly, marking the location of the destroyed ships.

-

"Second wave launching," reported Alborg as he sent the next barrage of hyperspace dark matter missiles toward their next designated target. "All ships are firing force beams and direct energy projectors targeting enemy vessels from the first missile wave which weren't destroyed. Those screens have to be close to going down."

"How many did we get?" demanded Fleet Commodore Dreen. He could see the remains of the novalike explosions so he realized they'd had some success. At any moment the black ships would be firing back. His eyes searched the viewscreens for any signs of the deadly black antimatter spheres.

"Seventy-eight," answered Laylem. "We got seventy-eight of them, and a number of others have been damaged."

"Force beams and direct energy cannons are firing," added Alborg as his hands flew across his console. He picked out a target with a screen bloated with absorbed energy.

-

More dark matter energy flooded across the screens of the Vorn cruisers. Space lit up with brilliant flashes of light from exploding dark matter warheads. At the same time, a second round of lesser energy from the Lakiams struck the already engorged screens of those dark vessels not destroyed in the first missile attack. More Vorn screens collapsed, releasing nearly incalculable amounts of energy.

The dark matter missiles killed additional Vorn vessels. Ship after ship died as their hulls were turned into plasma and glowing gas, leaving very little wreckage behind.

-

Military Commander Mardok stood paralyzed in the Command Center of the Reaper. This was a calamity; his fleet was being blown apart by weapons of unheard of power! For a moment, Mardok was at a loss as to what action he should take.

All ships fire our black antimatter beams, sent Prince Brollen, seeing Mardok failing to carry out his duties. *Our black antimatter spheres will be too slow. Target the enemy ships and continue to fire until I order you to stop.*

Prince Brollen then turned toward Military Commander Mardok. With another quick thought, he ordered two guards to escort the military commander to his quarters and to ensure he stayed there. With sadness, Prince Brollen knew Mardok would have to face deletion. He had not fulfilled his duties at a critical juncture, and such rampant failure could not be tolerated in the Vorn civilization.

-

Fleet Commodore Dreen flinched as fourteen of his battlecruisers blew apart under the deadly attack of the black beams. "All ships jump!" he ordered hurriedly.

The jump coordinates had already been calculated, and all hyperdrives in the fleet were on standby. On the main viewscreen, he saw numerous Lakiam battlecruisers vanish into hyperspace, and then moments later he felt the Basera jump.

In what seemed like the blink of an eye, the ship exited hyperspace a few million kilometers away from the black fleet. Looking at the viewscreens, he could see brilliant flashes of light where the black fleet was. He was seeing the light from his battle with the enemy that was only just now reaching this area of space.

"How many more of them did we get?"

"One moment," said Laylem as he studied his sensors. "Between the missile strike and our energy weapons, we took out sixty-seven more. That's one hundred and forty-five total."

"How many ships did we lose?" He had expected the enemy to use their black antimatter spheres, not those deadly black beams. He wouldn't make that mistake again.

"Twenty-seven," replied Laylem, looking expectantly at the commodore.

Dreen nodded his head as he thought over his next move. "In order to force them to withdraw, we need to destroy one of their big ships."

"That will be difficult," Alborg said as he studied the nearby tactical display. "The three motherships are in the heart of their formation, surrounded by cruisers."

"The black fleet is still on course for Kanop," reported Laylem.

Fleet Commodore Dreen knew he had no choice. They needed a victory against the black ships, no matter how costly. "All ships, this is Fleet Commodore Dreen. We will jump into point-blank range of the black fleet. Half of our fleet will target their cruisers, and all other ships will focus their fire on target Alpha Prime." Before they had originally engaged the black fleet, each mother ship had been given a designation.

With a deep sigh, Dreen knew he was about to lose a lot of valuable warships. "Alborg, I want to target as many of the cruisers between our fleet and our target. Once the path has been cleared, we will fire dark matter missiles until the target has been destroyed or we run out of missiles."

"I'll set it up," Alborg answered solemnly. "I'm pretty sure we can do this, but it'll cost us a lot of dark matter missiles."

Fleet Commodore Dreen didn't have to be told how important those missiles were. It would take months to replace what he had already used and the ones he was about to. The only good thing was, the enemy didn't know how short the Lakiams were on dark matter missiles or how long it took to produce them.

-

Prince Brollen faced a quandary. He was outnumbered by over two to one, and the enemy had already demonstrated they had a weapon dangerous to Vorn ships. The prince stood in the middle of the spacious Command Center, contemplating what he should do. He didn't have the training of a military commander, and, in that regard, Military Commander Mardok was sorely missed. However, Mardok had demonstrated his inability to command in the heat of battle when the fortunes of war were not going his way.

Total cruiser losses are one hundred and forty-five, and we destroyed twenty-seven enemy warships, reported the Vorn standing in front of the sensor console.

Prince Brollen turned to study one of the tactical displays. The enemy had not fled, merely retreated a few million kilometers. No doubt they were deciding upon their next move. *All ships*, Brollen broadcast telepathically. *I expect the enemy to return and attack shortly. When they do, we will use our black antimatter beams to annihilate their vessels. If we can destroy enough of their ships, they will withdraw, and we can complete the harvesting of this system.*

Brollen turned his triangular-shaped head back to the viewscreens. A few wisps of glowing gas still marked where Vorn warships had died. This was the second time a harvesting fleet under his command had suffered losses. He was becoming concerned that the harvest of this galaxy might not be as simple and easy as first believed.

Enemy ships are jumping! sent the Vorn at the sensor console.

Standby to fire weapons! ordered Prince Brollen as he prepared for combat. He was confident his black matter beams could still destroy this enemy fleet.

-

"Fire!" ordered Fleet Commodore Dreen as the Basera exited hyperspace within easy combat range of the black fleet.

"Missiles launched," confirmed Alborg.

"Enemy are firing," warned Laylem as his sensors went wild.

They had come up with a simple strategy. The first wave of missiles from all ships would be targeted on the cruisers between the Lakiam fleet and target Alpha Prime. The second and third wave of missiles would all target the massive mothership in the hope the release of so much energy would cause its screen to collapse, destroying the vessel. If two waves of missiles weren't enough, they would continue to fire until all dark matter missiles were expended.

On a nearby viewscreen, a Lakiam battlecruiser exploded as an enemy black beam blew it apart. On other screens, brilliant explosions marked the death of enemy cruisers as their energy screens were overloaded.

"Six more of our battlecruisers have been destroyed," reported Laylem as the friendly green icons on the tactical screens swelled up and vanished.

"Firing force beams and direct energy cannons," called out Alborg.

"All ships, hold your positions and continue to fire!" ordered Commodore Dreen determinedly. On the tactical display, he could see more of his battlecruisers dying. But in order to win this engagement, he had to destroy the mothership they were targeting, even if it meant the sacrifice of a major portion of his fleet.

-

In space, the battle intensified. A Vorn black antimatter beam slammed into the main part of a Lakiam battlecruiser, setting off massive explosions and blowing out a large portion of the hull, sending the ship adrift, out of control. The next beam cut completely through the ship, leaving it to be destroyed by Vorn antimatter missiles. Other Lakiam vessels were blown apart rapidly as the deadly black antimatter beams performed their lethal work. They cut right through defensive energy screens as if they were not even there.

In the Vorn fleet, forty-seven cruisers died in the first wave of dark matter missiles. Then force beams and direct energy fire took out eleven more.

The Lakiam fleet launched its second wave of missiles. Every one was aimed at a single Vorn mothership. In the center of the Vorn formation, a glowing star was born. Missile after missile exploded, releasing torrents of energy, which were rapidly absorbed by the ship's powerful screen. Then another wave arrived and another. The mothership's screen glowed brilliantly with all the energy it had absorbed. Then the final wave of missiles arrived, and, in a titanic release of energy, the screen collapsed. The Vorn mothership didn't explode; it was simply vaporized from the intense amount of energy that struck its hull from all sides. For the first time in Vorn history since coming to this universe, a mothership had been destroyed.

-

"Target is down," cried out Laylem exuberantly. "There's nothing left of it. The released energy from the screen vaporized the vessel completely."

"Jump us out," ordered Fleet Commodore Dreen. His heart was pounding, and he took several long deep breaths. On the viewscreens, Lakiam battlecruisers were still dying rapidly from the deadly black beams.

"Jumping," reported Jalad as the Basera transitioned into hyperspace.

-

Prince Brollen stared in shock at where the Hetel had been only moments before. Now a raging fire of dying energy marked the vessel's location.

"*Hetel has been destroyed*," reported the Vorn at the sensor console.

For a moment Brollen stood frozen, and then his multifaceted eyes shifted to one of the tactical displays, showing the enemy fleet. It still had not fled. No doubt its commander was already planning the next attack. For the first time since leaving the Conclave Habitat, he spoke out loud. "All ships are to enter hyperspace and rendezvous at System X-42-397." Prince Brollen didn't trust the use of telepathy to hide his deep concerns over what had just happened.

Moments later the Reaper, the Scythe, and the remaining Vorn cruisers transitioned into hyperspace, leaving the system of Kanop far behind.

-

"They're gone!" called out Laylem as he watched the last red threat icon vanish from his sensors. "We beat them!"

Fleet Commodore Dreen let out a deep sigh. Yes, they had beat them, but the last battle had cost him 117 battlecruisers, all destroyed within two minutes. He had never been in a battle so violent and so intense. What frightened him the most was many more such battles were probably in his future.

"Contact Kanop and inform them we have driven off the Destroyers of Worlds, and the Kanop people are safe."

Dreen leaned back in his command chair, his pulse returning to normal. They had their victory, and just possibly the enemy would pause in their attack on the Enlightened Worlds and their colonies. It would take time for the Lakiams to build sufficient black matter warheads to give the galaxy a chance at defeating the black ships. Even then they had no idea of the actual strength of the enemy or how many there were.

"Jalad, set a course for Kanop. We'll use their shipyards to repair our vessels. As soon as repairs are finished, we'll set a course for home."

-

In hyperspace, Prince Brollen watched silently as Military Commander Mardok was led to a disposal chute, which connected to one of the vessel's reactors. Without a comment or a thought, he allowed the two guards to open the chute and toss him in.

Prince Brollen still reeled from the disaster in the food system they had just left. Over two hundred of his cruisers had been destroyed as well as the Hetel. It was the worst disaster the Vorn had suffered since coming to this universe. It would be necessary to once more halt the harvest of this galaxy until sufficient forces could be amassed to ensure success. This had now become a battle for survival. Without the food resources in Galaxy X241, the Vorn would starve. There wasn't enough time or resources to go to another galaxy. Besides, most of them had already been picked clean.

Turning, Prince Brollen headed toward his quarters. He had much to think about. He had some concern over what would happen to him when he returned and reported this disaster. He had just lost a mother ship with a considerable amount of harvested food on board. There was a chance, a small one at least, that, upon his return to the Conclave Habitat, he could face deletion. He had failed in the harvest and, in doing so, had failed the Vorn race.

Chapter Eighteen

Fleet Admiral Kurt Vickers was in the Command Center of the Lakiam battlecruiser Aurelia along with Mara and Tarnth. Over the last week Kurt had made it a point to take both on tours of Newton, showing them the people and the relaxed lifestyle most led. He had also put together a command crew, drawing on experienced people from across the fleet. He had moved Captain Randson from the Star Cross to the Aurelia as its commander. Andrew was currently in Engineering, working with its crew. Several of Lomatz's engineers and technicians had agreed to stay on board the Lakiam vessel to help instruct the new crew on how its systems functioned.

"Your people are intriguing," commented Mara as she showed one of Kurt's people how the ship's advanced sensor systems functioned. "Much different than I imagined."

"How so?" Kurt was curious to hear what Mara thought of Newton.

Mara paused, turning to face Kurt. "Your people are not as barbaric as I expected. This world, in many ways, is similar to Lakiam. Your people have been careful how they treat the environment on the planet and wish to live in harmony with nature. Your cities are well laid out, and your government voices the will of the people. All are positive indicators of a civilization well on its way toward becoming a Protector World and eventually an Enlightened one."

Kurt nodded, pleased with Mara's assessment. "Our home world isn't like this. When we set up the Newton colony, we took into consideration everything we did wrong on Earth. We didn't want to commit the same mistakes here."

"A wise decision," responded Mara as she walked to the navigation console, where another crewmember was struggling with a hyperjump simulation. "It is the same with many of the more advanced colony worlds. That's what separates a race with the potential to find Enlightenment from one who never will."

"Are there older civilizations who never became a Protector World or reached Enlightened status?"

"Oh, yes," answered Mara, nodding her head. "There are many. Some civilizations advance to a certain stage and stagnate. Numerous small empires are scattered across the galaxy, some very similar to the Gothan Empire, except they don't have Profiteers. They become embroiled in petty wars and lay waste to entire solar systems."

"Why don't the Protector Worlds become more involved in preventing such acts?" Kurt had known other small empires were in the galaxy; he just didn't know a lot about them or how many there were.

Mara paused as she considered her answer. "Too many Enlightened Worlds and Enlightened World colonies need protecting. Some of these empires do occasionally threaten an Enlightened World system. When that happens, the Protector World responsible for defending that particular Enlightened species becomes involved. While there are a lot of Protector Worlds, there are many more Enlightened Worlds and their colonies."

"You're saying the Protector Worlds don't have the ships to enforce peace across the galaxy." Kurt had thought most of the galaxy was civilized with just isolated pockets, such as the Gothan Empire, causing trouble.

Mara nodded her head. "Yes, that's correct. Many times a Protector World is responsible for up to one hundred Enlightened World civilizations and their colonies. There are entire sectors where barbarism prevails, and those areas are avoided."

Kurt took a moment to take in all of this and then asked his next question. "How many intelligent species are there in our galaxy?"

Mara looked to Tarnth, unsure if she should answer.

"You should be more concerned about learning the functions of this ship than a galactic history lesson. Even the youngest Lakiam knows the answer. Since you have promised to free us after we take care of High Profiteer Creed, I'll answer. Across the galaxy are over eight thousand Enlightened World civilizations, with one hundred and seventy-three Protector World civilizations defending them. In addition there are twelve hundred small empires, comprising anywhere from ten to three hundred star systems. Most of these are at a static stage of development. In the future a few of these may make it to Protector World status. Plus we can count tens of thousands of what we call barbaric worlds, planets similar to your Earth. As Mara said, some sectors of the galaxy are deemed too dangerous to explore or enter."

"How would you classify Newton?" Kurt was curious to hear Tarnth's opinion, as he didn't voice it very often.

Tarnth was silent for a long moment. "You're in the beginning stages of moving toward Protector World status," he answered grudgingly. "If not, I would never have agreed to teach you how to operate the Aurelia."

An alarm sounded on the comm console, indicating an incoming message. Mara stepped over and sent the message to Admiral Vickers, who was sitting in the command chair.

"Admiral, we may have a problem," Colonel Simms said hurriedly. "The light cruiser Justin exited hyperspace a few moments ago. It came directly from Kubitz. Captain Edison reports that High Profiteer Creed has disappeared from the Gothan Empire. Avery Dolman told Marvin Tenner he's headed here."

"Damn!" swore Kurt, his eyes widening in concern. "We're not ready yet. Does Edison know how many ships High Profiteer Creed has in his fleet?"

"Possibly over one hundred," Simms replied. "Dolman says rumors going around Kubitz indicate four other small Profiteer clans are involved as well as Dacroni Clan Leader Jarls."

"All ship commanders will meet in two hours," Kurt said. Turning toward Mara and Tarnth, he asked, "Is the Aurelia ready for a battle?"

Tarnth looked at Mara, who nodded. "If you trust Mara and me to operate most of the systems with some minor assistance from your crew, we can do it. This ship is highly automated, and its computer can handle most of what will need to be done."

Kurt had hoped for that answer. "Very well, we'll set out for the Proxima Centauri System later today." Kurt just prayed they could get there in time to respond to any attack in the Solar System. He was deeply concerned that, this time, High Profiteer Creed would leave nothing behind.

-

On Earth, President Marlen Stroud sat in the Oval Office of the White House, smoking a Cuban cigar. A special informant had notified him earlier in the day that High Profiteer Creed would shortly be returning to the Solar System with a massive Profiteer fleet. Months back, after returning from Newton, Stroud had been contacted by several individuals who said they represented Creed's claims to Earth's riches. Stroud had often wondered if these two men were actually from Earth. He had heard there were many humanoids within the galaxy who could pass for an Earth Human.

He had worked out a deal with the two supposed associates of High Profiteer Creed. If he would identify where all the main caches of Earth's gold were hidden, High Profiteer Creed would arrange for Stroud to have absolute control over the planet and the Solar System once Creed left. Marlen would rule as Creed's representative with the agreement that gold would continue to be mined on Earth and 70 percent of it turned over to the Profiteer on a yearly basis. In return, Creed would leave a few warships in orbit to ensure the people of Earth obeyed whatever Stroud demanded and would not nuke the planet.

Standing up, Stroud walked to the large window overlooking the city. He had brought in more workers at higher wages to speed up construction. It had been necessarily cut back on the reconstruction of several bombed-out cities, but he was president, and his capital must look the part. It wouldn't hurt if a few lowly civilians suffered a little while longer.

As he puffed on his cigar, he thought over what one of Creed's associates had told him earlier. The High Profiteer was on his way back to Earth and would arrive in the next day or two. As long as there was no resistance, everything would be peaceful. The Profiteers would collect the gold and whatever other valuables they wanted, and then they would leave.

Stroud nodded to himself. Former President Mayfield should have worked out such a deal. It would have saved millions of lives, and the world would have been far better off.

-

In space, High Profiteer Creed was growing impatient for the fleet to reach Earth. He hadn't revealed to the other clan leaders that he had an inside source who knew where the main caches of gold were located. Once the fleet arrived above the planet, Creed would send down some of his small cargo ships to pick up the gold from the designated locations. The others could scrounge for their gold among the cities and the countryside. There would be plenty to keep them satisfied. Creed had furnished the other clan leaders a list of places where gold and other valuables were likely to be found. However, if Creed's plan worked, he would come away from the planet with the majority of the valuable yellow metal.

"We'll arrive at Earth in twenty-nine hours," reported Third Profiteer Holbat from Navigation.

"Excellent," replied Creed. With the size of his fleet and with Clan Leader Jarls's twenty-eight battleships, Creed wasn't even concerned about Fleet Admiral Vickers. If Vickers decided to show up before the looting of Earth was complete, his ships would be destroyed. That was one of the reasons Creed had brought such a large fleet. Nothing would stop the Earth from being thoroughly looted and most, if not all, of its treasure seized by the Profiteers.

"Some Class Two Defense Platforms are in orbit over Earth," Second Profiteer Lantz pointed out. "Also a number of dual-firing energy cannon satellites." This information had been reported back by the two Profiteer escort cruisers sent in to scan the system several months back.

"They won't fire on us," Creed said confidently. "I've already seen to that." If his sources on Earth were telling the truth, a Human by the name of Marlen Stroud was cooperating. He was also the ruler of the most powerful country on the planet.

"I'm still concerned about Admiral Vickers," said Lantz uneasily. "He's the wildcard in all this."

"He doesn't have that large of a fleet," Creed responded, his eyes shifting to Lantz, who was a constant worrier and very hesitant about taking risks. With the fleet Creed had, this raid on Earth was a sure thing. "If Vickers had a larger fleet, he would have brought more warships with him on his last trip to Kubitz. I don't believe he will risk a major confrontation with our fleet."

"Perhaps," Lantz said doubtfully. "But don't forget about what happened in the Julbian System. He had enough ships there to take the system away from us."

Creed's eyes turned red with anger. "We could have defeated Vickers in the Julbian System! We retreated so as not to take a substantial loss to our profit margin."

-

Lantz stayed silent. No point in aggravating the High Profiteer more. Also no point in mentioning the warships and the cargo vessels lost in that encounter, particularly the two largest cargo ships. The encounter with Vickers had been very expensive. If Creed really wanted to destroy Vickers and his ships, that might have been the best opportunity.

-

Fleet Admiral Aaron Colmes gazed at his latest orders from President Stroud with great concern. Under Colmes's command he had three battleships and three battlecruisers. Not a very powerful fleet. But when combined with the two large Class Two Defense Platforms over Earth and the energy cannon satellites, it was enough to deter most aggressors, particularly the Profiteers if they returned. However, the message he had just received from the president made no sense. His ships were to proceed to

Neptune and go into orbit. They were to stay there until otherwise ordered. If unknown ships were detected dropping from hyperspace into the Solar System, he was to take no aggressive action.

With a deep sigh, he folded his arms across his chest and stood in the Command Center of the Atlas, wondering what this meant. He still felt guilty about being put in charge of the fleet, particularly after Fleet Admiral Tomalson had fled the system with the Retribution, three other battlecruisers, and several cargo ships. All caused by the changes in government in the North American Union. He had known Marlen Stroud for years. They were not close friends, but Stroud had helped in advancing Aaron's military career. Aaron had never felt comfortable with some of the things Stroud asked of him. Most of the time it was small favors, like inside information on military maneuvers or what the fleet's current status was. Stroud had helped him to move up rapidly through the chain of command.

"What do you think is going on?" asked Tamara Scott. She was a talented XO and very confused about the current political situation on Earth.

"I don't know. We're supposed to take the fleet to Neptune and stay there until we receive additional orders."

Tamara frowned, shaking her head. "Sounds like we're being sent out of the way where we can't interfere with anything. Will you obey the orders? We'll be leaving the system nearly defenseless."

Colmes nodded his head in agreement. "Retreating is dangerous, but we're paid to follow orders. Let's get the fleet moving to Neptune." Then as an afterthought, he added, "Take the fleet to Condition Three just in case."

"Yes, Admiral," Captain Scott replied. "I think that's a wise decision."

-

A few minutes later the fleet was underway, leaving the Solar System wide open to attack. Only the defense platforms and energy cannon satellites still defended Earth. As long as the two defense platforms were intact, they should deter any aggression toward the planet.

However, orders were already on the way from the new military commander of the North American Union for the two crews on board the platforms to return to Earth. Supposedly maintenance teams would be arriving to service the platforms. For the next few days Earth would be defenseless as there weren't enough energy cannon satellites to stop an all-out assault, not without the fleet and the defense platforms taking the lead to stop an inbound enemy fleet.

-

The Star Cross dropped from hyperspace in the Proxima Centauri System. Along with it were the heavy battlecarrier Ranger, the light carriers Vindication and Wasp, and the battlecruisers Ceres, Vesta, and Trinity. In addition there were the warships purchased from Kubitz, which had been rebuilt and updated to current fleet standards. Those ships included the battleships Ipetus and Triton, and the four battlecruisers—the Dione, Rhea, Hyperion, and Pandora. However, the most imposing vessel was the Lakiam battlecruiser Aurelia, now combat ready and prepared to engage the Profiteers.

"Contacts!" called out Lieutenant Lena Brooks as warning lights flashed on her sensor console and a low-pitched alarm sounded. "Contacts are friendly. I have positive IDs on Fleet Admiral Tomalson's ships."

Kurt nodded. Strange not to have Andrew at his side; however, it was more important he command the Aurelia. Kurt trusted Andrew's judgment more than anyone else in the fleet, except for Henry. However, Henry was more valuable on the Vindication and was better suited for carrier operations. Looking at one of the viewscreens, Kurt could see the sleek outlines of the Lakiam battlecruiser. At 1,700 meters long, the vessel looked impressive. He wondered if Newton, even with Lomatz's help, could ever build a ship like her.

"Fleet Admiral Tomalson reports no evidence of Profiteer ships in the Solar System," reported Lieutenant Brenda Pierce.

"He does report some strange fleet movements. The six remaining warships in the Earth System have gone into orbit around Neptune."

"Neptune?" said Lieutenant Evelyn Mays from Tactical, looking confused. "That doesn't make any strategic sense."

Kurt let out a deep breath. "It does if you don't want the ships to engage the Profiteers. President Stroud may be avoiding a confrontation with High Profiteer Creed." This put Kurt in a quandary. What if he attacked the Profiteer and Creed in return nuked Earth?

Activating the ship-to-ship comm, he spoke to the commanders of both fleets. "All ships will go dark immediately. Full stealth mode and power at minimal levels. We'll continue to monitor the Solar System for the arrival of the Profiteer fleet. I believe President Stroud will attempt to negotiate with them. Due to the vulnerability of Earth and the other colonies in the system, we'll wait and see what the results of those negotiations are. As much as we want to destroy the Profiteer fleet, we don't dare put Earth in danger."

"So what now?" asked Lieutenant Mays. With the transfer of Captain Randson to the Aurelia, Lieutenant Mays was now also acting as Kurt's XO.

Kurt leaned back in his command chair, folding his arms across his chest. "Now we wait. High Profiteer Creed should arrive any day. We'll see what happens in the Solar System, and, if things go south, we'll jump in and engage the Profiteer fleet."

-

High Profiteer Creed had just entered the Command Center. In thirty more minutes the fleet would emerge from hyperspace inside the Earth System. Already he could see the piles of gold bars waiting for him. He would soon become the richest Profiteer in history!

"Everything's ready for emergence," Second Profiteer Lantz said as he saw Creed.

Creed sat down in his command chair as he studied the activity in the Command Center. Everyone was preparing for their arrival over Earth. If his people on the planet had succeeded in their mission, the planet would be wide open to plunder. The Profiteer ships would sweep in; cargo ships would land, and thousands of Profiteers would spread out across the planet, looting everything of value. Even the warships would be involved as shuttles of heavily armed Profiteers would be sent to the more highly prized targets.

-

The minutes passed quickly by. Creed studied the hyperspace sensor, seeing no signs of Fleet Admiral Vickers. The only ships showing on the display were the ones moving about in the Earth System. With satisfaction he saw six ships orbiting the eighth planet. Those would be Earth's warships. With a fierce grin, he realized his plan had succeeded. The evidence was in the location of those six vessels.

"Two minutes to hyperspace dropout," reported Third Profiteer Holbat.

High Profiteer Creed leaned forward expectantly. The fleet would drop from hyperspace just outside the orbit of Earth's moon. If danger was evident, then the fleet would reenter hyperspace and reassess the situation.

The last minute flew by, and suddenly the Ascendant Destruction emerged from hyperspace. For a moment static blurred the viewscreens, and then they cleared, showing a vivid view of space. On the main viewscreen was Earth, its blue-white globe nearly filling the screen.

"Contacts," reported Third Profiteer Bixt. "I have a large number of civilian ships. Most seem to be cargo ships and a few passenger vessels. No warships are in orbit around Earth. However, two Class Two Defensive Platforms and a number of energy cannon satellites are in place."

"Are the platforms targeting us?"

"No," answered Bixt, looking at Creed in surprise. "They seem to be shut down."

"Excellent, that's what I wanted to hear. All ships," Creed said over his ship-to-ship comm. "Earth poses no danger to us.

We will go into orbit and shortly collect the fortune that awaits us."

It didn't take long for the Profiteer fleet to go into orbit around Earth. For the most part, the comm channels were silent, except for fleeting messages from a number of cargo ships and passenger ships jumping into hyperspace and fleeing the system, no doubt bound for Newton, where they thought they would be safe.

"I have Clan Leader Jarls on the comm," reported Third Profiteer Lukon from Communications. "He wants to know if he can destroy those two defensive platforms as well as the energy cannon satellites. The platforms don't have their screens up and will be easy targets."

Creed thought for a moment. He had never promised he wouldn't destroy the platforms; he had only asked that they be shut down. "Yes," he replied. If somehow the platforms were reactivated, they could pose a threat. Better to eliminate that possibility now than regret it later.

Once the Profiteers from the other ships landed, it would be evident rather quickly to the North American Union President that Creed had no intention of following through on their agreement, at least not all of it.

-

Dacroni Clan Leader Jarls wasn't quite sure what was going on. All Earth warships in the system were orbiting the eighth planet, making no effort to resist the Profiteer fleet. The two defensive platforms, which could cause considerable damage, were shut down. It didn't make any sense to Jarls unless High Profiteer Creed was up to something. Jarls had already decided to keep an eye on the High Profiteer. Jarls strongly suspected there was more to this raid than Creed had let on.

"I want all our battleships to target the orbiting defense satellites and take them out. We'll fire two of our hyperspace missiles at the defense platforms and destroy them. Once we've done that, there won't be anything in orbit around Earth to interfere with the raid."

"What about those six warships?" asked Salas, gesturing toward the six red threat icons on the tactical display. "Three of them are battleships and could pose a danger."

"No, we'll leave them alone unless they move toward us. If they do, we'll destroy them."

Salas nodded his understating and passed on the orders to target the two defensive platforms and the energy cannon satellites.

-

From the twenty-eight Dacroni battleships, beams of light flashed out as energy projectors fired, striking the orbiting satellites. Bright flashes of light filled Earth's sky as the satellites were rapidly annihilated. Then Jarls's flagship launched two hyperspace missiles. One missile each struck the two large Orbital Defense Platforms, turning them into expanding fireballs, which lit up the night sky over the North American Union.

-

On Earth, President Marlen Stroud stared up in shock as two bright fireballs flared in the night sky. Other smaller fireballs indicated the destruction of all the orbiting defense satellites. Feeling nervous and betrayed, Stroud turned to face the two grim-faced men in black suits, standing in his office.

"The defense platforms were not to be destroyed," he said angrily. "I thought we had an agreement!"

"We do," replied one of the men. "High Profiteer Creed is just ensuring no incidents happen while the fleet's in orbit. By removing the defense platforms and the armed satellites, it reduces that possibility. I'm sure you see the common sense of taking such a precaution."

Stroud thought it over and had to agree it did make sense. He had already contacted the European Union, the Russian Collective, and the Chinese Conglomerate, asking them not to engage the Profiteers. He had informed them he was in the process of negotiating a settlement to allow the Profiteers to take their gold and leave. He had made the calls as soon as the Profiteer fleet appeared in the system. Neither of the other three major governments seemed pleased with Stroud's request, but they agreed to hold off on any aggressive action until the negotiations were finished.

"So what now?" asked Stroud, a little less sure of himself.

The two men looked at each other. "We go to Fort Knox to meet with High Profiteer Creed. If he's satisfied with the amount of gold stored there, we'll load it into our cargo ships and leave your system in peace, never to return."

"What about the two ships you're to leave in orbit to ensure I become ruler of the entire planet?"

"That's something you will have to talk to High Profiteer Creed about. I'm sure for the right price an arrangement can be worked out."

Marlen Stroud let out a deep breath. This wasn't going as he had planned. He thought an agreement had already been made. "Let's go to Fort Knox. There's enough gold stored there that even your High Profiteer will be satisfied."

As they left the White House, Stroud felt confident that, sometime within the next few days, the planet Earth would have its first world leader, and that leader would be Marlen Stroud.

Chapter Nineteen

Across the planet, swarms of Profiteer shuttles set down in major cities. They landed in schoolyards, parking lots, parks, and everywhere else with room to do so. The entire world waited fearfully to see if President Marlen Stroud of the North American Union had succeeded in working out a deal with the Profiteers. Would the world be allowed to go on in peace, or would war break out?

In the United Kingdom, that question was answered early as Profiteers opened fire on innocent civilians in the streets of London. They mercilessly killed everyone in front of six large jewelry stores marked as potential targets to plunder. The Profiteers set up a perimeter around all six sites and began hauling out everything of value. Other Profiteers fanned out, seizing young men and women to be sold at the slave auctions on Kubitz. Young nubile women were brutally handled and taken to the nearest shuttle to be placed on a detainee ship for transport to Kubitz. Women such as these were in high demand by the pleasure houses on the black market world. Young men who could be trained to fill various labor positions were rounded up as well and loaded onto the shuttles.

The British Prime Minister, hearing of the mayhem and death in the streets, sent in the army to take on the Profiteers. This was a brutal invasion, and the prime minister was determined to meet the enemy, particularly since innocent civilians were being slaughtered. He might reap severe consequences for his actions, but he saw no other viable choice. British citizens had died and were being abducted, and he was determined to stop it.

In Australia, the Perth Mint was struck. Ten shuttles and a small cargo ship set down. Profiteers loyal to High Profiteer Creed attacked the guards and, in just a short time, reached the vaults. Setting explosive charges, they blew them open. It didn't take long before the first antigravity sleds of precious metals, including a large quantity of gold, were headed for the cargo ship.

All across Australia, wherever major deposits of gold or precious metals were stored, Profiteer shuttles put in an appearance. With reluctance, knowing it was probably useless, the Australian government gave the order to deploy the military into the streets of the country's cities. They were confused as to how the Profiteers had known exactly where the gold was.

All across the world it was the same. In China, Russia, Germany, France, South Africa, South America, the Profiteers went after the gold, killing anyone who got in their way. In less than an hour after their first appearance, heavy fighting broke out across the world between the Profiteers and the worlds militaries. Most world governments felt, since the Profiteers had nuked the planet twice before, they would probably do it again, and this time it would be the end of everything. So they might as well fight. At least they could take a few of the hated enemy with them.

-

At Fort Knox, President Marlen Stroud stood beside High Profiteer Creed as the first massive gold vault was opened. Stroud nodded in satisfaction, seeing the gleaming pallets of gold bars. This should ensure the Profiteers left the North American Union alone. Stroud had already heard fighting was breaking out in other countries, where they had decided to resist the Profiteers. He knew it was useless to resist the Profiteers due to their superior weapons. The other governments were just sending their brave men and women to their deaths.

"See," said Stroud, gesturing toward the gold. "There's enough gold here to set you up for life." Stroud was confident this gold haul would encourage the Profiteer to allow Stroud to rule the world. "Remember, our agreement is for 70 percent of all future gold mined on Earth to be sent to your Kubitz account. I can make you a very rich man."

"We'll see," commented High Profiteer Creed as he gazed greedily at the gold bars. "We must sample the gold first to test its purity. If it's acceptable, then perhaps an agreement mutually beneficial to both of us can be worked out."

Stroud smiled, pleased to hear the Profiteer's words. Stroud had been right: the Profiteers could be reasoned with. Of course it helped that Stroud had provided a list of where most of the planet's gold was stored. It didn't bother Stroud that he had betrayed the other leaders of the world and was the direct cause of the deaths of many of their citizens.

-

High Profiteer Creed gazed wide-eyed at the pallets of gleaming yellow gold that lay in the vault, and this wasn't the only one. The Human leader told him how much gold was in the vaults, and Creed had nearly fainted. The amount Stroud had mentioned was beyond belief. If what the Human had told Creed was true, the total amount of gold in just this facility alone would be worth over 240 billion credits. Add that to his share of the gold his Profiteers were seizing all across the planet, and his take from Earth could easily be over five hundred billion credits! He wouldn't only be the richest Profiteer in history, he could actually afford to buy Kubitz if he wanted.

From now on, wherever High Profiteer Creed walked, people would whisper and point, mentioning his exploits, and how he was the richest and most successful Profiteer ever. He was assured a spot on the ruling council on Marsten if he wanted it. Anything he wanted or desired, he could have!

Creed walked over and placed his hand on one of the pallets in the vault. He marveled at the feel of the gold beneath his hand. The Human had offered him 70 percent of all gold mined on the planet in the future. Creed found it difficult to grasp the total riches being offered to him. Picking up one of the gold bars, he smiled, thinking about how Second Profiteer Lantz would react when he found out the value of all the gold. There was no doubt in Creed's mind that his second officer would go out and buy a pleasure house of his own. Creed would enjoy the look on Lantz's face when he showed him just how right it had been to mount this raid.

"High Profiteer, there's a problem," spoke up Profiteer Lagan, who was testing the gold. "This isn't what it appears to be."

The grin faded from High Profiteer Creed's face as he turned toward Profiteer Lagan. "What do you mean, there's a problem? I know what gold feels like." He still held the bar of gold he had picked up in his right hand. "This is gold!"

Profiteer Lagan shook his head. "It feels like gold and looks like gold, but it is not. There's an outer layer of gold but, inside, is an alloy that has all the characteristics of gold, yet it's not real."

"So what's all this worth?" asked Creed, gesturing toward the vaults and feeling his world come crashing down.

"A few million credits at the most," Lagan replied. "Or course it will cost more that that for all the handling, transport, and smelting to free the gold from the alloy it covers."

Creed felt his anger boil. He had been duped by this Human leader. His dreams of becoming the most famous Profiteer had just been shattered. "So all this is worthless?"

"Yes, High Profiteer," Lagan answered with a nod. "It's best if we just leave it here and go on."

Creed turned his anger on the Human, standing near him. "Did you really think I would fall for this? How many other lies have you told? Is there fake gold at the other locations as well?" Creed was angry enough to kill the Human standing in front of him.

"I don't understand," stammered Stroud, looking around confused. "This gold was real."

Creed reached out and grabbed Stroud by the neck, squeezing. "I should kill you here and now for your treachery," he snarled. With disgust, Creed shoved Stroud to the floor, glaring at him. Gesturing to two nearby Profiteers, Creed gave an order. "Take this cowardly Human to one of the shuttles. He's to be taken to Kubitz and sold at one of the slave auctions."

"He's too old. He won't bring much," commented one of the Profiteers, who grabbed Stroud, jerking him back on his feet.

"Doesn't matter. I'm sure someone will purchase him for light labor. He could clean the rooms at one of the pleasure houses. That would be a fitting punishment for the treachery he's shown."

-

Stroud didn't know what to say as the two Profiteers led him back outside. Both were well armed, and Stroud knew, if he attempted to make a break for it, he would be killed. To be sold at the slave auctions, he thought, recalling the High Profiteer's chilling words. He had thought the slave auctions were something Fleet Admiral Vickers had made up. Even after the two captured cargo ship crews had returned and told their stories, Stroud had refused to believe them.

In the distance, he heard a loud explosion. Looking toward the north, he saw a bright glow in the night sky. The city of Louisville was in that direction. With a sobering thought, he realized he had been played by the Profiteers from the beginning. As he was taken on board the shuttle, he realized, instead of going down in history as the world's greatest leader and savior, he would be recalled as its greatest traitor instead.

Moments later the shuttle lifted off, taking President Marlen Stroud with it. He would be put on a detainee ship and shortly be on his way to Kubitz with the other captives rounded up across the planet.

-

Fleet Admiral Aaron Colmes fumed at the videos coming in from Earth. The Profiteers were attacking everywhere. All across the planet, cities were in flames, and world militaries were engaging the Profiteers. Occasionally an orbiting warship would fire a beam weapon toward the surface in support of Profiteers fighting Human forces, devastating entire city blocks.

"We can't stay here," said Captain Tamara Scott, her eyes shifting to the admiral. "It's our sworn duty to protect Earth. People are dying there. Military people are dying, and we're sitting out here at Neptune."

Colmes let out a deep and ragged breath. "We were ordered to stay here."

"Screw our orders!" cried out Tamara, pointing at the front wall of the Command Center. "Look at the viewscreens." On them scenes from various media stations were being displayed. Buildings were on fire, and Profiteers were shown firing beam weapons on helpless civilians. Military forces fought back but, in many instances, were being slaughtered by the superior weapons of the Profiteers.

Colmes closed his eyes, wondering what Fleet Admiral Tomalson would do. As soon as he considered that, he knew what must be done. He had never fully trusted Marlen Stroud. He wouldn't sit here and let his world die under the hands of the Profiteers.

Activating his ship-to-ship comm, he spoke to the commanders of his other five ships. "The Profiteers have attacked Earth, and people are dying. We were ordered by President Stroud to stay here at Neptune and wait for further orders. Those orders haven't come. I intend to violate the president's orders and go to Earth and engage the Profiteers. I can't ask the rest of you to do the same as it would be putting your careers on the line. All I can do is ask you to do what your conscious is telling you. I'm going to Earth. Fleet Admiral Colmes, out."

Aaron turned toward a grinning Captain Scott. "Tamara, activate the hyperdrive and put us just outside the Moon's orbit. We'll choose targets of opportunity and see if we can't take out a few of those Profiteer warships."

"It's the right decision, sir," Tamara replied as she moved to carry out the admiral's order.

Colmes just hoped he was doing the right thing. "Activating the shipwide comm he announced, "All crew, go to Condition One. We're going to Earth to engage the Profiteers."

Moments later the Atlas entered hyperspace, only to emerge a few seconds later just outside the Moon's orbit. A minute later, the sensor alarms sounded as five more ships exited hyperspace nearby.

"It's the rest of the fleet," Tamara said with a tear in her eye. "They came after all."

Colmes sat up straighter in his command chair. It was time to see just how good of a fleet admiral he was.

-

On board the Star Cross, Lieutenant Lena Brooks saw on her long-range sensors the six ships orbiting Neptune suddenly vanish and then reappear just outside the Moon's orbit. "Admiral, I believe those six warships are about to engage the Profiteers."

Kurt stared at the tactical display long and hard and, after a moment, realized Lena was right. The six ships had formed into a V formation and were moving directly toward the orbiting Profiteer fleet.

"Something's gone wrong," he said as he activated his ship-to-ship comm. "All ships, it appears as if something serious has occurred on Earth. The six Earth warships we were monitoring orbiting Neptune have jumped back to Earth and are in an attack formation. They are moving to engage the Profiteers." Taking a deep breath, Kurt continued. "I don't intend to let them fight alone. All ships standby to enter hyperspace. We have a planet and some brave ship crews who need rescuing. Five minutes to hyperspace entry. All ships go to Condition One. I want every Profiteer ship in the Solar System destroyed!"

Kurt leaned back in his command chair, taking a deep breath. Perhaps at last he would get his shot at High Profiteer Creed and the Ascendant Destruction. No doubt Creed was there, leading the raid. Kurt intended to ensure this was the last Profiteer raid Creed ever led.

-

The five minutes passed, and then all twenty-four warships in the Proxima Centauri System entered hyperspace. They were barely over four light-years from Earth. The trip through hyperspace would take a little more than eight minutes.

-

Fleet Admiral Colmes swore as the Atlas shook violently, and a number of red lights flared on the damage control console. Smoke hung in the air, and the ventilation system was having a hard time clearing it out.

"We have hull breaches in sections seven and twelve, and we're bleeding atmosphere," Captain Scott reported as she scanned the console. "We've lost two energy projectors, and one of our missile tubes is disabled. There's also a fire in cargo bay three. The fire suppression system has activated and the fire should be under control shortly."

"Continue to fire our hypermissiles," Colmes ordered. They didn't have many of them, only what Fleet Admiral Vickers had furnished them immediately after their refit.

On one of the viewscreens, he saw a Profiteer escort cruiser's screen suddenly flare up as a number of hypermissiles struck it. With a furious explosion, the ship blew apart as its screen was overloaded as a single hypermissile breached its hull.

Colmes took a deep breath. One down and one hundred more to go.

-

On Earth, High Profiteer Creed entered a shuttle so he could return to the Ascendant Destruction. He had just been informed the small fleet of Human warships had left the eighth planet and were now attacking the Profiteer warships in orbit. Clan Leader Jarls was in the process of moving his battleships to engage the enemy and remove this last aggravating obstacle. Creed had already decided, when they finished looting the planet, he would give the order to nuke it, sterilizing its surface. The destruction of an inhabited world was strictly prohibited by the Controllers, but, in this instance, it would allow him to get his revenge on Fleet Admiral Vickers. Even if the other clans and Jarls refused to participate, his own ships were quite capable of carrying out the attack. He would deal with the consequences of his actions later.

With relief he learned most of the other raids at the targets the Human leader had suggested had contained large quantities of gold. Not as large as Fort Knox supposedly had but enough to make this raid a success. If he could just have another forty hours, the Profiteer fleet could strip Earth of most of its wealth. This time, thanks to the traitorous Human leader, they knew where most of it was. It would also give Creed the credits needed to pay the hefty fine for destroying the planet.

-

Fleet Admiral Colmes sucked in a deep breath as a massive explosion occurred in his fleet formation. The battlecruiser Knolls had suffered a catastrophic failure of its energy screen when multiple hypermissiles struck it, releasing torrents of energy. With growing despair, Colmes saw a number of Dacroni battleships moving in to engage what was left of his fleet. The Knolls was the first to die, but it wouldn't be the last.

"Take us in," he ordered, looking at Captain Scott. "Maybe we can take a few of them with us." Even as he spoke, the sensor alarms sounded.

"Sir, we have numerous ships exiting hyperspace just behind us," reported the sensor operator. "They're already in attack range."

"More Profiteers," muttered Colmes, feeling helpless. "They must really be afraid of us to commit so many ships to our destruction."

"They're not Profiteer ships," added the sensor operator excitedly, his face glowing with renewed hope. "They're from Newton. I have confirmed IDs on the Star Cross and the Retribution. Fleet Admirals Vickers and Tomalson are both here!"

"They're moving up to support us," said Tamara as she stared wide-eyed at the bright green icons now showing on the tactical display. "There's also a massive ship with them which we can't identify."

"Put it up on a viewscreen," ordered Colmes. Instantly on the primary viewscreen appeared a ship larger than Colmes had ever seen before. It was obviously a warship and a very powerful one. "I don't know where Fleet Admiral Vickers got that ship, but I don't think the Profiteers will like it."

"Admiral, I have fleet Admiral Tomalson on the comm. He asks that you fall back into their formation."

Colmes nodded. Perhaps he wouldn't die today after all.

-

Dacroni Clan Leader Jarls took one look at the main viewscreen in his Command Center and felt an icy chill run down his back. "I want a confirmation on the identity of that large ship." He thought he recognized who had built it; he just wanted to verify the bad news.

Salas took a moment as he checked the ship's database. Then he turned toward Jarls with a strained and confused look on his face. "It's the Aurelia, a flagship in the Lakiam fleet."

Jarls's face turned pale as he gazed at the viewscreen. "Pull our ships back toward Earth and recall all our raiding missions on the planet."

"It will take a while to get them all to their ships."

"I don't care how long it takes. Get them started back now. Tell the leaders of the different raiding groups they have twenty minutes to return. If they're not on their respective ships by that time, they'll be left behind."

Salas looked confused. "It's only one ship. Surely we can handle one Lakiam vessel."

Jarls shook his head. "You've never seen a Lakiam vessel in battle. I have. I once watched as two Lakiam ships destroyed an entire Profiteer fleet that was encroaching in the outer regions of an Enlightened World system they were responsible for protecting. They have a single missile that's capable of taking down an energy shield and destroying the ship as well. We can't fight something like that and still hope to have a fleet left when it's over. All we can hope for is to move closer to Earth and let the other Profiteer clans fall victims to the Aurelia's weapons while our raiding groups return."

"Ships are pulling back," Salas replied after sending the order.

-

Kurt watched the tactical display, seeing with surprise that the Dacroni battleships were pulling back.

"Dacroni battleships are retreating toward Earth," Lieutenant Brooks reported. "The other Profiteer ships are maintaining their positions."

Lieutenant Mays looked toward the admiral. "I suspect the Dacroni recognized the Aurelia and want no part of it."

Kurt nodded his agreement as he activated his ship-to-ship comm. This made things a lot more even if the Dacroni battleships stayed out of the fighting. "All ships are free to engage the Profiteers. All carriers, launch your fighters and bombers. Let's make these barbarians realize they should never have returned to Earth."

"Admiral, I've located the Ascendant Destruction!" reported Lieutenant Brooks excitedly. "It's in low orbit directly over the North American Union."

Kurt felt his pulse race. With any luck at all High Profiteer Creed was on Earth. If they could destroy the Ascendant Destruction, perhaps they could capture the High Profiteer and bring him to trial for the crimes he had committed.

"The battlecarriers and light carriers are launching their space wings," Brooks added as numerous small green icons appeared on her sensors. "The squadrons of fighters and bombers are forming up and advancing toward the Profiteers."

"Aurelia is firing," called out Lieutenant Mays.

On one of the primary viewscreens, several bright energy beams leaped from the Lakiam vessel to strike a nearby Profiteer escort cruiser. The beams tore right through the ship's defensive screen and slammed into the hull. Moments later the ship blew apart as too many essential systems were compromised.

"Profiteer escort cruiser is down," reported Lieutenant Brooks. "We're entering weapons range."

This was what Kurt had been waiting for. "All ships, open fire! Show no mercy to the enemy, for they will show you none."

With a devilish grin, Lieutenant Mays fired a full salvo of hypermissiles at a nearby Profiteer battlecruiser. As soon as the missiles struck, lighting up the enemy ship's screen, she fired the ship's powerful particle beam cannon. The beam hit the already-stressed energy screen and then penetrated. It struck the heavy armor of the ship's hull, tearing all the way through the warship. Secondary explosions shook the battlecruiser, blasting open huge rents in the hull.

Without hesitation, Lieutenant Mays fired both of the large kinetic energy cannons on the bow. The ship shook slightly from the recoil as a pair of two-thousand-pound projectiles hurled toward the damaged Profiteer battlecruiser at 10 percent the speed of light. The two rounds hit the enemy ship with the force of a large nuclear explosion. Moments later two glowing fireballs were all that remained of the enemy warship.

"Profiteer battlecruiser is down," reported Lieutenant Brooks.

-

On Earth, Major Nathan Aldrich looked up into the night sky, seeing the sudden appearance of countless fireballs in orbit. He had a full platoon of Marines, stealthily following a group of Profiteers taking a large group of captive young women toward their shuttle.

"What are those explosions?" asked Marine Corporal Lasher, looking up at the bright flashes.

Major Aldrich grinned as he heard a message over his comm. "Fleet Admiral Vickers and Fleet Admiral Tomalson have returned. They're engaging the Profiteer fleet in orbit."

"Do they stand a chance?" asked Private Malone. "Supposedly over one hundred Profiteer warships are up there."

"Command seems to think they do," Aldrich answered. "I'm also receiving reports General Braid has taken over the military command because General Fuller has disappeared."

"Fuller was a patsy for President Stroud," commented Lasher disgustedly. "It doesn't surprise me that he ran."

"There's also a rumor that President Stroud has been taken prisoner by the Profiteers and that former President Mayfield has taken command at the emergency headquarters in Canada."

"Wow, things are really moving!" commented Lasher as they went around a street corner.

The Profiteer shuttle was just ahead, sitting in the playground of an elementary school.

At a quick signal from Aldrich, the Marines took cover behind some abandoned vehicles. On the rooftops near the school, half a dozen Marine snipers waited. Nathan had been hoping for an opportunity to separate the captives from the Profiteers, but time had run out. "All units, standby," he said as he took careful aim with his assault rifle. The Marines were using armor-piercing rounds, which should go through the light armor the Profiteers wore. "Fire!"

Aldrich squeezed off a shot as he peered through the scope on his rifle. The Profiteer he targeted grabbed his chest with a shocked look on his face and fell to the ground. All around Nathan other Marines fired, including the snipers on the roofs. More Profiteers fell, then they began returning fire with their energy weapons. The young women screamed and took off running. Several of the Profiteers turned their weapons on the women, killing some of them. The snipers must have seen this because their next rounds put the offending Profiteers to the ground.

Nathan ducked as an energy beam struck near him. He heard several of his Marines scream out in pain, then the firing died down, and then it stopped completely. Looking over the vehicle he hunched behind, he saw all the Profiteers were down. Most of the young women were still running.

"Move in and check for survivors," he ordered. Aldrich could see half a dozen young women on the ground, not moving, but over thirty others had been freed. Shaking his head at the lives lost, he walked toward the schoolyard just as the shuttle took off, streaking upward. In moments it was gone. Several of his Marines took out their pistols and walked from one prostrate

Profiteer to the next, putting several rounds in their heads. Nathan said nothing. The Profiteers deserved whatever they got. The taking of prisoners was not a priority.

-

Captain Andrew Randson watched in awe as the Aurelia blew up its third Profiteer battlecruiser. Tarnth was leaving the smaller escort cruisers to the Newton ships. "The Dacroni mercenaries run from us," he commented as he watched the Dacroni stay just outside the range of his weapons.

"I would suggest we forge ahead of the fleet," said Mara. "Our shields can handle anything the Profiteer ships can attack us with."

Andrew thought for a moment. No doubt Dacroni Clan Leader Jarls had recognized the Aurelia and retreated rather than engage it. Already countless Profiteer shuttles rose from Earth to rendezvous with the orbiting ships. "Do it," he ordered. "We need to ensure the Dacroni never return to Earth again."

-

Tarnth allowed himself to grin. While he didn't approve of the situation he and Mara were in, it was satisfying to watch the Profiteer ships die from the Aurelia's weapons. The ship had been dishonored by the black ships; now that honor had been redeemed.

-

On Earth, President Mayfield stepped into the operations room at the secret command bunker in Canada. With a smile he spotted General Braid issuing orders to the military forces of the North American Union.

"I see your esteemed replacement is missing," Mayfield said as he stepped near Braid.

"Yeah. He disappeared as soon as the Profiteers fired their first weapon."

"I'm glad to see you, Mr. President," Colonel Stidham said, striding over to Mayfield and saluting.

"Where are the other Cabinet members?"

"In the Cabinet meeting room," Stidham replied. "They're waiting for you."

Mayfield looked at several viewscreens, showing cities on fire. "What's our current situation?"

"There's fighting all across the planet. Nearly every nation is resisting the Profiteers. So far no nukes have been used," reported General Braid. "You should know both Fleet Admiral Vickers and Tomalson have jumped into the system and are currently engaged against the Profiteer fleet."

Mayfield looked concerned. "They can't take on a fleet that large."

Stidham grinned as he changed the view on one of the viewscreens. It showed a gigantic ship engaged against the Profiteers. Even as they watched, a nearby Profiteer battlecruiser exploded, sending debris flying across space. "They have, and they're winning. We haven't identified that ship, but it seems to have more firepower than all of our ships combined. Its energy shields are impenetrable."

Mayfield gazed at the screen for nearly a minute, watching the powerful ship. "I will say one thing for Vickers. He never ceases to amaze me. Now I'll go speak with the Cabinet."

As Mayfield left the room, Stidham turned toward General Braid. "What'll he do?"

"He has them over a barrel. They made a bad decision supporting Marlen Stroud, and now the world is paying for it." Looking at another viewscreen, General Braid could see downtown Dallas. Buildings were on fire, and soldiers fought Profiteers in the streets. "I suspect we'll have a new Cabinet soon."

-

President Mayfield entered the Cabinet room, seeing the stunned looks on the faces of most of the Cabinet members. "Does anyone object to me taking back the office of president?"

No one replied.

"Very well, all in favor raise your hands."

Very tentatively everyone in the room raised their right hands.

"All this is being recorded so it will count as a legitimate vote. Former President Stroud has been taken prisoner by the Profiteers after he attempted to give them all the gold at Fort Knox. Unbeknownst to him, I had it removed before I left office to keep it safe from the Profiteers. In orbit above us, Fleet Admirals Vickers and Tomalson are fighting the Profiteer fleet and winning. I expect the Profiteers to be driven off shortly."

"Our gold is gone again," groaned Dwight Michaels, shaking his head in disbelief. "Who did you give it to this time?"

"That's none of your concern," Mayfield said coldly. "I expect all your resignations on my desk within the hour. Any of you who refuses to tender your resignations will be charged with treason and will spend the rest of your lives in prison."

Mayfield looked from one shocked face to the next, but no one challenged him. "One hour," he reiterated as he turned and left the room.

"What do we do?" asked Connie Saxon. "He can't force us to resign."

Dwight Michaels shook his head. "He can, and we will. He's right. With what President Stroud tried to do, we could all go to prison. I prefer to spend my retirement in comfort at home with my family." Standing up, he addressed the others. "I'm going to my office to write out my resignation. I suggest the rest of you do the same."

-

Above Earth, Fleet Admiral Vickers felt the Star Cross vibrate and heard a ringing sound strike the hull.

"Energy shield is down to 74 percent," reported Lieutenant Mays as she pounded a nearby Profiteer escort cruiser with the ship's energy projectors.

"Continue to fire," ordered Kurt. "Lieutenant Pierce, contact our bombers and direct them to take out the hyperdrive on all the detainee ships. Once that's done, they're to focus on the cargo ships."

"Message sent," Pierce said. "I also sent it to Rear Admirals Wilson and White."

"That's fine. They can coordinate the attacks." Kurt looked at one of the primary viewscreens, showing the night side of Earth. Even from space, some of Earth's cities were aglow with fires. Although no nukes had been used, the planet was once again suffering a lot of damage. Hundreds—perhaps thousands—of people were dying.

"Admiral, the Ascendant Destruction is nearly within range," reported Lieutenant Brooks.

Kurt's eyes went instantly to one of the viewscreens, showing the hated Profiteer vessel which had wrought so much destruction on Earth.

"Lieutenant Styles, take us in. Ignore all other enemy ships around us. I want the Ascendant Destruction!"

-

In space, Captain Anders led his squadron of ten Scorpion bombers on their attack run. A large detainee ship was ahead of them with only a few light energy batteries for protection and no energy shield.

"That ship may have abductees from Earth on it," he cautioned over the squadron command channel. "Target the Engineering areas only, and let's ensure it doesn't leave this system with our people."

"They're not leaving," swore Lieutenant Davis as he launched a single Hydra missile equipped with an explosive warhead toward the ship.

"I've got secondary Engineering," added Lieutenant Jamie Schmidt.

Looking out his cockpit window, Anders saw several telling explosions against the hull of the Profiteer ship. It seemed to tremble and then went dead in space.

"Target neutralized," commented Lieutenant Davis smugly. "That ship's not going anywhere."

Captain Anders quickly scanned the detainee ship, seeing both Engineering sections were heavily damaged. The ship was repairable but not without a shipyard. "Good shooting. Let's go to our next target." Adjusting course, Anders pointed his bomber at a large cargo ship. There were still plenty of targets to be taken out.

-

The battle grew more heated with every passing minute. Profiteer ships were blown from space by the Aurelia, one after another. Seeing the devastating firepower from the massive vessel, the Profiteers were trying to stay out of its way, while taking on board their shuttlecraft.

The light cruiser Concord came under fire from two Profiteer battlecruisers. The shield erupted in brightness as powerful hypermissiles and energy beams struck it. One energy beam penetrated and then half a dozen more. The hull was blown open in several areas, and secondary explosions shook the ship. Emergency bulkheads slammed shut, sealing some of the crew inside the damaged areas. Fire suppression systems came on to control the raging inferno, spreading through several decks. Then a Profiteer hypermissile penetrated deep inside the ship, and moments later the Concord died as it was turned into a fireball by the nuclear blast.

Other Human ships were on the losing end of their battles as well. The battlecruiser Vesta exploded, sending debris into the shields of several nearby ships when it strayed too near a Dacroni battleship. The battlecruiser Far Star died when it was struck by a large piece of debris from a destroyed Profiteer warship.

-

Kurt flinched each time one of his ships was lost. But the Aurelia was destroying Profiteer vessels far quicker than the Profiteers were destroying the Human ones.

"In range!" called out Lieutenant Mays.

"Fire!" ordered Kurt, his eyes glowing with determination. "I want that son-of-a-bitch dead!"

On the main viewscreen, the Ascendant Destruction appeared. Across its screen massive hypermissile explosions released torrents of energy. The screen held, and the Profiteer ship returned fire with its own missiles. The Star Cross shook violently, and a shower of sparks erupted from a console. Damage control people hurried to put out the small fire and work on getting the console back in operation.

"Lieutenant Mays, fire our antimatter hypermissiles. Lieutenant Pierce, inform all ships the use of antimatter weapons is now authorized." Kurt had been waiting until they were at point-blank range before deploying these much deadlier weapons.

On the screen, Kurt watched with anticipation as the first fifty-megaton explosion rocked the energy screen of the Ascendant Destruction. Then a second and a third explosion pounded the Profiteer ship. Suddenly the Star Cross fired its particle beam cannon, and the bright blue beam passed completely through the Ascendant Destruction's energy screen, impacting the armored hull. The beam's impact set off a massive explosion, hurling glowing debris into space. The energy screen around the Profiteer ship seemed to flicker.

"Firing KEW cannons," called out Lieutenant Mays, sensing the weakness in the Profiteer ship's energy screen.

The two KEW rounds penetrated the screen, and dual massive explosions rocked the Ascendant Destruction. For a moment the ship seemed as if it would survive, then, in a brilliant explosion, the Profiteer flagship blew apart.

"Ascendant Destruction is down," reported Lieutenant Brooks breathlessly.

Admiral Vickers leaned forward, his adrenaline rush coming to an end. He just hoped High Profiteer Creed had been on board that ship when it died.

-

Dacroni Clan Leader Jarls recoiled in shock when he saw the Ascendant Destruction explode. "How much longer on our shuttlecraft?"

"They're all on board," reported Salas. "The last one is being secured."

"Let's get out of here! This battle's lost." Even as he spoke, he saw the Aurelia blow apart two of his battleships. "Jump now before that thing destroys us all!"

Almost instantly Jarls's flagship jumped into hyperspace. He felt anger at losing to Fleet Admiral Vickers once more. At least High Profiteer Creed had paid Jarls a large fee up front so all wasn't lost on this raid. He hoped his shuttle crews had succeeded in bringing some gold and captives to their respective ships. If so this raid could still turn out to be very profitable.

"What now?" asked Salas. "As near as I can tell, we lost four of our battleships to that Lakiam vessel."

"Consider us lucky," Jarls answered back. "We could have just as easily lost all of them." Once they got back to Dacron Four, Jarls would have the damage to his ships repaired. Perhaps it was time to leave Fleet Admiral Vickers alone. To fight him was too costly in ships and crews. There were better ways to make a profit.

-

In space, the other Profiteer clan leaders saw the Dacroni mercenary ships flee into hyperspace. On their viewscreens, the monster ship bore down on them. Without a moment's hesitation they too jumped out, leaving stranded shuttles in orbit that hadn't made it to their ships. A single detainee ship and a few cargo ships also jumped out, but most remained. They were drifting powerless as their engineering sections had been destroyed or disabled by the Scorpion bombers.

-

On Earth, in the secret command bunker in Canada, the operations room erupted in loud cheers and clapping when it was announced the Ascendant Destruction had been destroyed, and the Profiteer fleet was in full retreat.

"Fleet Admiral Vickers did it again," commented General Braid with a huge grin. "We've won, and this time it will be permanent."

President Mayfield nodded. He didn't mention the possible menace from the black ships. That would be dealt with later. For now, he needed to clean up the massive mess President Stroud had made of the world in his attempt to negotiate with the Profiteers.

-

Aboard the Star Cross, Kurt let out a long sigh of relief. The battle was over, and Earth was once more free of the Profiteers. A few enemy shuttles still had to be dealt with; and they were being escorted to ground by Lance fighters. Also numerous Profiteers remained on the surface and were being rapidly rounded up by Earth's military. Once their fleet had withdrawn, they had thrown down their weapons and surrendered.

"What now?" asked Lieutenant Mays.

"We spend a few days in orbit, and then we'll go home." Kurt wasn't sure what was in store for Newton next. The black ship menace remained, and he needed to work out some deal with Mara and Tarnth. Kurt really wanted to find a way to encourage them to stay instead of going back to Lakiam.

Glancing at the main viewscreen, he saw the glowing gas and twisted wreckage that represented the Ascendant Destruction. There was no doubt in his mind that, after today, the Profiteers would never be a danger to Earth or Newton again.

Epilogue

In the Oval Office of the White House, President Mayfield, General Braid, Secretary of Homeland Security Raul Gutierrez, and Fleet Admiral Tomalson were all together once more.

"The world's a mess," Raul said as he gestured toward a thick stack of reports he had brought in. "Most of the world blames the North American Union for what happened in this most recent Profiteer attack."

"And they should," Mayfield answered with a deep sigh. "Stroud was nearly the end of us all. If Fleet Admirals Vickers and Tomalson hadn't arrived when they did, I fully believe the Profiteers would have nuked us into oblivion."

"So what now?" asked General Braid. "In the shape Earth's in, it'll be all we can do to defend ourselves."

"We won't be alone for much longer," Tomalson said. "We're forming an alliance with the Julbians and possibly two more nearby worlds. It will allow for trade and should help our world to recover. Admiral Vickers has also made several more of his ships available to defend the Solar System, and he's moving four Class Two Orbital Defense Platforms from Newton to Earth."

"We're also opening up Newton to increased colonization from more countries across the world," added President Mayfield. "Since they now have their independence, they'll take more people."

"It will be easier with all the detainee ships we captured," Tomalson said. "They're currently at Newton for refurbishment and being changed over into passenger liners. Each one can carry twelve thousand colonists."

The four men fell silent as they thought about their future. It would still be years before Earth fully recovered, and, until then, it would be up to Newton to protect the system and to be the shining light of hope for the Human race.

-

On Kubitz, Marvin Tenner was attending one of the slave auctions. For the last hour a number of Humans from Earth had been placed on the selling block. His people had purchased every one so far. Now an older man was brought up. Tenner recognized Marlen Stroud. The man looked worn and haggard and seemed confused as to where he was.

The auction began with no bids. The price was lowered, and one of the reps from a small pleasure house placed a minimum bid. Stroud's eyes seemed to clear as he looked hopefully in Tenner's direction.

No other bids were offered, and Stroud was sold at the minimum bid. As he was led out, he looked desperately at Tenner. Tenner met the man's eyes and slowly shook his head. What Stroud didn't know was that Tenner had arranged for the ex-president to be sold to this particular pleasure house. He would be put to work, but the work wouldn't be that hard. He would also be on round-the-clock surveillance. Marlen Stroud would never be a danger to Earth again.

-

On Newton, Kurt had just finished speaking to Mara and Tarnth. After much discussion they had agreed to stay for three more months. During that time they would teach Kurt's people how to operate the two Lakiam battlecruisers as well as the four Andock vessels. At the end of that time, the Star Cross would deliver the pair to Kubitz, where they would find passage back to Lakiam. Enough ships from various worlds across the galaxy traded at the black market world that it would be relatively easy to book passage back to Lakiam space.

"So they agreed to stay a bit," commented Keera, as she snuggled up to Kurt. They were sitting on the comfortable couch in their apartment.

"It's because of the black ships," Kurt answered. "Even the Lakiams agree with us. The more worlds that can fight the Destroyers of Worlds, the better. I think both of them have been impressed by what they've seen here on Newton."

"What about Lomatz? I still don't like the idea of so many of the weapons dealer's people coming to live here," Keera said.

"The first of his people should be arriving next week. He's been busy on the island, getting it ready. I was over there yesterday, and they've already built housing, businesses, and set up a number of automated factories. As much as I hate to say it, his people can teach us a lot."

Keera sat up and stared into Kurt's eyes. "Just don't let them off the island. I don't want Newton to turn into another Kubitz."

"Don't worry about that. We're taking precautions to ensure that doesn't happen. Lomatz's people will be allowed to travel on Newton, but only for short periods of time and only after their travel plans have been approved. Perhaps after a few years, we can reduce the restrictions and someday eliminate them completely."

"What will we do when the black ships finally come here?"

Kurt let out a deep sigh. "We should have time to prepare. Both Mara and Tarnth are in agreement on that. They say we live in a backwater section of the galaxy that's sparsely inhabited. It may be years before the black ships make their way here, and, by then, we'll be ready. We'll continue to add to the defensive grid, and build bigger and more powerful ships."

-

Keera leaned back, snuggling against Kurt. She felt his hand slide to her back, moving gently up and down. Her breathing got heavier, and she could feel her excitement building. Turning her head, she kissed Kurt, enjoying the special relationship they had. If anyone could find a way to stop the Destroyers of Worlds, it would be Kurt. However, right now she had other plans, and Kurt knew exactly what they were.

The End

If you enjoyed The Star Cross: The Dark Invaders and would like to see the series continue, please post a review with some stars. Good reviews encourage an author to write and also help sell books. Reviews can be just a few short sentences, describing what you liked about the book. If you have suggestions, please contact me at my website, link below. Thank you for reading The Dark Invaders and being so supportive.

For updates on current writing projects and future publications, go to my author website. Sign up for future notifications when my new books come out on Amazon.

Website: http://raymondlweil.com/

Follow on Facebook at Raymond L. Weil

Other Books by Raymond L. Weil
Available at Amazon

Moon Wreck (The Slaver Wars Book 1)
The Slaver Wars: Alien Contact (The Slaver Wars Book 2)
Moon Wreck: Fleet Academy (The Slaver Wars Book 3)
The Slaver Wars: First Strike (The Slaver Wars Book 4)
The Slaver Wars: Retaliation (The Slaver Wars Book 5)
The Slaver Wars: Galactic Conflict (The Slaver Wars Book 6)
The Slaver Wars: Endgame (The Slaver Wars Book 7)

-

Dragon Dreams
Dragon Dreams: Dragon Wars
Dragon Dreams: Gilmreth the Awakening
Dragon Dreams: Snowden the White Dragon

-

Star One: Tycho City: Survival
Star One: Neutron Star
Star One: Dark Star
Star One

-

Galactic Empire Wars: Destruction (Book 1)
Galactic Empire Wars: Emergence (Book 2)
Galactic Empire Wars: Rebellion (Book 3)
Galactic Empire Wars: The Alliance (Book 4)
Galactic Empire Wars: Insurrection (Book 5)

-

The Lost Fleet: Galactic Search (Book 1)
The Lost Fleet: Into the Darkness (Book 2)
The Lost Fleet: Oblivion's Light (Book 3)
The Lost Fleet: Genesis (Book 4)

-

The Star Cross (Book 1)
The Star Cross: The Dark Invaders (Book 2)

-

(All dates are tentative)
The Lost Fleet: Search for the Originators (Book 5) October 2016
The Star Cross: Galaxy in Peril (Book 3) December 2016

ABOUT THE AUTHOR

I live in Clinton Oklahoma with my wife of 43 years and our cats. I attended college at SWOSU in Weatherford Oklahoma, majoring in Math with minors in Creative Writing and History.

My hobbies include watching soccer, reading, camping, and of course writing. I coached youth soccer for twelve years before moving on and becoming a high school soccer coach for thirteen more. I also enjoy playing with my five grandchildren. I have a very vivid imagination, which sometimes worries my friends. They never know what I'm going to say or what I'm going to do.

I am an avid reader and have a science fiction / fantasy collection of over two thousand paperbacks. I want future generations to know the experience of reading a good book as I have over the last forty-five years.

Printed in Poland
by Amazon Fulfillment
Poland Sp. z o.o., Wrocław